D1588448

LIGHTS OUT IN LINCOLNWOOD

LIGHTS OUT IN LINCOLNWOOD

GEOFF RODKEY

SIMON & SCHUSTER

London · New York · Sydney · Toronto · New Delhi

First published in the United States by Harper Perennial,
an imprint of HarperCollins, New York, 2021

First published in Great Britain by Simon & Schuster UK Ltd, 2021

1 3 5 7 9 10 8 6 4 2

Simon & Schuster UK Ltd
1st Floor
222 Gray's Inn Road
London WC1X 8HB

Simon & Schuster Australia, Sydney
Simon & Schuster India, New Delhi

www.simonandschuster.co.uk
www.simonandschuster.com.au
www.simonandschuster.co.in

A CIP catalogue record for this book
is available from the British Library

Hardback ISBN: 978-1-4711-9742-0
Trade Paperback ISBN: 978-1-4711-9743-7
eBook ISBN: 978-1-4711-9744-4

Printed and bound in Great Britain by CPI Group (UK) Ltd, Croydon, CR0 4YY

LIGHTS OUT IN LINCOLNWOOD

OCTOBER 2019

TUESDAY

THE ALTMANS

"We're out of yogurt."

It was less a statement than an accusation, which Dan delivered in a tone of wounded sorrow as he stared into the open refrigerator. Its top shelf, where the big tubs of Greek yogurt usually sat, was desolate except for some leftover olives in a plastic Whole Foods tub and that two-year-old jar of pineapple salsa he'd bought by accident and couldn't bring himself to throw out even though nobody in the house wanted anything to do with a salsa defiled by fruit.

The target of his accusation wasn't listening. Jen sat at the kitchen table in front of a mug of coffee, wearing the Michigan T-shirt she'd slept in and staring dead-eyed at her phone. On its screen was a chunk of text from an article in the Nutrition and Fitness section of the *New York Times* app titled "How to Stop Yourself from Crying."

Upon seeing the headline as she scrolled, Jen's initial reaction had been amused contempt: *When did the* Times *start running articles that* Woman's Day *rejected?*

But that had quickly given way to a second, much less cynical thought: *Maybe this could help.*

Unfortunately, three paragraphs in, she'd realized the article was pitched exclusively to readers who didn't want to quit crying so much as they just wanted to quit doing it in front of other people. Jen did her crying alone, usually in the upstairs bathroom on school days when nobody was home, and the *Times* apparently felt this was either not a problem at all or so grave as to be beyond its capacity to fix. It was hard to tell which.

Either way, by the time Dan issued his yogurt indictment, she'd stopped even trying to read the article. Her eyes were still fixed on the screen, but her mind had wandered off to wrestle with the binary choice that had come to dominate her weekdays: *Will I or won't I?*

No. Not today.

Well, maybe—

No! Jesus.

But—

"Didn't you go shopping yesterday?"

Having failed to engage his wife's attention through passive aggression, Dan was trying again, without the passive part this time.

"I thought you were going to—Jen . . . ? *Jen!*"

Finally, she turned her head from the phone. "What?"

"Why didn't you go shopping yesterday?"

"I did! I got dinner." Dinner had been lasagna and sautéed spinach carried out from Delectables, an overpriced gourmet place on Hawthorne Avenue that only sold prepared foods. She'd chosen it late Monday afternoon over more versatile shopping alternatives for a simple reason she didn't dare articulate to Dan: it was possible to drive to Delectables and back by executing only right turns.

"Why didn't you get breakfast stuff?"

"I was working! I put in a Fresh Direct order. I don't know why it hasn't come yet." Jen's laptop was on the table, halfway between her and Max. She moved her coffee mug to clear a path and dragged over the laptop. Before she opened the screen, she reached out and smacked her fourteen-year-old son's free hand.

Max was wearing a pair of massive blue headphones that dwarfed his skull, making him look like some kind of cyborg monkey as he shoveled cereal into his mouth while watching a martial arts video on his phone. Its cracked screen lay flat beside the cereal bowl, little pinpoints of splashed milk speckling the image of a shirtless, steroid-swollen man in a Mohawk who was conducting a tutorial on the mechanics of an elbow smash to the face.

"What?" Max snapped.

"Quit staring at your screen," Jen scolded him as she clicked on the Fresh Direct link in her browser bar.

"You're staring at yours!"

"I'm staring with a purpose."

"So am I!"

What his mother didn't know, because Max would've sooner cut off a finger than explain it to her, was that the elbow-to-the-face video was no idle entertainment. It was source material in a research project with serious implications for his future.

"I think we should *all* stop staring at our screens," Dan declared.

Jen's irritation at this—as if her husband wasn't about to spend the entire commute into Manhattan staring at *his* screen—was compounded by her simultaneous realization that $137.54 worth of food was still sitting in her Fresh Direct cart. Somehow, she'd failed to complete the order.

"Shit."

"What?"

"I forg—" *Bad idea, don't admit that.* "It takes forever to schedule this stuff." She clicked on the next available delivery window and quickly finished the transaction as the headache she'd woken up with reasserted itself in a stab of pain just behind her left eyeball. "Eight to ten tomorrow night."

"Tomorrow *night*? What are we going to do until then?"

"Go to the store like normal people?" The words came out in a snarl. Jen knew counterattacking was a poor choice, but it was tough to act strategically with an invisible icepick digging into her skull.

"*Who's* going to go to the store?" Dan felt secure enough in his occupation of the moral high ground to ratchet up his tone from aggrieved to indignant.

"Do *you* want to?"

Dan sucked in his breath. For Jen to suggest that he buy weekday groceries, five minutes before he left for work with no chance of getting home prior to dinner, wasn't just logistically absurd. It was a violation of their marriage contract. According to the unwritten rules governing their relationship, Jen maintained the shopping list and bought all the groceries except on special occasions. Even then, they both knew it was a bad idea to let Dan shop alone. The pineapple salsa was proof of that.

And assuming he did have both the time to shop and the mental bandwidth to make a list (which he *didn't*, given that he was facing a highly stressful workday of creative demands he hadn't yet figured out how to meet), if Dan accepted such a major off-loading of his wife's household responsibilities onto his own plate, what would he get in return? If Dan bought groceries on a Tuesday, would Jen blow the leaves on Saturday? Would she file the insurance claim for Chloe's out-of-network therapist appointment? Would she—*what the hell, let's put all our cards on the table here*—quit chasing the financial crumbs of short-term consulting gigs and actually commit to going back full-time so he didn't have to keep shouldering ninety percent of their income burden?

This was some nonsense.

"When would I go to the store? We have to break two new stories today! The room could go till midnight!"

Jen slammed her laptop shut, conceding defeat. "Settle down! I'm going to the store! Jesus."

"I mean, is that a problem?"

"No. I'm on a deadline, but—whatever. It's fine." She got up from the table and gritted her teeth against the headache as she retrieved a pad of Post-its and a pen from the countertop.

"A deadline for what? The Rutgers thing?"

"Yeah. That's why I didn't get to the store yesterday." The Rutgers thing had been over for a week—*did I submit the last invoice? need to check on that*—but Dan didn't know this, so Jen figured it was safe to reanimate its corpse in the service of clawing back a little moral advantage. "What do we need besides yogurt?"

"Granola, fruit, milk . . ." Dan had reopened the fridge and was scanning its contents with mounting concern. "OJ . . . cold cuts . . . every kind of cheese . . . Jesus, what am I going to eat for breakfast?"

"There's eggs."

"I don't have time for eggs! I'll miss the eight eleven."

"You don't start until ten."

"I don't have anything to pitch yet! I need to get in early and do some thinking. Shit . . . I'll just eat at Barnaby's."

"You have time for Barnaby's, but not eggs?"

"It's quiet in the mornings—I can work there awhile and take the eight fifty-two. Do you have cash?"

"I did, until Chloe's ACT tutor took it all." Jen looked up from her list. "Max, what food do you need?"

Engrossed in a step-by-step walkthrough of an open palm strike to the chin, Max failed to hear the question.

"Max!"

No response. Dan added his voice to Jen's. "*Max!*"

Still nothing.

"*MAX!*"

The yelling finally reached a volume loud enough to penetrate Max's headphones. He pulled the muff off one ear. "What?"

"What do you need from the grocery store?"

"I dunno. Cheese sticks? More cereal." He let the muff drop back against his ear, shutting out his parents again.

"Don't get him more of that cereal," Dan warned Jen. "It's terrible for him."

"It's the only thing he'll eat for breakfast."

"If you don't buy it, he won't eat it."

"Then he won't eat anything! Look how skinny he is."

Chloe entered the kitchen, her still-damp hair carrying the strawberry scent of shampoo. She'd paired a bright blue halter top that showcased her toned upper arms with a simmering scowl so hostile that Dan instantly stepped back to give her a clear path to the fridge.

"What a skinny little *loser*. Right, Mom?" Chloe spat out each word through a clenched jaw as she yanked open the freezer door.

Dan and Jen exchanged a look. Their daughter was loaded for bear, and neither of them knew why.

"You okay, sweetheart?" Dan asked.

"Yeah. I'm fine! For a *loser*."

Jen narrowed her eyes in an expression that was equal parts weariness and pain. "What point are you trying to—"

"*Jesus!*" Chloe exploded in fury as she stared into the open freezer, which was only slightly less empty than the fridge. Her head spun around to glare daggers at Jen. "You didn't get more acai bowls? What am I going to eat for breakfast?"

"I have a *job*, Chloe!" Jen shot back. "I have more responsibilities than just—"

"*I have an AP Gov test first period! What am I going to eat?*" Chloe yelled so loudly that Max had to turn the volume on his phone up three more ticks.

"Why are you being so emotional?" Jen yelled back.

Chloe let out a noise that fell somewhere between a snort and a wail. "Huh! Yeah! I wonder why?"

It was clear to Dan that whatever massive mother-daughter fight was brewing, he wasn't implicated in it—and past experience had taught him that any attempt to mediate was not just likely to fail, but would risk expanding the conflict beyond its current borders.

He decided to flee. Before he did, he offered Chloe a spot in the lifeboat.

"I'm going to Barnaby's," he told her. "You want to come? I'll buy you breakfast."

Having made the offer on impulse, Dan was just beginning to calculate the level of paternal self-sacrifice involved in eating breakfast with his daughter while being completely unprepared for the ten a.m. writers' room when Chloe rendered the issue moot by rejecting his offer with a snarl. "I have a gov test! Emma's picking me up."

"Okay! All good." He put a gentle, supportive hand on her tense upper back as he slipped past her to fetch his messenger bag from the counter.

"If you treat me like a human being, I'll make you eggs," Jen told her daughter in a voice too bitter to accomplish anything except further escalation.

"I hate eggs!"

"Gotta go—love you both—please don't fight!" Dan called out over his shoulder as he escaped to the mudroom and the garage beyond.

"Thanks for your help, have a super day!" Jen told the back of her husband's head. Then she returned to her daughter with a weary sigh. "Will you please tell me why you're so pissed off?"

"You don't know? You *seriously* don't know?" Chloe's voice quivered. Her volatile emotional state had multiple overlapping sources: yesterday's sectional tennis final, Friday's BC calculus quiz, this morning's AP Government exam, last Sunday's practice ACT test, this Saturday's actual ACT test, record low acceptance rates at elite US colleges, the supplemental essays for her early decision application to Dartmouth, climate change, Josh Houser's Instagram feed, the absence of enlightened global political leadership, the absence of acai bowls in the freezer, and above all her mother's capacity for casual, apparently oblivious cruelty.

Jen winced as she watched Chloe's upper lip tremble. Her daughter had just posed a single-question, pass-fail exam, and Jen knew she was about to flunk it.

"Is it about the sectional?"

"It's about the *essay!*"

"What about it?"

"OH MY GOD!"

"Chloe! If you don't tell me, I can't help—"

"I can't believe this!"

Over at the table, Max dialed his phone's volume up to maximum and shifted his seat by thirty degrees to move the altercation out of his line of sight so he could finish watching "Top Five One Punch Knockouts" in peace. He had his own battle to fight. And unlike his sister's never-ending cold war with their mother, he planned to bring his to a swift and decisive conclusion.

Max had done his homework. He'd spent the past two weeks watching how-to martial arts videos on YouTube and doing push-ups in his bedroom after dinner. He was almost ready for the reckoning. All he had to do now was figure out how to goad Jordan Stankovic into taking another swing at him.

It was 7:54 a.m. on the last normal Tuesday morning in Lincolnwood, New Jersey.

DAN

Sitting inside his Lexus with the windows up, Dan could still hear Chloe and Jen going at it in the kitchen. As he hit the clicker that raised the garage door, he rolled down his window to monitor the noise level in case Judge Distefano was walking his dachshund next door. The Altmans were yellers—it was more or less genetic on Jen's side of the family—but Dan preferred to deceive himself that their neighbors in the other four houses on Brantley Circle's little cul-de-sac didn't already know this.

The elderly, dignified judge and his equally dignified wiener dog were nowhere in sight, but the front yard of the Mediterranean-style McMansion directly across from the judge's house was being patrolled by the Stankovics' asshole schnauzer, Dazzle. The mechanical rumble of the Altmans' garage door sent her into a frenzy of borderline-psychotic barking that more than overwhelmed the muffled strains of Jen and Chloe's fight.

Dazzle's owner, Eddie Stankovic, was in his driveway, dressed in Giants sweats and leaning his big frame against the side of his black Corvette while he sucked on a vape box. If he noticed that his dog was losing her shit loudly enough to wake everyone within a half-mile radius, he gave no indication of it. As Dan pulled his car out of the drive and Dazzle frantically mirrored its movements along the perimeter of the invisible fence connected to her shock collar, Eddie smirked and waved.

"Hey, Hollywood!" he yelled over the din of his dog and the lowering garage door. "Where's my money?"

Dan leaned his head out of the car window and shook it in mock helplessness. "I'm trying, man! Business affairs is a bitch!" Then he waved goodbye and switched on the radio, cranking up *'80s on 8* to drown out Dazzle as he exited the cul-de-sac and turned right onto Willis Road.

Eddie had been beating the where's-my-money? joke into the ground for two years, although after all that time, Dan still wasn't sure if his neighbor considered it a joke or a legitimate demand for creative compensation from *Bullet Town: NYC*, the CBS police procedural-slash-paean to vigilante justice on which Dan was a supervising producer. Unlike most of his friends and acquaintances, who combined their vicarious excitement over Dan's midlife career transition from securities law to screenwriting with a near-total lack of interest in watching the show, Eddie was a rabid fan.

Too rabid, in fact: almost from the minute he learned Dan had been hired as a story editor on *Bullet Town: NYC*'s first season, Eddie had started bombarding him with pitches for potential story lines whenever they crossed paths while taking out the recycling. Eddie's ideas mostly involved murder via dry cleaning accessories. He owned Capo's Cleaners, a seven-location chain whose delivery vans sported a giant cartoon head of an Edward G. Robinson lookalike growling, *I'm gonna show you a clean you can't refuse!* The company's advertising borrowed so liberally from Hollywood mob movies that two different studios had sent Eddie cease-and-desist letters, copies of which he proudly hung in frames next to the cash registers at all seven locations.

Eddie's ideas for *Bullet Town* were terrible, and Dan had never repeated them to anyone at the show. But when the showrunner, Marty Callahan, wrote three bloody corpses hanging from a dry cleaner's garment conveyor into the first season finale, Eddie refused to believe it was a coincidence. Next to all of his cease-and-desist letters, he hung giant blurry screenshots of the carnage under a caption that read *CAPO'S ON* BULLET TOWN: NYC! Then he began to pester Dan for money.

Putting his meathead neighbor's dumb joke to bed was the least of the many things Dan looked forward to about eventually leaving *BT: NYC* for another show—an actually *good* one, ideally created by Dan himself, and the kind of prestige drama that his friends and relatives could be expected to watch non-ironically.

But that was a long-term goal. In the short term, Dan needed to come up with replacement plots for the two story outlines the network had rejected on Monday.

Dead or Alive's "You Spin Me Round" came on the radio. As he guided his Lexus downhill, past the genteel homes of Upper Lincolnwood, he began to twitch his head in time with the music as his fingers tapped a beat on the steering wheel.

Guy murders his obnoxious neighbor?

Again?

He'd already killed off a fictional Eddie in episode thirty-seven, although the real Eddie had failed to recognize his own speech patterns, wardrobe, and marketing practices once they'd been laundered through the character of a pizza chain owner named Lenny. Dazzle the schnauzer had also gotten her mortal reward, in episode fifty-four.

What else you got, Danny Boy?

He heard the taunt in the voice of his boss, Marty—Dan's old friend, recent savior, and more recent nemesis, a six-foot-three man-child with a goofy grin that masked a bottomless insecurity. Occasionally, it exploded into rage; Dan had seen flashes of that over their three-plus years working together, but Marty had never directed it at him until last May, when in the course of a single conversation about his contract renewal, Dan managed to fall from his perch as Marty's golden boy to a near-pariah who, despite being the workhorse of *BT: NYC*'s writing staff, almost hadn't been brought back for the fourth season.

Five months and ten episodes later, Marty still wasn't over it. As a lifelong people-pleaser, this meant Dan wasn't, either. But the freeze had been slowly thawing, and Dan suspected that if he could crack these two replacement stories, the creative offering might finally persuade Marty to get over his pissy grudge.

Reaching the stoplight at Hawthorne Avenue, Dan shifted his foot from the gas to the brake. He took a long, deep breath of the crisp October air, and as he paused to let it out, he felt the familiar flutter of creative anxiety in his gut.

I've got nothing.

He let the breath out in a whoosh.

Two hours. Plenty of time.

Of all the gifts his career change had bestowed on Dan, his optimism was perhaps the most surprising to him. He'd always been self-confident in a narrow sense—even back in his old life on the existential treadmill of corporate law, with its mandatory suits and eleven-hour workdays billed in six-minute increments, he never doubted his ability to handle whatever life shoveled onto his plate.

He just refused to believe that things ever worked out, for himself or anybody. Corporate Law Dan was a grim fatalist with a profound skepticism about the notion that the moral arc of the universe bent toward justice.

But now—after a miracle of self-reinvention that saw him trade his dreary Talmudic parsings of Rule 105 under Regulation M of the Securities Exchange Act for a career in which he got paid mid-six figures to dream up lurid sadomasochistic fantasies involving a deranged fictional cop, assemble them into a sequence of cause and effect, and watch Ray Liotta perform the results on a soundstage in Queens—he possessed a faith in karmic fairness that his old self would have considered dangerously naïve. New Improved Hollywood Dan believed that life unfolded according to a plan which—given sufficient inputs of talent and hard work—could be controlled, or at least directed.

It was a solvable puzzle. All of it.

Episodes eighty-four and eighty-six? Solvable puzzle.

Dan's strained relationship with Marty? Solvable.

Even Jen and the kids were solvable.

But Jesus, they'd been a handful lately.

Chloe was a basket case of anxiety over grades, tennis, and her last-ditch third swing at the ACT before the Dartmouth early decision deadline. Max seemed trapped in the personality-distortion field of puberty, both desperately in need of guidance (or, at a minimum, some kind of extracurricular that didn't involve staring at a screen) and totally uninterested in accepting it, at least from his parents.

And Jen was barely holding it together. Her career was a mess, and her compensatory decision to assume managerial control over Chloe's college application process, while well-intentioned, had ignited a psychodramatic mother-daughter trash fire that Dan worried was doing more harm than good.

If nothing else, it was the reason his wife had been putting away half a bottle of wine a night recently. He couldn't blame her for that. Psychologically, Jen's problem was obvious: she'd spent the last seventeen years devoting herself to the kids, and now that they were getting old enough not to need her anymore, she was mentally stuck between the two stools of full-time parenting and full-time work. Hopefully, the end of the college admissions melodrama would set her free to finally put the focus back on herself. She'd had a great career going before she stopped out to be a full-time mom. And sure, maybe she'd stayed out a little too long. But she was still young and talented enough to get back on track. She just had to put herself out there, quit spinning her wheels on short-term marketing projects and get across the river to network in Manhattan.

What Jen really needed was a *Bullet Town: NYC* of her own. A professional rebirth. A new and improved Jen.

She'd get there eventually. So would the kids. Chloe might be stressed, but she was a badass. In a couple months, all that stress would pay off when she got in early to Dartmouth. Max would figure things out, too. He was a good kid. Awkward, a little insecure, even worse at sports than Dan had been at that age. But he was smart, with a sharp sense of humor and a strong creative streak. That movie he'd made at arts camp over the summer had showed some real promise. If he could just keep building on that, he'd eventually come out the other side of puberty as the capable young man he was destined to be.

Notwithstanding all the recent bickering and foul moods in the Altman household, fundamentally all four of them were fine.

More than fine. They were blessed.

Dan parked his car in the New Jersey Transit lot at the Upper Lincolnwood station, then crossed the street to Barnaby's. It was a recent addition to the two-block cluster of businesses on Hawthorne, run by a couple of hipster refugees from Bushwick who had impeccable design taste and served high-end breakfast and lunch items that were almost delicious enough to justify their prices. Dan ordered a large coffee and an organic yogurt with granola and berries, gave the server behind the counter his name, and took a seat at one of the small tables along the exposed brick side wall. Then he pulled his black leather Moleskine from his messenger bag, slipped off the elastic closure, and looked at the notes he'd scrawled during last night's commute home.

Every episode of *BT: NYC* unfolded according to a strict formula. In the cold opening, a New Yorker was murdered. In Act 1, Detective Vargas was assigned the case. By Act 3, he'd solved it. In Act 4, the feckless criminal justice system botched the prosecution, and the murderer went free. In the Act 5 climax, Vargas murdered the murderer, leaving no evidence of his involvement and ensuring that justice had been done in a manner that only seemed fascist if you thought about it too hard.

Several op-ed writers had done just that over the first two

seasons, but for the show's 9.1 million remaining viewers (not terrible, although well off its season one peak of 12.3 million), the story arc was as satisfying as it was predictable.

Even so, the lower ratings had brought increased meddling from the network, which had just rejected two of Marty's most recent story outlines on the grounds that their templates—"disgruntled-ex-wife-murders-successful-former-husband" and "pompous-critic-gets-offed-by-righteously-angry-subject-of-bad-review"—had already been used in at least four episodes each.

This statistic was unsurprising to anyone familiar with Marty's marital history, his views on the state of professional television criticism, and his habit of using Detective Vargas as a proxy for the exorcism of his personal demons. Nevertheless, it left the writers' room with a pair of gaping holes that needed filling ASAP. So far, the only options Dan had come up with were:

Crooked cop shaking down produce stand guy—Vargas poisons
    w/exotic Chinese veg?
Mossad agent shot by Hamas Uber driver—Vargas has to work
    w/hot Israeli cointel
School principal runs pedo ring—Vargas asphyxiates w/black-
    board eraser (retro?)

None of these seemed promising, even by the eroding standards of season four. If Dan wanted the glory of bailing out the writing staff—as well as the satisfaction of finally redeeming himself in Marty's eyes—he needed more and better. And he needed it by the time the writers' room convened at ten.

He tucked his AirPods into his ears, cranked up a live version of "The Core" from Clapton's *Crossroads 2*, and uncapped the monogrammed Waterman pen that he'd received as a gift on his fiftieth birthday. Pushing his glasses up on the bridge of his nose, he narrowed his eyes in a determined glare.

Time to kick ass.

It was 8:07 a.m.

CHLOE

Emma Schroeder's white Jetta was idling at the foot of the Altmans' driveway. Still red-eyed and glowering from the breakfast fight with her mom, Chloe stalked down the drive, her racket bag and overstuffed backpack on either shoulder. She flung open the passenger door, shoved the rackets in the back, and sank into the seat with her pack on her lap, slamming the door with enough force to compel Emma's question:

"What's the matter?"

"My mom is *such* a dick."

Emma shook her head as she steered out of Brantley Circle. "That's a gendered insult. Women can't be dicks."

"Fine, whatever. She's a fucking bitch."

"Okay, that's misogynistic."

"How? I'm a woman! She's my *mom*."

"Yeah, but you've internalized this totally toxic social norm where any woman who acts assertively gets called a bitch. Which is how the patriarchy—"

"*Emma!*" She was Chloe's best and most supportive friend, but in the six months since she'd started hanging out on Twitter, she'd developed an exhausting habit of dragging their conversations into rabbit holes of sociocultural critique. "Can we just talk about why I'm mad?"

"Okay! Sorry. Tell me what happened. But first, take a deep, cleansing breath."

Chloe filled her lungs, then pushed the air out in a sharp huff. "Okay, that actually helped," she admitted.

"Right? So, what's up?"

As she spoke, Chloe unzipped an outer pocket of her backpack and took out one of the protein bars she'd wound up grabbing for her breakfast. "You know how the Dartmouth supplemental is, like, 'Talk about an episode in your life where you showed resilience?' And I was going to write about that crazy thing that happened with my backhand where I basically forgot how to hit it?"

Emma nodded. "You got the yips." Emma didn't play tennis, but she was a forward on the varsity basketball team, so she could relate to Chloe's problem on a sports-psychology level.

"Right. And the more I tried to fix it, the worse it got. I went to, like, two different pros, saw a therapist, tried that visualization shit—"

"But you got over it. Right?"

"I *thought* I did. For, like, a week. Then yesterday, it came back again! Right in the fucking middle of sectionals!"

"Ohmygod! Why didn't I know this already?"

"I just didn't want to deal." Chloe pressed her eyes shut and swallowed hard. "I mean, it's like, whatever. Lydia won, and so did both the doubles, so we're still in the tournament. But, like, not only did I totally choke—it blew up my whole essay! Because it was going to be all, 'I had this crazy problem, and I worked my butt off, and I *fixed* it—'"

"'Cause you've got grit! Admissions people eat that shit up."

"Yeah. Except I have no grit. Because I can't hit a fucking backhand!"

"Well, but . . . maybe it's just, like, a different *kind* of grit—"

"That's what I started thinking," Chloe agreed through a mouthful of protein bar. "Right? Like, emotional maturity grit. So last night, I rewrote it to be, like, 'Sometimes you work your butt off, and it's *still* not enough. But as long as you worked your absolute hardest—'"

"You gotta be okay with the outcome. 'Cause you did your best. Totally! Focus on the effort. That's good shit."

"Right? *Right?* So I go to bed thinking, like, maybe the essay's actually better this way. Like, it's more real or something."

"Sounds good to me."

"But then after I went to sleep, my mom went on the Google Doc and *shit all over me*. Like, not even just the essay—like, me as a human being."

"She did not!"

"Oh, yeah. She was, like, 'You sound like a total fucking loser.'"

"Ohmygod!"

"I mean, she didn't say 'fucking.' But she was, like, 'You're a loser, and you should throw this whole thing out and write about *math class*.'"

"Ohmygod, Frenchie . . . I am so sorry. That sucks so much."

"It gets worse." Chloe's voice was starting to break. "This morning, I come down to breakfast, and she's, like, 'Why are you so emotional?'"

"Are you kidding me? After she wrote that shit?"

"Right? I was, like, 'You called me a loser!' And then— ohmygod! She was, like, 'No, I didn't.'"

"Whaaaat? Was she trying to gaslight you?"

"Basically! It was the craziest thing—she was, like, 'You're misinterpreting me.' And I was, like, '*Read what you wrote!*' I swear to God, I think she might've been too drunk to remember writing it."

Emma laughed in disbelief. "Holy shit! Your mom was wasted on a Monday night? That's, like, intervention time."

Chloe shook her head, recoiling from the idea. "No, I mean, she's not—I'm totally kidding. Like, she drinks a lot. But not, like, *a lot* a lot." She stuffed the rest of the protein bar in her mouth, then crumpled the wrapper in her fist. "But, like—" She struggled to get the words out past the protein bar. "Would *your* parents shit all over you like that?"

"No, they'd have Linda do it." Linda was Emma's college admissions consultant. "Except they pay her too much to actually shit on me? So she'd probably just, like, rewrite my essay until I had no idea what it even meant anymore."

Chloe sighed. "I don't know. Maybe I shouldn't ED to Dartmouth."

"That's crazy! Where would you ED?"

"I don't know. NYU?"

"Do they have a supplemental?"

"I think so. But it's not bad. It's, like, one essay."

"I feel like you can do better than NYU. What's their ACT?"

"I forget. I'd have to check Naviance." Chloe pulled an apple out of her bag, then rummaged in another pocket for her phone. "But it's definitely lower. So I wouldn't have to take the ACT Saturday and risk getting a shitty score—"

"But there's no way that'll happen. Right? I mean, your practice scores—"

"Ohmygod! I didn't tell you this? I took a practice test Sunday and got a *twenty-nine* on the math."

"*Holy shittles!* How did that happen?"

"I don't know!" Chloe had finally found her phone. "I swear to God, this has been the worst week of my li—*AAAAAH!*"

"What?"

Chloe straightened her shoulders, squirming back against the seat as her eyes stayed riveted on the screen. She pressed her thumb on an Instagram notification. "Josh replied to my comment!"

"The one from last night? What did he say?"

"'IKR . . .' then a laughing emoji . . . then 'Do u know any good ones . . .' then a winking emoji."

Emma scrunched up her nose, confused. "Wait, what did he post again?"

"This selfie of, like, half his face, and he's lying on the floor, and the caption is, 'TFW u swam a three mile set and can't stand up."

"And your comment was . . . ?"

"'Awww poor baby,' crutch emoji, 'somebody needs a massage therapist.'"

"And he said?"

"'IKR, do u know any good ones?'"

"So he's basically saying, 'Give me a massage'?"

"Right? How should I reply?"

"Don't."

"At all?"

"It took him, what? Twelve hours to answer you?"

"Nine. And a half. But I don't think he's on Insta that much. He might not even have notifications on."

"So what? Don't reply until at *least* lunch."

"But what do I say then?"

"Then you neg him. Be, like, 'I know this amazing three-hundred-pound Swedish guy named Hans.'"

"Savage! I like that."

Emma squinted as she looked through the windshield. They were driving down an empty residential side street. Up ahead on Broadmoor Avenue, the traffic was bumper-to-bumper in the direction of the high school. "Hey, isn't that your brother?"

Just off the curb a short distance from the corner, Max was standing hunched behind a parked car, straddling his mountain bike with his fist against his mouth. As the Jetta closed the distance between them, he lowered the fist and exhaled a cloud of vapor twice the size of his head.

"Ohmygod, he is *such* a little criminal." Chloe lowered the window and bellowed, "*Max Altman! You're under arrest!*"

MAX

His sister's yell startled him so much that Max nearly fell over when his flinch jostled the bike hard enough to send its front wheel spinning backward into his leg. He managed to stay on his feet, but only at the price of looking like an idiot. As the Jetta stopped at the corner a few feet ahead, he flipped Chloe off. She leaned out the window and yelled back at him.

"You said you were quitting!"

"I'm tapering!"

This wasn't true, unless it was somehow possible to taper up.

"You'd better be! Or I'm telling Mom!"

Max scowled at the Jetta as it turned up Broadmoor, merging into the line of cars headed for the high school. His fight-or-flight response had been on a hair trigger lately, and Chloe's surprise shout had just flooded his mental circuits with an adrenaline surge of fear that was combining in unpleasant ways with the head rush from his fourth Juul hit of the day. Suddenly, his arms and legs felt so shaky that he wasn't sure he could pedal straight.

My sister's a dick.

He took a deep breath, trying to settle his nerves. Rationally, he knew it was silly to fear an unprovoked attack. In the two and a half weeks since Jordan Stankovic had punched Max in the side of the head while they waited in line for slices at Mario's Pizza, his assailant hadn't even made eye contact with him, let alone threatened him again.

But Max's limbic system wasn't big on rationality. His fingers trembled as he zipped the Juul into the chest pocket of his jacket. Dismounting the bike, he lifted it over the curb onto the sidewalk. Better to go on foot until the shakes went away.

He turned onto Broadmoor, and the whole school arrival scene opened up in front of him. Hundreds of kids, borne by cars, buses, bikes, and skateboards, were funneling into the Gothic-arched maw of Lincolnwood High's century-old building. Up ahead on the sidewalk, Max spotted the familiar logo of Dennis Gerdes's *Attack on Titan* backpack. He quickened his pace, catching up with Dennis and Andy Ko just before they reached the crosswalk at Grove Street.

"What up?"

"Yo." His friends gave him perfunctory nods before returning to their conversation. "Just hang out on the roof and snipe people," Dennis was telling Andy.

"No way, dude. They'll come up through the building next door and pick me off from behind."

Ugh. "When are you going to quit playing COD?" Max asked them.

Andy snorted. "When are you going to start again?"

"You should get back into it," Dennis told him. "New maps dropped yesterday!"

Max rolled his eyes. "Ohmygod. *So* exciting. My dick gets hard just thinking about it."

"Your loss, bruh," Andy said with a shrug. Then he and

Dennis returned to their COD talk. Max fell in behind them, simmering in silence.

It was no exaggeration to say that the Call of Duty multi-player was the root of all his problems. Until his three closest friends—Dennis, Andy, and Ben Schwartz—had all gotten way too into it while Max was away at summer camp, he'd been the alpha in their group. When they played D&D, he was the dungeon master. When they played poker—a game Max had introduced them to!—he usually won. And even though they all pretended to look down on him for it, the fact that he had a Juul addiction gave him street cred none of them possessed.

If he'd had a fair start when the locus of their social lives unexpectedly moved to the COD multiplayer, he might've been able to sustain his dominance, or at least hold his own. But by the time he got back from Camp Meadowlark, they all had six weeks' worth of combat experience on him, and Max—who, owing to an embarrassing lack of hand-eye coordination, had always sucked at video games—never caught up. He was the weak link on any team, with a kill–death ratio that lagged far behind his friends.

The situation was aggravating but tolerable, right up until school started and Andy brought Grayson Oliver into it. Grayson was a braying jackass on the freshman football team who was so obnoxious that he only had one friend in their entire class: big, dumb, lumbering Jordan Stankovic. Jordan and Max had been next-door neighbors for most of their lives, but other than a brief Pokémon-related dalliance in the second grade, Max had largely avoided socializing with him. Jordan was just no fun at all. He had the personality of a lump of three-day-old mashed potatoes that had somehow become sentient, and in the absence of charisma or better options, he loped around after Grayson like a needy puppy.

There was no good reason to hang out with either of them. But somewhere around the second week of school, Andy had bonded with Grayson in study hall over COD and invited him—without bothering to clear the invite with Max or anyone else—to join their cadre's nightly deathmatch. When Grayson showed up, he brought Jordan along.

Jordan sucked at COD. But he sucked just a little bit less than Max did.

From there, it was a rapid and psychologically punishing descent to the fateful afternoon in Mario's Pizza when a round of COD-inspired trash-talking led Jordan to crudely insult Max's manhood. Max countered with a put-down so withering that the enraged yet verbally incompetent Jordan struck back with a fist to the side of Max's skull.

The assault came as a shock to everyone, bystanders included. Physical violence among the town's adolescent boys was rare, and Max—who responded not by counterattacking, but by fleeing the scene before anyone could register the tears welling in his eyes—expected his friends to close ranks around him in the aftermath, shunning Jordan out of solidarity.

Instead, something like the opposite had happened. Dennis, Andy, and Ben all agreed that what Jordan had done was totally uncool. But then they quickly drew a curtain of embarrassed silence around the incident—except for Grayson, who told the entire freshman football team about it at practice that week—and continued their nightly deathmatches with Max's assailant, while giving no thought at all to the feelings of his victim. Within a couple of days, it was like the whole thing had never happened.

Except to Max. The incident haunted him day and night. It wasn't the trauma so much as the fact that it shattered his sense of place in the hierarchy of Lincolnwood High's freshman class. Prior to the punch in the head, Max placed himself somewhere in the lower part of the upper fiftieth percentile—not an obvious baller like Mike Santiago or Jack Metcalfe, but still higher status than Dennis, Andy, or Ben, and much cooler than Jordan or Grayson.

Plus, he'd gone into that school year with some real upward momentum. Summer camp in Maine had been a massive success. Not only had Max been the de facto leader of Cabin Six and the writer, director, and star of a short film, *Attack of the Killer Mosquitoes*, that triggered peals of laughter when it was shown to the whole camp at Arts Night. He'd also enjoyed an unexpected end-of-summer hookup with Anna Schwartzman, who was both a year older than him and the kind of girl he'd previously considered unattainable.

Entering high school in September, Max was riding so high that he'd started to fantasize about making a play for Kayleigh Adams. He'd had a secret crush on her since seventh grade, and she'd always seemed way out of his league—in the social order, Kayleigh was pretty and well-liked enough to flirt with the ninetieth percentile. But the ego boost from his directorial debut and his summer mini romance had left Max with both a heightened sense of the possible and a road map for achieving the kind of performing-arts-based success that might compensate for his lack of athletic ability.

Kayleigh's nose ring and the streak of dyed magenta in her hair indicated she was probably artsy enough to be won over by that kind of thing. All Max had to do was figure out how to replicate his filmmaking success in the context of school. He'd already started daydreaming about how to make that happen when Jordan's fist threw a wrench into everything.

If character is revealed through action—as Max's summer filmmaking teacher had drilled into him—then those few seconds in the pizza place had been life-altering. Max had outed himself as someone who, when physically attacked, would respond not by standing up for himself, but by running away like a little bitch. The fact that he'd been victimized by such a low-status clown as Jordan only multiplied the shame.

It didn't matter that the story probably hadn't spread as far as Kayleigh, or that even loudmouthed Grayson quit teasing him about it after a couple of days. The fact that Max knew himself to be a coward was so devastating to his self-esteem that he'd come to view kicking Jordan's ass as his only route back to mental and social health.

His YouTube research had yielded a best-in-class option for taking down a much larger opponent: a karate chop to the nerve endings at the base of the neck, which if delivered with proper form (*full twist at the hips, weight moving forward, keep the shoulder horizontal*) should be sufficient to literally bring Jordan to his knees. The only remaining question was how to instigate a second fight. He couldn't strike without warning—the YouTubers had been unanimous that only bullies threw sucker punches. So he had to get Jordan to come at him first, verbally if not physically. That was challenging, not least because Jordan seemed determined to ignore him. Engineering a showdown would require some creativity.

But if there was one thing Max still had confidence in, it was his imagination. As he peeled off from Dennis and Andy and guided his bike through the before-school crowd on the fading buzz of his Juul hit, he conjured his adversary in his mind's eye and began to brainstorm possible opening lines.

Yo, Jordan—we've got some unfinished business.

So, Jordan—I couldn't help noticing you haven't apologized to me yet.

Hey, Jordan—remember that conversation we started at Mario's a couple weeks ago? It's time to finish it.

None of those felt right. But given enough time, he'd figure it out. Max locked up his bike at the rack on the edge of the parking lot and joined the stream of kids heading into the building.

It was 8:27 a.m.

JEN

The house had been silent since Chloe slammed the front door on her way out. Jen sat slouched at the kitchen table, arms folded against her chest, staring unfocused at the black screen of her laptop. It had gone to sleep.

Sooner or later, she'd have to wake it up, open the Google Doc, and figure out what she'd written last night to set off her daughter.

She had a hazy memory of having read and rolled her eyes at Chloe's latest draft of the Dartmouth supplemental. But why had Jen wound up reading it in the first place? As best she could recall, she'd only gone online to check Everlane for winter sweaters.

A Google Docs notification must have popped up while she was browsing, and she'd clicked over to it. And then apparently left a comment or three.

How bad could it have been? I was sober enough not to buy any sweaters.

Or was I? Did I buy sweaters last night?

Jesus, my head hurts.

She dragged her index finger across the laptop's trackpad, bringing the screen to life. Scanned her inbox to confirm the absence of purchase receipts. Then she got up, plodded to the sink, turned on the faucet, and let the water run cold as she fetched a drinking glass from the cabinet. She filled it to the brim, then gulped down most of it before stopping abruptly when her stomach threatened to reverse gears.

I've got to quit doing this.

She half filled the glass and took it back to the table. Sat down again in front of the computer.

Her desktop image was a picture from their end-of-summer trip to Nantucket. All four Altmans stood grinning on a dock. The oversized sunglasses Max had refused to take off looked a little absurd, but his smile—usually the weak link in any family photo, a pasted-on grimace that came off as more pained than happy—actually seemed genuine. Jen wondered, not for the first time, if she should use the picture for their holiday card.

Then she shifted her gaze to Chloe and remembered why she was sitting there.

Shit . . .

How bad could it be?

She opened her browser and hovered over the Google Docs tab for a moment before losing her courage and clicking to the *New York Times* instead. She scrolled down the home page, so distracted that she was on her fourth headline before she realized she'd already read them all.

She clicked over to Weather Underground. Low sixties and sunny for the next two days, then a bad stretch of heavy rain Thursday. A remnant of that hurricane coming up from the Gulf.

Just get it over with.

Jen opened Google Docs and selected "Dartmouth Supplemental 3" from the top of the list.

There were only two comments in the right margin. The first was Jen's, from Monday at 11:14 p.m.:

NOOOOO MESSAGE CAN NOT BE "ACCEPT
DEFEAT"—ur brand is POET WARRIOR—this makes u
sound like a loser—if u can't spin as victory then trash this
and write about how u used to suck at math

Underneath it was a response from Chloe at 7:27 a.m. today:

I love you too mom

Ouch.
What the hell was I thinking?
I mean, she DID sound like a loser.
But, Jesus, don't SAY that, you idiot.
Jen stared at the two comments for a while. She tried revising her opinion of the situation.
It's not that bad. Chloe overreacted.
But the dull ache spreading in the pit of Jen's stomach said otherwise. Her emotional hangover was starting to act as a force multiplier on her physical one.
I should go back to bed.
I should take a shower.
I should have a drink.
None of those things happened downstairs. She deleted her comment on the doc, pushed back from the table, stood up, and left the kitchen, not sure yet what path she'd take when she got to the second floor.
A moment later, she reached the top of the landing. At the end of the long hallway, the door to the linen closet loomed like a demonic portal in a Stephen King novel.

Don't open it.

You have to.

One way or another, you've got to get rid of it.

She walked down the hall to the door. Turned the knob, drew it back, bent over, and reached deep into the gloom of the lower shelf, behind the spare guest room sheets.

She pulled out a one-liter bottle of Stolichnaya. It was half empty.

Think like an optimist, Jennifer. It's not half empty. It's half full!

Hahahahahaaaaaahhhhfuck.

She walked back to the stairs. Took three steps down, sank her butt onto the top step, and set the bottle next to the wall on her right.

Then she had a good cry.

Jennifer Anne Riehl, Michigan '91, Wharton '96, Deloitte, AmEx, class mom (K–4), Ridgefield Avenue School PTO Treasurer (three consecutive terms), was not the kind of person who drank vodka out of the bottle before noon on a weekday while unshowered and wearing sweatpants.

And yet somehow, it kept happening.

When is this going to end?

Today?

Is it over? Am I finally done?

Is this the first day of the rest of my life?

The answer was yes. But not in the sense Jen imagined.

It was 8:44 a.m.

DAN

The fifty minutes Dan spent staring at his notebook in Barnaby's were unproductive. By the time he left to catch the 8:52 train, he'd only come up with two story ideas that felt even halfway viable:

> celeb chef murdered—Vargas loves his gnocchi?

> artist impaled on his own sculpture—OR artist is the perp?—
> performance artist—murder IS the performance?

Neither was likely to work. The former didn't go anywhere plotwise, and Marty would inevitably shoot down the latter on the grounds that it was too highbrow. He'd probably accuse Dan of sniffing his own farts, which had become Marty's go-to put-down ever since their falling out.

That, and calling Dan "Princeton boy." Which was particularly galling, seeing as how they'd first met when Marty lived down the hall from him freshman year, and the whole sequence of events that led to Dan writing for *Bullet Town: NYC* began when they reconnected at their twenty-fifth reunion.

Fucking Marty . . .

I've got to give him something better than this.

As Dan hurried toward the Upper Lincolnwood station, he

tried to quiet the whine of creative anxiety in his head with the thought that he could spend the forty-minute trip into Manhattan playing "Victim or Perpetrator?" It was an idea-generating exercise in which he imagined his fellow commuters as characters on *BT: NYC*, and over the years, it had been good for a surprisingly large number of ideas. In season three alone, the show had killed off almost a dozen riders of the Lincolnwood–Bergen line, most of them dispatched by their co-passengers.

Dan trotted up Forest Street and crossed the tracks to the inbound platform just as Pete Blackwell arrived from the other direction, coming downhill on foot from his family's mansion on Mountain Avenue.

"Hey!" Dan greeted him with a grin as their paths converged on the platform. "You're getting a late start." In Lincolnwood's commuter taxonomy, Pete was a 7:18, not an 8:52.

Pete rolled his big brown eyes in the direction of his genetically blessed hairline. "Tess's shower backed up, so I had the rare pleasure of spending my morning snaking her drain." It was very on-brand for Pete Blackwell to do his own plumbing. The only non-asshole hedge fund founder Dan had ever met, he had a net worth rumored to be in the ten figures, a face and build that belonged on a modeling runway, and a home listed on the National Register of Historic Places—yet he somehow managed to convey such an unassuming charm that nobody in Lincolnwood resented him, at least not out loud.

The whole Blackwell family was like that. Tess, the oldest of their three daughters, was Chloe's age, and Jen had shared class mom duties more than once with Meg Blackwell, who actually *had* clocked time on a modeling runway before getting her master's in public health from Johns Hopkins and cofounding a charity that distributed antimalarial mosquito nets in Africa.

"The absolute worst thing about the Blackwells," Jen had once declared upon returning home from an evening spent assembling gift baskets for the elementary school faculty in Meg's massive-yet-somehow-still-cozy living room, "is that there's no worst thing about the Blackwells."

Although Tess Blackwell's angelic mane of thick, honey-blond hair apparently had its drawbacks, at least as far as their National Register of Historic Plumbing was concerned.

"Pulled a lot of hair out?" Dan asked with a sympathetic grimace.

"*So much* hair. I could've made a coat from it. By the way—thanks for the birthday invite! We're looking forward to it."

"You're coming? That's great! It's just a small thing this time—it's not like fifty-one's a milestone." When he turned fifty, Dan had thrown himself a cocktail party, and it was so much fun that he'd decided to do it again this year.

"After fifty, they're *all* milestones, my friend." The train was pulling in, and Pete had to raise his voice to be heard above the screech of the brakes.

"I guess so," Dan conceded as they headed for the nearest door. "It's mostly just an excuse to get people together. No gifts this time! Although I do love my pen."

"We will get you absolutely nothing, I promise," Pete said, patting him on the back as they stepped up into the train. Dan doubted that was true. Meg Blackwell was the kind of person who showed up to a no-gifts party not just with a gift, but an impeccably chosen one in a price range that walked the narrow line between thoughtful and extravagant.

As he settled into a rear-facing window seat and Pete continued past him down the aisle to a seat of his own, Dan savored the aftertaste of their exchange. One of the many dividends of his new career was that he'd become interesting to people like Pete and Meg Blackwell. Four years ago, Dan couldn't have imagined them actually attending a party at his house—they would've instantly RSVP'd with regrets, citing some ironclad yet unverifiable excuse. But lately, when they ran into each other at school curriculum nights, Pete actively sought out Dan to make small talk. Coming from a man so rich he didn't fly commercial and so handsome he could've played bass for Duran Duran, the attention was gratifying on a level that—as minor and silly as it might seem—felt like a validation of Dan's existence.

He retrieved his Moleskine from his messenger bag, propped them both on his lap, reinserted his AirPods, dialed up *Let It Bleed* for atmosphere, uncapped his Meg-Blackwell-gifted Waterman pen, and raised his head to look around for a suitable "Victim or Perpetrator?" candidate.

A retired couple sharing the *New York Times*.

Husband murders wife? Vice versa?

Done to death. No pun intended.

The train pulled out of the station. As "Gimme Shelter" conjured the apocalypse in his ears, Dan moved on to the next candidate—a stylish business-casual gay millennial in a purple baseball cap.

Advertising exec murders . . . ?

No. Too upscale.

Mom with eight-year-old in Hogwarts hat.

Mom kills kid? Ugh, no. Way too dark.

Kid kills mom? He's an evil genius?

Could be cool.

But then Vargas would have to kill the kid.

So, no.

Dan looked around. There were no other good candidates. He'd have to wait for more passengers to come on at the next stop.

He took his glasses off, pulled the bottom of his T-shirt out from under his V-neck sweater, and used it to wipe the lenses clean. Then he put them back on and returned to the ideas he'd written down back at Barnaby's, hoping to add more depth to them.

What if celebrity chef is a perp instead of a victim? And they poison someone?

Who would they poison? A presidential candidate? Too big.

Mayoral candidate? Running on a platform of . . . food labeling? Calorie counts?

Nobody gives a shit about food labeling.

The train pulled into the Lincoln Avenue station. Dan took out his phone and checked the time.

8:59 a.m.

A few dozen people boarded the train. On Dan's earphones, "Love in Vain" gave way to "Country Honk." It was a poor fit with his search for evil in the hearts of New Jersey commuters, so he swapped it out for the doom-laden chords of the first Black Sabbath album.

A mousy, Slavic-looking librarian type wearing John Lennon

specs and a puffy maroon three-quarter-length coat sat down next to him.

Librarian murders author?
No. Too close to Misery.
Librarian gets murdered?
By who?
A guy who read a book about murdering a librarian.

This one was worth writing down.

Creepy patron murders librarian—
reenacts murder in crime novel he checked out

Dan glanced to his right. Mousy Librarian had taken out her phone and was playing some kind of Candy Crush knockoff.

Doesn't read during commute.
Not a librarian.
Receptionist?
OR . . . maybe an incompetent *librarian?*
Who plays Candy Crush instead of reading books?

Librarian doesn't read books—creepy patron offended

The details might be wrong, but there was meat on this bone. Dan studied his seatmate out of the corner of his eye. She was laser-focused on her screen, mouth hanging open as her eyes followed the game in random, darting zigzags.

Sweet—simple-minded—no friends—lonely

He looked around for minor characters to populate the story. Two rows away, in a front-facing seat on the south side of the train, was a heavyset Asian twentysomething wearing Bose headphones and staring into his laptop.

> Vargas gets list of guys who checked out same book
> Nerdy programmer fits serial killer profile
> BUT turns out to be innocent

This was good. Dan drew five vertical slashes in his notebook to represent the act breaks, then pondered how to label them.

> CO: poisoning? / V finds book / nerd dead end? / ? / trial / V kills
> w/sequel plot?

9:08 a.m. The train pulled into Newark Broad Street.

Twenty people exited the car. Forty more replaced them. Mousy Librarian was forced to scoot over so close to Dan that their jackets touched, in order to make room for a bearded hipster with a Captain America shield backpack and a button on the chest pocket of his fatigue jacket that read STRONG FEMALE PROTAGONIST.

Dan sat up a little straighter and—leaving some empty space under his act-break schematic for the librarian murder idea— added a new line in all caps:

> MURDER AT COMIC CON

Brilliant.

Cinematic setting, tons of fun. Skewed a little young for the *BT: NYC* audience, but that was fine, as long as the tone condescended to Comic Con in a way that let the audience feel superior.

cosplay knight kills w/real sword

(Ninja? Reaper w/scythe? Thor w/hammer?)

montage: Vargas interrogates cosplay superheroes

one offers to help investigate (I'm a superhero!)

Dan looked up from the page. "Victim or Perpetrator?" had delivered for him once again. It was such good stuff that he had to resist the urge to play air drums along with the Sabbath song chugging in his ears.

Thank God for New Jersey Transit.

He caught his reflection in the window, experienced his usual reaction—*when the hell did I turn into a doughy middle-aged guy?*—but was so pleased with his creative breakthrough that he managed, for the moment at least, to accept his physical decline with compassion rather than beating himself up for not eating salads at lunch or waking up early to exercise.

Beyond his reflection, the Newark skyline passed out of view as the train entered the no-man's-land west of Jersey City. Dan let his mind wander as he watched fenced-in industrial equipment lots give way to an expanse of tall weeds, then open water bisected by the beginning of the seventy-five-foot-high viaduct that carried the New Jersey Turnpike over the Hackensack River toward Manhattan.

Dan turned his head to admire the massive, slender structure.

That's a big viaduct. . . . Maybe somebody gets thrown off it in the cold opening? Then Vargas could partner up with a Jersey cop who—

The music in his AirPods stopped.

In the same instant, the lights on the train car winked out.

The background *whirr* of the circulation fans faded away, and the steady rumble of track seams passing underneath stretched and slowed. The scenery out the window gradually stopped moving across Dan's field of view.

It was suddenly, disconcertingly quiet.

"Ugh!" Mousy Librarian huffed. Dan glanced at her. She was jabbing at her phone's newly dead screen in frustration.

"What the hell?" a woman exclaimed from somewhere behind him.

Dan pulled out his iPhone to check the time and turn his music back on.

The screen was black. When Dan tapped it, nothing happened.

The eerie silence in the car began to fill up with mutters, grunts, and whispers of confusion and complaint. Dan kept tapping his screen.

Still nothing.

Oh, come on!

As he held down the side power button to restart his phone, he looked across the aisle at Nerdy Asian Programmer, who was glowering at his laptop while he tapped its unresponsive keyboard.

Someone in the back of the car called out, "Does anybody's phone work?"

The answer seemed to be no.

Dan kept pressing down his power button, but the glowing white apple refused to reappear.

"What the heck is going on?" someone exclaimed.

Dan scowled. *This better not be serious. I've got to get to work.*

As he craned his neck, surveying the other frustrated passengers, a distant whine reached his ears from somewhere to the southeast.

In the space of a few seconds, it climbed in volume and pitch until it sounded like the shriek of a Nazi dive bomber in some World War II documentary.

Then a woman at the front end of the car screamed in terror. *"OHMYGO—!"*

Other voices joined hers, but their cries were smothered in the roar of an explosion so thunderous that Dan felt it vibrate in his chest cavity.

The two-hundred-plus people in the car uttered a collective gasp of shock.

Then everybody began to move at once.

JEN

Sitting atop the stairs next to the half-empty bottle of vodka—her imaginary friend, domestic companion, and pitiless shitlord—Jen contemplated the sequence of events that had gotten her into this mess.

It was a long story. But there was plenty of time for it. She had nothing on her agenda except shopping, banking, figuring out how to heal the pain she'd just inflicted on her overstressed daughter, and fundamentally changing the trajectory of her life.

She'd made some poor choices. But even as she considered herself a horrible and possibly irredeemable person, in Jen's self-telling, she wasn't the story's villain.

Oddly enough, alcohol wasn't, either.

The real villain was Erin Fucking Tiernan.

To be fair, Jen had liked to drink long before she ever met Erin. And as with most things Jen enjoyed—tennis, school, arguing about politics—she was good at it. But other than the occasional cringe-inducing hookup in her late teens and twenties, and that too-close-for-comfort brush with a DUI on a post-college trip to Napa with her former sorority sisters, it had never been a problem. By the time she and Dan got married in '99, she was mostly down to weekends only, and she rarely had more than three, or maybe five, in an evening.

Then she got pregnant with Chloe in the summer of 2001, and for nine months, she didn't have so much as a glass of wine.

Which was a real feat, considering that those months coincided with the biggest trauma of her life.

She was eleven weeks into the pregnancy and twenty minutes into her workday on the twenty-sixth floor of the World Financial Center when the first plane hit the North Tower a few hundred feet from her desk. In the shock and confusion that followed, she didn't get out as fast as she should have. When she finally made it home on foot to her and Dan's two-bedroom walkup in the Flatiron District, there were ashes in her hair and images in her head that would keep her up at night for months.

But in the short term, the post-traumatic stress paled next to her anxiety over the effect that breathing in toxins from the Trade Center fire was having on her unborn child. The week after the attack, when even the air outside their apartment two miles north of Ground Zero was so thick with scorched-chemical stink that they couldn't leave the windows open, AmEx moved Jen's division into temporary offices on Wall Street, just a few blocks from the still-burning rubble. Both the HR department and the federal government swore the air was safe to breathe, even as Goldman Sachs next door was warning their pregnant employees to stay home.

Then came October's anthrax scare, the cherry on top of Jen's prenatal-terror sundae.

Through it all, she never picked up a drink. But by the time Chloe was born in April 2002, the Altmans had closed on a house in Lincolnwood. And when Jen's maternity leave ended in July, she didn't go back to AmEx. Her plan to raise kids in the city while balancing motherhood with a career was no longer operative on either count. Partly because it eased his guilt over the long hours he was clocking on the Wilmer Hale partner track, Dan was on board with Jen's decision to become a stay-at-home mom. So was Dr. Rosenzweig, the psychiatrist she'd started seeing.

"I mean, when I ask myself," Jen explained to the owlish, Talbots-clad woman who bore an uncanny resemblance to a nonjudgmental version of her mother, "'What's more important? Being there for my daughter, or increasing retention on the Platinum Card by another three percent?' It's kind of a no-brainer."

"Sounds like you're making the right decision," said Dr. Rosenzweig.

"I think I am," agreed Jen.

It took her a decade to fully appreciate how wrong that decision was. But full-time motherhood's drawbacks—the brain mush, the loss of external validation, and the absence of sustained human contact with anyone who could complete a sentence and didn't shit themselves every few hours—were already starting to weigh on her in ways that made a predinner glass of wine increasingly mandatory by the time the Altman family, now grown to include serial-reflux-barfing baby Max, moved into the house on Brantley Circle in late 2005.

Next door, in a newly built 4,500-square-foot trophy home with four-year-old Eliza, eighteen-month-old Henry, and seldom-seen investment banker John, was Erin Tiernan.

It was a perfect match. Chloe and Eliza, born just a few months apart, instantly became best friends. Max and Henry wound up spending countless hours playing together, too—or, more accurately, playing in parallel, since they were too young and too Y-chromosomed to forge the kind of bond that the girls enjoyed. But circumstance kept them in close proximity, because their mothers were even more inseparable than their sisters.

Jen was smitten with Erin from the start. She was funny, fiercely intelligent, and even played tennis at Jen's level, not that it was possible to get a match in except on the odd weekend morning when they could pawn the kids off on their overworked husbands. Erin's recently abandoned career in entertainment journalism left her with a large catalog of unprintable celebrity gossip and a snarky contempt for the hypervigilant, competitive-mothering types who looked down their noses at anyone negligent enough to feed her kids nonorganic snacks or use her car stereo for anything less intellectually stimulating than Baby Mozart.

That was the dominant ethos on the tidy, rubber-surfaced playgrounds of Lincolnwood—earnest, overprotective, judgmental, and blithely dismissive of any marker of female self-worth independent of motherhood. Jen found the atmosphere so oppressive that it triggered an almost adolescent urge to rebel. Erin not only shared that urge, she operationalized it. She didn't just offer Jen a witty partner in the mockery of sanctimonious Übermoms like Stephanie Andersen and Lisa Cohen— she showed Jen how to give a big, decadent middle finger to the whole value system.

It started with White Wine Wednesdays. They were innocent enough at first—just a glass or two after they got back from the midweek Mommy and Me swim class at the community center. That time frame meant the bottle never got uncorked before four p.m., which wasn't *too* scandalously early. And it offered a welcome decompression after they'd just had to endure Stephanie and Lisa's smug post-class chatter in the family locker room about how they were pureeing their own organic baby food.

"Shouldn't we wait until five, though?" Jen asked on that first Wednesday.

Erin shrugged as she filled her glass. "It's five o'clock in Nova Scotia."

Jen didn't argue. As a statement of fact, it was unassailable.

Once they'd institutionalized White Wine Wednesdays, Erin's follow-up proposal for culturally defiant recreation was Friday Funday. This one was a little harder for Jen to justify, because it started at lunch and involved margaritas.

"I just feel a little weird day-drinking when there's no football game involved," she confessed.

Erin looked bemused. "Is that a Michigan thing?"

Jen nodded. "You didn't tailgate in college?"

"Only for the Yale game," Erin replied. Then she countered with her own collegiate self-justification.

"This whole 'no day-drinking' taboo is such Puritan bullshit that even the Puritans didn't buy it. Did you know that for the first hundred years Harvard was a college, they served their students beer for breakfast?"

"Seriously?"

"Yes! And it wasn't just college kids. Beer for breakfast was totally normal back then. The Founding Fathers had a pretty good buzz on twenty-four seven. And those guys led a rebellion! And wrote two constitutions! What do you have to do today? Change a diaper and read *Goodnight Moon* out loud six times in a row?"

"Okay, sold," Jen conceded. "But I'm only having one."

She wound up having three that first Friday, and not without some trepidation. "Wait!" she yelped, putting a hand over her glass to block Erin's second refill attempt. Then she gestured toward the kids, who were playing a primitive version of hide-and-seek around the backyard jungle gym a few feet away. "What happens if somebody cracks their head open and we have to go to the emergency room?"

"I'm fine to drive," Erin promised. "And the hospital's easy from here. It's all right turns."

"That sounds a little sketchy."

Erin rolled her eyes. "First of all, nobody's going to crack their head open. The girls are too careful, and the boys are too timid. Second: in the highly unlikely event that somebody does, I was a camp counselor for three years. So I'm qualified to administer first aid for as long as it takes Boris from Lincolnwood Taxi to show up."

"So 'Boris from Lincolnwood Taxi' is our designated driver?"

"Sure. Why not?"

"Is there an actual Boris? Do you know this man personally?"

"No. He's a composite. But there's definitely a Lincolnwood Taxi. And they're very prompt. I took one home from the country club last weekend."

Boris quickly became a code word ("Is Boris on the clock yet?" "Time to call Boris." "Don't let me get Boris'd—I have a homeowners' association meeting at six."), and Friday Funday became a ritual alongside White Wine Wednesdays.

Which gradually began to spill into other days of the week.

"It's a little screwed up that we do this," Jen observed one sunny Tuesday as they sat on a playground bench in Memorial Park, drinking chardonnay out of sippy cups.

"No, it isn't," Erin promised her. "It's actually the smartest thing we've ever done."

"I just wonder if I'm drinking too much."

"As long as you don't drink every day, it's fine."

Jen thought for a moment. "I *do* drink every day."

"Wine with dinner doesn't count. Ask the French. They're the healthiest people on earth."

There was a limit to what Erin could talk Jen into. Despite intensive lobbying, Jen drew the line at Monday Bloody Monday, which would've consisted of Bloody Marys during morning nap time.

"You're welcome to do it without me," Jen told her.

Erin snorted. "I'm not going to drink alone! That would be fucked up."

Occasional episodes of self-restraint notwithstanding, Erin and Jen's secret society of semi-inebriated stay-at-home moms held its regular covens for almost three years. They might've kept it going indefinitely if it hadn't been for the 2008 financial crisis. Lehman Brothers collapsed, taking John Tiernan's job with it. Suddenly, the man who'd been an even more spectral presence in his household than Dan was moping around all day every day, and the long-running weekday afternoon party in the Tiernans' massive open kitchen came to an abrupt end.

The drinking continued, but now it mostly took place in the Altmans' basement rec room, paired with what felt to Jen like an endless marital-financial therapy session with an increasingly

brooding, fearful Erin. Her fun-loving outlaw disposition cur-
dled so thoroughly that Chloe began to quiz Jen about it: *Why
is Eliza's mom angry all the time?* When John got a new job in the Bay
Area and the Tiernans left town after the school year ended in
2009, Jen felt almost as much relief as sorrow.

Distance broke the spell. Erin had obliterated Jen's taboo
around day drinking, but she'd left intact the one around drinking alone, which—outside of Jen's predinner glass of wine—she
never seriously contemplated breaching. When her drinking
partner went away, replaced in the McMansion next door by the
sweet but too-dim-to-socialize-with Kayla Stankovic, so did the
worst of Jen's drinking. Within a year, she'd lost ten pounds, was
working out three days a week, enjoyed a perfectly collegial relationship with fellow third grade class mom Lisa Cohen (whose
parenting philosophy actually began to seem pretty sensible),
and occasionally wondered what the hell she'd been thinking
during that whole Erin Tiernan phase. They were still Facebook
friends, but Erin's snarky commentary about congressional Re-
publicans and her smug neighbors in Atherton didn't play nearly
as well online as it did in person. Eventually, Jen stopped clicking
"like," and the Facebook algorithm took care of the rest, slowly
erasing Erin from Jen's timeline and, by extension, her life.

By the time Max started school full-time and her autonomy
over substantial chunks of her day returned, Jen no longer felt
the urge, let alone the compulsion, to drink outside of socially
acceptable hours. She frequently woke up hungover after weekend dinner parties, but it was nothing serious.

Then Max entered second grade, Jen decided it was finally
time to go back to work, and things started to go downhill. She'd

always considered herself a blue-chip talent, and in her twenties, almost everyone she encountered professionally agreed. Her initial ascent from management consulting to business school to the middle rungs of consumer marketing at American Express had been nearly frictionless.

But taking ten years off turned out to have been a disastrous career move.

It wasn't just the optics of having prioritized life over work for so long, or the fact that she'd let her professional network wither to the point where she initially had trouble just finding contact info for people who'd once been her closest work allies. In the ten years she'd been out, the business world had gone through such rapid evolution that when she tried to come back, she discovered she didn't just lack critical skills. She didn't even know what those skills were.

She had to google "SEO" just to figure out what the abbreviation meant.

She didn't have a LinkedIn page. Apparently, that was a source of shame.

What the hell? Why didn't somebody tell me?

For the first time since junior high, Jen felt incompetent. It took eighteen months for her to find a full-time job. When she finally did, it sucked. She wound up doing business-to-business marketing for a midsize financial services firm run by a pack of frat-boy mediocrities who made her life so miserable that after less than a year on the job, Dan—who'd been a tireless advocate of her going back to work—started begging her to quit, not just for her own mental health, but to spare him and the kids the collateral damage from her unhappiness.

Jen refused, on the grounds that if she bailed out without another job lined up, she'd never recover professionally from the stain on her résumé.

Then the frat boys downsized her, which looked marginally less bad on paper, but felt infinitely worse. After that, no amount of wine at dinner was sufficient to anesthetize the wound to her ego.

Vodka did the trick, though.

Jen discovered this almost by accident. After the frat-boy debacle, she started picking up short-term consulting projects from former peers who'd lapped her professionally. The second person to hire her for one of these was Rick Beasley. He was a few years younger than Jen, and he'd worked underneath her during her last two years at AmEx. They'd always been friendly, but she never thought of Rick as an equal, mostly because he was dumb as a sack of hammers.

Yet, while Jen was killing a decade as a class mom in the suburbs, Rick was failing upward. By the time Jen reconnected with him, he was a senior VP at a late-stage internet startup, and he hired her on a weekly to put together a series of PowerPoint decks for his company's sales team in advance of a minor product launch.

From their first meeting, it was clear that Rick now considered himself Jen's superior in every respect.

She figured she could handle it. She'd had years of professional experience managing the egos of fragile men. But everything that came out of Rick's mouth seemed designed to rub his superiority in her face while offering input that was as arrogant as it was contradictory.

"Here's how we do things around here—and it's a higher RPM than you're probably used to . . ."

"Don't just give us pretty pictures. We need hard numbers."

"This is dry as dust. You gotta visualize those numbers for us! Tell us a story, Jenny!"

Nobody had called her Jenny since elementary school. When she pointed that out to him, Rick laughed. Then he kept doing it.

She left their fourth meeting—which ran thirty minutes long, because Rick was forty minutes late—having suppressed so much rage that toward the end, her eyelid began to twitch. She missed an uptown subway by seconds, and the one she finally caught arrived at Penn Station three minutes after the train she'd planned to take back to Lincolnwood departed.

She had almost an hour to kill before the next one. As she emerged from the subway turnstile into the underground passageway under Madison Square Garden, she was so consumed with impotent fury that she'd started to visualize kicking random commuters in the shins.

Then she passed Tracks, the underground bar. It was narrow, dark, and sad, which matched her mood perfectly. She put away three vodka gimlets in forty minutes. The effect was magical. By the time she got on the train back to New Jersey, everything was *fine*.

Granted, driving home from the train station was a little problematic. But once she reached the garage, she practically skipped into the house.

She'd discovered a miracle cure. Vodka was a solvent capable of neutralizing every negative emotion that weighed on her: frustration, resentment, insecurity, inadequacy, even the self-loathing caused by drinking too much.

Vodka fixed every problem, including itself.

It was good for her marriage, too. When Dan started his absurd new screenwriting hobby, Jen's new vodka hobby made her infinitely more tolerant of it. When he insisted on making the uncharacteristically reckless choice to abandon his mid-six-figures-a-year partnership at Wilmer Hale for a mid-five-figure lottery ticket as a bottom-rung writer on some brainless murder-porn cop show, drinking gave her an emotional buffer against the fear of financial ruin that otherwise would've crippled her. And when his writing career took off, Jen was able to drown her envy over the fact that Dan's job fulfilled him in ways she knew her own career never could, even in the unlikely event that she managed to pull it out of the ditch.

Did it bother her that Dan seemed to prefer spending time at work to time with her and the kids? Was she jealous that whenever they went out with friends, people quizzed Dan incessantly about his new glamour job, while rarely remembering to even ask Jen what she'd been up to lately?

Yes and no. It depended on how much she'd been drinking.

And that could be tough to calibrate. The line between not enough and too much was strangely elusive. Worse, it usually didn't reveal itself until after she'd crossed it.

She had to be careful. She couldn't drink too much or too frequently. When she did, covering her tracks was critical. She developed an elaborate logistical framework for both acquisition (not buying liquor from just anywhere, or leaning too hard on any one store, lest the people behind the counter grow suspicious of her habits) and disposal. Tossing an empty fifth of Absolut into the blue recycling bin in the garage was a nonstarter. So was nonchalantly pulling it out of the back seat of her Volvo and dumping it in a public garbage can. What if somebody saw her?

All empties had to be carefully wrapped, then hidden in advance of being discreetly eighty-sixed on a weekday morning, usually in a trash can on the periphery of one of three area parking lots.

The one behind the Whole Foods was the best.

There were other complications. Obviously, Dan and the kids could never know, or even suspect anything. So she couldn't get *too* shitfaced, and on drinking days, she had to be careful to stay out of smelling range of them until her predinner glass of wine could mask the scent.

Thank God for the predinner glass of wine. Not for the alcohol content so much as the camouflage.

It went without saying that she couldn't go out in public less than sober. Or, in the worst case, any more than mildly buzzed. Anything kid-related was a bright-line *no*, especially parent-teacher conferences.

Drinking and driving was also nonnegotiable, except when absolutely necessary. Chloe's tennis pickups were a huge pain in the ass, and doubly so under winter road conditions. Fortunately, Max had no extracurriculars to speak of, so she didn't have to chauffeur him around, although the fact that he was constantly at home presented its own logistical complications.

Work phone calls had to be planned around. Not being sober for those was definitely suboptimal, although sometimes it couldn't be helped.

The work itself was a mixed bag. There was an argument to be made for the beneficial effect of alcohol on creativity. This was somewhat less true where spreadsheets were concerned. Emailing while sloshed was risky at best.

All things considered, there was no question that drinking made life much more complicated. *Too* complicated, in fact. Eventually, Jen figured that out.

What she couldn't figure out by that point was how to stop.

This wasn't quite true. Stopping was easy. She could go weeks without drinking. She just couldn't stay stopped.

And the drinking days turned into a real crapshoot. Most of the time, she just got a little tipsy. But occasionally, she blew way past the line, then had to feign illness, leave money for pizza delivery on the kitchen counter, and hide in bed when the kids came home. Dan started to get suspicious—more than once, she'd made the mistake of picking up the phone after overserving herself, and she'd had to invent a phantom lunch date with a degenerate class mom to explain away her slurred speech.

For some reason, Mondays tended to be particularly bad. On one of them—what was it? three years into her Better Living Through Alcohol experiment?—she found herself nursing a Bloody Mary at ten a.m. while designing a marketing funnel for the local community center's adult education program. Looking through their old promotional materials, she came across a half-page photo of the center's swimming pool and flashed back to the Mommy and Me swim classes she'd attended there alongside Erin Tiernan.

Holy shit . . . I finally made Monday Bloody Monday a thing.

She decided to message Erin on Facebook. They hadn't communicated in forever, but Erin was Erin. She'd find it funny.

Jen typed Erin's name into the search box. Her page popped up. Jen skimmed the posts.

Wow . . . Lots of changes in Erin Tiernan's life. Eliza and Henry looked so grown up! Henry was playing lacrosse. Eliza was in the school musical. Seemed like she might be going through a goth phase. Was that still a thing kids did? Apparently yes, at least in the Bay Area.

Erin and John were . . . divorced? Predictable. But still. She was dating a new guy. He looked like a dork. That was surprising. They seemed happy, though.

Then, a one-sentence status update: *Five years today.*

What did that mean? Five years since what? The divorce?

Five years today had over a hundred likes. Jen skimmed the comments.

"Congratulations!"

"So proud of you!"

"One day at a time!"

"Keep coming back!"

Jen's heart rate skyrocketed as she realized what it meant.

Erin Tiernan's in AA.

Oh, that is fucked up . . .

That is seriously fucked up.

She must've really gone to pieces.

Jen's eyes drifted from the laptop screen to the Bloody Mary sitting beside it on the kitchen table. Beads of condensation clung to the lower end of the half-empty glass.

Why is my heart beating so fast?

That was the day the crying started in earnest. Since then, it hadn't really stopped.

Neither had the drinking. Over the past year, Jen had spent more days sober than not. But she couldn't string together more than seven or eight in a row.

She started to think about getting help. Nothing too drastic, because she didn't want Dan and the kids to find out. She secretly went back to Dr. Rosenzweig for a few sessions. It was a waste of money. Her surrogate mother, now borderline elderly and much more judgmental-seeming, had no actionable advice except "go to AA."

Which was ridiculous.

Still, Jen eventually got desperate enough to google "Lincolnwood AA." There were two non-evening meetings a day, at seven a.m. and noon, both down at the Episcopal church on Hawthorne. After a few weeks of equivocating, she showed up at the noon meeting on a Tuesday and quickly discovered that the only thing worse than crying alone was crying in a room full of strangers.

Worse still, they weren't all strangers. Her next-door neighbor, Judge Distefano, was there. His wife had just died of Alzheimer's, and he raised his hand and talked about it in front of thirty people in a way that made Jen simultaneously heartbroken and embarrassed, like she was eavesdropping on some intensely private conversation she had no business hearing.

She never went back. But every time she saw Judge Distefano—which was much too often, because he was retired and seemed to spend half his waking hours walking his dachshund, Ruby, around the neighborhood—he smiled at her in a way that made her cringe inside. She couldn't tell if he was being sweet or just condescending to her as a hopeless drunk who'd refused to join his cult of hand-holding cliché parrots.

AA made her skin crawl. And she didn't need it to quit drinking. She just needed a kick in the ass—some kind of definitive, this-far-and-no-further wake-up call.

Like calling her daughter a loser in a Google Doc, then forgetting she'd done it the next morning.

There weren't a whole lot of bright lines left in Jen's sense of acceptable conduct when it came to alcohol, but hurting her kids was one of them. And screwing up Chloe's college application process—which had been the primary focus of both their lives for much of the past year—was absolutely unthinkable.

This isn't who I am. I'm better than this.

It's over. For real this time.

I'm done.

Jen dried her eyes and stood up from her perch atop the stairs. She grabbed the Stolichnaya bottle by the neck like a naughty child and marched it through her bedroom into the primary bath. She unscrewed the top and poured the rest of it into the sink. Then she wrapped the empty in a plastic CVS bag, tied it up, and took it downstairs to the garage, where she left it in the trunk of her Volvo en route to its final resting place in the garbage can at the back of the Whole Foods parking lot.

Her head was still throbbing from the hangover. *Good.* She deserved it. The pain only fueled her resolve.

No more.

Remember this feeling, Jennifer.

Because you never want to feel this way again.

She went back inside to finish her shopping list. Shit was going to get done today. She'd go to the bank, stock the fridge, wrap up the loose ends of the Rutgers thing, send out some feelers to start looking for a real job, make Chloe's favorite parmesan chicken for dinner, and figure out how to articulate her apology in a way that her daughter would accept as legitimate and heartfelt.

The shopping list finished, she bounded back up the stairs, practically reveling in the stabbing cranial pain that every step triggered. She stripped off her clothes, paused to scowl at her booze-eroded body in the mirror—*time to fix that too*—*maybe I'll start running, become an endorphin junkie*—and got in the shower, turning the water temperature almost to scalding.

It hurt, but in a good way. Like a purification ritual.

She'd just started shampooing her hair when the lights went out.

DAN

A plane had crashed, somewhere very close, and they were all in danger.

Dan hadn't actually seen anything, but he'd heard the keening whine of the aircraft, followed by an explosion, followed by screams from the commuters at the south-facing windows. Now the entire rush-hour-stuffed train car was losing its collective shit in a manner that suggested the fiery aftermath posed an imminent threat to all of their lives.

Dan tried to stand in his seat, but there was no room—the luggage rack over his head was too low for him to straighten up, his messenger bag was taking up every bit of the narrow space in front of him, and Mousy Librarian had him boxed in on the left. She was standing with her back to Dan and her arms spread to grip the seatbacks on either side, causing her long puffy coat to hang like a curtain that made it impossible for Dan to see past her.

"*Open the doors!*" someone was yelling from the back of the train.

Up front, a woman kept screaming, "*OH GOD OH GOD OH GOD!*"

Someone else—*is that Pete Blackwell?*—was trying to calm her. "It's okay! We're okay!"

That was a minority opinion. The prevailing mood in the car was panic teetering on the edge of hysteria.

Dan shoved his bag against the wall below the window, then

took another shot at standing. This time, he managed to squirm in a half turn to face the train's interior by putting his left knee up on the seat while he pivoted on his right foot. Then he tilted his head almost ninety degrees to peer around Mousy Librarian and try to catch a glimpse of whatever was happening out the south-facing windows.

The AirPod fell out of his left ear.

Shit!

He looked down. No sign of it on the seat. It must've fallen to the floor in the row behind him.

Another round of screams erupted from the south side of the car.

"OH GOD OH GOD!"

"IT'S GOING TO BURN US!"

"WE'RE UNDER ATTACK!"

Fear surged through the train like an electrical charge. Mousy Librarian whipped around, her wild eyes making contact with Dan's for a split second before she looked past him and gestured—

"Open the window!"

"What?"

He turned his head to see what she was pointing at. On the upper right corner of the window a few inches away from his eyes was a U-shaped red metal EMERGENCY EXIT bar.

PULL TO REMOVE RUBBER MOLDING, it read.

But standing like he was, hunched under the luggage rack with his back to the window, he wouldn't be able to pull off the molding even if he could get a grip on the handle. He needed to turn his whole body around.

He also felt a competing—possibly irrational, yet strangely insistent—urge to locate his missing AirPod.

Dan began to shift clockwise, putting his foot back down on the floor and bending his knees awkwardly to negotiate the 270-degree turn that would leave him facing the window. As he turned, he kept his eyes down, hoping to catch a glimpse of the little white earpiece.

"I just dropped my—"

"*OPEN THE FUCKING WINDOW!*" Mousy Librarian shrieked. He looked back at her, startled—and got a brief glimpse of her eyes burning with fury, so close to his that he could see tiny red veins spiderwebbing the whites around her dark brown irises.

Then he hit his head on the luggage rack.

"*Fuck!*"

"*OPEN IT!*"

"I'm trying!" He'd misjudged Mousy Librarian. She wasn't mousy at all. She was a bitch on wheels.

A few feet away in the aisle, people were yelling and pushing as they tried to shove their way toward the back of the car, away from whatever it was that had so terrified the passengers up at the front windows.

With a heroic twist that nearly blew out his knee, Dan managed to turn all the way back around to face the window. But then his wedged-in messenger bag blocked him from getting his right knee up and completing the maneuver.

AirPods are back-ordered at the Apple Store. It'll take weeks to—

"DUDE! OPEN THE WINDOW!"

Hipster Captain America was screaming at him now, too.

"I am!" Dan examined the window. There were instructions posted above the glass. He looked up at them.

"OPEN IT!"

"HANG ON!"

Don't they realize how hard this is?

All around him, people were screaming. He tried to block out the noise and focus on the words in front of him.

1. LOCATE RED HANDLE ON WINDOW.
2. PULL HANDLE. REMOVE RUBBER MOLDING COMPL—

"OUT OF THE FUCKING WAY!"

The librarian climbed onto the seat and forced herself into Dan's physical space, squeezing in beside him as she grabbed for the emergency exit handle.

"Jesus! What the—"

Her outstretched fingers got a grip on the red handle, and she yanked it back with everything she had. It popped loose from its retaining screws and hit Dan square in the cheekbone.

"AAAUGH!"

"The doors are open!" someone yelled.

Disoriented by pain, Dan briefly lost the thread of events. Mousy Librarian was attacking him—*or the window? or both?*—and there was yelling, and commotion, and someone kept bellowing, *"The doors are open!"*—and suddenly she'd pulled away and her elbow was no longer pinning Dan against the seat back.

He looked up. The emergency exit handle, which just a second ago had been the Ring of Power to his seatmate's Gollum, was banging free against the pane on its half-pulled rubber line. Through the window, Dan could see commuters running down the track bed in the direction of Newark.

He turned around to see Mousy Librarian shoving her way down the aisle behind Hipster Captain America. They were headed for the car's rear exit door.

The rows of seats on either side of Dan were already empty.

As he started to bend down to scan the floor for his missing AirPod, a voice called to him.

"Dan!"

It was Pete Blackwell. He was in the aisle, headed for the rear exit door. The car was empty now. Over Pete's shoulder, Dan caught a glimpse out one of the far windows of a billowing cloud of orange fire.

His stomach dropped at the sight.

"Let's go," Pete told him.

It wasn't a suggestion. Dan grabbed his messenger bag. Before he followed Pete into the aisle, he paused for an instant.

What about the AirPod?

A second wave of panicky commuters from the next car was barreling up the aisle toward him. To search the prior row, where the AirPod had most likely landed, he'd have to swim upstream against the mob.

He followed Pete in the opposite direction, down the aisle to the open door. After a few steps, it occurred to him that the right side of his face was throbbing with pain. He put two fingers to his cheekbone.

His fingertips came away smeared with blood.

Mousy Librarian had busted his face open.

JEN

As soapy water ran in rivulets down her face, Jen cracked an eye just wide enough to confirm that the bathroom lights had gone out.

Oh, COME ON.

Is a hurricane hitting Bayonne?

Did a squirrel climb on a transformer in Maplewood?

You're a power company. You have ONE JOB!

The upstairs windows provided just enough natural light to allow her to finish showering and get dressed in the bedroom. As she leaned over to pull her socks on while sitting on the bed, a wave of nausea made her briefly reconsider the decision to power through her hangover. But she shook it off, determined to stay on her game at least until the fridge was full of groceries.

She unplugged her phone from its charging cord on the nightstand. It was off, so she held down the power button for a few seconds before sticking it in a jeans pocket and heading downstairs.

Back in the kitchen, she took one last survey of the darkened fridge and freezer—*the good news is there's not much in there to spoil*—before adding a few final items to the shopping list, which had spilled over onto a second Post-it.

She folded over the sticky backs and pocketed them. Then she took her handbag from the countertop, went to the mud-room, bent over to put on her tennis shoes—*gaaah there's that hangover again*—grabbed a fleece jacket from one of the wall pegs, and slipped it on. Transferring the phone to her jacket pocket, she entered the garage.

The button on the wall didn't work—*duh*—so she raised the garage door manually, flooding the space with sunlight. She got in the Volvo, tossed her bag on the passenger seat, and pressed the ignition button.

Nothing happened.

She pressed it again. Still nothing.

Well, this is just a banner fucking day.

Jen pulled her phone from her pocket. It was still off. She pressed hard on the power button as she reached out with her free hand to fish in her bag for her wallet. When she found it, she set the phone down on the dash, then rifled through the wallet until she located her AAA card to call for a jump.

She picked up the phone again. It was still off. She sighed, exasperated, as she thumbed the power button a third time while staring at the screen.

Seconds passed.

Too many seconds.

Seriously?

SERIOUSLY?

My car AND my phone died?

AND the power's out?

The thought crossed her mind that these things might somehow be related.

But she quickly dismissed it, because it made no sense.

CHLOE

Chloe had breezed through the multiple-choice section of her AP Gov exam and was three paragraphs into what she considered a bold but textually defensible five-paragraph dunking on the current Supreme Court for failing to hold itself to the standards of judicial review established in *Marbury v. Madison* when the lights went out in Mr. Unger's windowless interior classroom, rendering it so dark that she could no longer see her handwriting on the page.

The twenty-plus kids in the class uttered a dozen varieties of exasperated noises.

"Gaah!"

"Come on!"

"Mr. Unger! This is ridic!"

"Shhh!"

"What?"

"Mr. Unger?"

"Shhh! We're taking a test!"

"Not anymore."

"Can you even see?"

"No."

"Mr. Unger!"

"I think he went to get coffee."

"Can somebody turn on a light?"

"The power's out, genius."

"Use your phone!"

"It doesn't work."

"Mine either."

Chloe squinted as hard as she could at her exam. It was hopeless. She couldn't see the page well enough to even finish the sentence she'd been writing.

This is SO unfair. She'd been crushing it. For the first time all week, something had been going right. *And now this?*

"Does anybody's phone work?"

"Wuuut?"

"This is crazy, fam."

"Somebody go get Unger."

"I can't even see the door!"

"It's right there."

"Super helpful, Sean. Great."

Chloe set her pencil down and slumped back in her seat. The movement jostled her desk, and she heard the faint wooden trill of her pencil rolling. She shot her arm out to stop it, only to hear it fall to the floor. Reaching down, she swept her open hand back and forth until she found the pencil. When she brought it up again, a quick probe with her thumb revealed that the lead had broken off.

That was the final insult. Only the knowledge that Josh Houser was sitting two rows away kept her from bursting into tears of frustration.

This is the worst week of my life.

MAX

Three floors below his sister, Max stood on a volleyball court in the northeast quadrant of the gymnasium, dressed in his PE uniform and cursing his gym teacher's approach to education.

What did Mr. Farmer think was the point of the volleyball unit? Was it to teach his students how to play volleyball? Or just humiliate the ones who didn't already know? If it was the former, how come he hadn't bothered to show them how to hit an overhand serve?

Statistically speaking, Max knew underhand was a much safer bet. But since his sole aspiration for his serve was to avoid ridicule, and the only kids in the class who served underhand were girls, he was stuck with overhand, the mechanics of which mystified him. Two days into the unit, he still couldn't tell if you were supposed to hit it with an open palm or a closed fist. And since Mr. Farmer didn't consider instruction to be part of his job, Max was on his own in figuring it out.

His effort the previous day had been a complete disaster. Monday's serve had come off his knuckles at an almost perpendicular angle to the net, nearly hitting Madison O'Rourke in the face and triggering howls of laughter from both teams.

Max's only consolation had been that there were four simultaneous games going on—and Kayleigh Adams was playing on the opposite end of the gym, so she hadn't witnessed his humiliation.

Back in September, he'd been thrilled to discover his secret crush was in his gym class. By now, though, he couldn't remember why he'd ever considered that a plus. He wasn't athletic
enough to impress her physically, and he didn't know her well
enough to hang out next to her and drop clever wisecracks about
the existential absurdity of gym.

Kayleigh's presence offered nothing but peril. And today she
was on his team. Another failure at the service line would be
devastating to his already fragile self-image.

Why the hell hadn't he practiced serving the night before?
Chloe had played a couple seasons of volleyball, and there was
still a ball somewhere in their garage. Max had come home after Monday's debacle with the intention of tracking it down and
smacking some practice serves against the side of the garage. But
then he'd fallen into a bottomless well of street fight videos on
YouTube, and the evening got away from him.

Now he was about to pay the price. The rotation was carrying him inexorably toward the service line. He'd been praying the 9:23 dismissal to the locker room would arrive before his
turn did. But he was up next, and according to the wall clock, it
was only 9:16.

A kid on the opposing team spiked the ball out of bounds a
few feet from Kayleigh. She and Max both moved to retrieve it.

Kayleigh got there first. When she turned and tossed the ball
to him—a little clumsily, because she was no athlete herself—
she gave him a shy smile.

For a brief, aching moment, he felt his heart begin to soar.
But then from the other side of the net came Grayson Oliver's
horselike chortle:

"Cover your balls, yo! We don't know where this one's going!"

As Kayleigh turned away to take her place in the middle row, Max saw her wince at the insult. His spirits plummeted again.

"Grow up, Grayson!" one of the other girls scoffed, which just made Max feel even more pathetic. He took his spot on the line and weighed the ball in his hand as he surveyed the court.

Everyone was staring at him—mostly out of self-preservation, because Grayson was right. Nobody, least of all Max, could predict where the ball was headed when it left his hand.

He took a deep breath.

Then the lights went out with a soft *pop*, plunging the gym into darkness and leading him, for the first time in his fourteen years on the planet, to consider the theological possibility of divine intervention in human affairs.

DAN

"What the hell is going on here?"

Pete Blackwell shook his head, bewildered, as he took in the scene. He and Dan were in the middle of a drawn-out caravan of hundreds of train passengers trudging west along the shoulder of the Newark–Jersey City Turnpike like refugees fleeing a war zone.

Whatever had disabled the train, phones, and possibly even the crashed airliner had also knocked out all the cars and trucks. The turnpike's four lanes were cluttered in both directions with stopped vehicles. Drivers stood in the road, chattering in confusion, staring at the flames and smoke rising from the plane wreckage a mile to the west, or just gaping openmouthed at their dead phones.

"Am I still bleeding?" Dan asked Pete.

Pete squinted as he surveyed his companion's face. "Little bit, yeah."

Dan dabbed at the swollen cut with a wadded-up Kleenex. "Think it needs stitches?"

"Maybe? Depends on how you feel about facial scars. But here—" From his jacket pocket, Pete produced an immaculate white square. "Take my handkerchief."

Dan held up the bloody Kleenex in reply. "I'm good. Thanks."

"Take it. Seriously."

Dan shook his head firmly. "I'm fine." There was a dull ache in his stomach that he suspected was due less to acute trauma than to his feelings of shame over the lack of grace under pressure he'd displayed on the train. Dan felt a strong urge to compensate by taking some kind of heroic action, and accepting another man's handkerchief felt like the opposite of heroism.

"You sure we shouldn't go back and try to help the people from that plane crash?"

"What are you going to do, bleed on them?"

"I dunno—help them to safety?"

"I really don't think that was a survivable crash. And even if it was"—Pete gave the strap of his carbon fiber backpack a referential tug—"I'm not packing anything that'd do a third-degree burn victim any good. Except maybe my handkerchief." He extended it again. "Which you desperately need. Here—"

"I don't—"

"Yes, you do! C'mon! You'll make me feel less stupid for having it. I've been carrying these things for years, and I never use them."

"You don't blow your nose?"

"I mean, I would. Theoretically. I just never have to. C'mon, take it."

Dan finally relented, stuffing the soiled Kleenex in his pocket and accepting the clean linen from Pete's outstretched hand while marveling at the physiology of a man whose nose never ran. A corner of the soft fabric was tastefully monogrammed with the initials *PDB* in navy blue thread.

"Thanks. I'll wash it and get it back to you."

"Just toss it. I've got plenty."

Where does a guy go for monogrammed handkerchiefs? Pressing it to his wounded cheek, Dan began to wonder if he should get some, too. During allergy season, he went through a packet of Kleenex every other day.

A woman's exasperated yell interrupted his thoughts. "We can't just leave it here!"

The voice came from a few yards up the road. In the middle of an intersection clogged with disabled cars, a fiftyish couple in denim and sweats were arguing over a rust-streaked Camry that had died attempting a left turn.

The man shook a phone at his wife. "You wanna call a tow, Marjorie? Be my guest!"

Pete shook his head again. "What. The hell. Is going on?"

As they walked, Dan tried to formulate an answer, but quickly slipped back into ping-ponging between the self-recriminatory poles of *why was I so worried about the stupid AirPod?* and *why didn't I just stop to look for it?* while his brain force-fed him the image of Mousy Librarian shrieking in his face, her red-veined eyes bulging in grotesque condemnation of his lack of manhood.

"I lost an AirPod."

"What, on the train?"

"Yeah. I was bent over to try to see out the window, and it fell out of my ear."

"Shit. Those things are back-ordered for weeks."

"I know! Right? I feel like I should've stopped and looked for it."

"Give yourself a break. It's hard to think straight in a situation like that."

"How much danger do you think we were actually in?"

"From the plane crash?" Pete shrugged. "Not that much. It was pretty far away from the tracks."

"See, that's what I thought. But—Jesus, the woman next to me was out of her fucking mind."

"Textbook case of mass panic. Could've been worse, though."

"How's that?"

"If she'd popped you half an inch higher, you'd be picking prescription glass out of your eyeball right now."

"Jesus." Dan reflexively pushed his eyeglasses up higher on his nose. "Good point. I hadn't thought of that."

"Always look on the bright side."

As clichés tended to do, the comment reminded Dan of Marty Callahan. He glanced back over his shoulder at the Manhattan skyline. "I wonder if I should be trying to get in to work right now."

"Something tells me not a lot of people are making it to the office today."

"Yeah, but my boss can be a real dick about stuff like that."

"Isn't he your college buddy or something?"

"Yeah, but we, uh—the relationship's been a little sideways lately."

"How so?"

"Kind of a long story. You know how *Bullet Town*'s basically a franchise? Like, our show spun off from the original *Bullet Town*? Which Marty also created?"

"Uh-huh . . ."

"Well, he's been trying to do a third one. *Bullet Town: Boston.* And at the end of last season, my contract was ending—I had a three-year deal, so if I was going to come back, the studio had to renew it. And the thing about a deal like that is—"

"Holy shit." Pete stopped in his tracks.

Dan stopped, too. "What?"

As annoyed turnpike refugees rerouted around them like a stream bypassing a pair of rocks, Pete slipped his backpack off, unzipped a compartment, and pulled out an iPad. He examined it closely.

"Is it working?" Dan asked.

The taller man frowned and shook his head. "No." He raised his head and surveyed the scene, taking in the stopped cars, the plane crash, and the diaspora of commuters.

"What are you thinking?" Dan asked.

"I'm thinking . . ." Pete's eyes unfocused for a moment as he frowned thoughtfully, like he was performing a complex calculation in his head. "I'm going to run home."

"What?"

"Yeah. I'm going to run." He put his backpack over both shoulders and tightened the straps.

"In those shoes?" Pete's leather brogues looked expensive enough to be comfortable, but not nearly comfortable enough to run the eight miles home.

"Yep. Want to come?"

"Not sure I'm in the best shape for—"

"Okay. See you!"

Pete took off, leaving Dan so stunned that it took him a moment to realize Pete had dropped his iPad on the ground.

"Pete! Your iPad!"

"Keep it! Or toss it!" Pete yelled over his shoulder from twenty yards away.

Bending at the knees to keep his messenger bag from slipping off his shoulder, Dan picked up the abandoned piece of technology and looked it over. It was a little dusty, and the screen wouldn't light up. But it was otherwise intact.

Dan raised his head and squinted up the turnpike. Pete was well over a hundred yards away, loping toward Newark in a long, athletic stride. With growing unease, Dan watched him disappear from view behind a cluster of walkers.

What kind of bullshit rich-person entitlement is that?

Am I supposed to carry this home for him?

Should I just leave it here?

Why did HE leave it here?

Why is he running home in dress shoes?

Should I be running home?

That seemed impractical. Dan had bad knees, and he couldn't remember the last time he'd done any cardio more strenuous than twenty minutes on an elliptical machine. In the end, he wiped the dust off the tablet with his sleeve, stuck it in his bag, and resumed his slow march toward Newark.

Under the circumstances, carrying Pete Blackwell's iPad back to Lincolnwood was the most heroic action he could think to take.

JEN

The last thing Jen wanted to do was to knock on Judge Distefano's door.

But if she was going to salvage anything productive from this ridiculous morning, she didn't have a choice. The food shopping had to get done, and with the power outage rendering her cable-based land line as dead as her cell, she needed to borrow a neighbor's phone to call AAA for a jump.

And that neighbor could only be Frank Distefano, because the other three houses on Brantley Circle were empty.

She'd started at the Stankovics', even though she knew Kayla's help would come at the price of at least ten minutes of self-awareness-free monologuing about how hard it was to winterize a swimming pool, or how bad the service was at the nail salon on Hawthorne, or who would win the current season of *The Bachelor*. But Kayla must've been out getting collagen injections, because all that the knocking on her door accomplished was to send Dazzle into a fit of canine hysteria so frenzied that as Jen listened to the schnauzer hurl herself against the other side of the front door, she wondered if it was possible for a dog to give itself an embolism.

Then she tried the Mukherjees. But Arjun was never home on weekdays, and Anu must've been out running errands while Zaira was at pre-K.

Next up was Carol Sweeney, the busybody divorcée with

grown children, who must've been at a meeting of the Arts Council, or the Friends of the Botanic Garden, or one of her other six dozen volunteer committees. It occurred to Jen, standing on the front porch of the mid-century Craftsman from which Carol had ejected her podiatrist husband Patrick for sleeping with his receptionist, that it had been at least two years since Carol had pestered her to join a committee.

Was that just attrition? Or had Carol somehow sussed out Jen's drinking and no longer considered her reliable?

It was a paranoid thought. It was also irrelevant. Carol wasn't home.

That just left the judge. Like Carol's place, his postwar Cape was a relic of a less ostentatious era in Lincolnwood's architectural history. From the outside, it was tidy and well-kept. But its interior hadn't been updated since Frank and his late wife, Natalie, moved in around the time the Beatles appeared on *The Ed Sullivan Show*. As Jen pressed the ancient doorbell, she prayed the house wouldn't smell as musty as it had the last time she'd been inside, when she brought him a casserole after Natalie died.

Ruby answered first. Compared to Dazzle, her barks were almost polite. When the judge opened the door in his cardigan and house slippers, the dachshund quickly backpedaled to observe Jen from behind her owner's legs.

"Good morning, Jennifer!" The Honorable Francis V. Distefano's eyes crinkled with warmth behind his reading glasses as he gave her his usual inscrutable smile, the one that could mean anything from *hello, neighbor!* to *I'm so sorry you're a pathetic drunk who won't go to meetings.*

"Hey, Frank. Sorry to bother you——"

"Never a bother, kid. What can I do for you?"

"Does your phone work? My car won't start, and I need to call a mechanic."

"Sure! C'mon in." He pushed the screen door wide and stepped back to give her space to enter. As Jen crossed the threshold, Ruby slipped past her and took a few hopeful steps onto the porch.

"Ruby——we already went out this morning, sweetheart." The judge half closed the screen door, and the dachshund reluctantly retreated back inside.

To Jen's relief, the house mostly smelled like lemon Pledge with just a hint of senior-citizen funk. With Ruby at his heels, Judge Distefano led his guest past the living room and down the entry hall into the worn linoleum and cracked Formica of the time-capsule kitchen.

"The land line usually hangs in there even when the power's out." An ancient beige rotary-dial phone was mounted on the side of a cabinet. The judge picked up the receiver and put it to his ear.

Then he frowned. "Either I'm deafer than I thought," he said as he handed Jen the receiver, "or we're out of luck."

The weight and feel of the vintage receiver, with its overstretched spiral cord dangling almost to the floor, triggered a sense memory of childhood. Jen held the phone to her ear, half expecting to hear the voice of Emily Miller, her elementary-school best friend.

There was no Emily Miller on the other end. Nor was there a dial tone.

"Aaah, rats." Jen jiggled the nubby prongs on the wall unit a few times before hanging up in resignation.

"That's strange," the judge said, gazing at the phone with mild concern. "Doesn't usually happen. We didn't even lose service after Sandy. Who'd you need to call again?"

"Triple A. My car won't start."

"Think it's the battery?"

"I guess so? But my knowledge of cars pretty much ends at popping the hood open, so . . ."

Ruby took a couple of tentative steps toward Jen, who bent over and held out her hand for a sniff. The dog quickly retreated, declining the offer.

"You want a jump?" the judge asked. "I got cables. I could pull my car into your garage—"

"No, I don't want to inconvenience you." Jen stopped trying to entice Ruby and straightened up. Bending over had aggravated her headache.

"It's no trouble. All I got on tap today is reading a book about Gettysburg. And I already know who won."

"That's really sweet of you. But I'll be fine. I'm sure the power will come back soon."

"Well, if it doesn't, just knock. Happy to help." They returned to the front door together.

"Thanks, Judge. I really appreciate it."

"That's what neighbors are for. And give those kids of yours a kiss for me."

"I'll try. They're getting a little too old to put up with it."

"Don't let 'em give you that nonsense. They're never too old."

"Will do. Thanks again."

He held the screen door open for her. "My pleasure. Take care of yourself, Jennifer."

There it was—the gentle smile that made her feel like an object of pity.

Fucking AA people with their smug superiority complexes.

Back at home, Jen returned to the garage and tried to start the car again. It was every bit as dead as before.

What the hell?

I mean, what the hell?

She hadn't stuck around to discuss the situation with the judge, but the fact that his land line was dead made everything that much odder.

Why didn't her laptop work? The iPhone she could blame on a power surge. But her laptop hadn't been plugged in. Yet somehow it was dead, too.

She needed information. But with no internet, no TV, and no car radio—

The radio.

The one with the hand crank, that generated its own electricity. They'd bought it after the blackout of 2003, and they'd used it all through Hurricane Sandy.

Where the hell did we put that thing?

She got out of the car.

The radio wasn't where Jen expected it to be, in the kitchen cabinet with the flashlight. But the flashlight worked—*thank God something works*—so she took it down to the basement to search the big walk-in storage closet.

She found the radio on the lower shelf with the emergency supplies they'd bought in the aftermath of Sandy, more or less at random—a first aid kit, three more flashlights, batteries, candles, safety matches, rain ponchos (*rain ponchos? what were we thinking?*), half a dozen gallons of bottled water, and an assortment of canned food. She put her flashlight facing out on a chest-high shelf, cranked up the radio, and turned it on.

Nothing. Not even static. It was as dead as everything else.

She took it upstairs to the kitchen and tried again. Still nothing. She turned the crank twenty times to make sure it was fully powered. It didn't do any good.

This is getting seriously weird.

I feel like I'm in a Stranger Things *episode.*

Her eye fell on the half-empty bottle of cabernet next to the toaster oven.

No.

But—

NOOOOOOOO.

She briefly considered pouring the wine down the drain. But Dan might want a glass when he came home from work that night.

And anyway, there was no need to pour it out. It wasn't actually tempting. She was done with alcohol. That was nonnegotiable.

So now what?

Somehow, she had to get to the store and buy groceries.

How far is Whole Foods? A mile? Two?

She could walk it easily. Getting back would be more challenging. The hill was steep, and she'd be loaded down with groceries. But it'd be good exercise.

And they needed food. Whatever was happening with the power (and the phones . . . and the car . . . and the radio) might end up being a real hassle.

Not as bad as Hurricane Sandy. But bad enough.

The grocery list would need revising. She couldn't buy more than she'd be able to carry two miles uphill. And whatever she got would have to last them at least until Fresh Direct came through with the order she'd placed. Maybe even longer.

How long? And what do we already have?

Jen returned to the basement for a closer look at the emergency supplies.

She cast the flashlight beam across the dust-coated tops of six big jugs of Poland Spring on the bottom shelf. They were all a year past their expiration date.

Does water actually expire?

Seems like BS.

Probably a plot by Poland Spring to get you to buy more water.

She moved on to the next shelf. There were ten cans of tuna. Four Costco-sized jars of peanut butter. Canned artichoke hearts. String beans. Tomatoes . . .

And way in the back, behind the tomatoes, a fifth of Crystal Head vodka.

Oh, Jesus.

THAT thing.

It was a leftover from Dan's fiftieth birthday party. Jen considered Crystal Head a silly gimmick—the bottle was shaped like a human skull and cost twice as much as it should—but Dan had insisted on stocking it, because it was his boss's favorite brand. Of course, Marty Callahan had never showed up, which

Jen could've predicted. She'd only met him and his Ukrainian model-actress-whatever wife, Marina, a couple of times, but it was obvious to Jen (if not to Dan) that they were far too fabulous to socialize in the New Jersey suburbs.

Even so, Dan had kept the Crystal Head in the freezer all night just in case Marty showed, so it had never been opened. Instead of returning it to the Bottle King the next Monday, Jen had hidden it in the basement as her emergency stash.

Then she'd forgotten about it for almost a year.

Now here it was, smirking at her from the gloomy depths of the shelf. She pushed the canned goods aside and pulled it out, weighing it in her hand.

The symbolism of a skull-shaped bottle of her favorite liquor materializing out of the darkness on the same day she'd resolved to quit for good was about as subtle as a baseball bat to the head.

Skull-shaped vodka. What is this, Drunk Hamlet?

Maybe it's a sign.

A sign of what?

That Marty Callahan's an overgrown teenager?

That you hoard vodka like a crazy person?

Why would God put this in front of me on the day I finally decide to quit?

Oh, Jesus Christ, Jennifer.

God does not want you to drink a marketing gimmick.

Even Satan's rolling his eyes at this thing.

She shook her head in self-disgust and took the bottle upstairs to pour it out.

CHLOE

Lincolnwood High's entire student body had been milling on the front lawn and adjacent faculty parking lot for at least forty minutes, and everyone was getting restless. Per the standard fire drill procedure, which Principal Slavitt had opted to follow for lack of a better option, the students had initially lined up according to class. But as time passed and the less rule-bound kids got impatient and drifted off in search of their friends, the lines had gradually lost all coherence.

Now the teachers were starting to slip away, too, gathering in small groups of two or three to whisper their irritation at the administration for having no clue as to how to handle a building-wide power outage that had also taken out both land lines and cellular service. District policy was not to close school without informing parents, but without recourse to phones, texts, or email, there was no way to get the message out short of sending up signal flares. Consequently, for the past however many minutes—the sudden failure of everyone's phones had robbed most of them of the ability to tell time—students and faculty alike had been stuck in an increasingly restive limbo.

Chloe's opinion of the situation had improved over time. Having a test disrupted when she was acing it was infuriating, and the fact that most of her classmates had the opposite reaction only compounded her irritation. Even before Mr. Unger had hustled them all in single file from the third floor down to the front lawn, chronic underperformers like Sean Hollister had started lobbying him for a do-over. The thought that her first decent academic performance in weeks might get tossed on a technicality threatened to make Chloe's head explode, and once they got outside, she joined the pack of whining seniors surrounding Unger to plead various sides of the case.

At first, the whole fiasco felt like just another layer in the shit sandwich of failure that the universe had been feeding her all week.

But then things started to turn around. Mr. Unger capitulated, offering a voluntary retake while promising nobody's grade would get hurt either way, and that anyone who'd been happy with their performance to that point could pick up where they left off as soon as the power came back on.

Even better, Josh Houser was one of the AP Gov underachievers, and lobbying Mr. Unger put him and Chloe face-to-face with something to argue about. Once Unger's surrender lowered the stakes, the argument devolved into friendly teasing.

"It wasn't even that hard a test!" Chloe told Josh.

"Are you kidding? You must be some kind of, like, politics genius. Hey!" Josh's eyes widened. He had great eyes. They were bright blue, flecked with what looked like little shards of gray. Next to his swimmer's body, they were the hottest thing about him. "Would you tutor me?"

"Seriously?" Chloe couldn't tell if he was joking.

"Yes! Oh, my God, that'd be *so* awesome! How much do you charge?"

Chloe smirked as she looked up at him. That was another great thing about Josh—he was two inches taller than her. At five eleven, she couldn't say that about a lot of guys.

"I'm insanely expensive," she told him in a faux-haughty voice. "I doubt you can afford me."

He smirked right back at her. "Do I have to pay in cash?"

"You mean, like, do I take Venmo?"

"No, like . . . What's it called when you, like . . . y'know, trade stuff for other stuff? Instead of money?"

"Bartering?" It occurred to her that Josh might be a little dimmer than she'd previously estimated. He'd only been going to Lincolnwood since the beginning of junior year, and he'd quickly fallen in with the über-popular, stuck-up jocks like Tom McCarthy and Brett Mazursky. So despite the fact that she'd been crushing on him for months, he and Chloe had never really hung out. This conversation was already just a few sentences short of qualifying as the longest one they'd ever had.

"Bartering! Yes! You are *so* smart! See, that's why I need you to tutor me."

"Yeah, but, like, what are you offering as barter? Like, a bushel of wheat?"

"Totally! I have a really big backyard. I can farm it."

"Think you can get a harvest in before the makeup test? 'Cause that's, like, a day."

He laughed. "Maybe! I guess I should go plant some crops, huh?"

"I don't think—agriculture's usually more of a long-term thing? How about livestock? Do you have a cow? Or some chickens?"

He laughed again, and she started to worry that she was being *too* funny. Guys didn't like that.

"I mean, I would've!" he said. "If I knew I was going to need them." Then a faintly lascivious smile crept across his face. "Wait! I got it: massage."

She felt a flutter in her stomach. Was she reading that smile right? "Oh, really? Are you a licensed massage therapist?"

"I *should* be. I have the magic fingers."

Chloe felt her face start to flush. She briefly considered backing off the flirty suggestiveness and trying to work in Emma's Swedish-massage-therapist-named-Hans joke.

But then she decided to go for it.

"You know, that is reeeeally tempting."

"I know, right?" His smile widened. "You'd be amazed at how good it feels."

Chloe was definitely blushing now. The twinkle in Josh's eye seemed unmistakable. This was getting interesting.

It was her turn to banter.

She blanked.

What do I say next?

WHAT DO I SAY?

OH SHIT, I'M RUINING IT—

"Can you believe this madness?" Emma appeared at Chloe's elbow, unwittingly saving her.

"Heeey! Josh, do you know Emma?"

"Yeah. Of course! What's up?"

"Just staring at my bricked phone like the rest of us." She held up her useless iPhone. "How bizarre is this?"

"Really bizarre."

"Yeah. Super bizarre."

"Did you know *cars* aren't working?"

"Whaaaat?"

"Check it out." Emma turned and gestured toward the distant intersection at Broadmoor and Grove. Two cars stood at right angles to each other. Both drivers were outside of their vehicles, conversing as one of them leaned, arms crossed, against the front hood of his BMW.

"Their cars died," Emma explained. "They can't move them."

"Shit." Josh's mouth hung open slightly as he stared in concern at the immobilized cars. "I hope I can get to swim practice."

Chloe's mind flashed on tomorrow's state tennis semifinal.

"Do you think this is more than a one-day thing?"

"I dunno. Why?"

"We've got semis tomorrow. We're supposed to drive all the way to Rumson."

It seemed hard to believe that whatever had happened would disable the school district van that Coach Kaniewski drove to tournaments. Then again, it also seemed hard to believe that a power outage could screw up her phone when it wasn't even plugged in.

If the semi gets pushed to Thursday, I'll have an extra day to fix my backhand.

But I'll have to reschedule the ACT tutor.

And when am I going to do that reading response for AP Lit?

When's the physics quiz?

Depending on how long it lasted, this power outage could really screw a lot of things up.

"Hey, uh—"

Chloe snapped out of her reverie. Josh was watching her with a little smile and those killer eyes.

"If they call off school, what are you guys doing today?"

Chloe raised her eyebrows as she smiled back at him.

The situation might create some problems. But there was opportunity in it, too.

MAX

"It's an EMP, dude," Dennis declared. "It's gotta be."

Over in the faculty parking lot fifty yards from his sister, Max had only just begun to wonder about the cause of the power outage. Up until a few minutes ago, all of his mental energy had been devoted to staying warm and being angry at Mr. Farmer, who'd sent the whole class out to stand in the windy, fifty-five-degree weather wearing nothing but their gym shorts and T-shirts.

Protected from the elements by a sweatsuit and enough body fat to insulate a harbor seal, Farmer had maintained his position that everybody should tough it out and quit bellyaching right up until Mackenzie Whitelaw's teeth started to chatter. At that point, he relented and went inside with Mrs. Mansfield, where they somehow found a pair of flashlights that they used to escort the kids back into the locker rooms to change clothes.

Max's locker was just down the hall from the gym, and before heading back outside, he'd managed to dash over to it in the semi-darkness and fetch his coat and backpack in anticipation of school getting dismissed. That seemed imminent now—Vice Principal Figueroa had just trotted over from the main entrance to give the teachers on that side of the building a whispered update—so Max had tracked down Dennis, standing with his geometry class, to see what his plans were for the rest of the day.

Dennis had a theory about what was going on, based on

some obscure video game called *Dark Age* that Max had never heard of, let alone played.

"What's an EMP?" Max asked him.

"Electromagnetic pulse. It's, like, this huge wave of electrical energy. Fries anything with a circuit board. So, like: the power grid, phones, internet, basically any car made after, like, the seventies or something. 'Cause their shit's all electric. Which is probably why those cars died." Dennis pointed to the stalled cars on Broadmoor.

"So what causes it?" Max asked.

"Could be a bunch of shit. Like, in *Dark Age*, it was nukes. The Chinese sneak-attacked us."

"Dude, if we got nuked, I think we'd know it."

"Nuh-uh! You can, like, set them off way up in the atmosphere so you just get hit with the EMP and nothing else. And it doesn't *have* to be nukes. Like, after I played the game, I read up on EMPs. And this is the crazy shit: it could just be the sun."

"What?"

"Like, a solar storm. 'Cause the sun's basically this giant-ass nuclear weapon that's permanently going off. Right? And sometimes it'll just, like, throw off a ton of random energy. Like a solar storm. And a big enough solar storm could send this massive EMP shooting across the solar system. And just totally fry everything on Earth."

"So if that happens, how do you fix it?"

"You can't, dude. That's why the game was called *Dark Age*. Shit just went totally medieval. Society collapsed. Like, overnight."

Before Max could process the implications of this, Vice

Principal Figueroa began to bellow an announcement from atop the short steps that led to the side door.

"Listen up, people! Obviously, this is a very unusual situation. It's not clear what happened or how long the power's going to be out—"

"Try forever," Dennis muttered.

"But we can't conduct classes in this environment. So while we're not able to contact your parents directly, we're going to go ahead and dismiss you. Those of you who are bus passengers, please meet Mr. Garcia at the front entrance to—"

"Snow day, muthafuckas!" Andy Ko descended upon Max and Dennis, clapping them both on the shoulder. "Poker game at my house."

Max had just enough time to enjoy a glimmer of relief at the prospect of his friends finally moving on from the COD multiplayer when Andy's next sentence knocked him back on his heels:

"Grayson and Jordan are in, too."

"What the fuck? Why would we play with *them*?"

Andy grinned. "'Cause they'll suck, bruh! We'll take their money!"

"No way. No *fucking* way! I'm not playing with those idiots!"

"Duuude . . ." Dennis moaned as Andy made an exasperated noise with the back of his throat. "Don't be like that. He's not going to hit you again."

"Fuckin' A he's not!" Max's adrenaline surged at the thought.

"Can't you just get over the whole thing?" Andy whined at him. "It was your fault anyway."

WHAT?!

"Fuck you, Andy!"

"What? You said it yourself!"

"No, I didn't!"

"Yeah, you did." Dennis insisted. "You shouldn't have dick-slapped him about that thing with his dad."

"No, it—that wasn't—*fuck* you guys!" Max was spluttering with rage now. "It's *our* poker game! You can't just invite them without asking us!"

Andy shrugged. "Yeah, I can. It's my house."

Three minutes later, Max was huffing up the Grove Street hill on his bike, wrenching the handlebars from side to side for momentum as he stomped down on the pedals.

The whole thing was unbelievable. He'd never felt so betrayed in his life.

Poker was Max's thing! Andy, Dennis, and Ben wouldn't even know how to play if it weren't for him!

And now they were throwing him over for those dumb fucking meatheads?

Fucking traitors!

By the time he got to Walker Street, his chest was burning from the exertion. He turned right and slumped back onto the seat to catch his breath. Halfway down the block, he steered over to the curb, came to a stop, and unzipped his jacket pocket.

He needed a hit. Gulping air, he scanned the street in both directions to make sure there was nobody around who could narc on him for vaping. Then he pulled out his Juul.

Traitors! Backstabbers!

He glowered at the device cupped in his hand. Its battery light wasn't showing green.

It wasn't showing anything.

He double tapped it. Nothing.

What the hell?

He tapped it a few more times, with increasing urgency. Still nothing. It was dead.

He tried to hit it anyway.

Nothing.

FUUUUUCK!

Max stared in wounded disbelief at the finger-length rectangle of plastic and metal in his palm. Unlike his so-called friends, the Juul had never let him down before.

CHLOE

"I don't know, Frenchie." Emma sat in the driver's seat of her Jetta, the door open and one foot on the pavement. "You really want to hang with those people?"

"Not most of them." Chloe nibbled a cuticle on her fingertip as she stood by the open car door, surveying the student parking lot. The next row over, Josh was talking to Tom McCarthy and Brett Mazursky. "Just, y'know . . ."

"One of them?"

"Yeah."

Emma sighed. Chloe winced.

"I'm sorry—"

"No. I get it."

"I mean, he's not like—"

"He's definitely the least annoying of them."

"Right? Like, if he hadn't fallen in with those guys when he first got here and didn't know anybody—"

"Yeah. No. I get it."

"It wouldn't be long. Just for a little. Like, I have practice at three thirty anyway." As school dismissed, Coach Kaniewski had sought out Chloe and the rest of her teammates to tell them practice was still on, the urgency of the state semis having outweighed the inconvenience of the power outage. "And I have to eat lunch at some point. So, like, we'd just go for a while."

"Yeah. Okay."

Chloe put a hand on Emma's shoulder. "Thank you so much!"

Emma put her hand over Chloe's. "Like, what are friends for, right?" Then she reached forward and turned the ignition key back and forth for the umpteenth time, to no effect. "I'm going to be *so* ripshit if my car's dead."

"Don't worry. I'm sure it's fixable. Like, all the cars can't be dead." As Chloe looked around, she didn't see any evidence for her assertion. But she quickly forgot about that, because Josh was on his way over with Tom and Brett.

"What up?"

"Just watching Emma try to start her car."

"Sucks, huh?"

"Totally."

Josh nodded in sympathy. "This is the weirdest shit ever. Hey, so we're going to go hang at Brody's. Want to come?"

Brody Kiplinger went to Lincolnwood Academy, the local private school. His parents owned a mansion on Mountain Avenue but seldom seemed to be there, as a consequence of which it had become the apex of Lincolnwood's teen social firmament. Neither Chloe nor Emma had ever been inside. If asked, they both would've claimed this was by choice. Emma considered Brody the personification of wealthy cis white male privilege, and Chloe just thought he was a dick. But until now, their objections to hanging at Brody's had been purely theoretical, because they'd never been invited.

The two girls exchanged a look. Then Chloe answered for both of them.

"Yeah! Totally."

DAN

Is this a big deal?

Or not?

The further Dan walked toward home, the more confused he became about just what he and the thousands of people he passed, from the outskirts of Harrison through downtown Newark and into the suburbs, were experiencing.

Was it some kind of slow motion 9/11? The first stage of an alien invasion? Or just a very comprehensive power outage?

For the first couple of miles, he sensed they were on the more dire end of the spectrum. The mood of the crowd trudging west on the turnpike was somber and fearful. Unsettled by Pete Blackwell's unexplained departure, Dan's thoughts during that first stretch were mostly devoted to Jen and the kids.

Are they okay?

Is this . . . whatever it is . . . happening in Lincolnwood, too?

Is Jen freaking out? Is she having 9/11 flashbacks?

Dan stopped at a gas station to try to call home. Its land line was out, which only left him more unsettled.

But once he entered Newark, the atmosphere changed. The urban center was too far removed from the plane crash for most of its residents to have experienced it as anything but a rumor. And while the city's entire technological infrastructure had failed, it had done so without any immediate misfortune greater than a few minor car accidents and stalled elevators. The blackout had sent most of Newark into the streets, yet there was no buzz of panic or distress. People just seemed confused.

That made them chatty, especially with Dan. His busted-up face gave him an aura of Guy Who Just Went Through Some Shit, and as he made his way across the city, strangers kept pressing him for information.

"What happened to your face, yo?"

"I was on a train outside Harrison when a plane crashed right next to us."

"Holy shit! You was in a plane crash?"

"Not *in* it. But, y'know—next to it."

"Was it bad?"

"Yeah. It was a passenger jet. Couple hundred people."

"Damn! Is that got to do with all this? Power going out and such?"

"I don't know. Hey, can you tell me where Lincoln Avenue is?"

"Three blocks that way. Turn left at the Dollar Store."

"Thanks."

"Take care of yourself, brother!"

The widespread respect that accrued to Dan by virtue of his injury—on a couple of occasions, people seemed to stop just short of saying *thank you for your service*—both flattered him and made him feel like a fraud. Even so, he saw no point in explaining the full context. *Oh no, see, what actually happened was that I got popped in the face because the woman next to me wanted to jump out the window, but I was too busy trying to find my AirPod to pull the emergency handle for her* was just too big a mouthful. And anyway, he didn't want to ruin a well-meaning stranger's vicarious experience of the calamity.

So when passersby stopped to quiz him, he tried to maintain a posture of quiet stoicism. And with the memory of Mousy Librarian's contempt still clinging to him like an itchy sweater, he kept an eye out for opportunities to be heroic amid the crisis.

But it wasn't that kind of crisis. Other than a constant supply of flummoxed drivers who didn't know what to do with vehicles that had failed down to their power locks in the middle of the street, the closest Dan came to encountering a stranger in need was an elderly Latina muttering in despair over a cart full of groceries at the front door of a five-story apartment building.

He deduced that she needed help carrying the bags upstairs, but she didn't speak English, and his *Dora the Explorer* level proficiency in Spanish didn't give him the verbal tools to erase her look of wary hostility. After a few fruitless attempts to persuade her of his good intentions, Dan gave up, regretting his decision to take French in high school. The odds of his finding an elderly Frenchwoman in distress anywhere near East Newark were vanishingly long.

In the end, the only act of heroism he managed to perform was carrying home Pete Blackwell's iPad. And it didn't even weigh very much.

By the time Dan reached Lincoln Avenue, which cut a straight line from a working-class Latino neighborhood of downtown Newark through six miles of steadily rising incomes before reaching its geographic-socioeconomic peak atop the ridge half a mile from Dan's house in Upper Lincolnwood, his concern for his family had mostly receded in favor of worrying about his job.

Is the power out in Manhattan? Is the writers' room still happening?

An image of the room popped into Dan's head. Marty holding court at the head of the table, slouched in his Aeron chair, whiteboard on the wall behind his head . . . Sumaya, the writer's assistant, perched at Marty's elbow with her fingers poised on the keyboard of a MacBook . . . Adam Fineman in his usual spot by the door, doing that weird thing with his pen . . . Sara Gutierrez, twirling her hair in silence . . . Bobby O, cracking open a Red Bull . . . and the chair next to Bobby—Dan's usual spot—conspicuously empty.

Bobby and Adam lived in Brooklyn. Had they made it in to the office? Were the subways running? The show was in production on one of Sara's episodes, shooting on the soundstage in Queens. Had the power gone out over there, too?

If production shut down for even a day, it'd be a real headache. Marty would be preoccupied with putting out fires. The last thing he'd want to do would be to sit in the room all day trying to beat Bobby's and Adam's mediocre pitches.

Especially when Dan was carrying the good shit right there in his Moleskine.

He started to game out how he could get himself into the city. Lincoln Avenue would take him to within a few blocks of the train station where he'd parked his Lexus. By then, maybe New Jersey Transit would be running again. If not, the Lexus was highly reliable. Only six thousand miles on it, and he'd just had it serviced. Surely—if nothing *truly* bad had happened—he could get his car to start. Then he'd drive to the city, parachute into the room, and save Marty's bacon with "Death at Comic Con" and "Mousy Librarian Gets What's Coming to Her."

That wouldn't be the actual episode title. But Dan would get his emotional revenge, and it would be sweet.

He figured he should minister to his injury before he tried to get in to the office, so a few blocks after he turned onto Lincoln Avenue, he went into Luisa Farmacia for first aid supplies. But their Polysporin was overpriced, their Band-Aids were off brand, and they were only taking cash. So Dan decided to save the seventeen dollars he had on him for future contingencies.

A mile up the road, he tried Eldridge Urgent Care, but left empty-handed when they asked for seven pages of paperwork and a twenty-dollar copay.

After he passed two more drugstores that had locked their doors due to the power outage, he began to despair of procuring first aid before he reached his car.

Then he decided it might be better this way. If Dan showed up in front of Marty still bleeding from an undressed facial wound, it'd be tough to argue that he was insufficiently committed to his job.

Dan had just started mulling this over when he encountered the cop, headed the other way down Lincoln Avenue. It was an Essex County sheriff's deputy, and both his uniform and his height conveyed such authority that Dan stopped him in the hope of learning something useful.

"Excuse me, sir? Do you know what's going on?"

The cop gave Dan a blank look. "The power's out."

"Yeah, but—do you know why?"

"I, uh . . ." The cop lowered his chin and furrowed his eyebrows in a thoughtful look. "I don't have any information on that at the moment. What happened to your face?"

"It's kind of a long—Did you hear about the plane crash?"

The cop's eyebrows reversed direction. "You were in it? The one on the golf course?"

"I don't—What?"

"The plane? That landed on the golf course?" The cop jerked his thumb to the southwest, beyond the avenue.

"A plane landed on a *golf course*?"

"Yeah. At the country club in Short Hills. Seven thirty-seven. Heard the pilot put it down right on a fairway."

"Oh, wow. I didn't know anything about that."

"It's pretty wild. Apparently, everybody got out okay."

"Did you see it?"

"No." The cop shook his head, lightly but rapidly. "I just heard about it. From a guy. So, you were on *another* plane?"

"No, I was on a train. Into the city. A plane went down next to the tracks."

"Where was that?"

"Outside Harrison. Almost to Jersey City. Have you heard anything else?"

"About what?"

Dan shrugged. "Anything?"

The cop shook his head again, slower this time. He took a long breath, then puffed out his cheeks as he exhaled. "I'm just headed back to headquarters to see if there's any, y'know . . ."

Dan waited for him to finish the sentence. He didn't. Instead, the sheriff's deputy turned the question back on Dan.

"Have *you* heard anything?"

"Not really. No."

"Okay. Well, take care. Maybe get that cut looked at." The cop started to walk away.

"Wait—"

"Yeah?"

"Do you know where I could do that? Get this looked at?"

"You try urgent care? Back that way?"

"I did, yeah," said Dan. "It was a little . . . bureaucratic. I was thinking maybe if there's a hospital that—"

"I wouldn't." The cop shook his head firmly. "I'd stay away from the hospitals right now. I just came from Memorial—they got their hands full. All their equipment's down. ICU and everything."

"Don't they have backup generators?"

"Yeah. But those are down, too."

"Oh, geez."

"It's a real mess. I'd steer clear."

"I will. Okay. Have a good day."

"You too."

Dan resumed his walk. As he turned the conversation over in his head, his sense of the situation's gravity began to shift again.

A world in which planes landed on golf courses . . . hospitals had no functioning equipment . . . and cops were wandering around clueless . . . was not normal.

It was *very* not normal.

As Dan kept walking, he began to feel light-headed, then nauseous.

Am I in shock?

No. I'm just hungry.

He felt this way before lunch all the time. It was a blood sugar thing.

Is it lunchtime yet?

He instinctively moved his hand to his hip pocket to check the time on his phone. Then he remembered his phone was dead. He didn't know what time it was.

He didn't know a lot of things. Like where Jen and the kids were. And whether they were okay.

Dan's feet, unused to walking such a long distance, were starting to hurt. Despite the discomfort, he quickened his pace.

JEN

The Crystal Head vodka bottle was grimy with dust, which made cracking it open and pouring it into the sink unappetizing. So when Jen came up from the basement, she tied it up in a plastic Rite Aid bag and left it on the counter to dispose of on the way to Whole Foods. Then she sat down to revise her shopping list.

Jelly to go with all of the peanut butter in the basement. Mayonnaise and celery to go with the tuna. Red onion.

Something special to make Chloe for dinner as a peace offering.

How am I going to cook with the power out?

She checked the oven. It wouldn't turn on. Unless the power came back before dinner, that meant Chloe's favorite, parmesan chicken, was out.

The gas burners on the stovetop still worked, although they had to be lit with a match. She could stir-fry a Thai chicken with basil and serve it over rice. That was a decent second choice. Max didn't like stir-fry, but he didn't like anything except pasta and burgers.

Jen went to the pantry cabinet. Not much to work with. They were out of rice. And pretty much everything else.

She sat down again, next to the tied-off plastic bag that entombed the vodka bottle, and looked over the shopping list again. Rice was already on it.

What else? What's good in a power outage . . . that I can cook on a stovetop . . . and isn't too heavy to carry home?

She drew a blank. Her hangover wasn't conducive to organized thinking.

There were only two ways to fix a hangover. Time, and the thing Jen absolutely wasn't going to do under any circumstance.

She went back to the list and tried to concentrate. Her eyes stared at the words, but couldn't assemble them into meaningful thoughts.

Fuck it. I'll figure it out at the store.

She put the list in her pocket and stood up. Then she turned her attention back to the Rite Aid bag.

Am I going to carry that thing all the way to Whole Foods?

No. That's ridiculous.

I should smash it. Throw it off a cliff. Shatter the fucker on a rock.

Some kind of ceremonial destruction seemed appropriate. She was quitting forever. This was a big fucking deal.

I need a ritual.

Jen vaguely recalled—among the dozens of articles she'd googled over the past couple of years about addiction, dependency, and breaking bad habits—reading something to the effect that symbolic rituals could be helpful in making a decision stick.

There was nothing symbolic about just tossing a bag in the garbage.

Especially when the bottle inside it was so grimy.

She couldn't smash a grimy bottle. She'd get her hands dirty.

Jen untied the bag, took the bottle out, and washed the exterior in the sink.

The skull's blank, sunken eyes stared up at her from between her hands.

Drunk Hamlet. You evil little fucker.

Where could she shatter it? There were no cliffs between here and Whole Foods. There wasn't even so much as a drainage ditch.

Memorial Park was out of the question. What if some little kid came by and cut herself on the broken glass?

Maybe I should bury it in the backyard.

Or hide it back down in the basement.

Emergency vodka.

Oh, Christ, not that idea again.

She'd gone the "emergency vodka" route at least half a dozen times. It never worked. It was too easy to declare an emergency.

Get real, Jennifer. If you keep it around, you'll drink it.

The thing was, though . . .

Was her last drink on earth really going to be a glass of Two Buck Chuck? That she only half remembered?

That just seemed pathetic. No ritual to it at all.

I'll shop better if I take the edge off this hangover.

SHUT UP, JENNIFER.

You deserve this hangover.

It's not about that, though.

It's about the power of symbolic ritual to reinforce a change of habit.

A clean break with the past.

A totem. A talisman. A symbolically meaningful goodbye.

Or am I just kidding myself?

Look, the power's out, the car won't start——the day's already ruined.

SHUT UP!

This is ridiculous.

She stared at the bottle. The bottle stared back.

Ten minutes of internal monologue later, she was seated at the kitchen table, congratulating herself on the aesthetic perfection of Jennifer Riehl's Last Drink Ever. It was a vodka on the rocks, poured into her finest highball glass from a gleaming personification of Death and perfectly chilled via the ideal ratio of vodka to ice.

So this is goodbye.

She raised it to her lips and took a long sip, savoring the familiar burn as it slid down her throat.

We had some good times. I'll give you that.

It occurred to her that she should enumerate them. Forget the bad shit for a moment and focus on the good, back in the early days before it all went south.

This is a funeral. We don't speak ill of the dead at a funeral.

Remember the first time?

Kelly's lake house. Summer '85. Three cans of Old Style, a bonfire, and Billy Shober's tongue in her mouth.

Jen smiled to herself.

Goooood times.

There were others. So many others.

Michelle's basement. Brad's Camaro. Both proms. That whole summer after high school, working at the ice cream shop on Lake Michigan.

Rush week. The road trip to the Ohio State game.

Rum on spring break in the Bahamas.

Wine on her honeymoon in Santorini.

Bar nights at Wharton.

The Guinness she drank every night when she was breast-feeding Chloe. So good. And medically prescribed! The pediatrician had recommended dark beer while nursing.

Jen tipped the glass back, the half-melted ice cubes tumbling against her lips.

Shit, that wasn't enough.

Just a tease, really.

She looked at the bottle. It was nearly full.

What if that was my . . . Second to Last Drink Ever?

Oh, for fuck's sake.

Get up and get to the store!

She looked at the clock on the stove.

But there was no clock. The power was out.

She shook a couple ice cubes into her mouth and chewed them pensively.

Aesthetically speaking, Jen's Absolutely Positively Last Drink Ever was a real disappointment. The ice cubes, transplanted from a defrosting freezer to a bowl that had been left for too long at room temperature, had lost all their potency. They floated atop the vodka like dead minnows, shrinking so fast that they barely clinked as Jen raised the glass to her lips.

Not only that, but Skully—as she'd recently christened him—was no longer gleaming. When Jen tried to poetically contemplate his visage, the eyes staring back at her were smudgy with her own fingerprints.

Somewhere along the way, the symbolic clarity of the

moment had blurred into what was starting to feel like just another Tuesday.

I gotta get to the store.

Can't drive like this, though.

Oh, right.

Can't drive anyway. Gotta walk.

Shit, that's a hike. Especially with groceries.

Did I eat breakfast? I should definitely—

The thought was interrupted by the *click-creak-shwuuush* of the front door opening.

FUCK—

Instantly, she was up and moving, her heart pounding from fear of exposure. She flung open the undersink cabinet and shoved the bottle inside, way in back, next to the Drano. The rest of the drink went down her throat. The highball glass went in the back of the dishwasher.

She slammed it shut and turned around as her husband entered the room.

DAN

One look at Jen, and Dan realized he'd been right to worry about her. She looked positively shell-shocked. Back in the day, it had taken her ages to get over the trauma she'd suffered on 9/11, and this whole situation was clearly retraumatizing her.

Or at least his busted face was.

"Ohmygod!" she yelped, clapping a hand to her mouth in horror. "What happened to you?"

"I'm okay! It's just a cut." He set down his messenger bag and strode toward her, arms out to envelop his wife in a protective, comforting hug.

She darted away like a scared rabbit.

"I'll get you a Band-Aid!"

"It's fine! Don't worry! It looks worse than it is." Dan wasn't sure if that was true. He had yet to get a look at his own injury.

She half ran down the short corridor to the bathroom and ducked inside, shutting the door in his face when he followed her.

"Hey—" Dan tried to turn the doorknob. It was locked.

"Hang on! I'm getting you stuff!"

He knocked. "Are you okay?"

"Yeah. Just—let me—we gotta clean you up—"

"Don't worry about me! What about you? Are you okay? Can you let me in?"

"I'm fine! You're the one who—hang on, I'm just looking for—"

From the other side of the door, he heard the sound of the medicine cabinet banging shut. "Why aren't you at work?"

"I was on the train when the power went out," he explained to the closed door. "Then a plane went down right next to the tracks. Everybody freaked out, it was like a mass panic. Pete Blackwell was there—then *he* freaked out and ran home, and I spent the last I don't know how long walking back here—"

"Wait—start over. *Where* were you?"

"On the train. Almost to Jersey City. Can you open this door?" He twisted the knob back and forth for emphasis.

"Yeah! Just a sec."

Finally, Jen opened it. She had both hands raised in front of her chest, holding a damp, wadded-up Kleenex in one and an open bottle of rubbing alcohol in the other.

"Hold still." She reached out with the Kleenex to dab at his cut.

Dan caught a strong whiff of the rubbing alcohol and recoiled, putting his hand up to block hers.

"Jesus, not *that*! It'll hurt like hell!"

"You gotta clean it!"

"Don't we have peroxide?"

She looked at the bottle in her hand. Then back at the open medicine cabinet behind her.

"Yeah, that'd be better. Let me get it."

"Wait—can I have a hug first?"

"Just—gimme a sec." She seemed oddly lukewarm on the hug offer, sidestepping away from him and back toward the medicine cabinet.

He followed her into the little room. "Are you doing okay? I know it's been a really scary day."

"Yeah . . ."

"Holy shit!" He finally got a look at himself in the mirror. There was a swollen red bruise under his right eye, crowned by a blood-crusted open cut a quarter of an inch long. "Do you think I need stitches?"

"Maybe?" She set the bottle of rubbing alcohol down next to the sink and turned her shoulder away from him, toward the cabinet.

"Honey—" Dan held his arms out. She turned back to him, her lips pressed together in a pained look, and hugged him tightly.

Her heart was beating so fast that Dan could feel it through her rib cage. He rubbed her back, trying to calm her. "Oh, babe. I'm so sorry. I know how scary this must be for you."

"Yeah . . . Tell me what happened to you again?"

"I was—" Dan stopped in midsentence. "Wait." He pulled back from the clinch. "Where are the kids?"

"School," she said out of the side of her mouth as she turned back to the medicine cabinet and pulled a bottle of peroxide from the shelf.

"You sure? How long's the power been out here?"

"Since, like . . . nine, I guess?" She unscrewed the peroxide cap, plucked a fresh Kleenex from the box over the toilet, and saturated the tissue with the disinfectant.

"There's no way the kids are still in school. I just came up Hawthorne. There were teenagers wandering around all over."

"Can you step back?"

Dan did as he was told. Jen reached out at half an arm's length to wipe his cut with the peroxide-soaked Kleenex.

"Don't worry," she told him, still talking out the side of her mouth. "Max is probably at Dennis's. And Chloe's with Emma."

"You really think they're okay?"

"Why wouldn't they be?" She opened a Band-Aid from a box in the cabinet, squeezed a bead of Neosporin onto the pad, and carefully applied it to his cheek.

He watched her, confused. "Because of everything that's going on?"

"Like what everything?"

"Planes crashing, cars dying, all the phones down—"

Jen held up a hand. "Wait. Start over. *What's* going on?"

Dan caught a whiff of Jen's breath. It was pungent.

"Have you been drinking?"

She screwed up her face in an indignant look. "No! Oh my God, no! It's, like, ten in the morning!"

"I think it's closer to noon."

She picked up the open bottle of rubbing alcohol. "You're probably smelling this."

"Oh. That makes a lot more sense."

"Right? Here—go sit in the living room. Tell me everything that happened."

They went to the living room. She curled into a corner of the couch with her knees up and her hands folded across her chest. Dan sat as close as her position would allow him to get, resting an arm on her knee, and told her everything he'd been through that morning.

"Holy shit."

"Right?"

"Yeah. That's really scary." She reached out and rubbed his arm affectionately.

"You think I should've gone back for the AirPods?"

"I dunno. Maybe? Those things are a bitch to replace. They're back-ordered for weeks."

"Right?" He put his hand over hers. "How are *you* doing?"

"I'm fine."

"Because I was worried this would kick up, y'know, all the 9/11 memories and—"

"No. That's sweet. But no. I'm fine."

Dan leaned over to kiss her. She drew back a little before letting herself be kissed.

He sniffed, then straightened up with a look of alarm. "You *really* smell like booze."

"I told you. It's the rubbing alcohol." She waved her hand in the direction of the bathroom.

"It's your *breath*, Jen."

"Then it must be left over from last night."

That was an alarming thought. "How much did you drink last night?"

"I don't know. Like, two glasses of wine?"

Dan shook his head. "That doesn't make sense. And it doesn't smell like wine. It smells like vodka."

He watched her carefully. She squeezed her eyes shut and sighed.

"Have you been drinking?"

"I just—it's been a *really* hard morning, okay?"

"I thought you said you were fine."

"I'm not. I'm really not." She sat up, her face starting to wrinkle with emotion. Then she put her head in her hands and started to sob.

"Oh my God! Honey." He put his arm around her.

"I'm sorry . . . ! I'm so sorry. The truth is . . ."

She turned to face him. The odd lack of affect she'd retreated into after her initial look of horror when he came home was gone now. In its place was what looked like genuine anguish.

"I don't know how to tell you this . . ."

"It's okay." He rubbed her back some more. "I know how hard this must be for you. If I'd been through what you went through back then—and now all of a sudden, planes are falling out the sky again—"

"Yeah . . . Yeah." She slowly nodded, the anguish receding from her face. "I think I must be in shock or something? With all the, the whole 9/11 thing—"

"It's okay. It's okay." He drew her to him, and she buried her head in his chest.

He stroked her hair softly. They were silent for a moment.

"Seriously, though," he said. "How much did you drink?"

She pulled back and stared at him. He stared back at her.

Then she kissed him. Not softly, but insistently.

Hungrily. Her mouth opening to his.

Jesus, she tastes like vodka—

She slipped a hand between his legs.

"Let's go upstairs," she whispered in his ear.

"Oh. Okay!" As Jen led him from the room by the hand, Dan

flashed back to an article he'd read once about all of the people who'd reacted to 9/11 by running out and having sex with strangers. Apparently, it had been a very common reaction.

But until now, it had never really made psychological sense to him.

CHLOE

"You know what's going on, right?" Tucker Number One said. He sat slouched in one of the Kiplinger living room's red leather club chairs, his legs splayed wide, with one hand attached to a can of Bud Light perched just above his crotch. "It's a glitch in the simulation."

"What does that even mean?" Tess Blackwell asked. She was on her third raspberry Smirnoff Ice, coupled with several hits of indica, and her words were starting to get slurry.

"You don't know about the simulation?" Tucker Number Two looked incredulous.

Or is that one Parker?

Chloe wasn't sure. Parker and the two Tuckers all went to Lincolnwood Academy and seemed to be more or less the same person, which was making it difficult for her to keep them straight.

"It's totally badass!" Probably Tucker Two sat up and leaned forward over the massive mahogany coffee table, energized by the simulation topic.

"Sooooo badass," echoed Brody, without looking up from the joint he was constructing on the opposite side of the coffee table.

"Okay, so, it's like: reality isn't real. 'Cause we're—"

"Dude!" Tucker One barked. "Let me tell it."

"Sorry." Tucker Two shrank back, acknowledging his place in the hierarchy of Tuckers.

"It's like this." Tucker One pulled himself ever so slightly up out of his bro slouch so he could properly address his lecture to the couch that contained Tess, Cressida Cohen, and some Academy girl named Alexis. "Did you see *The Matrix*?"

"No."

"Aww!" Josh chimed in. He was sitting with Chloe and Emma on the other couch. "You gotta! It's fire."

"So, *The Matrix* is, like . . ." Tucker One paused for a moment, daunted by the task of coming up with an adequate plot summary. Then he shrugged it off. "Whatever. Doesn't matter. Basically, the deal is: the whole fuckin' world is, like, one big computer simulation. That's being run by, like, superior beings."

"Like we're all just characters in their video game or some shit," Brody added as he unscrewed the cap on his weed grinder.

"Right. So when weird shit like this happens—" Tucker One made a sweeping gesture with his beer can, taking in the entirety of the cavernous living room, the natural light from its eight-foot windows not quite strong enough to banish the gloom in its corners. "It's not real. It's just, like . . . a glitch in the simulation."

"Like, reality's an app, and it got hung up or some shit," Tucker Two added.

"Huh." Tess's mouth hung open.

Cressida slowly nodded. "Wow . . . That's trippy."

"It's *complete* bullshit," Emma declared. She crossed her arms against her chest as she fixed Tucker One with a look of disdain.

"No, it's not!" Tucker One insisted. "It's, like, probably true."

"Yah," said Brody. "Like, one of the smartest guys on Earth said we're almost definitely in a simulation. Like, the odds are."

"Really? Who was that?" Other than Chloe, Emma was the

only one in the room who was sober. But unlike Chloe, who was abstaining due to her impending tennis practice, Emma seemed to be doing it to prove a point, to herself if not to the rest of the group.

"I forget his name. He's, like, a computer guy. There's this YouTube video—" Tucker One picked up his phone to search for the video, then realized he couldn't. "Shit! I did it again."

This had been a chronic occurrence, and not just for the Tuckers. All of the kids still had their phones within arm's reach, and every few minutes, one of them would compulsively check it like an amputee trying to scratch an itch in a limb that no longer existed.

Emma gave Tucker One a smug grin. "Persuasive argument."

With the exception of Chloe and Josh, the rest of the room scowled at her.

"It's fuckin' true!" Tucker One snarled. "Like, the guy who came up with it's a lot smarter than you."

"Or maybe he just smokes a ton of weed," Emma replied as a distant cheer erupted from the Beer-Pong-by-candlelight game being played in the basement rec room below them.

"Actually, I think that dude *does* smoke a ton of weed," Brody admitted.

"Doesn't mean he's wrong." Tucker One relaxed back into his entitled slouch. "And it makes sense. I mean, what the hell? How often does the power go out and fuckin' *cars* don't even work?"

"So fuckin' weird." Tucker Two shook his head in wonder.

An awkward silence fell over the room. There had been almost as many of these silences as there had been reflexive phone checks. Chloe couldn't tell if all the conversational dead spots were a side effect of involuntary technological withdrawal, or if Brody Kiplinger and his friends were just fundamentally boring.

Then again, she wasn't exactly being chatty herself. She kept trying to think of something clever or flirty to say to Josh, without much success. And he wasn't giving her a whole lot to work with. He was almost as quiet as that girl Alexis, who literally hadn't said a word all afternoon.

Or was it still morning?

She gave Josh a nudge with her elbow.

"Do you know what time it is?"

He reached for his phone, then stopped himself.

She grinned. "Made you look!"

He chuckled as they held eye contact for a moment. He had a great smile. And those awesome eyes.

Plus a little bit of a horse face. But that didn't bother her. There was a name for that kind of profile. A much nicer one than "horse face."

Roman? Is that it? A Roman nose?

Something like that.

Emma, sitting on the opposite side of Chloe from Josh, leaned in to whisper in her ear.

"I can't believe how boring this is."

As she said it, they heard the sound of the heavy front door opening, its creak sending an echo through the high-ceilinged entrance hall. Evidently, Brett Mazursky was back from his mission to liberate a twelve-pack of beer from the fridge in Mr. Mazursky's basement man cave.

Still hunched over his joint-in-progress, Brody called out, "Yo, Berserksky! Gimme one of them beers!"

To everyone's surprise, the person who entered the room wasn't Brett Mazursky. It was Tess's father, Mr. Blackwell—the richest man in town and a legit billionaire, according to the rumors. Sweaty, flushed, and moving with a painful-looking limp, he scanned the group of kids until his eye fell on his daughter.

"Tess, honey? We need to go."

At the sight of her dad, Tess's eyes grew as wide as they could get, given the constraints of indica and Smirnoff Ice. She got to her feet, quickly but unsteadily, and started toward him at the threshold of the entrance hall.

"Mr. Blackwell?" Brody's eyes were even wider than Tess's. He'd hurriedly shoved the half-made joint, grinder, and baggie of weed under the coffee table.

"Yeah?" As his daughter passed him on her way to the door, Pete Blackwell paused to look back at Brody.

"Please don't tell my parents."

"Where are they?"

"London."

"When are they supposed to come back?"

"Tomorrow."

Mr. Blackwell considered this, then nodded. "Good. That's good." He started to follow his daughter out, then seemed to realize Brody was in need of more explicit reassurance. He paused again.

"Don't sweat it, Brody. Just don't do anything stupid. Okay?"

Brody nodded vigorously. "We won't! I promise."

"Cool. We'll see you."

Then both of the Blackwells were gone, followed by the sound of the front door opening and closing again.

"Jeeeeesus," Brody said, his head briefly disappearing as he retrieved his weed from under the coffee table.

"Don't trip," Tucker One told Brody. "Tess's dad is super chill."

Cressida shook her head. "You don't know him. Like, he *seems* chill? But he's a total control freak."

"Whose dad isn't?"

"No, but, like—have you ever been to their weekend place? In Pennsylvania?"

"No."

"Ohmygod." Cressida rolled her eyes. "First of all, it's amazing. Like, it's huge. Right on this lake. And I think they, like, own the lake? But the thing is—her dad turned the whole basement into this, like, bunker. With, like, food and guns and all kinds of shit."

"So he's like a whaddayacallit?"

"Survivalist."

"Yeah."

"Basically. Tess said it's, like, in case of the apocalypse or whatever. Like, he's totally paranoid."

"Having a bunker is pretty badass," Brody pointed out.

"We have guns," Parker piped up. "My dad has a shitload of them."

"Seriously?"

"Yeah. Like, hunting rifles. Two shotguns. A Glock—"

"Can we not talk about this?" Cressida asked. "It's freaking me out."

"You started it."

"No, I didn't! I just said—"

Emma leaned in to whisper to Chloe again. "I am *so* fucking out of here."

Chloe followed Emma to the front door. "Why are you leaving?"

"Are you kidding? They're idiots! And now they're talking about their daddies' *guns*?" Emma screwed up her face in disgust.

"They're not that bad."

"They are, though. Tess was the only one who was even half-way nice. And she was barely out the door when Cressida started talking shit about her family. Plus, do you notice how none of the girls ever call the boys on their bullshit? They're like fucking geishas."

Josh came out of the living room. "Everything okay?"

"Yeah. We're just, um . . ."

"I gotta jet," Emma explained. "It was cool hanging out, though. Thanks."

"Yeah. Totally. You need a ride or something?"

The girls looked at him quizzically.

"Oh! Right. Duh." He turned to Chloe. "Are you going, too?"

Chloe thought about it. "I don't know. I kind of need to eat before tennis."

"Eat here," Josh said. "They've got tons of food. We can raid the fridge."

Chloe looked at Emma, who granted her approval. "You should stay."

"You sure?"

"Totally. I'm just going to go home."

"How?"

"I'll walk. It's not that far."

"What about your car?"

Emma shrugged. "It's not like they're going to tow it."

"Okay." They hugged. "Love you!"

"Love you, too, Frenchie. Bye, Josh!"

"Take it easy!"

Emma shut the heavy front door behind her. A portentous *thunk* echoed through the big entrance hall. Chloe looked at Josh. He gave her a lopsided smile under that Roman nose and those killer eyes.

"Eats?"

"Yeah. Where's the kitchen again?"

"This way."

She followed him, watching with thirsty approval as his swimmer's body strode down the corridor into the shadows.

JEN

Jen swished a big slug of Listerine around in her mouth, then—after a half second during which she contemplated swallowing—spat it out in the sink.

That should take care of the smell.

Barely dressed in the undies and T-shirt she'd pulled on en route to the bathroom, she surveyed herself in the mirror.

Could be worse. The bad lighting helps.

She closed her eyes, took a deep breath, and sighed heavily.

I've got to stop. This is ridiculous.

Should I have come clean with him?

Jesus, no. Do you really want to open that can of worms?

She padded back to the bedroom and climbed into bed, snuggling up to Dan under the covers.

"So that was nice," he said.

It was one of his two standard post-coital lines, the other one being *we should do this more often.*

"Mmmm-hmmm," she agreed, laying her head on his chest.

From Jen's perspective, the sex itself had been lackluster. She'd opted for what the internet porn world labeled "reverse cowgirl," a term whose cutesy misogyny made her roll her eyes, and a position that didn't do a whole lot for her. Dan liked it, though. In fact, he liked it too much. It was low on Jen's list largely because it tended to be over too soon.

But she'd chosen it because it accomplished her overriding

goal of keeping her vodka-fragrant mouth on the opposite end of the bed from her husband's nose.

Now, having successfully distracted him from the subject of her drinking with literally the oldest trick in the book, she felt like she was mostly in the clear. The only loose end was Skully, sitting in the darkness under the sink.

Where am I going to put that bottle?

And why isn't Dan talking?

It was so quiet that with her head on his chest, she could hear his heartbeat in her ear. The silence worried her.

Is he still thinking about the booze?

"You okay?" she asked.

"Yeah. I'm just wondering where the kids are."

Oh, Jesus, the kids.

I'm a horrible person.

As if in response to the thought, she felt a pinprick of pain deep inside her sinus cavity. With the alcohol beginning to recede from her bloodstream, the hangover was creeping back in.

"You don't think they're still in school?" she asked.

"How could they stay open with the power out?" As Dan breathed, Jen's head rose and fell against his chest. "I should've gone by there on my way home. It was just a few blocks out of the way."

"I'm sure they're fine. Chloe's probably just avoiding me after this morning."

"What was that fight about?"

"Her Dartmouth essay."

"Oh, Jesus. . . . Thank you for dealing with that."

"Don't thank me. I'm screwing it up."

"No, you're not—"

"I am, though. Really. I was going to make her favorite dinner tonight as a peace offering." Jen grimaced. The hangover was definitely returning, with accrued interest. There was no avoiding it.

Unless she added more alcohol to the equation.

If he stays up here, and I go downstairs—

Dan gave a sudden start, jostling her head. "Did you go shopping?" There was a sharp edge of alarm in his voice.

"When would I have gone shopping?"

"Before the power went out."

"There was no time!" Jen lifted her head from his chest and glared at him in self-defense. "I barely managed to shower—"

Rather than argue, Dan leaped out of bed.

"We've got to get to the store! How much cash do you have?"

He grabbed his pants from the floor, his underwear still nested in the legs.

"What's the hurry—"

"Everything's closing! This could be worse than Sandy! We've got to find someplace that's still open!"

Trying to cram his leg through both his pants and his underwear at the same time, Dan got hung up and almost fell over, managing to avoid a pratfall only by lurching butt-first back onto the bed.

"How are you going to get there?"

"I'll ride my bike! You should come, too. Help me carry stuff."

Just the thought of such an excursion made Jen's stomach pucker with nausea.

Did I eat breakfast?

She was trying to manufacture an excuse for not accompanying him when they heard the distant *creeeaak-clop* of the door to the garage directly below them.

One of the kids must've just come home.

Dan stood up and called out to them. *"Max? Chloe?"*

Zipping his pants, he took three quick steps to the window and looked out over the driveway.

"Ohmygod!"

"What?"

"Max was home this whole time!"

Dan grabbed his shirt and ran from the room.

Jen groaned. She was in no condition to match her husband's frantic energy.

But if I can get him to leave the house without me . . .

Reluctantly, she got to her feet and started to look for her jeans.

MAX

Leading his bike by the handlebars, Max paused at the top of the driveway to scan the property next door for a sign of his nemesis. Jordan Stankovic was nowhere in sight.

Of course he's not home. He's at Andy's, playing poker with my so-called friends.

It had been a rotten morning. Max had spent the last half of it lying on his bed, stewing over both his friends' betrayal and the sudden disruption of his nicotine supply. He couldn't think of a good solution to either problem, and the lack of nicotine was starting to affect his mood.

After he came home—avoiding his mom, who he could hear banging around in the basement doing God knows what—he'd tried swapping out the Juul pod for a fresh one from the box hidden in the back of his desk. It didn't do any good. Neither did trying to recharge the device from the wall outlet. The outlet was dead, and so was his Juul.

This threatened to become a crisis. Just six and a half hours without a hit, which was as long as he had to last to get through a school day, was enough to make his brain itch. He hadn't gone more than twelve hours in months. Twenty-four was unimaginable. He needed to source a replacement before withdrawal set in.

But Juul devices weren't cheap. A new one would cost at least twenty bucks. And while he still had the fifty-dollar bill his grandmother had mailed him for his birthday, he was reluctant to break it in case he decided to show up at Andy's poker game after all.

Laying a crisp fifty down on the card table in the Ko family living room, while everybody else was fronting their little piles of small change, definitely seemed like a baller move. The trouble was, Max couldn't figure out what his follow-up move would be.

Sit down and just start playing with them? That'd be like admitting defeat.

And what if nobody could change his fifty? Or what if they did, and then he lost money and couldn't get it back? Trading a crisp fifty for a Ziploc bag of nickels, dimes, and quarters was the opposite of a baller move.

He fantasized for a while about challenging Jordan to go high card for the full fifty. That'd be baller for sure. But it was way too risky. If Jordan said yes and Max lost, he'd be even further humiliated.

Then he tried to imagine walking into the room and—without a word, like a stone killer—delivering his karate chop to Jordan's neck. The thought of it was satisfying. Unfortunately, though, he hadn't trained for that scenario. There were no YouTube walkthroughs of a standing attack on a target who was sitting at a table. Probably because it was a bitch move. So that was out of the question.

He switched to fantasizing about calling Jordan out, challenging him to a fight in Andy's backyard. But Max hadn't trained for that, either. The karate chop to the neck gambit relied on Jordan not really expecting it. A totally fair fight, with both sides primed to throw down, would require a completely different strategy. And Max couldn't even start doing the You-Tube research on that, because the internet was down.

Why didn't his laptop work? Even with the power out, it should've been able to run on the battery. But it was bricked.

Pondering that question led Max back to Dennis's electromagnetic-whaddayacallit theory. What if Dennis was right? What if all the electronics on the planet had just been fried by some freak solar storm? Or a Chinese nuke?

What if society was about to collapse?

That could be pretty cool.

At least, it seemed like it for the first couple of minutes. Max's mind wandered off into a hazy fantasy that featured him and Kayleigh Adams living in sin together, surviving by their wits (well, mostly his wits) in the ruins of civilization.

But when he tried to add enough believable detail to mas-turbate to the fantasy, it quickly went off the rails. Where would they live? How could they get rid of their parents? And what would they do for money? Or food? Given any sustained consid-eration, the prospect of an actual, real-life, not-a-movie-or-a-video-game apocalypse was terrifying.

Martial law. Mass starvation. Armed gangs roaming the streets . . .

It didn't take long for Max to scare himself into action. If the apocalypse really was coming, he needed to lock down his nicotine supply ASAP.

Sticking Grandma's fifty-dollar bill in his pocket, he headed for the garage. As he pulled his bike out, his eye passed over a basket of sports equipment on the wall shelf. Nestled between a basketball and a pair of lacrosse sticks was a scuffed-up volleyball. Max made a mental note to practice his serve when he got back from buying a new Juul. If society didn't collapse, sooner or later he'd have to go back to gym class.

He'd finished surveying the area to confirm Jordan's absence and was coasting down the driveway into the street when a voice called out behind him.

"Max! Wait!"

He braked to a stop and looked back. His dad was hobbling toward him with a weird-looking limp that Max guessed must be due to his not wearing shoes.

"Where are you going?"

"Just out."

"When did you get home?"

"A while ago."

Dad reached the bottom of the driveway and stepped gingerly onto the asphalt in his socks.

"So was school canceled?"

"Duh. The power's out."

"Did they say anything?"

"About what?"

His dad gestured with his hands, taking in the whole neighborhood. "Whatever's going on."

Max briefly considered relaying Dennis's EMP theory, but decided against it on the grounds that it might slow his departure.

"I dunno." He shook his head. "I gotta go."

"Where?"

"Just out for a bike ride."

"Wait a minute. I'll go with you."

"*No!*" This was a Juul run, not some Father-Son Quality-Time nonsense that'd inevitably lead to stupid questions about why he didn't want to sign up for a coding class, or join the cross-country team, or some shit.

"Come on! I need your help carrying groceries."

"I'm on a bike!"

"I will be, too! Just give me a minute. I gotta pump my tires."

"Dad, *no*—"

"Ohmygawd, Altmans! What is *happening*?"

At the sound of the South Jersey–accented bleat, they both turned their heads toward Willis Road.

Jordan's mom was trudging up the street toward them.

DAN

"Hi, Kayla." Dan tried not to wince at the sight of Kayla Stankovic marching uphill in yoga pants and an athleisure top that she'd somewhat incongruously paired with platform shoes and several heavy necklaces.

"What's goin' *on* here?" She wailed again, so loud that she alerted Dazzle to her presence. The schnauzer let loose a frantic round of barks from behind the front door of the Stankovic McMansion.

"Weird, right?" Dan called back to Kayla, doing his best to sound friendly but not approachable.

"It's *crazy*! I had to walk all the way home from Ridgelawn!" She was headed straight for them. Some amount of polite conversation was unavoidable now.

Max hopped onto his bike pedals. "Bye!"

"Wait!"

Too late. His son was already halfway to Willis Road. "Back soon!" Max yelled over his shoulder.

Kayla replaced Max on the asphalt in front of Dan, determined to relate the events of her day. "So I'm literally in the dentist chair when the lights go out. Miles from home! And my car wouldn't start—I had to leave it there! It's in a one-hour spot. They better not be writing tickets, or I'm gonna go apeshit. This is unbelievable! Thank God I was just getting a cleaning.

Can you imagine if they'd been drilling a cavity?" She jabbed a finger into her open mouth for emphasis.

"Yeah, that'd really be—"

"Worst thing is, they only got halfway through the cleaning. You know how, like"—Kayla ran her tongue across the top of her teeth, which had the effect of bulging her collagen-inflated lips out even further than usual—"when they clean your teeth, it's, like, sharp afterward? On the edges? I got that on the right, but not the left. Feels so weird, I swear to gawd."

The Stankovics' front door opened. Eddie appeared in the entryway, holding a vociferous Dazzle back by the collar. In a practiced motion, he flung the dog backward into the house, then slammed the door before she could launch a counterattack.

"Eddie!" Kayla moaned at her husband. "Carry me inside! My feet are killing me!"

"Suck it up," he told her as he sauntered toward them. "You're, like, three steps from the door."

"Don't be an asshole. Feel sorry for me." She greeted him with a fierce hug. "I had to walk all the way from Dr. Liebowitz's."

"Told ya not to go to that guy." Eddie peered at Dan from over his diminutive wife's head. "What happened to your face?"

Kayla turned back around, seeming to notice Dan's injury for the first time. "Oh, shit! You okay, Dan-O?"

"Yeah, it's nothing. I was just, uh, on a train and—"

"Somebody stole your shoes?" Eddie nodded at Dan's sock-clad feet.

"No, I was—I saw Max out the window just now, so I ran out to talk to him."

"Can you believe what a fuckin' clown show PSE and G is?" Eddie asked.

"What do you mean?"

"I mean this whole power outage."

"You think it's the power company's fault?"

"Who else would it be?"

"I dunno. But I don't think the power company can knock out cars."

"Don't put it past 'em. Those people could fuck up a one-car funeral."

"But what about the cell phones? And the airplanes?"

Kayla's eyes widened. "Ohmygawd, you hear about the plane crash? Crazy!"

"I saw it," Dan told her. "I was right there when it went down."

"On the river?"

"What river?"

"What's all this?" asked Eddie.

"A plane crashed in the Passaic River!" Kayla told him.

"It *did*?" This was news to Dan, and hearing it made his stomach drop a little.

"Right in the river? No shit? Like that guy Sully?" It was news to Eddie, too.

Kayla nodded. "Yeah. Except this time, it didn't go so good. Comin' home, I passed a guy who saw the whole thing." She turned to Dan. "You saw it, too?"

"No, I saw a different crash. Outside Jersey City. And I heard there was a third one. On a golf course in Short Hills."

"Oh shit. Oh *shit*." Some of the color left Eddie's face. "That's some enemy action right there." His eyes darkened. "I bet it was the fuckin' Muslims."

"What, like ISIS?" his wife asked him.

"Yeah." Eddie looked over his shoulder, casting a suspicious glare at the Mukherjees' house next door. "Did Arjun go into work today?"

Kayla smacked him in the arm. "Eddie! Not all Muslims are terrorists!"

"Also, they're not Muslim," Dan pointed out.

"What?"

"The Mukherjees. I'm, like, ninety-nine percent sure they're Hindu."

Kayla gave Dan a blank look. "Isn't that kinda the same thing?"

"No. They're completely different religions."

Eddie looked skeptical. "Are they, though?"

"Yes! Definitely. You can google it."

"If I could"—from his hip pocket, Eddie produced his dead phone and waved it at Dan—"we wouldn't be standing here."

"Good point," Dan admitted.

The Altmans' front door opened, and Jen came out. As she started toward the threesome in the street, Kayla called out to her.

"Hey, babe! Can you believe this shit?"

Jen shook her head. "Totally bizarre."

"We should get going," Dan reminded his wife as she approached.

"Where you headed?" Eddie asked.

"We've got to get groceries before everything closes."

"Too late. Nothing's open."

"You sure?"

Eddie nodded. "I came home up Fairmont. D'Angelos is closed. So's the Whole Foods."

"Is *anything* open?" Jen asked.

"Gas station by the parkway. But the pumps don't work. All the guy's got is junk food and cigarettes."

Kayla glared at her husband. "You didn't buy cigarettes, did you?"

"I had to! My vape died."

"Eddie! You *promised* me——"

"It was an emergency!"

"That's not an emergency!"

"There's got to be something open," Dan insisted.

"Nah," said Eddie. "Registers don't work. You can't take credit cards. Whaddaya gonna do? You gotta close. All my stores closed. At least, they should've."

Kayla smirked. "Think Novak remembered to lock the door this time?"

"He better have."

"I don't know why you hired that idiot."

"He's family!"

As Eddie and Kayla bickered about nepotism at Capo's Cleaners, Dan fixed Jen with a concerned look. "What are we going to do for dinner?"

Jen looked pained. "Tuna salad?"

"Will Max eat that?"

"No. But there's peanut butter."

"You should come to our place!" Kayla told them. "We got tons of food. I just did a Costco run on Saturday."

Eddie nodded. "Yeah, come by! We can grill." Then his eyes widened. He looked at Kayla. "Shit, we *have* to grill! All those steaks are gonna go bad."

"Ohmygawd, they're gonna rot!" Kayla screwed up her face. "I *told* you not to get so many!"

"How was I supposed to know the power'd go out?"

Kayla turned to Jen and Dan. "You gotta come over! My idiot husband bought too much mail-order steak."

Eddie nodded energetically. "Seriously. I got three hundred bucks' worth of rib eyes in the freezer. Totally choice. We'll have a fuckin' feast."

"The thing is . . ." Dan turned to Jen as he searched his brain for a creative excuse. Even in a food shortage, sharing a meal with the Stankovics didn't appeal to him.

"And we can make margaritas!" Kayla chirped excitedly.

"In!" Jen raised her hands in the air like she was signaling a touchdown.

"You can't make margaritas," Eddie told his wife. "The blender don't work."

"They don't have to be frozen," Kayla explained. "We'll make the classic kind. Just need Triple Sec and lime juice."

"I can bring Triple Sec," Jen offered. "I think we've got a whole fifth of it."

"Yeah, but, honey—" Dan put a hand on his wife's arm and fixed her with a meaningful look. "Now that I think of it . . . don't *we* have food in the freezer that's going to spoil?"

Jen clearly understood what he was getting at.

Which made it all the more irritating when she cut his legs off.

"Are you kidding?" she replied with a snort. "The freezer's empty. We barely have ice."

"You'll love these steaks," Eddie assured Dan. "They're Omaha!"

"Steaks and margaritas!" Kayla crowed. "And *everybody's* invited!" She made a circular motion with her index finger that took in all five houses on the cul-de-sac. "The whole street!"

Dan understood this as a pointed reference to Eddie and Kayla having been left off the guest list for his fiftieth birthday party, the existence of which had been impossible to keep secret once the guests' cars had filled all of Brantley Circle and half a block on Willis Road in either direction.

It was just one of the many reasons that dinner at the Stan kovics promised to be unpleasant for him.

"Can't wait!" Jen beamed.

"Super," said Dan.

"Awesome possum!" Kayla grinned. "Come over at, like . . . I dunno. Whenever."

"Before the sun goes down," Eddie suggested. "So we can still fuckin' see."

"Don't worry about that," Kayla assured them. "We got torches and shit. We're going to get through this together!"

She meant it as a promise, but Dan couldn't help hearing it as a threat.

JEN

"What did you want to do, eat peanut butter and tuna fish?"

Dan finished spooning dollops of peanut butter from the jar into a bowl. "Is this seriously all we have?"

"There's a box of protein bars." Jen pointed toward the pantry cabinet.

"Save those for the kids," Dan said. But through a mouthful of peanut butter, it sounded more like *Shave shosh shur re shids.*

"I can't believe you're eating it like that," Jen told him as she watched him work his jaws over the mouthful of goo.

With considerable effort, he swallowed. "I just need to get my blood sugar up. Are you coming or not?"

"Do I really need to? You heard Eddie. Nothing's open."

"You're going to take Eddie's word for it? The guy who doesn't know the difference between Muslim and Hindu?" Dan filled a glass in the sink and took a long drink of water.

"What?"

"Never mind. *I'm* going to go. And I could really use help carrying food if I find someplace that's open." He shoved another spoonful of peanut butter in his mouth.

"Well, if you do, call me and I'll come down."

Dan briefly paused his mastication to glare at her, incredulous. "*How re herw wou I raw rou?*"

Jen sighed. "Sorry. I forgot for a sec."

He swallowed again. "Just come with me."

"I can't."

"Why not?"

Because I have to get rid of the vodka.

"Because what if Chloe comes home?"

"What if?"

"Somebody should be here for her."

Dan capitulated. "Whatever. Just give me all your cash."

"What cash?"

His glare returned. "Oh my God. You didn't go to the bank?"

The look he was giving Jen made her want to mash the bowl of peanut butter into his face.

"When would I have gone to the bank?"

"Don't yell at me!"

"Don't yell at *me!*"

He sighed. "This is a real problem. How much money do you have?"

They spent the next few minutes pooling their cash. She had eleven dollars in her wallet. Dan had seventeen. His change dish upstairs yielded another five bucks in quarters. He left the rest behind on the grounds that carrying it was more trouble than it was worth.

"I don't understand," he told Jen in a voice dripping with condescension, "why you don't just get, like, a thousand bucks in cash when you go to the bank so we have it around."

"I do! But then I end up giving it all to the ACT tutor! Do you have any idea how much that guy's costing us? It's three hundred bucks a session!"

"And she got a twenty-nine on the last practice test? That's bullshit. We should be able to claw some of the fee back. It ought to be performance-based."

"Couldn't agree more."

"Do the kids have money?"

"Probably. You want to search their bedrooms?"

A light search of both kids' rooms yielded nothing except a Ziploc bag of change on Max's dresser and some dirty glassware that should've been brought down to the dishwasher. Dan extracted the quarters from Max's stash.

"How much have you got?" Jen asked.

"All in?" Dan made a mental calculation. "Thirty-six seventy-five."

"That's not going to go too far."

"I'll bring the checkbook, too. Just in case."

Jen watched him finish his bowl of peanut butter, trying to stifle her impatience. By now, her headache, dry mouth, and general irritability were making a strong argument in favor of a maintenance hit of vodka. But Dan was standing in front of the cabinet where she'd hidden the bottle.

"You're sure you're not coming?" he asked her.

"I just want to do right by Chloe. We were in a really bad place when she left this morning." Jen thought for a moment. "If they have any prepared foods, get some chicken Milanese."

Dan's incredulous look returned. "Are you serious?"

"What?"

"We have thirty-six dollars, and the stores are closing for God knows how long. You think I'm going to spend twenty bucks on chicken Milanese?"

"Okay, whatever—"

"Are you all right?"

"I'm fine."

"No, I mean seriously."

"I'm fine! Will you get out of here?"

"Why are you so hostile?"

"I'm sorry. It's just—it's been a really stressful day."

He stared at her with a mix of irritation and concern. For a long moment, she was sure he was going to bring up the drinking again.

But then he just shook his head and went to the garage.

It took him forever to pump up his bike tires and ride away.

When he was gone, she hurried back into the kitchen and fetched Skully from under the sink.

This is definitely the last day I'm doing this, she thought as she brought the bottle to her lips.

CHLOE

Only the gas stovetop in Brody Kiplinger's kitchen was still functional, so Chloe and Josh boiled water in a pot, then put in half a box of pasta they found in a cabinet. The cooking instructions were to boil it for twelve minutes, which they had to time using the antique grandfather clock in the Kiplingers' formal dining room.

The hands on the clock pointed to just after one fifteen when they put in the pasta.

"What time's your practice?"

"Three-thirty."

"Cool."

Awkward silence.

"This is a really nice house."

"Yeah."

More awkward silence.

"So you're, like, really good at tennis, huh?"

"I mean, I guess. Yeah." Chloe wasn't sure what her optimal level of self-confidence should be. She didn't want to be a geisha, like Emma had accused the other girls of being. But she didn't want to come off like a ball-buster, either. And in any case, she wasn't too confident about her tennis game at the moment.

"You're, like, number one, though? On the team?"

"Yeah. But . . . ugh."

"What?"

"You don't want to hear about it."

"No, I do! Tell me." Josh leaned back against the kitchen counter, set his beer down, and looked at her with an expression of what seemed like genuine interest.

She explained her mysteriously disappearing backhand. Even before she'd finished, he was nodding.

"I totally get that."

"Really?"

"Yeah! It happened to me with baseball once."

"Ohmygosh. I forgot you played baseball."

"Yeah. I'm not as good at it as swimming. But I'm still varsity. I pitch. And a couple years ago—this is so crazy, but it's, like, totally what you're going through—I forgot how to throw to first."

"You forgot how to *throw*?"

"But only to first base. Like, if somebody hit a comebacker to the mound, I'd go to field it, and my brain would be, like, *wuuuggghh*. And my throw would, like, go into the dugout. Or pull the first baseman off the bag."

"That's awful!"

"I know!"

"So what did you do?"

He shrugged. "I just started swimming a lot more."

"Gaagh!"

"No! I'm kidding. But, like, seriously—I had to just take some time off. And when I came back, I was fine. It was like it never happened."

"The thing is, though? We're in the semis of the team tournament. So I basically have to fix this by tomorrow."

"You can! You totally can. You just have to stop thinking."

"What do you mean?"

"I mean, like . . . your brain knows how to do it. Like, deep down, you've got the muscle memory, right?"

"I wish."

"You do, though! You're just letting some other part of your brain get in the way of it. So you have to, like, not think. And let the muscle memory take over. It's like the Force. Don't think it. Just feel it."

"Huh . . . But how do you not think about it? It's, like, impossible."

"No, it isn't. Just—" He stepped toward her. "Here, show me your backhand."

"My racket's back in the hallway. Should I—?"

"Don't worry about it. Just pretend. Get in position."

He stepped behind her. She played along, placing her feet hip distance apart, bending her knees, and stacking her fists in front of her, holding an imaginary racket.

"Okay. Now what?"

"The ball's coming. What do you do?"

She stutter-hopped, turning sideways as she pulled her arms back.

"Okay, now right there—that's where you start freaking out, right?"

"Totally."

"So when you're like this . . ." He put his body up against hers, his arms and legs mirroring her position, and the physical contact made her heart race. "Just don't think."

"So what do I think about?"

His mouth was so close she could feel his breath on her ear. "I don't know," he said. "Me?"

She turned her head a little further toward him.

And just like that, they were kissing.

MAX

No matter how many times Max had bought vape products from the gas station across from the parkway on-ramp, his stomach still got fluttery on the way there. When he U-locked his bike wheel to its frame by the side of the building, his fingertips tingled with nervous energy.

The little store was empty except for the South Asian–looking middle-aged guy who perched on the tall stool behind the register whenever he wasn't out pumping gas. Before approaching the counter, Max selected a protein bar. It always felt more legit to buy at least one non-vape item, too.

He put the bar down on the rubber mat beside the cash register.

The guy slid off his stool. "Three."

"Can I, uh, get a Juul, too?"

"What flavor?"

"Not the pods—the device."

The guy turned to the shelf behind him, selected one of the thin white boxes, and set it down next to the protein bar.

"Thirty-three."

Ouch!

Max suspected he was getting price-gouged. But considering that he was underage, it seemed unwise to try to haggle. He handed over his birthday fifty.

"Got smaller?"

Max shook his head. "Sorry."

The guy pulled out the register drawer and counted Max's change.

Mission accomplished.

He stuck the protein bar in his back pocket and went outside. As he walked to his bike, he set to work on the Juul box's sealing sticker, picking at it with a fingernail until it yielded. Then he slid out the plastic tray and extracted the device.

Even before he inserted the pod he'd brought along, a sense of well-being settled over him. All his nervousness was gone. So was the brain itch of nicotine deprivation that had started to plague him over the past hour. Anticipating the hit was almost as pleasurable as the hit itself.

But the battery light wasn't going on.

The Juul didn't work.

It was brand-new.

And it doesn't work?

WHAT THE FU—

No. Wait. It just needs charging.

Max stilled the panic rising in his gut with the memory of his first Juul purchase a year ago. It hadn't worked out of the box that time, either. All he had to do was go home and charge it, and everything would be fine.

He was two blocks away from the gas station when the flaw in that logic revealed itself: as long as the power was out, he couldn't charge the Juul. For the rest of the long uphill ride home, only the slim hope that he might be able to animate the device with a portable phone charger—assuming he could find one back at home—kept him from either screaming at the top of his lungs or bursting into tears.

Life was just not fair at all.

DAN

The streets of Lincolnwood were dotted with bicyclists and pe-destrians, most of them looking bewildered and moving at speeds which suggested that, like Dan, they were less concerned with reaching a specific destination than with foraging for sup-plies and information.

Both were in short supply. Nothing was open in town except Barnaby's, which was only taking cash for their remaining in-ventory of sixteen-dollar prosciutto sandwiches and nine-dollar cold-pressed juice.

It was crowded inside. Dan spent a few minutes at the display case, pretending to ponder the options while he eavesdropped on the bearded thirtysomething owner, who was telling a cus-tomer his theory that the power outage was due to budget cuts at the Princeton Plasma Physics Lab.

"It's like Chernobyl over there," he said as he retied a white half-apron over his Sonic Youth T-shirt. "They've been doing fu-sion research on a test reactor that's basically held together with duct tape. This kind of shit was inevitable."

"Wow. That's wild stuff. How much are these scones?"

"Eight-fifty."

Despite Dan's hunger—the bike ride into town had burned up what little energy the peanut butter had given him—he left empty-handed. With just $36.75 on hand to feed his entire family for an indeterminate period of time, he could no longer afford Barnaby's.

After he left the restaurant, he crossed over to the New Jersey Transit lot to visit his Lexus. The key remote didn't work, which was unsurprising. Dan propped his bike against the front bumper, opened the driver's side door with the physical key, and sat down behind the wheel.

The car refused to start, or to show any other sign of mechanical life. While also unsurprising, this proved unexpectedly upsetting. For the first time since he'd escaped the train with Pete Blackwell, Dan felt genuine panic stirring in his chest.

What the hell is going on?

And why was Jen drinking alone in the middle of the day?

That was pretty nuts. She smelled like a distillery.

I guess it's understandable. If I'd been next door to the towers on 9/11—

Dan's thoughts were interrupted by the sight of a man trying to steal his bike.

"*Hey!*"

It was a twitchy young blond kid in a zippered hoodie. He had the bike by the handlebars and was trying to back it out of the narrow space between the Lexus and the rear bumper of the car in front of it when Dan opened the door, which startled him. The kid's first instinct seemed to be to run off with the bike, but Dan was blocking him from behind, and the cars ahead of him were parked bumper to bumper.

By the time the kid figured out the geometry and started trying to maneuver the bike around the corner of the Lexus's passenger side, Dan had gotten his hand on the seat.

"That's my bike!"

"Sorry, dude!" He did look sorry, but only that he'd been caught. "I thought it was abandoned."

"It's not."

Time slowed to a crawl as both men considered their next move.

Dan's heart was pounding. The kid couldn't make a clean escape, but he wasn't letting go of the handlebars.

He was tall and skinny. Probably unarmed, or he would've flashed a weapon by now.

If the altercation turned physical, who would come out on top?

Not having been in a fistfight since the sixth grade, Dan wasn't sure how to calculate the odds. The kid's eyes looked a little crazy. Almost desperate.

Is he on drugs?

If he was a meth addict, that'd definitely give him the upper hand. He'd be jacked up. He might even bite.

On the other hand, Dan was equipped with the strength of righteous anger. It was his bike.

"Don't overreact, dude," the kid told him. "It's all good."

But the kid didn't let go of the handlebars. Instead of replying, Dan just stared at him.

Is there a cop around here?

Are cops useless now? The one on Lincoln Avenue definitely had been.

The kid's head turned slightly. He looked past Dan, toward the intersection of Forest and Hawthorne.

"Check it out!" he exclaimed.

Does he think I'm an idiot?

Dan wasn't about to get suckered by a misdirection trick so clichéd that it had cropped up in at least half a dozen episodes of *Bullet Town: NYC.*

But it wasn't a misdirection. The kid let go of the bike and ran down the passenger side of the Lexus toward Hawthorne Street.

Dan stepped forward and grabbed the handlebars. His property secured, he turned to see what had sent the kid running.

A black 1972 Chevy El Camino with gray hood stripes was slowly weaving its way through the maze of cars stalled at the intersection of Hawthorne and Forest. Dan could hear the low mutter of its engine.

Just a few hours ago, a '72 El Camino traveling down Hawthorne at five miles an hour would have been a banal sight, except possibly to fans of vintage car-truck hybrids. Now it was the object of such fascination that ten men followed in its wake, both on foot and bikes. As Dan watched, the twitchy kid joined the procession.

After a moment's consideration, Dan manually locked the Lexus, guided his bike down the narrow space between the parked cars, and took up the pursuit of the mysteriously functioning automobile.

JEN

There was just enough light coming through the window of the little downstairs bathroom for Jen to decant the vodka from the Crystal Head skull into the plastic bottle of rubbing alcohol she'd just rinsed out.

It almost all fit, but not quite. She was slurping a skooch off the top when the sound of the garage door slamming froze her in place.

Her eyes darted to the bathroom door to make sure it was locked.

"Dan?" *Could he be home that soon?*

"No!"

It was Max. She heard him slamming drawers in the kitchen. Then he clomped upstairs.

She capped the rubbing alcohol bottle, now filled with vodka. There was still a little bit left in the glass skull, so she put it to her lips, tilted her head back, and sucked out every last drop.

Ritually speaking, she was aware this was pretty trashy behavior. But that was okay, because Skully no longer had to bear the symbolic weight of Jen's Last Drink Ever. That honor now belonged to the margarita (or two, or maybe three) she'd have at the Stankovics' that evening.

A margarita felt like an excellent vehicle for bringing down the curtain on Jen's relationship with alcohol. Tequila was festive yet sinister, in a Día de los Muertos kind of way.

The vodka she was about to stash in the medicine cabinet was just that—medicinal. It was strictly for emergency use only. She'd probably never even drink it. Once she got a few days' worth of sobriety under her belt, she'd almost certainly dump it out in the sink.

In the meantime, she congratulated herself for devising such an ingenious hiding place. It'd be a comfort just knowing the vodka was there, perfectly disguised and only steps away from the kitchen.

Not that she'd need it. When she got up tomorrow, she was going to make a fresh start.

The first day of the rest of my life.

As long as this fucking power outage doesn't get in the way.

It wouldn't. She was determined to quit for good this time. The power outage might even help. With Dan and the kids around, it'd be that much harder to drink.

Jen put the plastic bottle back in the medicine cabinet next to the peroxide. Then she bagged the empty—*Skully, I hardly knew you*—and, after listening to make sure Max was still upstairs, took it to the garage and hid it in the trunk of the Volvo next to the other bagged empties.

Mission accomplished, she returned to the kitchen and pondered how to kill the remaining—*hours? minutes? how the hell do I tell time?*—before she could go over to the Stankovics' and get Margarita Tuesday underway.

Her thoughts quickly returned to Chloe, and she felt a pang of regret.

What can I do to make it up to her? Cooking dinner's no longer an option.

I could rewrite her Dartmouth supplemental for her.

No, I can't. It's in the cloud.

When's the last time we printed? How many drafts ago?

Maybe after we get back from the Stankovics', I can sit down with her and work on it.

I'd have to stay sober. Stick to one margarita. Or two, if I eat enough to—

OH SHIT, they're grilling steak.

Chloe doesn't eat red meat. She'll be furious.

Why didn't I think of that?

In a matter of seconds, the warm fog of alcoholic detachment washed away in an acid rain of self-disgust.

You fucking idiot. What were you thinking?

I'm a terrible parent.

As she ruminated on her sins, they multiplied.

What's the matter with you? Look at yourself! You just poured a bottle of vodka into a—

Max stormed in, looking surly.

"Hey, sweetheart!"

"Do we have a phone charger?" He went to the utility drawer and yanked it open.

"I don't. Chloe might. But she probably took it to—"

Before Jen could finish the sentence, Max slammed the drawer and stormed back out again.

"Are you okay?" she called after him.

"Fine!" he snarled over the sound of his feet on the stairs. Jen considered following him up to his bedroom to ask why he was so upset.

Instead, she stayed rooted in place, marinating in her self-loathing.

I'm the worst parent on earth.

Her laptop was on the table in front of her. She flipped it open. Banged a few buttons.

Still dead.

What the hell is happening, anyway?

DAN

The El Camino's Pied Piper journey through downtown Lincoln-wood had attracted several dozen bicyclists and pedestrians by the time it ended in the little parking lot behind Borough Hall. The car's driver guided it into a spot across from the two dozen townspeople who were already clustered around the rear entrance, hoping to get answers from their local municipal officials. Once Dan and the other El Camino followers joined them, it was a good-sized crowd, and they all watched with interest as the driver door opened and the car's owner emerged.

He was a pontytailed graybeard in a Hawaiian shirt and cargo shorts. Dan recognized him at once. The guy was a fixture at the Astro Diner on Hawthorne, holding court most mornings at the window booth by the counter with a bottomless coffee and a copy of the *New York Post*, from which he habitually read aloud to the waitress, the owner, and any customer unwise enough to make eye contact. Dan's sense had always been that behind his boisterous extroversion, Ponytailed Hawaiian Shirt Guy was desperately lonely, and the diner folks tolerated him out of pity.

Now, having just won a lottery that paid out in human attention, he glowed with delight as a crowd of mostly white males converged on him.

"I don't know!" his voice boomed in answer to a question from one of the men closest to him. "She just started right up! Chevy El Camino, baby! Don't make 'em like they used to!"

Dan walked his bike to the edge of the cluster of men surrounding Ponytailed Hawaiian Shirt Guy so he could listen in on their conversation. It didn't take long for him to conclude that neither the driver nor anybody else in the group had any useful information. They were just jockeying for position in the hope of riding shotgun.

Barry Kozak appeared to be a lock for that honor. He was a corroding brick wall of a man who'd spent almost two decades as Lincolnwood's police chief before flaming out in a blaze of corruption unearthed during the investigation into a pair of sex harassment accusations lodged by a department secretary and a rookie patrolwoman in late 2017. The next autumn's municipal elections had turfed out all of Kozak's enablers on the city council in favor of a new generation of reformist, largely female political leadership led by a former pharmaceutical executive whose name Dan could never remember.

Since his public disgrace, Kozak—who, to the disgust of female acquaintances who followed local politics much more closely than Dan did, had somehow managed not only to dodge criminal charges for his sexual and fiduciary malfeasances, but also to keep his pension—had continued to haunt the bars and restaurants of Lincolnwood like an embittered ghost, sharing tales of persecution with anyone who'd listen. Ponytailed Hawaiian Shirt Guy must've been among Kozak's supporters. He kept calling him Chief and clapping him on his hulking back while Kozak muttered advice about the husbanding of scarce automotive resources that Dan couldn't overhear across the three layers of rubbernecking men.

Eventually, Dan gave up and began to wander through the

still-growing crowd in search of someone he knew well enough to talk to. He recognized a number of people by sight from school parent nights, youth sports leagues, Temple Beth Shalom, and the gym, but he didn't strike up a conversation until he came across his Brantley Circle neighbor Carol Sweeney. She was on the edge of the lot by Borough Hall's back door, dressed in bike shorts with a helmet under her arm and nodding in concern at an elderly woman who was upset that her trash hadn't been picked up that morning.

"Absolutely, Gloria! You need to raise your voice! This administration has to make good on its promise to be responsive to its constituents!"

"Hi, Carol."

Carol nodded curtly at him. "Dan. You know Gloria? Runs the Botanic Gardens."

"Hi," Dan said. Gloria nodded back, her lips pursed.

"What's going on?" Carol asked.

"I was about to ask you the same thing."

"We're getting stonewalled is what's going on!" Carol jerked an indignant thumb toward the doorway. "They locked us all out! Said they need to 'marshal an appropriate response.' Can you believe that?"

"Wow," said Dan. "That's . . ."

Perfectly reasonable was how he would've finished the sentence, if it hadn't been clear that Carol would take offense at such an opinion.

"These are our elected representatives!" She jabbed an angry finger at the ground to emphasize each syllable. "And I'm not just some random voter! I'm the chair of the Arts Council!

I should be in there!" She looked closer at Dan, then modulated her tone. "What happened to your face?"

"Long story. You hear about the plane crash outside Jersey City?"

Carol's eyes widened. "Jersey City? I thought it was just the one on the Garden State."

"There was a plane crash on the *Garden State*?"

"You didn't hear about it? Jumbo jet. Horrifying."

"I think we're under attack," declared Gloria from the Botanic Gardens.

The conversation was cut short by a surge of human energy in the direction of Borough Hall's back door. It had just opened, and a uniformed police deputy was dragging a podium onto the short sidewalk.

Behind the deputy came a small delegation of officials: the well-dressed mayor, whose name still escaped Dan; a heavy-set middle-aged woman in a police uniform whom Dan recognized as Kozak's successor without being able to recall any other biographical details except that she had two last names; a pale, frightened-looking little man in a sport coat whom Dan suspected was the borough administrator; and a massive, shark-faced skinhead in a suit whom Dan knew as the absolute worst parent he'd ever encountered in over a decade's worth of youth sports.

Steve something. Shrecklich? Is that it? Huge asshole.

Dan had once seen him reduce a teenage soccer referee to tears during a girls' ten-and-under game, for no defensible reason. Since Chloe had quit playing soccer, Dan's only sightings of Steve were at the gym. He was the kind of guy who grunted theatrically with every rep and never reracked his weights.

How did that jackass get elected to city council?

Dan was still wondering this when the mayor stepped up to the podium, gripping it with both hands. She began to speak in a voice loud enough to be heard all the way back at the El Camino.

"First of all, I want to thank you all for coming out, and for the concern you're showing our community. I truly believe we are at our best in moments like this, when we all come together and support each other as neighbors."

"Why's the power out?" somebody in the back yelled.

The mayor replied with a sympathetic grimace. "I wish I had all the answers for you already. Unfortunately, whatever's happened, at the moment the source of the problem remains both mysterious and challenging. But I have no doubt we will get through this together! And as with everything that our borough does, we are committed to transparency and open communication. If you have any issues, do not hesitate to call me directly—"

"The phones don't work!" someone yelled.

The mayor paused to nod thoughtfully, acknowledging the validity of the observation. "Or you can email—"

"There's no email!"

The mayor stopped nodding. "Or just come by the—"

"Quit locking the doors!" Carol Sweeney bellowed, with surprising fury.

The mayor gritted her teeth and narrowed her eyes as Steve the Asshole Sports Dad, who'd been standing behind the mayor with the other officials, took a step forward and reached out to put a hand on her upper arm.

She instantly drew back from his touch, then turned to shoot him a look of unmistakable hostility.

Steve raised his eyebrows at the mayor.

The mayor glared back in reply.

The entire crowd seemed to stand up straighter and lean forward, closely monitoring the nonverbal communications of its civic leadership.

The mayor adjusted her grip on the podium. The beginnings of a mirthless smile briefly appeared at the corners of her mouth before vanishing again.

"Under the statutory requirements of the state of New Jersey," she announced, "our borough—like *every municipality in the state*—has a designated emergency management coordinator, tasked with helping to direct our response."

Steve stepped up to loom beside the mayor, a full head-plus taller than she was. In response, she shifted in his direction and lowered her shoulder slightly, as if to protect the podium from his encroachment.

"I want to emphasize that the coordinator's job is to work *with* our borough's elected officials *and* its chief of police—"

Dan craned his neck to get a glimpse of Chief Hyphenated Last Name. She was standing behind Steve and the mayor, shoulders squared, hands clasped behind her in a military pose as she stared poker-faced at the back of Steve's shiny bald head.

"—for the common welfare of our community and its citizens, who have entrusted us with this solemn responsibility. And now . . ." The mayor paused to take a deep breath. "Our emergency management coordinator, attorney Steven Shreckler, would like to address you."

She stepped to her left, yielding the podium. Shreckler took her place, set his jaw, and addressed the crowd in a booming voice that managed to sound simultaneously angry and nervous.

"First of all, let me assure you that the government of Lincolnwood will do *whatever is necessary* to maintain order, ensure your safety, and secure our borders from any transient populations who seek to take advantage of our resources. *We will protect you.*"

A few people in the crowd exchanged bemused looks. Nobody seemed to have previously considered the threat posed by transient populations. Either that, or they couldn't figure out what the phrase meant.

"To facilitate our local government response, I have officially declared a *state of emergency* for the borough of Lincolnwood. During an initial review of our community's most urgent operational concerns, Mr. Blavatnik, director of the Lincolnwood Water Department, identified a critical deficiency in our municipal water delivery. As you know, Lincolnwood's water is sourced entirely from groundwater—"

Dan did not know this, having always assumed the town's water supply came from the big reservoir in the forest preserve atop the ridge a mile from his house. He took a quick glance around the parking lot, wondering if this came as news to everyone else—and encountered unanimous expressions of wide-eyed concern.

"This water enters our system via a series of electrical pumps. At the moment, both the pumps and their backups are nonoperational."

A murmur of alarm rippled through the crowd. Shreckler raised a hand, as if to silence them.

"In order to preserve resources," he continued, "I have directed law enforcement to take possession of all bottled water supplies in the community, both commercially available and privately held——"

They're confiscating WATER?

The murmur of alarm rose to an agitated whine. This seemed to anger Shreckler, who raised his hand again.

"There is *no need to panic*——"

The crowd showed signs of disregarding his recommendation. Standing at Shreckler's elbow, the mayor's eyes had narrowed to slits. She appeared to be grinding her teeth.

Undaunted, he continued:

"Once we collect and inventory all drinking water supplies, the borough will distribute them on an as-needed basis. In the meantime, when you return home, I advise you to put aside a quantity of water for personal use, *limiting your consumption to drinking only*——"

The panic commenced in earnest as everyone in the crowd made a snap decision to return home and open their taps as fast as possible. As Dan turned to flee, a woman's jacket caught on his handlebars when she ran past. She tumbled to the ground in a complicated tangle that included Dan and his bike.

Ow! Shit!

Up at the podium, Shreckler's bald head had turned a bright pink.

"*Do not panic!*" he demanded of the rapidly dissolving mob.

The mayor was shaking her head with undisguised contempt.

Dan managed to regain his feet. His kneecap hurt like hell.

The woman who'd plowed into him was already up and sprinting away.

"Refrain from showering, washing clothes or dishes . . ."

Dan hopped on his bike and followed the crowd as it poured onto Hawthorne Street in what looked like an odd parody of an Ironman competition, with bicyclists and runners competing in tandem while wearing street clothes.

"Do not water your plants or lawns, do not operate toilets . . ."

The last thing Dan heard behind him as he left the now-empty lot was the sharp hiss of the mayor's after-action review of her emergency management coordinator's performance.

"I fucking told you not to do that!"

CHLOE

"You seriously don't have to walk me all the way to practice."

Chloe and Josh were walking hand in hand down Forest Street toward the center of town.

We're holding hands in public. Omg!

To her pleasant surprise, he hadn't even let go when all five Blackwells rode past them, apparently having decided to bike it out to their weekend-place-slash-survival-bunker with their big yellow lab in tow. It loped alongside Mr. Blackwell on a retractable leash.

"No, it's cool," Josh told her. "The courts are, like, right by my house."

"Really? Where do you live?"

"On Baker. Across the street from that playground next to the courts."

"Random! I had no idea."

Chloe knew exactly where Josh lived. She'd practically been stalking him for the past two months. Maybe someday she'd confess that to him.

Right now, it was way too early for that kind of admission.

But omg!

The past two hours had been magical. In the shadowy light atop the silk duvet on Mr. and Mrs. Kiplinger's California king, Chloe had just experienced the first orgasm of her life that wasn't self-administered. And while her feelings for Josh as a person were difficult to disentangle from both her raw physical attraction and her newfound appreciation for his manual dexterity, it was possible she'd just found her soul mate.

She didn't want to get ahead of herself. She had no idea where this was going. The relationship had barely started. It might not even be a relationship.

But if it's not, why's he holding my hand in public?

She smiled to herself as she readjusted the racket bag on her shoulder.

"Sure you don't want me to carry that?"

"You're sweet. But I've got it."

She smiled at Josh. He smiled back.

Omg those eyes!

"Hey, check it out."

Josh pointed down the hill. Two and a half blocks below them, a stream of bicyclists was zipping up Hawthorne.

"Weird—ohmygosh, is that my *dad*?" Chloe squinted at the semidistant figure, huffing along at the tail end of the group.

It definitely looked like Dad.

But why would he be riding his bike through town on a Tuesday afternoon?

"Is there some kind of charity bike ride going on?" Josh asked.

"On a Tuesday?"

"Yeah, I guess not. Check it out—there's runners, too."

"They don't really seem dressed for it."

"No. . . . This is weird. I hope everything's okay."

"Me too." Chloe squeezed Josh's hand a little tighter.

"Must have something to do with the power outage," Josh said.

"Yeah," Chloe agreed.

"You're lucky you can still practice," he told her. "There's no way I can swim with the power off. The pool's in the basement."

"That sucks."

"I know. I should go for a run. Get some cardio in."

They walked in silence until they reached Hawthorne. By then, the flow of people moving north on the avenue had dried up. Everything felt normal again.

Normal, and yet completely different. In more ways than one.

"Hey, so, uhh—"

"Yeah?" She adjusted her grip on his hand, hoping her palm didn't feel too sweaty to him.

"If there's, like, no school tomorrow? You want to hang out?"

Omg!

He gave her a shy smile. She returned it, trying not to look too excited. "Yeah. I mean, I'm probably going to have semis tomorrow. But I could hang in the morning."

As she said it, the thought entered her mind that if there was no school tomorrow, she should probably spend the time doing ACT prep and revising her Dartmouth supplemental. But the idea left as quickly as it had come when she realized that as long as there was no power, she couldn't access either the practice tests on PDF or the Google Docs where all of her essay drafts were stored.

"Hype! I can come by your house. Where do you live?"

"Brantley Circle."

"Where's that?"

"It's off Willis."

"Where's Willis?"

"Straight up Hawthorne. You know where Delectables is?"

"No."

"How about the furniture store?"

He shook his head. "Is that, like, by the church?"

"No. That's down on Harris."

"You sure?"

"The Catholic church? Yeah."

"No, the one—I *think* it's Catholic . . . ?" He shrugged, giving up. "What's the address? I'll just Google Map it."

"Mmmm, no, you won't."

"Oh shit. You're right." He laughed. "What if you just come by my place?"

She smirked at him. "Do you seriously not think you can find my house? It's, like, three turns. I can draw you a map."

"I guess? I'm just, like, *really* bad with directions."

She rolled her eyes. "You want me to come to your place instead?"

"That would be *awesome.*"

"Like, what time? Ten?"

"Yeah. Although . . ."

"What?"

"How will I know when it's ten?"

She laughed. "Look at a clock?"

"What clock?" he protested. "The power's out!"

"You are, like, sadly helpless."

"I know! Right? It's embarrassing. Will you forgive me?"

He stopped and turned to her, slipping his arm around her waist.

She tilted her chin up, closing her eyes as his lips met hers.

Omg . . .

They made out for a full half minute, until some sophomore boys walking up the other side of the street yelled, "Get a room!" at them. They broke the clinch, traded bashful smiles, and continued walking in the direction of the municipal tennis courts up the street from Josh's house.

As they walked in silence, Chloe contemplated Josh's apparent inability to overcome minor logistical challenges and quickly decided it was endearing. It might even be the kind of thing that'd become a running joke between them.

My boyfriend is so hopeless without me.

"Boyfriend"?

Quit future-tripping!

But omg . . .

Under the circumstances, it was hard to resist the temptation.

JEN

Unable to think of anything more productive to do, and in order to distract herself from the two questions that kept pushing themselves to the front of her mind—*what qualifies as a vodka emergency?* and *when's the earliest I can head over to the Stankovics'?*—Jen had carried all of the Altmans' post-hurricane supplies up from the basement. The flashlights, batteries, candles, rain ponchos, gallons of water, and canned goods were spread out on the kitchen table to be tabulated along with a full inventory of the food they had on hand.

She planned to tackle that just as soon as she finished her own personal, private inventory of their alcohol. Not because she planned to drink any of it, but just so she knew what they had.

She started at the bottom of the pantry, where they kept the beer and wine:

Seven bottles of red. Four white. Three IPAs.

She dragged the low stool from the pantry floor over to the fridge, hopped onto it, and opened the double cabinet above the fridge where they kept the household liquor:

Half a fifth of gin. Unopened fifth of bourbon, plus half an open bottle. Almost full fifths of Triple Sec, rum, crème de menthe. Half a fifth of vodka—

Is that legit? Or did I water it down?

She vaguely recalled watering down a household vodka at one point, for reasons that now escaped her.

Was it that fifth? Or another one?

She was about to open the bottle for a closer examination when she heard the clattering of metal in the garage. She slammed the cabinet shut, hopped off the stool, and was returning it to the pantry when Dan burst into the room.

He was wild-eyed, dripping sweat, and so frenzied that he almost knocked her over as he lurched toward the sink.

"Look out!"

"Jesus!"

He threw open a lower cabinet and pulled out their largest cooking pot.

She watched him, bewildered. "What are you—"

"The water's going to run out!" He shoved the pot into the sink and opened the tap. As water began to flow into it from the faucet, he pulled three more pots from the cabinet and dumped them on the countertop.

"How do you know—"

"Fill all these up!" he yelled as he turned and squeezed past her again, this time on his way to the front stairs.

She followed him. "Dan! Will you settle down and—"

"Aaagh!" As he made the hairpin turn from the hall to the stairs, he suddenly faltered, nearly crumpling to the floor.

"What's the matter?"

"Leg cramp! Shit!" Bent over, panting and clutching his left thigh with an anguished grimace, he hesitated for a moment. Then he straightened, grabbed the banister, and began to lurch up the stairs while cursing through his teeth.

"Shit! Shit! Shit!"

Jen went after him. "Let me help you!"

"Stay down there and fill the pots!" he yelled over his shoulder.

She disregarded his instructions, following him up to the second-floor landing as he hopped on one foot to the bathroom door and twisted the knob.

It was locked.

"*Busy!*" Max's voice was a startled half shriek.

"Open up!" Dan yelled, jiggling the lock as he continued to gasp for breath and hop on one leg. "It's an emergency!"

"I'm *busy!*"

"Dan—will you please calm down—"

"Max!" He pounded on the bathroom door. "Fill the tub with water! Do you hear me?"

"Yes!"

"Fill it with water!" Dan repeated as he turned and staggered past Jen. "Go back and fill the pots!" he told her.

He disappeared into the main bedroom. A moment later, she heard the hydraulic rumble of the taps opening in the bathtub.

Annoyed, she went back downstairs. The giant pot was overflowing in the sink. She swapped it for the others. Then, for good measure, she filled the plastic salad spinner, their largest serving bowl, and the Brita pitcher from the fridge before heading back upstairs.

As she reached the landing, Max opened the bathroom door. Behind him, she heard the tub filling with water. They made eye contact. Then, without a word, he turned his back and exited to his bedroom, moving with an odd, bow-legged gait.

Jen entered the vacated bathroom and checked the tub

there. Confirming that it'd take a few more minutes to fill, she continued on to the bathroom in the main bedroom.

The tub was filling with water as a red-faced, still-panting Dan stood on one leg, clutching the edge of the sink with one hand while the other was twisted behind his back, tugging at the ankle of his jackknifed bad leg as he tried to stretch it.

"What the hell, dude?"

"Water's going to run out. The—*gagh!*—town pumps don't work."

"Where'd you hear this?"

"Borough Hall. Mayor gave a . . . I dunno, press conference."

"The new one? What's her name again?"

"Can't remember. What do I do to fix a leg cramp?"

"I don't know. Try massaging it."

Dan sank to the floor, lying on his back with his bad leg bent sideways above him as he kneaded the thigh with both hands. "I gotta get in shape. . . . *Gagh!* This isn't helping."

"You should roll it out."

"With what?"

"One of those big rubber things they have at the gym."

"Do we have one?"

"No."

"Great advice, honey. Thanks." He abandoned his attempt at massage, sat up, and pinned his leg underneath his butt in a second stab at stretching the muscle.

"Don't they have backups?"

"What?"

"For the water. Don't they have backup pumps or something?"

"Those are down, too. Did you fill the pots?"

"Yeah."

"Good. Is the—*mmrf!*—other tub filling?"

"Yeah. Are you okay?" Her husband's face was a florid shade of red.

"Not really. I think I'm having a coronary. Did Chloe come home yet?"

"Nope."

"Think she's okay?"

"Why wouldn't she be?"

"Things are getting fucked up out there. We might have to leave town."

"And go where?"

"I dunno. Wellfleet?"

"Oh, *Jesus*—"

"What?"

"There's no way I'm going to your mother's." The invocation of her mother-in-law's summer home on Cape Cod triggered a pang of guilt as Jen's own mother materialized in her mind's eye.

Should I have called my mom? Are the phones working in Boca?

"She won't be there! She's in Newton. And if the alternative—"

"How would we even get to the Cape? The car won't start."

"I don't know. Ride bikes?"

"Dan, look at yourself. Do you feel like a three-hundred-mile bike ride is doable right now?"

Max entered the bathroom. "What can I eat for lunch?"

"Kinda late for lunch, isn't it?" Jen asked. She certainly hoped it was. Margaritas at the Stankovics' couldn't come soon enough.

Shit, did I eat anything today?

"Have a protein bar," Dan suggested to Max through his grimace.

Max stared at his writhing father. "What's wrong with you?"

"Leg cramp."

"Sucks. What kind of protein bars do we have?"

"Chocolate chip, I think? But don't spoil your dinner," Jen warned.

"What's for dinner?"

"We're grilling steaks at the Stankovics'."

Max's face soured in disgust. "I'm not going to the Stankovics'!"

"You have to. There's nothing to eat here."

"No! *No!*"

"Buddy, calm down—"

"*NO!*" Max's voice rose to a yell. "I fucking *hate* the Stankovics!"

"Hey! Watch your language—"

"Then you can go hungry," Jen snorted.

"*This is bullshit!*" Max roared as he stormed out of the room.

"That wasn't helpful," Dan admonished Jen.

She shook her head, puzzled by her son's outburst. "What's up *his* butt?"

MAX

Max slammed the front door so hard that the entire house shook. He stomped down the porch stairs, hands clenched into fists, breath seething from his nostrils. The multiple indignities of the past few hours, layered on top of early-stage nicotine withdrawal, had produced a boiling rage.

First his friends had stabbed him in the back. Then his Juul died. Then he wasted thirty bucks trying to replace it. Then his dad tried to bust in on him while he was jerking off, half a minute after he'd finally—*finally!*—managed to achieve an erection without internet porn, which had turned out to be surprisingly difficult.

Then, with his dick still aching from having to shove it back in his pants, his mom had just casually dropped the dinner-at-Jordan's bomb on him like it was no big deal.

Un-fucking-believable!

He needed to hit something.

At the foot of the porch stairs, he pulled up short. Walking made his junk hurt, and there was no point in continuing to move until he'd decided what inanimate object he was going to punch. As he stood there cataloging his options, he heard the interior door to the garage open. A moment later, his dad appeared, limping down the driveway with his bike. Seeing Max, he paused.

"You okay?"

"Fine. Where you going?"

"To look for your sister. Think she's at Emma's?"

Max pondered the question. "No. . . . Probably tennis practice."

"Good idea. I'll check there first." His dad hopped on the bike and pedaled out of sight, weaving unsteadily from his leg cramp.

Max sat down on the porch steps with a heavy sigh. Then he remembered he was starving. He was about to get up and head back inside for a protein bar when the Stankovics' front door opened.

His pulse quickened. But it wasn't Jordan who emerged. It was Mr. Stankovic. He gave Max a curt nod as he pulled a box of cigarettes from the front pocket of his Giants hoodie. Then he took out a smoke and lit up.

Max sat up a little straighter. The cost-benefit analysis around dinner at the Stankovics' had just changed.

If I go over there, maybe I can steal a cigarette.

But I'd have to deal with Jordan.

How bad would that be?

Jordan wouldn't try any shit in front of adults. He didn't even seem inclined to try shit when adults weren't around. As Max thought about it, the only serious barrier to his attendance at a Stankovic cookout was his own sense of pride.

Do I really have to avoid him now if I'm going to fight him later?

As he watched Mr. Stankovic exhale a thick cloud of smoke into the air, Max—for what felt like the hundredth time—began to replay the critical seconds in Mario's Pizza.

"Learn to pull a headshot, you pussy-ass bitch."

The first half of the sentence had stung because it was true:

Max couldn't pull a headshot to save his life. But the second half was just idiotic. And the self-satisfied grin on Jordan's face when he said it—like stringing the words *pussy*, *ass*, and *bitch* together made him the cleverest boy in the world—demanded retaliation.

Max's first instinct had been to disparage Jordan's mental capacity while mirroring his sentence construction:

Learn to read, you fucking moron.

But as Max had started to open his mouth, the memory of a similar but much more personal insult popped into his head.

His bedroom window overlooked the Stankovics' backyard, and for the past decade, he'd been an unseen witness to Jordan and his dad's games of father-son catch. These ran the gamut from football to baseball to lacrosse, but the two things they all had in common were Jordan's incompetence and Mr. Stankovic's vocal disgust in pointing it out.

When it came to catching and throwing, Jordan was an even more hopeless klutz than Max. The critical difference was that Max's dad didn't take his son's lack of athletic prowess personally. Mr. Stankovic did. And in contrast to Dan, who offered nothing but positive reinforcement during his halfhearted efforts to improve Max's skills, Jordan's dad seemed to operate on the assumption that if he could just make his kid sufficiently ashamed of his ineptitude, Jordan would magically blossom into an All-Pro.

So when Max had asked himself, *What's the meanest thing I can say to wipe that smug grin off this dickhead's face?* what had come out were the same words he'd been hearing through his window for years:

"Learn to catch a ball, Dorothy!"

It had worked much too well. Five seconds later, Max was

stumbling down the sidewalk away from the pizza place with his left ear ringing, spots in his eyes, and the whole side of his head feeling like it was on fire. Jordan wasn't agile, but he was big, and he'd put his whole weight into the punch.

For all the times Max had rerun the episode in his head, until this moment—as he watched Jordan's dad suck down a possible solution to Max's nicotine problem while patrolling their front stoop like a lazy gorilla—he'd never really made a good-faith effort to see the episode from Jordan's point of view. Even when Dennis had shaken his head mournfully upon hearing the backstory and declared it "some ice-cold shit," Max had refused to even entertain the possibility that in weaponizing his inside knowledge of the Stankovic father-son psychodrama, he'd been hitting below the emotional belt.

But now, whether out of empathy or just the self-justification necessary to put himself in the same orbit as that pack of cigarettes, Max began to reflect on the weight his words might have held for Jordan.

Learn to catch a ball, Dorothy.

Mr. Stankovic hadn't just said it once. He'd said it a hundred times.

What if Jordan was actually gay? Insulting him like that would be pretty cruel. Like, years-of-therapy cruel.

Even if he wasn't gay, it was pretty harsh.

Jordan played freshman football. Was he as bad at it as he was at catch? Did he even want to play football? Or was he just doing it to make his dad happy?

He probably sucked at it. As far as Max knew, Jordan sucked at everything.

That must be hard. . . .

Wait, what?

Fuck that guy! He punched me in the head!

This train of thought had gone far enough. Pitying Jordan might be useful insofar as it allowed Max to rationalize enduring his company long enough to eat a steak and hopefully steal a cigarette from his asshole dad. But there was no reason to go overboard with it.

The front door opened behind Max.

"Hey, buddy." His mother's lower legs entered his field of vision, less than a foot from his head.

"I'll go to the Stankovics'," he told her.

"Great! Glad to hear it." She stepped in front of him and waved to Jordan's dad. "Hey, Eddie!"

Mr. Stankovic waved back with his cigarette hand. "Wazzzz-uuup?"

"You guys need help making dinner?"

"Nah, we're good! But the bar's open if you want a margarita!"

Jen looked back at Max. "I'm going to go help Mrs. Stankovic with dinner."

"He just said they didn't need it."

"Yeah. . . . They probably do, though. Want to come?"

Max shook his head. "I'll come over when Dad gets back."

He watched his mom trot across the lawn, wondering if she expected him to believe she wasn't going over there just for the margaritas.

DAN

The tennis courts were an easy downhill ride from the house, but even so, Dan had to stop his bike twice on the way there to try to stretch the cramp out of his quadriceps. It kept seizing up with a kind of pain that made him feel like he was getting stabbed in the leg with a meat skewer. He chalked it up to his lousy fitness regimen and swore to himself that when this crisis passed, he'd start going to the gym more often.

Pedestrians and cyclists still populated Lincolnwood's streets in much higher numbers than usual, but there was none of the agitated frenzy that had accompanied the mob's departure from Borough Hall. While some of the faces Dan passed were anxious, and a few were inquisitive, most of them just looked tired. A lot of the walkers were in disheveled business attire and trudged with a weary determination that led Dan to conclude they'd traveled on foot the long way around from Manhattan, up north to the GW Bridge and then back down the turnpike. With the sun getting low in the sky, they were probably trying to make it home before dark.

As he turned onto Baker Avenue and approached the little park that contained the municipal tennis courts, he was struck by how ordinary the scene looked. The adjacent playground was half full of the standard complement of mothers and toddlers. Just beyond it, four of the six courts were occupied by the girls' varsity team. Dan quickly spotted Chloe trading shots with the number two singles player, Lydia Weissman. Their coach, Bob Kaniewski, was monitoring a doubles match on the far court, and Dan waved to him before pulling to a stop on the other side of the chain-link fence from Chloe.

Lydia had just hit an approach shot deep to her backhand. Chloe returned it with a low, flat shot down the line, then pumped her fist when it rocketed past Lydia and landed just a few inches inside the baseline.

Turning around, she saw Dan.

"Hey!" he called.

"Hey," she replied, walking over to him. "What are you doing here?"

"Just checking in. Everything okay with you?"

"Fine. What happened to your face?"

"It's, uh . . . kind of a long story. I'm okay, though."

"Good. Tell me about it later?" Chloe nodded her head in Lydia's direction. "Kind of in the middle here—"

"Yeah! Sure! Just wanted to, y'know—touch base."

"Cool. Thanks." She pressed a stray ball against the outside of her foot with her racket head, then lifted the ball in the air and caught it in a practiced motion. "I'll see you at home, okay?"

"Yeah. Of course. Sorry to interrupt."

"No problem!" She took three steps toward the service line, then turned back to him. "Dad!"

"Yeah?"

"I fixed my backhand!"

"That's great, sweetheart!"

Beaming, she lowered her voice to a thrilled half whisper. "I'm hitting the *shit* out of it. They better not cancel semis."

Then she turned away again and trotted up to the line to serve. Dan watched her hit a service winner, feeling a little sheepish for having interrupted her.

"One more thing?" he called out before the next point.

She turned, but didn't reapproach him. "Yeah?"

"We're having dinner at the Stankovics'."

Chloe wrinkled her nose. "*All* of us?"

Dan nodded.

"Ugh."

"They have something we don't," he explained. "Food."

"Mom didn't go to the store?"

Dan shrugged. "She couldn't. The car died."

His daughter rolled her eyes and shook her head in mild contempt as she returned to her game. Dan guided his bike over to Coach Kaniewski, who'd moved to the bleachers to make notations on a clipboard.

"Hey, Bob."

"Hey, Dan! She's on fire today." Kaniewski nodded in Chloe's direction. "The old Chloe's back! Tearing the cover off the ball."

"That's great!" Dan lowered his voice so as not to be overheard by any of the girls on the team. "Think you'll get the semi in tomorrow?"

"We're acting as if," the coach replied, matching Dan's hushed tone. "Figure it's the best thing for the girls psychologically. Between you and me, though? Unless somebody waves a magic wand, I have no idea how we're going to get to Rumson."

"What do you think is going on?" Dan asked.

"Honestly? You want my real opinion?"

"Sure."

Coach Kaniewski's eyebrows knitted together with concern as he stared at the ground. Then he raised his eyes to meet Dan's. "I think it's aliens."

"Like . . . from space?"

The coach nodded gravely.

"Interesting."

"That's an understatement." Kaniewski sighed. "Just hope they're friendly. Got a bad feeling, though. You ever see that Tom Cruise movie? This is how it starts."

"Well, that's a chilling vision, Bob."

"Sorry to bring you down."

"No! I mean—hey, I asked."

"What do *you* think it is?"

Dan weighed the various theories he'd heard over the course of the day. "I dunno. Some kind of terrorism, maybe? But honestly, I have no idea. Totally stumped. Hey, unrelated question—what do you do for a leg cramp?"

Kaniewski recommended Gatorade, bananas, and several stretching exercises. The first two weren't an option due to both availability and financial constraints, but Dan dutifully performed the stretches next to the bleachers before getting back on his bike for the uphill climb home.

The exercises were just effective enough to get him back up the Willis Road hill without collapsing. When he reached the house, aching and sweaty, Jen had already left for the Stankovics'. Dan stripped off his damp clothes and entered the shower stall in the main bathroom. In his absence, the water pressure had fallen to little more than a fast trickle.

By the time he gave up and left the shower three minutes later, cleaner than he'd been but less clean than he wanted to be, it had stopped flowing entirely.

MAX

Max's earlier mental contortions had turned out to be unneces-
sary, because Jordan didn't show up to his own cookout. "I'm so
sorry Jordie's not here to hang out with you!" his clueless mom
bleated at Max when he and his dad arrived at their neighbors'
back patio. "He's staying over at his friend Grayson's. You know
Grayson, right?"

Ugh. "Yeah."

The bad news was that Mr. Stankovic's cigarettes hadn't shown
up, either. This wasn't quite true—the box of Camel Lights
had made brief appearances on the two occasions when Mr. Stankovic pulled it out of his sweatshirt pocket to retrieve a smoke.
But both times, the box had disappeared back into his hoodie
even before he'd lit the cigarette off a burner on his gas grill.

Still, like all of the other adults except Dad and Judge Distefano, Mr. Stankovic seemed pretty hammered, so Max hadn't
given up hope yet. He'd finished his steak, which had been delicious. But instead of excusing himself to go home—not that
there was anything to do at home—he was still biding his time
in the torchlight around the big patio table along with almost the
entire population of Brantley Circle: his parents, the two Stankovics, Judge Distefano, Mrs. Sweeney, Mr. and Mrs. Mukherjee,
and their toddler, Zaira.

The adults were talking about city government, or some shit.

"What I don't understand," Dad was saying, "is why a guy

who wasn't elected to anything and isn't even on the police force is suddenly calling all the shots."

"He's the emergency management coordinator," Mrs. Sweeney replied, drawing out each syllable in a sarcastic, tipsy slur.

"But what even *is* that?" Dad asked.

Mom patted Dad's arm. "Try keep up, honey." The head start she'd gotten on the margaritas had left her so schmizzed that words were going missing from her sentences. Dad kept giving her dirty looks.

"I'll give you the nickel summary," Judge Distefano offered. His forearms were propped on the table, hands wrapped around a can of lemon-lime seltzer. "Sometime around—I think it was post-Sandy, but maybe it goes all the way back to 9/11? I forget. Either way, the state of New Jersey mandated that every municipality's gotta have an Emergency Operations Plan. Supposed to be a playbook you run when things get screwy. Mostly, it's about as helpful as taking your shoes off at the airport. When I was on the council, we had to recertify it at one point—"

"You were on city council?" Mr. Mukherjee asked. He was a skinny, high-strung guy, and he looked really young. If he hadn't had a daughter, Max would've guessed he was still in college.

The judge nodded. "Just one term. Before I realized it was a dumb way to spend my golden years. Anyway, my recollection of the EOP is it was a glorified phone book. Basically a list of numbers and a Post-it note that said, 'Everybody grab your ass.' Please excuse my French," he added with a nod to little Zaira.

"She's asleep," Mrs. Mukherjee assured him.

"No, I'm not," protested Zaira, squirming forward to grab another tortilla chip from the bowl on the table.

"So to make sure whatever kabuki theater's in the EOP gets carried out," the judge continued, "they assign an emergency management coordinator. Most towns give the job to the chief of police, village manager, what have you. And day to day, there's not much to it. But it comes with a part-time salary. In Lincolnwood, I think it was something like fifteen K a year. And for reasons best known only to himself, Barry Kozak—back when he was still chief of police—gave the job to his drinking buddy, Steve Shreckler."

Mr. Stankovic perked up. "My boy Shrek!"

"You know him?" the judge asked.

"Yeah, we play hoops together on Saturdays."

"Well, correct me if I've misjudged his character, but he always struck me as a grade-A jackass."

"Little bit, yeah." Mr. Stankovic admitted. "Throws a lot of elbows in the paint."

"And if memory serves," the judge added, "he had no experience in emergency management. Or anything, really, other than filing nuisance lawsuits on behalf of con artists."

"C'mon!" Mr. Stankovic protested. "Shrek's got a legitimate legal practice!"

"Everybody's entitled to counsel," said the judge. "Even if they're scumbags. It's just that if I were in private practice? And my entire client list was scumbags? At some point, I might take a step back and reflect on my career choices. But that's neither here nor there. According to statute, Shreckler's the emergency coordinator. So the council's stuck with him."

"What kind of authority does that give him?" Dad asked.

"This is the whole problem!" said Mrs. Sweeney. She leaned

over the table and lowered her voice like she was sharing some kind of secret. "*Nobody knows!* They don't even know who's supposed to be in charge! What I heard from Stan Altbauer was, after the power went out this morning, the mayor and the chief of police were just sitting down with the heads of department to try to get a handle on things when this Shreckler character shows up at Borough Hall, crowing about how the EOP makes him some kind of dictator the second he declares a state of emergency."

"Attaboy, Shrek!" Mr. Stankovic crowed. "Takin' the wheel!"

"The crazy thing is, legally speaking, he ain't wrong," the judge said. "My recollection is, that EOP was pretty loosely worded. Statutory authority was so wide, you could drive a tank through it. Declare martial law if you wanted to."

"But *nobody even knows*! 'Cause they can't *find* the damn thing!" Mrs. Sweeney was practically yelling, which Max chalked up to the margaritas. "They turned the whole mayor's office upside down, looking for a hard copy of the emergency plan. But they only had it on PDF! And all the stinkin' computers were down! So they spent two hours going back and forth, yelling themselves hoarse about what they *thought* it said. And 'cause this Shreckler bozo was apparently the only one who ever bothered to read it, he wound up bigfootin' the mayor and the chief!"

"Sounds good to me," Mr. Stankovic declared. "Lemme tell ya, if bad shit goes down—"

"Eddie! Language around the kids!" His wife gestured toward little Zaira, who squirmed in resistance when her mother tried to cover her ears.

Mr. Stankovic rolled his eyes, but rephrased his comment.

"If bad stuff goes down—I'd *much* rather see Shrek in charge than Mayor MeToo or that Gwen Bitchy-Carpetmuncher."

"*Eddie!*" his wife howled.

Mrs. Sweeney looked indignant. "I'm sorry—are you referring to *Chief of Police* Gwen Bugatti-Kleindienst?"

"That's what I said: Gwen Bitchy-Carpetmuncher!"

"*Eddie!* It's 2019!" His wife smacked him hard on the arm. "You're not supposed to say that!"

"Do your knuckles drag on the ground when you walk, Edward?" Mrs. Sweeney asked.

"Just a little bit," Jordan's dad said with a chuckle. Then he pulled his hard pack of Camel Lights from his sweatshirt, plucked out a smoke, and tossed the box on the table as he leaned forward to catch a light from one of the votive candles scattered around the remains of the meal.

The cigarettes!

Max's heart began to race as he stared at the pack, which had landed between the bean dip and the bowl of chips.

Mrs. Stankovic smacked her husband for the third time.

"No smoking in front of the kids!"

"Or the adults," added Mrs. Sweeney.

Mr. Stankovic got up and retreated to the edge of the patio to smoke his cigarette, leaving the pack behind on the table.

"I don't care who's in charge, as long as they get the water back on," Zaira's drunk mom declared.

As the adults kept talking, Max began to formulate a plan.

If I go over and stand next to Zaira and her mom . . .

"Get real," Zaira's dad told his wife. "The city council's useless! Planes are falling out of the sky!"

. . . grab a tortilla chip, and pretend to scoop up some bean dip with one hand . . .

"How many plane crashes *were* there?" Dad asked. "I counted, like, four."

. . . while my OTHER hand flips open the box of cigarettes and palms a smoke . . .

"There were *plane* crashes?" the judge wanted to know.

. . . It's a risky move. I'll be right in the middle of everybody. And I'd have to pretend I like bean dip. Mom won't notice, she's wasted. But if Dad's paying attention . . .

"Lots of them," Zaira's dad told the judge. "Like at least ten."

"Ten?"

Do it now!

His heart racing, Max stood up and made his move.

DAN

"I saw three go down just from my office window," Arjun declared of the plane crashes.

Here we go again, thought Dan. Arjun had already spent twenty minutes recounting his walk home from Midtown in excruciating detail, despite the fact that nothing interesting had happened to him. In contrast, Dan had spent less than five minutes telling his own story, which was much more dramatically compelling and had even resulted in a head injury.

Yet underneath the resentment, Dan felt a prickle of anxiety spreading in his gut at the mention of the plane crashes. His sense of the situation's gravity had ebbed and flowed all day. Now it was starting to flow again.

"What about the cars?" Carol Sweeney wanted to know. "That's the thing that creeps me out."

"Didn't you tell me you saw one that worked?" Kayla asked.

"Yeah," Carol replied. "Denny Burgholzer's old pickup-car thing. Whatever you call it."

"El Camino!" Eddie interjected from the shadows between the citronella torches, where he'd retreated to smoke. "Sweet ride."

"What's up with that? Why would it still run?"

"Probably 'cause it's old," Eddie suggested. "If he had a horse, that'd still work, too. Hey, speaking of horses—Judge, does your Mustang still run?"

As Dan turned to look at the judge, his eyes met Max's. His son was standing across the table from him with a tortilla chip in his hand and an odd grimace on his face. Max quickly broke the eye contact, fixing his weird stare on the bowl full of bean dip that lay between them.

"Nah, I got rid of it," the judge told Eddie. "Been downsizing ever since Natalie passed."

Kayla reached out to pat the judge on the hand. "God rest her soul. She was *such* a beautiful person."

"Thank you, sweetheart."

"Whatever's happening," Arjun declared, steering the conversation back to the present, "it's *way* beyond local government. The feds are going to have to step in."

"The feds," Eddie snorted. "Good luck with that. Those clowns can't even clean up after a hurricane."

"You okay, Max?" Dan asked. His son was glowering at the bean dip like it had stolen money from him while his right arm twitched in an odd motion.

"Whuh? Yeah." He scooped up some dip with the chip he was holding, then paused with his hand still suspended over the bowl, like he wasn't sure what the next step in the process was.

"They've still got a military," Arjun told Eddie. "Who else is going to go after the monsters who did this? The state of New Jersey?"

Max continued to hold the loaded chip in midair.

"How's that bean dip?" Dan asked him.

His son's eyes widened. The question seemed somehow traumatizing. He looked from Dan to the bean-dip-smeared chip in his hand, then back again.

"It's, uh, y'know—" Max's oddly positioned right arm started to jiggle and twitch.

"Who we gonna go after?" Eddie asked Arjun. "We don't even know what this is yet."

Why is my kid such a weirdo? Dan wondered. *And what's he doing with his hand?* It was obscured behind the bowl of chips.

"S'fuckin' terrorists!" Jen suddenly roared, much too loudly.

Dan swiveled his head to stare at his wife with equal parts concern and embarrassment. She was drunker than he'd seen her in ages.

They were going to have to have a serious conversation about this in the morning.

"S'obvious!" Jen opined, her unfocused eyes squinting in the general direction of Eddie.

"I agree," Anu declared. She pressed her hands over her daughter's ears. As Zaira squirmed, Anu stage-whispered her suspicion to the group. "It's the effing Muslims! It *has* to be."

"I'm going home." Max shoved the chip in his mouth and stepped away from the table. "Bye!"

"Thanks for comin', sweetie!" Kayla purred. "Next time I'll make sure Jordan sticks around to keep ya company."

"It's fine!" Max vanished into the darkness. Dan turned his full attention to the adults' conversation, which had taken an awkward turn with Anu's Muslim accusation.

"It's *definitely* the effing Muslims," Arjun declared.

Kayla looked from Arjun to his wife and back again, her mouth slightly open as she puzzled over the situation. "No judgments, you guys . . . but aren't you Muslim?"

"No!" Anu looked appalled.

So did Arjun. "We're Hindu! It's a completely different religion!"

"Oh! Okay."

"That's cool," said Eddie.

An uncomfortable silence followed. Dan tried to think of some way to fill it, but came up empty.

"This whole situation is just completely unbelievable," Carol finally declared.

"It's a heck of a thing," the judge agreed. He pushed his chair back from the table. "And on that note—it's past my bedtime."

"It's, like, seven o'clock!" Eddie snorted.

"I'm not a young man," the judge pointed out. "But this was great. Thanks for the steak—it was fantastic."

The rest of the group chimed in with their appreciation of the Stankovics' largesse.

"We're so glad you all came!" Kayla gushed. "Times like this, ya gotta come together."

"*Mi casa, su casa*," Eddie added. "Or us *casa*, you *casa*. Whatever the plural is. My Spanish sucks."

"Mind if I fetch a bucket and take home some of your pool water?" the judge asked. "Wouldn't mind being able to flush my toilet in the morning."

"Of course!" Kayla waved a hand at him. "Ohmygosh! Don't even ask!"

"*Mi* pool, *su* pool!"

Dan stood up. "Let me help you carry that, Judge."

"It's fine, Danny. Don't put yourself out."

"It's no problem," Dan assured him. "I need the exercise."

That wasn't true. In fact, after taxing his legs far beyond

their usual limits that day, Dan wasn't sure if he could carry a full bucket of water across the cul-de-sac without crumpling in a heap. But it seemed like the minimally heroic thing to do. And Dan wanted to solicit his one levelheaded neighbor's candid opinion of the situation out of earshot of the others.

Three minutes later, Dan was trying not to slop water out of the bucket he was hauling across Brantley Circle on his gimpy leg while the judge lit their way with a flashlight.

"Can I, ahh, ask a question?"

"Fire away, Danny."

"What's your best guess as to what's going on here?"

"That's a tough one. Short answer is, I dunno. But something tells me things are gonna get worse before they get better. Especially depending on how far this goes. It's lights out in New York. Is it lights out in Philly, too? DC? Boston? Chicago? Could be a real hell of a mess."

"I'm wondering if I shouldn't try to get out. Take the family somewhere."

"What's your gut tell you?"

"My gut says leave. But my brain can't figure out how."

They reached the judge's front porch. He held open the screen door and gestured with the flashlight beam as Dan heard the jingle of Ruby's dog tags from somewhere in the darkness.

"Just leave it right inside the door. I'll take it the rest of the way when the sun comes up. And thanks again."

"My pleasure." Dan carefully set the bucket down, then stepped back onto the porch. "Are you thinking of leaving?"

The judge shrugged. "Where would I go? Maria and Tommy

are both on the West Coast. That's a long way to drive even if my Prius would start. And at my age? *Yugghh.*" His dachshund materialized at his feet. "Nah, Ruby and I are gonna make our stand here. If I were you, though . . ."

Dan waited for him to finish the thought. "You'd what?"

"Well, if I could figure out where to go . . . I'd maybe take the wife and kids someplace this isn't happening."

In the silence that followed, the anxiety in the pit of Dan's stomach multiplied.

"Course that's easier said than done," the judge added.

"It sure is," Dan agreed.

"Night, Danny. Thanks again."

"Night, Judge."

The judge closed the door softly. Dan limped down the darkened porch steps, clutching the rail. His head felt detached from his body, like it was levitating in a fog of dread.

When he reached the street, he saw the irregular light of a flashlight beam zigzagging in the second-story center window of his house.

He assumed it was Max, heading upstairs. But he was forced to revise the theory when a spasm of ragged coughs broke the silence, coming from somewhere behind the garage. For reasons Dan couldn't fathom, his son sounded like he was hacking up a lung.

CHLOE

Walking home in the moonlight, the neighborhood had been so quiet that Chloe could hear the sound of voices coming from the Stankovics' backyard even before she turned onto Brantley Circle. Hungry as she was, she'd briefly considered going straight to the cookout, but a quick sniff of her armpit persuaded her to go home and shower first.

Her lower back ached. She switched her racket bag to her other hand and readjusted her backpack for the final steps to her house. It had been an insane day, and even after the long walk home, her mind was still racing.

When's the physics review? Tomorrow? Is the quiz still Friday? Or not until Monday now?

How do I check Google Classroom with the power out?

How am I going to work on the supplemental?

Screw you, Mom.

And what about my reading response? Will I have to do it longhand?

What if they postpone semis until next week?

What if they postpone the ACT?

Ohmygod, what if they cancel it?

Get real. It's only Tuesday.

Could this thing last until Saturday?

What even IS this?

A simulation?

No. Ridiculous.

But maybe.

If it is, I gotta say: nice job on Josh's abs, Simulation!

And his butt. Ohmygod, swimmers' bodies.

I can't believe he fixed my backhand. He's, like, the backhand whisperer.

Or a sex therapist.

Ohmygod.

She entered the house. Other than the moonlight coming through the windows, the only illumination on the first floor was from a single flashlight, which Max had stood on its handle end atop the kitchen counter while he rummaged through a drawer.

"Hey."

"Hey."

"Did you eat already?"

"Yeah. The Stankovics grilled steak."

"Are they grilling anything else?"

"No."

"Seriously?"

"What? It's good."

"I don't eat red meat!"

"Sucks to be you." Having found what he was looking for, Max shut the drawer and headed for the mudroom, taking the flashlight with him.

"Where you going?"

"None of your business."

"Bring the flashlight back!"

"There's more on the table. Next to all that shit Mom brought up."

As she struggled in the darkness to locate the cache of flashlights on the kitchen table, she heard Max exit through the door to the garage.

Idiot.

Eventually, she felt her way to a flashlight and used it to examine the contents of the fridge and the mostly defrosted freezer.

What am I going to eat?

There's chicken tenders. Does the oven work? Brody's didn't. But his burners did.

She tried one of the burners on the stove and was relieved to smell gas when she turned it on. A quick check of the same drawer Max had just rummaged through revealed several books of restaurant matches.

I can pan-fry the chicken. No big deal.

She headed upstairs with the flashlight, mentally planning the next twenty-four hours as she went.

Shower, cook, sleep. Get up early. Take a practice ACT—

From somewhere in the backyard came the faint sound of coughing.

Max, you are such a delinquent . . .

She dumped her backpack on her bed. Pulled out her street clothes. Dropped them in a pile on the floor and then stripped down to her underwear.

Take a practice test, then go to Josh's. Get there by ten, we'll have what? Four and a half hours to mash before I leave for semis?

Where? At his place? Brody's?

No way am I taking him back here.

She retrieved clean clothes from her dresser and headed to the bathroom.

We'll have to get lunch somewhere.

Chipotle? Will they be open? Will the power still be out?

What if they postpone the semis?

Until when? Thursday?

If the semis are Thursday, I'll have to move my session with Kevin.

She locked the bathroom door, set the flashlight on its end like Max had done in the kitchen, and stripped off the rest of her clothes.

But what if he's booked Friday?

Jesus, this power outage.

Although no school is a net plus. As long as the semi doesn't——

What the——

The tub was full of water.

She opened the drain to let it out so she could shower.

Then it occurred to her to test the water supply. She opened the tub faucet.

Nothing.

Oh shit——

She quickly closed the drain. Then she turned around and opened the sink faucet.

Nothing.

SHIIIIT!

She tried the tub faucet again. Still nothing.

How am I going to shower?

I HAVE to shower. I stink! And I'm seeing Josh in the——

Wait. There's a full tub of water.

If it's clean, I can take a bath.

At room temperature?

Ugh. Suboptimal.

But still.

As she continued to ponder the situation, it occurred to her that the tub must've been filled intentionally. Realizing she'd need to get clean after practice, one of her parents had left her enough water to bathe in.

Must've been Dad. He's thoughtful that way.

Not like Mom.

Screw you, Mom.

Grateful for the solid her father had done her, Chloe carefully lowered herself into the tub.

JEN

She'd overdone it.

The margarita glass in front of her kept splitting in two.

So did Kayla across the table. Two-headed Kayla was laughing at something.

Jen squeezed an eye shut.

Just one Kayla now, lifting the margarita pitcher.

More booze splooshed into the glasses. Glass. Glasses.

Glass. Jen reached for it and got the spins.

She grabbed the table with one hand, between her thumb and forefinger.

That helped.

She drank more.

Kayla was saying something.

"Fine," Jen said.

A hand was on her shoulder, shaking her.

"Cut it out!"

Dan was staring down at her. He was saying something.

"I'm fine," Jen said.

"Everybody's leaving," Dan said.

Jen looked around. She was all alone at the table. Kayla was taking away the tortilla chips.

"Shuttin' it down," Jen declared.

They were halfway across the yard.

It was dark.

"We have to leave."

Dan kept saying that.

It made no sense. They'd already left.

They were home. It was dark.

Too dark. She bumped into a chair.

"Ow."

Her thigh hurt.

She was in the downstairs bathroom.

"What are you doing?"

She couldn't remember.

Dan had a flashlight. He wouldn't hold it steady.

He was irritating the shit out of her.

They were upstairs.

Jen had a flashlight of her own. The beam lit up the toilet in her bathroom.

She couldn't decide whether to sit and pee, or kneel and puke.

In another room, Dan and Chloe were yelling.

No way to sleep with that yelling. She needed to tell them.

Hallway. Flashlight beams everywhere. They made her dizzy.

She squeezed an eye shut.

Chloe was yelling.

"I'm sorry!"

She'd used all the water.

Dan was upset. He was telling Chloe they needed that water.

Jen agreed. She told Chloe what she thought of the situation.

Chloe was angry.

Dan was angry.

At Jen.

Ridiculous.

Jen didn't use the water.

Chloe was yelling at her.

Max was yelling at everybody.

Dan was being an idiot.

They were all annoying the shit out of her.

Jen told them what she thought of the situation.

She was in bed. The pillow felt soft and cool.

She was on her knees, hugging the toilet. The light was shaky.

Puke came out of her like a fire hose.

Her throat was burning. The sour tang of stomach acids in her mouth.

Dan was saying something.

She was in bed again.

Dan was still trying to talk to her.

She needed to sleep.

She told him that.

Still he talked.

She just needed to sleep.

So she did.

WEDNESDAY

DAN

It was still dark when Dan got out of bed. He didn't want to waste any daylight, and there was a lot that needed doing before they left town.

His legs were so sore from all of yesterday's walking and cycling that he had to stop and stretch just to make it to the bathroom. When he got there, he dry-swallowed two Advil. Then he washed his face and brushed his teeth using water he scooped from the tub after scanning it with the flashlight to confirm that his wife hadn't barfed into it during the night.

Back in the bedroom, he dressed in silence so as not to disturb her, snoring softly as she slept off her drunk.

Jesus, Jen.

What got into you?

Heading downstairs, his first stop was the garage to check the tires on all four bicycles. Jen's needed pumping, so he took care of that. Before he went back inside, he took a quick survey of the shelves, scanning them with the flashlight in search of anything that might be useful on a three-hundred-mile bike trip.

There was nothing except sports equipment and gardening tools. Cursing himself for not being more of an outdoorsman—*how come I never took the kids camping?*—he went back to the kitchen and inventoried their food supplies.

The ten cans of tuna and four big jars of peanut butter were the highlights, although they only had a fourth of a squeeze bottle of mayo and a few spoonfuls' worth of jelly to pair with them. After that, things went downhill. The canned vegetables were portable but unwieldy, especially if the four Altmans were limited to what they could carry on their backs.

Where can we get panniers?

It was a dumb question. A world where he could easily purchase bike luggage was a world where he didn't need to carry food and water hundreds of miles by bike in the first place.

Dan moved on to the pantry cabinet. The five protein bars would come in handy. Not much else would: flour, pancake mix, two cans of Campbell's Chicken Noodle, three boxes of pasta, some stale crackers, half a bag of pretzels, a third of a bag of pita chips, a cylinder of Quaker Oats a year past its expiration date, and a few bowls' worth of Honey Nut Cheerios.

Shit.

Then the freezer, which he opened and closed quickly to preserve what little cold air remained. Two frozen burritos, no longer frozen. Half a box of chicken tenders, ditto. Large Ziploc of reddish-brown sludge that must be leftover chili. Three sticks of butter. Bag of peas. Two pounds of ground coffee. Pints of lemon sorbet and vegan chocolate chip ice cream, both turning to soup. A nearly full reservoir of half-melted cubes swimming in water underneath the ice maker.

We can drink that.

Finally, the fridge. It was grim. There were ten eggs and not much else. Condiments and salad dressing, half a stick of butter, three beers, a third of a bottle of white wine, an unopened prosecco. A handful of olives. Pineapple salsa. Some shredded cheese in a bag. Small block of parmesan. A few cheddar slices. Four apples. Wilted lettuce. A corrupted lemon.

Dan shut the fridge door and took a few deep, slow breaths.

Stay calm. Think positive. Work the solution.

On the plus side, we'll have plenty of room to bring the canned goods.

Except we have to carry water, too.

There should be plenty of that, as long as nobody else took a bath.

Ugh, Chloe.

Don't point fingers. Think solutions.

How can we carry all the water?

Dan spent the next several minutes ransacking the kitchen for water bottles, then filling the half dozen he found with water from the pots on the counter. When he was done, there were still two medium pots, a salad spinner, and a Brita pitcher full of drinkable water. Plus whatever they could harvest from the ice maker in the freezer. Plus the six gallons of Poland Spring on the table.

Plus the mostly full tub in the main bathroom upstairs.

For the time being, they were good with water. They were so good that he decided he could spare some of it to clean the dirty pan and tongs he'd left in the sink after frying chicken tenders from the freezer for Chloe the night before.

In the wake of the bathtub fiasco, they'd actually had a nice little father-daughter bonding session while he made her dinner. He'd started by apologizing for losing his temper. She'd apologized in turn for using all the bath water.

Then, while she ate her chicken and the rest of Monday night's carryout lasagna and spinach, they'd tentatively addressed the drunk elephant in the room.

"Sometimes . . . your mom drinks more than she should."

"'Sometimes'? Dad, there's been a *lot* of sometimes lately."

"I know. But her work situation's really been weighing her down. I think she just feels stuck. And kind of isolated. And today was—I don't know if you realize how stressful 9/11 was for her—"

"What does that have to do with anything?"

"Well, anytime planes start crashing for no good reason—"

"*Planes* are crashing?"

Chloe hadn't known about the planes. He told her about them, and the news seemed to unsettle her.

"Should we be, like, seriously freaking out about all this?"

"No. We're perfectly safe. It's going to be fine. But when something like this happens, it kicks up all kinds of 9/11 memories for your mom. I think she's probably still got some PTSD."

"Yeah. I just . . . I dunno, sometimes I wonder if she has, like, a legit problem."

"With drinking?"

"Yeah. Like, even before last night."

The idea seemed borderline absurd. Dan and Jen had been married for twenty years. If she had a drinking problem, he'd know.

Then again, when he came home that morning, she'd been drinking alone. And she'd gotten absolutely plastered at the Stankovics'.

But it hadn't been a normal day for anybody. Far from it.

"I dunno . . . I don't *think* so? I'll talk to her in the morning."

"Would you? 'Cause she *really* pissed me off with that essay comment."

"What essay comment?"

That opened the floodgates. All of Chloe's frustrations with her mother, the majority of them centered around the college application process, had spilled out of her. Dan had mostly just listened sympathetically, pleased that his daughter was willing to confide in him but a little chagrined that it was happening at Jen's expense.

After promising his daughter that he'd intercede on her behalf with her mother, swearing up and down that nothing about the power outage would screw up her Dartmouth application, and offering his assurance that whatever had caused the power loss was both temporary and likely to be resolved in the next day or so, he'd gone to bed half believing it himself.

Now, though, as he carefully cleaned the pan in the sink with a bare minimum of water from one of the pots, his sense of mounting dread—*or is it just low blood sugar?*—made him feel shaky and weak.

We don't know what this is. Or how far it goes.

Is the whole East Coast like this?

The whole country?

The whole world?

Don't think problems. Think solutions.

We need money.

How are we going to get money?

The sun was coming up, and it was just light enough now to see without the flashlight. When he finished with the pan, Dan went to the table to fetch his notebook and pen from his messenger bag. He did his best thinking on paper.

Pete Blackwell's iPad was still inside the bag.

If I take it back to Pete, maybe he'll tell me why he ran home like that.

It wasn't a bad idea, except that going to Pete's would waste valuable daylight. They needed to get on the road.

Dan got out his notebook, pushed the canned goods to one side of the tabletop to clear enough space for writing, sat down, and opened the Moleskine.

Flipping to the first clean page, he passed the notes he'd taken on the train less than twenty-four hours ago.

MURDER AT COMIC CON jumped out at him.

Such a good idea. So's the librarian murder thing.

For a moment, Dan wondered how he could get the story pitches to Marty.

Is the post office open?

That was ridiculous. The power was out in the city, too. Production would've shut down. Everybody, even Marty Callahan, had much bigger fish to fry than breaking new *Bullet Town: NYC* stories.

Dan shook his head at the absurdity of spending even five seconds worrying about his job at a time like this.

Focus on the money. Solve the money problem.

He turned to a blank page and wrote down a single figure:

$36.75

What else have we got?

There was more change in the dish upstairs. And that Ziploc

bag on Max's dresser. Plus whatever else the kids might be holding. And the handfuls of coins sitting in both cars to feed the street meters.

So . . . what? Maybe another twenty bucks in change? Thirty, if we're lucky?
There's got to be more than that. We're rich.

By any conventional measure, this was true. The Altmans' house alone was worth well over a million. And their liquid assets—add up the Chase accounts, the Schwab account, the retirement accounts, the kids' college accounts . . . What did they amount to, the last time Dan checked everything? Two million? Two and a half?

But that was in a world with a functioning electrical grid.

Take away the electricity, and they had . . .

Thirty-six seventy-five.

Plus another twenty or so in small change.

And a few flimsy plastic cards inscribed with the logos of banks at which he didn't know a single employee and had no way of documenting his account balances.

Along with two books of blank checks that Dan strongly suspected nobody would cash unless the power came back, at which point it wouldn't matter anymore.

If I go to Chase or Charles Schwab . . . how do I prove I've got money with them?

Jesus Christ, I never should've gone paperless.

Calm down.

Don't panic.

Think solutions! What can I do to help us right now?

Dan pushed the air out of his lungs in an unsteady sigh. His blood sugar felt dangerously low, and it had been twenty-four hours since his last serving of caffeine. The possibility that he might faint entered his mind.

What can I do?

I can eat a burrito.

No. Save those for the kids.

I can boil eggs.

It made sense. Boiled eggs would travel well. And making them wouldn't dirty a pan as long as he was careful not to let the shells crack.

They could even reuse the water afterward.

Dan put one of the full pots on the stove, lit the burner with a match, and set it to boil. Then he pulled the tray of eggs from the fridge and put it down beside the stove. He was watching the pot, taking deep breaths to try to get his pulse rate under control, when Max walked in.

His son had a bad case of bedhead over an irritable scowl, and he smelled of crotch sweat.

Man up. Stay positive. You're the dad here.

"Morning!"

In lieu of answering, Max opened the fridge.

"Don't open that. You'll let the cold air out."

"What cold air?"

"Just—c'mon. Close it."

"What's for breakfast?"

"I'm making boiled eggs."

"Boiled eggs taste like ass!"

"You want a burrito?"

"No!" Max snarled with a ferocity that seemed entirely out of proportion to the situation.

"You don't have to bite my head off. I'm trying to be helpful." Dan watched his son, wondering why he was so surly, as Max shuffled over to the pantry and began to search it for breakfast options. "Are you feeling okay?"

"Fine."

He didn't sound fine. But Dan knew from experience that there was no point in trying to probe further. His son was a closed book.

Max took out the box of Cheerios.

"There's no milk," Dan warned him.

Max shrugged, then dug his arm into the box and withdrew a handful of Cheerios.

"Don't eat that—eat something perishable."

"Why?" Max asked just before he stuffed the Cheerios in his mouth.

"Because the perishable stuff won't travel. Cereal we can take with us."

"Where are we going?"

"Wellfleet."

Max screwed up his face in distaste as he chewed. "We're going to *Grandma's*?"

"It'll be good. She won't be there. She'll be in Newton." Dan thought for a moment. "Actually, if the power's on in Newton, we should just go there."

"Why would the power be on at Grandma's and not here?"

It was a reasonable question, and Dan was surprised to discover he couldn't answer it.

"Because . . . I mean, it can't be off everywhere."

"Why not? If it's an EMP?"

"A what?"

"An EMP. Isn't that what this is?"

"What's an EMP?"

"An electromagnetic . . . I forget what the P's for. Pulse? I think? It was in this video game. That Dennis played. And in the game . . ."

Oh, Jesus. Why's it always about video games with these kids?

Max kept talking, but Dan stopped listening, preoccupied with unpacking the assumptions behind his plan to leave town for his mother's second home on Cape Cod.

What makes me think the power's still on in Massachusetts?

Nothing. Except where else are we going to go?

And if we go to Wellfleet, the ocean's right there. So we can fish.

But when the hell have I ever done any ocean fishing?

We don't even own a boat.

"And how would we even get there?" Max was asking him.

"What?"

"To Grandma's. How would we get there?"

"Oh. We'd ride our bikes."

"*Bikes?* That's ridiculous!"

Chloe entered, looking and smelling much cleaner than her brother. "What's ridiculous?"

"Dad thinks we're riding our bikes to Grandma's."

CHLOE

"In *Massachusetts*?" The idea wasn't just ridiculous. It was the most batshit crazy thing Chloe had ever heard.

"Maybe we wouldn't have to go that far," Dad said. "We just need to get someplace where the power's on and our credit cards work. Then we can get a hotel room, and—"

"Dad! We're not going anywhere!"

"Sweetheart, we *have* to. We're running out of food here!" Apparently, he was serious. Which was insane.

"There's food in the freezer! And I have semis today!"

"You really think they're happening?"

"*Yes!* Coach Kaniewski said—"

"Then we can stop by the courts before we leave and see if —"

"No! Ohmygod, no!"

"Quit yelling!" Max whined. "Jesus!"

"Chloe—"

"Dad! I have semis! And test prep!" *And Josh!* "And my Dartmouth app! And homework!" *And Josh!* "And last night, you told me *everything was fine!*"

"I know, honey. I'm just kinda . . . reevaluating that."

"So, what? We're going to, like, go hide in a bunker like the Blackwells?"

"What about the Blackwells?"

"Their dad's, like, a crazy survivalist. Yesterday, he made them all ride their bikes to their, like, compound in Pennsylvania."

"How do you know this?" Dad asked.

"I saw them leave! I was . . ." *No point in getting too specific.* "Walking to tennis practice, and they rode by me on their bikes. All five of them. With their dog. And backpacks and stuff."

"How do you know where they were going?"

"They've got a place in Pennsylvania somewhere. On a lake or something. Where else would they have gone?"

"Do you know how to get there?"

"Dad! We're not going to go pound on the door of the Blackwells' survival bunker! We're not even friends with them!"

He looked a little offended. "I'm friends with their dad."

"Dude! Their dad hangs out with, like, billionaires and rock stars!"

"What rock stars?"

"Like that guy with one name who does charity stuff in Africa."

"Bono?"

"I guess?"

"Pete Blackwell's friends with *Bono*?"

"And he's totally paranoid! And if we show up at their compound, he'll probably just shoot us! Because we're not rock stars! And they're not our friends!"

"Seriously, though: do you know where their place is? Like, even the town?"

"*No!* And even if I did, we're not going there! Because *I have semis today!*"

"This is so totally fucked up," Max declared as he walked out of the room with the box of Cheerios.

Chloe stared at her father, who shut his eyes and sighed heavily. Then he turned away from her, back to the stove. The water was boiling. He took the lid off the pot, picked up a slotted spoon, and started to lower eggs into the pot from a tray on the counter.

She went to the fridge and searched it for something to drink. Finding nothing except alcoholic beverages—*great job, Mom! nice life*—she selected an apple, then sat down at the kitchen table to eat it as she watched her father stare at the boiling pot of eggs.

He looked so worried that Chloe's own level of concern started to rise dramatically.

"Should I be freaking out? Like, are we not going to be able to *eat*?"

He shook his head. "No. Don't worry. I'm going to do the worrying for us. Okay? You just . . . focus on the tennis and your college stuff. Okay?"

"Okay."

Dad looked back at the eggs.

"Do you have a watch?" he asked.

"No."

"You sure?"

"Dad, I have literally never owned a watch in my life."

He sighed. "Crap."

"What?"

"How am I going to know when the eggs are done?" He hobbled out of the room like he could barely walk. A moment later, Chloe heard him clomping up the stairs.

Sitting alone in the empty kitchen, she watched the blue flame lick the bottom of the pot across the room as she tried to decide how worried she should be.

What the hell is going on, anyway?

Dad had left a notebook open on the table next to her seat. She reached out, pressed her fingers to the page, and slid it close enough to read the single figure he'd written on it:

$36.75

What did *that* mean?

JEN

The yelling downstairs woke her up. Dan and the kids were going at it in the kitchen.

Shit. Ow. Bad night.

Her mouth was parched. Her stomach was queasy. And her headache was both global, in that her entire cranium felt like it was entombed in heavy concrete, and localized, in that a focal point of intense pain was throbbing half an inch behind the bridge of her nose.

It was as if some invisible imp was crouched on her forehead, hammering a masonry nail into her skull.

Floating underneath the physical symptoms, just beyond the perimeter of her consciousness, was a black fog of self-disgust. Its existence indicated that she'd done at least one regrettable thing the previous night, and possibly several. Eventually, she'd remember what they were.

But first, she needed water. Followed by Tylenol, followed by more water, followed by another four hours of sleep.

Jen forced herself up and out of bed. As her head's elevation changed, the concrete slab weighing down her brain gave a dizzying lurch, which triggered a wave of nausea. When the nausea receded, it left behind heartburn. Clenching her paper-dry mouth shut, she plodded to the bathroom and hit the light switch.

Nothing happened.

Then she saw the water in the tub and remembered.

Is it still—

She went to the sink, mentally crossing her fingers as she raised the faucet handle.

Nothing. Not even the hiss of air in the pipes. She began to groan, then stopped when the vibration of her vocal cords aggravated her headache.

The aftertaste in her mouth told her she'd probably puked the night before. She looked over at the toilet. The seat was up. The bowl was nearly empty of water, and there was evidence of regurgitation dotting the sides.

She had a vague memory of kneeling over the porcelain as Dan lectured her.

What was—

Shit. Chloe.

From the miasma of self-loathing, a memory surfaced. The upstairs hallway, unevenly lit by moving flashlights. Bits and pieces of her daughter's face, going in and out of the light as she snarled at Jen.

Oh, Jesus. I'm a terrible mother.

She looked in the mirror. Something akin to a meth addict's mug shot stared back at her.

Her stomach rumbled and puckered.

There was a bottle of Advil on the counter. She took it and the plastic cup that lived on the edge of the sink over to the tub, sank to her knees on the bath mat, filled the cup from the tub, and drank a full glass. Then a second one, which she used to wash down three pills.

When her stomach second-guessed the choice, she pushed herself back up on her feet, went to the medicine cabinet, and got out the big bottle of Tums. As she chewed the antacids, she managed to retrieve a few more blurry mental snapshots of her evening.

Chloe. Dan. Margaritas. Neighbors.

Did I make an ass of myself? Did I insult anybody?

Other than my daughter?

Jesus, I suck.

She trudged back to bed and curled up in the fetal position. She was just beginning to ponder the best way to apologize to Chloe when Dan came in. Jen feigned sleep as she listened to him open and shut his drawers. Then he came over to her side and did the same with her nightstand, just a few inches from her head.

She cracked an eye open at exactly the wrong time. He was staring down at her with a concerned look.

"Hey."

She shut her eyes again. "Hey."

"Do we still have that portable alarm clock?"

"Should be in there somewhere."

She reopened her eyes. He'd found the alarm clock.

"It works! No, wait. . . . It's definitely not four a.m." He shut the drawer where he'd found it and fiddled with the knobs on the back for a bit.

Then he just stood there, staring down at her like the physical embodiment of her conscience.

"Can I talk to you? It's important."

She sat up. The concrete entombing her head lurched again.

"I'm sorry."

"You don't have to apologize to *me*. But Chloe's really upset with you."

Jen started to cry.

"It's okay." Dan consoled her, holding her head gently against his stomach as he stroked her hair.

"I'm such a shit mother."

"You're a great mother. You just fucked up a little. It's okay. Everybody fucks up."

He stopped stroking her hair. For a moment, they were both silent.

"Can I ask you something, though? Serious question?"

Shit. Here it comes.

"Do you think you might . . . have a little bit of a . . . drinking problem?"

She flashed back to the T-shirt she saw once at a tourist trap on the Jersey Shore.

I DON'T HAVE A DRINKING PROBLEM. I DRINK, I GET DRUNK, I FALL DOWN. NO PROBLEM!

Hahahahaha—

"Jen?"

She withdrew her head from his embrace and looked up at him. He didn't seem angry. Just concerned.

What if I tell him the truth?

Do you really want to open that can of worms?

"Let's not get melodramatic. It was a stressful day. I just over-did it."

He nodded. "Okay. Apologize to Chloe, though, will you?"

"Of course!" She covered her face with her hands and massaged her skull.

"Can we talk about today for a second?" He wasn't done yet.

"What about it?"

"I was thinking we should leave. Get on our bikes, head for Wellfleet, or maybe Newton—"

"Are you out of your mind?"

"Maybe. I ran it by the kids and got a lot of pushback. Chloe actually thinks they're still playing the semis today."

"How the hell are they going to get to Rumson?"

"I know! It doesn't make sense. But she doesn't want to hear it from us. So—" He took a deep breath. "My plan is, once I feed the kids breakfast, I'm going to go into town. Try to get some information."

"About what?"

"Whatever's happening. Somebody's got to know by now. While I'm out, I'll look for food, too. Maybe try to get some camping supplies."

"We're going to *camp*?"

"I don't know! I just—we should be prepared. I talked to Judge Distefano last night, he thinks we should leave. And Chloe says yesterday she saw Pete Blackwell's whole family take off on their bikes for their weekend place in Pennsylvania."

"On bikes? That's ridiculous."

"Maybe it is, maybe it isn't. I don't know. I'm going to get some information. Then we'll make a decision. While I'm gone . . . just try to stay on top of things. Think about what we might pack. How we can get more cash. And don't let the kids wander off. Okay?"

"Okay." She appreciated that he had a plan. He always did. It was one of the reasons she'd married him. Dan's constant, neurotic weighing of options and gaming out of alternatives could get irritating day to day. But in a crisis, it was a plus.

"How worried are you?" she asked him. "About this whole situation?"

He thought for a second. "Scale of one to ten?"

"Yeah."

"Eight." Seeing the reaction on her face, he revised his estimate. "No. Seven. And a half." He looked at the little clock in his hand. "I gotta go check on the eggs." He started for the door.

"What eggs?"

"I'm boiling the eggs that were in the fridge."

"The kids hate boiled eggs." So did Jen. Just the thought of them made her want to retch.

"Yeah, but they travel well. And they don't make a mess."

"Dan?"

"Yeah?"

"Thank you."

"For what?"

"Everything. Being on top of all this."

"You're welcome. Just—this probably goes without saying? But don't drink today, okay?"

"Ohmygod, no! Are you kidding?"

"That's what I thought. Hope you're not too hungover."

"Too late for that."

"Well . . ."

"I know. I deserve it."

He shrugged and gave her a sympathetic wince. "You said it, not me."

Then he headed back downstairs, leaving her alone. Jen sank back into the bed—carefully, so as not to antagonize the imaginary imp who was still banging nails into her brainpan—and curled up again.

What am I going to say to Chloe?

How am I going to make it through this day?

MAX

Max sat at his desk chair, the empty Cheerios box lying on its side in front of him. He extracted the last few pieces of cereal from the dust at the bottom of the bag and chewed them angrily while he brooded over how to get more nicotine into his bloodstream.

There were much bigger problems, of course—chief among them society's imminent collapse from an EMP and his family's apparently total inability to handle that shit. But those were so big, and so impossible to solve, that Max couldn't stand to think about them for more than a few seconds at a time. Psychologically, it was much easier to focus on the nicotine situation, because that was at least solvable. And while failure would suck, it wouldn't suck as much as slow death by starvation.

Cigarettes were off his list. Mr. Stankovic's Camel Light had delivered a decent buzz, but at the expense of doing a real number on Max's lungs. He still wheezed every time he took a deep breath. It almost hadn't been worth it, especially now that it was morning and he was jonesing again.

He had one option close at hand: Juul pods. He could crack one open and lick the syrupy juice inside.

The trouble was, that might kill him.

Or maybe not kill him—Max wasn't sure if it was even possible to die of a nicotine overdose. But it could at least make him really sick. He had a vague recollection of learning somewhere that while you could definitely catch a buzz from licking Juul juice, it was crazy stupid to try it.

How stupid, though?

Max had no idea. Questions like these were what the internet was made for. With no internet, he was flying blind.

Fortunately, there was another option, assuming the seventeen bucks he had left over from yesterday's gas station fiasco was enough to cover the purchase: chewing tobacco, or whatever they called it. He'd never tried it before. He wasn't even sure how it worked, although it seemed like it must be pretty self-explanatory.

You just put it in your mouth and chew it. Right? Why else would they call it "chewing tobacco"?

Max decided to return to the gas station. If he couldn't score chewing tobacco there, he could ride his bike over to the public library and try to research how poisonous Juul juice was.

He'd never tried library research, either. But it also seemed self-explanatory. While he was there, he could learn more about EMPs, too. Dad didn't seem to know anything about them. If Max gathered enough information, maybe he could fix their busted electronics.

Maybe I could fix the Juul.

Or the whole power grid.

Maybe I could save the world!

First things first. Get the chewing tobacco.

Having laid his plans, Max decided to use the toilet. He went to the bathroom and locked the door. The window was cracked open to let in a chilly breeze, which told him Chloe must have recently vacated the premises.

The open window wasn't the only evidence of his sister's

presence. A faint whiff of air freshener was still hanging around. And there was no water in the toilet bowl—it was empty except for maybe an inch of cover at the very bottom.

Will a toilet still flush with no water in the bowl?

Max shrugged off the question as he settled onto the seat. That was the next occupant's problem, not his.

DAN

"That's *all* the money we have? Thirty-six dollars?"

"Sweetheart, there's no reason to panic. We're going to be fine," Dan told his daughter through a mouthful of boiled egg. "How's your egg? Is it done enough for you?"

Chloe picked apart her own egg with evident distaste. "I guess? These things are so gross."

"I love them with salt and pepper," Dan chirped. "They're good with hot sauce, too. You want some Tabasco?"

His daughter refused to be distracted by culinary issues. "Dad, seriously—how are we going to eat if we don't have enough money to buy food?"

"Sweetheart, we have *plenty* of money. Your mother and I have been very conservative, we have a lot of resources—"

"Then why did you write down 'thirty-six dollars' in your notebook?"

"You're not supposed to be reading that!"

"But why did you?"

"Because we're a little . . . light on cash." He took off his glasses and rubbed the lenses with the bottom of his shirt. "But it's not going to be an issue. I'm sure this will all be over soon."

His daughter stared at him in disbelief as he got up from the table, bent his leg like a flamingo, and began to stretch out his quadriceps while leaning against the countertop.

"A minute ago, you wanted to go beg the Blackwells to let us in their bunker! Or ride our bikes to Grandma's!"

"I was overreacting. And I apologize. When my blood sugar's low, I get irrational. The situation's not that drastic." He switched legs. "I'm going to go out in a few minutes and get us some answers. By the end of the day, we'll know a lot more."

"And what happens if we find out we're totally screwed?"

"Chloe, I *promise* you this is all temporary. You've got nothing to worry about except your tennis. And your Dartmouth app."

"And my ACT. And all my classes."

"Right. That's more than enough." He limped over and put a fatherly hand on her shoulder. "Okay? You've got a lot on your plate. Just focus on that and let me and your mother handle everything else. Okay?"

"Okay."

He gave the top of her head a kiss. "And beat the shit out of Rumson."

"I will. My backhand was fire yesterday."

"That's my poet warrior talking! Go get 'em!"

Dan hobbled out of the kitchen, silently congratulating himself on his acting job. He'd managed to convey an aura of confidence and optimism to his daughter despite the quivery sensation of dread in his gut that had been threatening to metastasize into a full-blown panic attack ever since he'd heard the news of the Blackwell family's departure.

Pete Blackwell wasn't just handsome, rich, and charming. He was also smart. And for the past fifteen minutes, Dan had been stewing over a memory he had of Pete on the sidelines at a peewee soccer game, offering investment advice to another dad in the wake of the 2008 financial crisis.

"The biggest mistake a lot of guys make," Pete had told the man, "is waffling. They can't decide whether or not to close out a position, so they don't do anything. And they think they're just postponing the decision—but doing nothing *is* the decision. It's like they're standing in the middle of the road with a truck coming at them, and they can't decide whether to jump left or right. So they just keep standing there. And they get hit."

Standing on the shoulder of the turnpike yesterday, Dan had watched Pete Blackwell make a decision—to get the hell out of town as fast as possible. Pete had seen a truck coming, and he'd jumped out of the way.

This morning, Dan had gotten out of bed intending to jump, too.

But his family wouldn't jump with him. Worse, they'd made him second-guess whether jumping was even the right choice. Now the four of them were standing in the middle of the road, hoping there wasn't a truck coming.

As Dan headed to the den in the probably vain hope of finding some piece of correspondence from Chase Bank that would help him prove they were holding his money, he tried to shake the metaphor from his mind.

Maybe there wasn't any truck. Maybe he was just being neurotic.

But the quiver in his stomach told him otherwise.

CHLOE

Right up until her father told her she had no reason to panic, Chloe hadn't seriously contemplated panicking.

The power outage was definitely annoying, and more than a little creepy. But truly scary, let alone life-altering? No way.

It just wasn't possible. She had too much going on.

Then Dad's transparent bullshitting, coupled with his head-spinning switch from let's-run-to-the-hills paranoia to don't-worry-your-pretty-little-head-about-it reassurance, set off major alarm bells. In a matter of minutes, the focus of her attention shifted from her carefully planned ACT-prep-then-Josh-then-tennis schedule to the much more chaotic, open-ended, and frankly petrifying question of how to survive a zombie apocalypse.

Or whatever the hell this was.

The first casualty was her appetite. It took an act of will to force down three hard-boiled eggs, which she only ate out of recognition that she might need the protein for tennis.

Like there's still going to be tennis in a zombie apocalypse.

Focus, Frenchie!

Remember what Coach K said. Act as if. Nobody's canceled anything yet.

She was finishing the last of her eggs when Dad limped past her on his way to the garage. "You okay?" he asked her in a tender voice.

"Fine."

Not fine! Freaking out here!

"Great! Love you! Beat the shit out of Rumson!"

"Okay!"

Good luck fighting the zombie apocalypse!

Then she went upstairs to her bedroom and quickly discovered that taking a practice math ACT test was next to impossible in her current state of mind.

"Antonio mowed 7 lawns and was paid $15 for each one. With the money he earned, he bought three graphic novels for $12 each —"

WHY DID I SPEND SEVENTEEN BUCKS ON THAT STUPID MOVIE SATURDAY NIGHT?

AND WHY DID I BUY EIGHT-DOLLAR POPCORN?

If I'd stayed home, I'd have a lot more than four dollars in my wallet right now.

I should tell Dad about the four dollars. We might need it.

Ohmygod. This is ridiculous.

FOCUS!

"Kanisha left her house at 8:00 a.m. on a Wednesday and traveled 527 miles—"

—to a place where the cars and phones still worked and she wasn't about to be eaten by zombies.

SHIT! FOCUS!

Then Mom walked in, looking like she'd spent the night in a ditch, and made everything a hundred times worse.

"Chloe? Can I—"

"I'm taking a practice test!"

"Can you just pause for a second and—"

"It's a timed test! *Get out of here!*"

Mom looked around for evidence of a functioning clock and saw none. "How are you timing it?"

"In my head! Leave me alone!"

"I just wanted to say I'm sorry."

"Okay! You said it! *Get out!*"

Chloe glared at her mom, but she wouldn't leave. She just stood there, looking like she might cry.

"I know you're upset. And you have a right to be—"

"*I don't have time for this!* Please leave!"

Mom's jaw tightened. For a moment, it seemed like she was gearing up to fight back. But then she hung her head and turned away.

"I'm sorry." She walked out.

"*Close the door!*"

Her mom closed the door behind her.

Chloe went back to the practice test.

"*In the standard (x,y) coordinate plane, a point at (−3, 4) is translated—*"

What if there IS no ACT?

Ever?

What if this is like The Walking Dead*?*

Nobody takes ACT tests on The Walking Dead. *They're too busy trying not to die.*

Three questions later, she gave up, put down her pencil, and let her mind spin out the various scenarios.

One thing became instantly clear.

If this is the zombie apocalypse, there's no fucking way I'm spending it with my mother.

Is it too early to go to Josh's?

If it is, I'll go to Emma's.

Either way, I've got to get out of here.

She stood up and headed for the bathroom to make herself presentable.

Halfway down the hall, she got her first whiff of the stink. When she entered the room, the smell was so pungent she had to cover her face with her hand.

The apocalypse had already arrived. It was sitting in the toilet bowl.

JEN

Jen slouched at the kitchen table, still dazed from the emotional beating her daughter had just administered. As she tried to neutralize her sour stomach with the stale remains of the pita chips, she surveyed their emergency supplies.

How long will this stuff have to last us? A week?

Forever?

How are we going to eat the peanut butter?

Why didn't you buy jelly to go with it? Or Nutella? Or anything?

You fucking idiot.

She looked around the room, taking in the dry faucet . . . the cold oven . . . the room-temperature fridge . . .

Nothing works.

NOTHING WORKS. No water, no power, no phones, no cars.

No money.

You should've gone to the bank Monday. And the store.

But you just stayed home and drank.

You fucking idiot. You fucked your whole family.

Think your daughter hates you now? Wait till she finds out she's going to go hungry and it's all your fault.

You fucking idiot.

Then she heard Chloe's scream, coming from the upstairs bathroom.

Oh, Jesus. Now what?

Dizzy, queasy, and almost catatonic with self-loathing, Jen

pushed herself to her feet and trudged off to find out what else had just gone to hell.

Chloe was banging on Max's bedroom door and screaming, *"Clean it up!"*

"Clean what up?" Jen hardly needed to ask—the bathroom door was closed, but the stink had been discernible from half-way up the stairs. As she approached, she covered her nose and mouth with her hand and swallowed hard against the stomach acid creeping up her esophagus.

Her daughter's face was twisted with revulsion, but at least it wasn't directed at Jen. "He took a dump in an empty toilet! It won't flush! It's just sitting in there!" Chloe turned back to Max's bedroom door and smacked it with an open palm. *"Clean it up!"*

"Leave me alone!" Max yelled from the other side of the door.

"Can't we just get a bucket of water and flush it out?" Jen asked.

"From where?"

"The tub in our room—"

"Dad said we have to save that! We're going to run out!"

A feeling of overwhelm began to rise from deep in Jen's gut. She pushed it down as best she could, trying to think of something useful to say.

"Can you just avoid the bathroom?"

"All my makeup's in there!"

"Why do you need makeup?"

Chloe's face underwent a rapid transformation from fury to chagrin.

"I'm . . . going out."

"To do what?"

"I'm meeting somebody."

A whole series of questions cascaded through Jen's mind.

Meeting who? Where?

At a nightclub?

I thought you were doing ACT prep!

What about tennis?

And your Dartmouth supplemental?

Jen was searching for a way to express her concern about Chloe's time management that was tactful enough not to trigger an explosion when her daughter exploded again anyway.

"*Ohmygod* it *stinks!*" She kicked Max's door so hard that the wall shook. "*Clean it up!*" she screamed one last time before retreating to her bedroom and slamming the door.

Against her better judgment, Jen went to the bathroom to investigate. Inside, the full horror of the situation quickly revealed itself. Back in the hallway a split second later, with the bathroom door shut firmly behind her, it took all the self-will she could muster not to throw up.

Something had to be done.

Jen went to Max's door and knocked twice, then tried the handle. As she expected, it was locked.

"Max? Can you please open this?"

A moment later, Max opened the door. "I had to go! And it's not fair! You know why there's no water in the bowl? 'Cause she took a dump before I did!"

"Will you just help me clean it up?" The thought of doing so threatened to make Jen heave up the pita chips.

Max was no more enthusiastic than she was. "Clean it up how? Where's it going to go if it's not the toilet?"

He had a point, the implications of which were obvious. This wasn't a one-off problem. Until the water came back, they couldn't flush any of the toilets.

What are we going to do?

Dig a hole in the backyard?

It was all too much. Jen retreated to her bedroom, collapsed onto the bed, and sobbed.

No toilets. No water. No nothing.

I can't take this. I can't even take a shower.

I can't fix the water. I can't fix the money. I can't fix my daughter.

I can't.

I can't.

I can't

I

can

have a drink.

Like a sleepwalker stepping off a ledge, she stood up and glided out of the room.

Inside the downstairs bathroom, she locked the door behind her and opened the medicine cabinet. In the dim light, the rubbing alcohol bottle was just visible between the hydrogen peroxide and the Band-Aids. It was full.

Jen pulled it out. Uncapped it and sniffed the clear, astringent liquid.

Definitely vodka.

Right? I didn't dream that?

She took a swig. Her stomach rebelled, bucking against the liquor like a horse that wasn't broken to the saddle.

Teeth sweating, she clamped her jaw shut and rode it out.

As her digestive system slowly submitted to her will, the corrosive stew of fear and self-hatred she'd been marinating in since she woke up began to lose its bite, diluted by the warm sensation of well-being radiating from her gut.

She was debating whether to take a second drink when she heard Max bounding down the stairs. He passed the bathroom door on his way to the garage.

"Max?"

No answer. The door to the garage opened, then slammed shut.

She capped the bottle, returned it to the cabinet, and followed him.

By the time she entered the garage, he was most of the way to Willis Road on his bike. Dazzle was at the farthest corner of her shock-collar perimeter, barking disapproval at the top of her lungs.

"Max!"

He didn't even turn his head. Dazzle did, but only for a moment. Then she went right back to hectoring Max as he turned and disappeared down the hill.

That fucking dog.

We're going to die of starvation, and the last sound we hear will be that fucking dog.

Having barked away the threat from Max, Dazzle turned her attention to Jen, standing at the threshold of the open garage. The dog trotted to the near end of her invisible fence, issuing warning barks as she approached.

Jen felt an odd compulsion to bark back.

How long before she realizes there's no fence anymore?

I should drown her in their pool.

Holy shit, the pool.

Two minutes later, Dazzle was backing away from Jen, her barks growing desperate and frightened at the presence of this human with the audacity to drag a massive plastic garbage bin on wheels into her backyard with one hand while wielding a bucket in the other.

Jen knocked on the sliding glass door. A moment later, Kayla opened it, her eyes a pair of slits under a backward Yankees cap.

"Shaddup, Dazzle!" she growled as the dog fled inside. "Ohmygawd, Jen, what did you do to me last night?"

Jen managed a smile. Her own hangover was submerging beneath a not-at-all-unpleasant vodka buzz. "Don't do the crime if you can't do the time. Can I borrow some pool water?"

Kayla eyed the wheeled bin with equal parts confusion and suspicion. "How much do you need?"

"Enough to flush our toilets until this is over."

"Yeah, I guess so."

Jen wheeled the bin over to the edge of the pool and began to bail water into it with the bucket, trying to bend only at the knees so as not to aggravate her nausea.

Kayla dragged over a patio chair and sat down to keep her company.

"So whaddaya do, fill up the tank with that?"

"No—you just pour it straight in the bowl."

"Huh." Kayla pondered this, then shook her head. "I don't think that'd work for us. We got really high-end toilets."

"A toilet's a toilet—you dump enough water in, it'll flush."

"How?"

"Gravity."

Kayla dropped the subject and leaned forward, hugging her chest with a frown. "Jen, can I tell you something?"

Her tone of voice put Jen on guard. "Sure," she said, praying she wasn't about to become privy to confidential information about Kayla and Eddie's marriage.

"I'm really scared."

"About what?"

"This whole thing. Like . . . what even *is* it?"

The bin was as full as Jen figured she could manage given the return trip across the lawn. She stopped bailing and turned to look at her diminutive neighbor.

Kayla was hunched over her knees, peering up at Jen with a plaintive, needy look.

Too needy. Half drunk, half hungover, and with a laundry list of urgent tasks starting to write itself in her head, Jen had way too much on her plate to indulge her neighbor's potentially bottomless need for emotional support.

Instead of commiserating, she just smiled. "We're going to be fine!"

"Really?"

"Yeah! Couple of days, this will all be back to normal."

"You're not freaking out?"

"Little bit. Not much. It'll be fine. Look at all the pool water you got! Don't worry, babe." Jen started to wheel the bin back toward her house, then paused out of guilt. Kayla looked like she was on the verge of tears.

"But if you're really feeling bad—"

"Yeah?"

"Take a Xanax."

Kayla's face fell. "I already did."

"Oh. Well, maybe take two. Thanks for the water!"

There were several close calls owing to the terrain and her impaired motor function, but Jen eventually maneuvered the garbage bin full of water across the lawn without losing more than a gallon or two.

She parked the bin inside the garage, then drew a bucket and took it upstairs. Back in the kids' bathroom, she dumped the water into the toilet bowl as fast as possible without triggering a backsplash, then watched with satisfaction as the rapid accretion of water pressure activated the flush.

Then she strode down the hall and knocked on Chloe's door. When her daughter answered, Jen smiled at her.

"Fixed!"

"Thank you."

"There's a garbage bin of water in the garage." Jen held up the empty bucket. "I'll leave this next to it. From now on, if you need to flush, take half a bucket and dump it in the bowl. Okay?"

"Okay." Chloe's look had softened almost to the point of being friendly. Jen decided to take a second run at an apology.

"Honey, I'm really sorry about last night—"

"I know—"

"I was overserved, and I shouldn't have gotten into it with you—"

"It's fine, Mom."

"And I'm even more sorry for that comment on the essay—"

"It's *fine*!" Chloe kept talking over her, trying to shut down the apology.

"It was a shitty thing to write. I was just trying to help. But I know it came off mean, and—"

"I get it! It's totally fine!"

"But it's not—"

"It's okay! Seriously! Apology accepted."

"You sure?"

"Yes!"

"Okay. I love you!"

"I love you, too."

"So . . . where are you going today?"

"Just over to Emma's. Then tennis."

"Okay. Good luck! Beat the shit out of Rumson."

"I will."

"I love you!"

"Love you, too."

Chloe shut the door. As Jen walked back down the hall to the stairs, she allowed herself a smile. That had gone surprisingly well.

Now it was time to kick ass. Solving the toilet-flushing problem was just the beginning. Jen was determined to spend the day making up for all of her prior negligence.

What's next?

Drinking water.

A plan was forming in her head for securing more of that. It was a little intricate, but she was confident she could pull it off.

Once the drinking water situation was locked down, she'd get to work on the food and the finances. Then she'd figure out how to get everybody showers.

Whatever was happening—*terror attack? alien invasion? power outage on steroids?*—Jen wasn't going to let it beat her. She'd carry the whole family through this crisis, all while making sure Chloe's Dartmouth app didn't get derailed.

She'd quit drinking, too.

Just not quite yet.

DAN

A house was on fire.

It was a big, rambling Victorian at the intersection of Crawford and Harris a few blocks south of Fairmont Avenue. Smoke was pouring out of the upstairs windows. From one of them, an angry tongue of orange flame kept darting out in irregular bursts, licking the exterior siding all the way to the roof.

His fingers cold and stiff on the handlebars in the chilly autumn air, Dan biked down Crawford toward the blaze with the vague idea that he might be able to help somehow, even as the thought was met with a memory of Pete Blackwell's gently mocking invocation of Monty Python as they fled yesterday's plane crash.

What are you going to do, bleed on it?

In any event, there were already more than enough hands available. Upward of twenty people were standing on the street and surrounding lawns, watching the conflagration with varying degrees of emotion. On the sidewalk, two older women were comforting a third as she wept. Beside them, three men stood in a half circle, observing the woman's grief with solemn concern.

Dan pulled up next to a beefy-looking guy in a red fleece, straddling a mountain bike at the edge of the scene.

"Should somebody go tell the fire department?" Dan asked.

"They're already here." Red Fleece pointed to two men about ten yards away, dressed in navy jackets with LINCOLNWOOD FD emblazoned across the back. They were standing there watching the house burn like everybody else.

"Isn't there something they can do?"

Red Fleece gave a mirthless snort. "Yeah—pray it doesn't spread."

They watched the blaze in silence for a moment.

"Do you, uh, know what's going on?" Dan asked.

"Shit's falling apart is what's going on."

"Yeah, but . . . why? What happened?"

Red Fleece shook his head. "Gotta be the Chinese. We're the big kids on the block. They had to take us out. So they Pearl Harbored us."

As Dan mulled over the theory's geopolitical implications, Red Fleece reached down and picked up a brown paper Whole Foods bag that Dan hadn't noticed sitting by the man's right foot. Two boxes of organic cereal were poking up over the top.

Dan stared at the bounty in hopeful disbelief. "Is the Whole Foods open?"

And will they take a check?

Red Fleece chuckled as he hung the bag from a handlebar. "Depends on what you mean by 'open.'" Then he rose up on the balls of his feet, eased himself onto his bike seat, and offered Dan some friendly advice as he pedaled away:

"Better get there before the cops do!"

Dan was a block away from the house fire, moving at a rapid clip in the direction of the Whole Foods on Fairmont, when it occurred to him that the moral implications of the moment required some interrogation.

Are people actually robbing the Whole Foods?

Am I going to rob the Whole Foods?

It was a discomfiting thought. In his entire adult life, Dan had never consciously violated a law more serious than speeding.

Then again, he'd never found himself in a situation remotely like this one. Things were getting serious. And while he owed a debt of obedience to civil society, he had an equally compelling obligation to feed his family.

As he turned up Fairmont, two blocks from the grocery store, he resolved to keep an open mind, consistent with his moral compass.

I'm not going to loot. I'm just going to look.

As he approached the Whole Foods building, he passed a man he knew vaguely—Scott Something, the father of one of Max's classmates. He was moving down the sidewalk at a half trot, weighed down by two of the large reusable vinyl bags that Whole Foods sold to their eco-conscious customers. Both bags were swollen with groceries.

"Hey—" Dan called to him, in a tone of voice that said, *Let's stop and talk!*

Scott didn't answer, or even make eye contact. Instead, he quickened his pace while willing himself into invisibility, like a guy leaving a porno store.

When Dan reached the Whole Foods parking lot, there were four men and a woman milling around the entrance while making a similarly concerted effort not to see each other. They were all white, a few years to one side or another of middle-aged, and clad in the preppy casualwear that was the unofficial weekend uniform of Lincolnwood residents.

Dan rode into the parking lot and executed a lazy arc that left him a discreet distance away from the group at the entrance. Then he dismounted and watched them.

All five were focusing their attention on the open hole left by a shattered pane on the bottom half of one of the two entrance doors. Shards of glass littered the concrete all around it.

To Dan's surprise, a brown paper grocery bag emerged from the hole, attached to a man's arm. After the man set the bag down atop the broken glass to one side of the door, the rest of his body followed in a labored crab-walk.

Once he cleared the hole, he pivoted, reached back inside, and pulled out a second bag.

Then he straightened up and race-walked away from the entrance with both bags, studiously ignoring the little cluster of people as he passed them.

As soon as he was out of the way, one of the waiting men stepped forward, crouched down on his haunches, and ducked inside.

A moment after he disappeared, another bag-laden arm materialized, and a second man exited. Once that guy was gone, the woman whose turn was next—for all their efforts not to acknowledge each other, the little cluster of people seemed to share a clear understanding of who was next in line—stepped forward and began to crouch down. But after getting a look inside, she backed off in a clumsy stagger. A second later, the reason why became apparent—someone else was exiting.

It was a thirtyish woman, and she was juggling three bags. The group unanimously glared at her, and Dan wondered what protocol she'd violated.

Are three bags too many? Was she supposed to alternate entrances and exits?

Whatever the rule, it was unspoken. Nobody was talking, or even acknowledging each other's presence.

By now, the little group had increased by three new arrivals, all of whom quickly sussed out the situation and joined the line. As he watched it grow, Dan debated with himself over whether to walk over and join it. On the one hand, there was no question this was criminal behavior. Just entering the store under these circumstances was indictable under the New Jersey burglary statute.

If I go inside, and the cops show up, I'll be trapped.

On the other hand . . .

Are the cops really going to show up? This town can't even put out a fire right now.

And if I wait too long, all the good stuff will be gone.

Pete Blackwell's warning about the dangers of waffling echoed in Dan's head.

Doing nothing is a decision.

Just standing here is a decision.

The clock's ticking. What are you going to—

"Hey!"

The voice startled Dan so much that he almost dropped his bike.

"Sorry to scare you. Dan, right?" It was one of the dads from Chloe's old youth soccer team. He'd walked up from the back of the parking lot.

"Yeah. Mike?"

"Yep!"

"Right! Simpson Thacher. M and A." They'd bonded on the

sidelines one Saturday morning years back over their mutual dissatisfaction with corporate law. "How's it going?"

"Not bad. I hear you're writing for TV now?"

Dan nodded. "Yeah. *Bullet Town: NYC.* Police procedural on CBS."

"That's fantastic!"

"Yeah, it's a good gig."

"I can imagine. Seriously jealous."

"Well, I got lucky. Right place at the right time."

"Good for you, man. That's awesome! You know, I've thought about writing for TV sometimes."

Oh, Jesus Christ.

"Really?"

"Yeah. It's always been kind of a . . . glimmer in the back of my mind. Got a couple ideas I've been kicking around. Can we grab coffee sometime? Or let me buy you a drink, pick your brain about how you made the transition?"

Ugh. Not another one of these.

"Sure. Maybe after all this is—" Dan gestured vaguely with his hand.

"Yeah. I mean, obviously." Mike stared at the crowd waiting in front of the door. It had now swollen to ten people. "So, what do you think is going on?"

Dan nodded toward the group. "You mean this specifically?"

"No, this is pretty self-explanatory. I mean in general."

"Oh. . . . Honestly? I have no clue. I was about to ask you the same thing."

Mike shook his head as he exhaled. "I'm stumped, too. I

mean, I assume it's some kind of terrorism? Or maybe the Russians? But I don't—"

He was interrupted in midsentence by an earsplitting crash, followed by the tinkle of shattered glass hitting concrete.

One of the new arrivals had taken it upon himself to ease the bottleneck at the entrance by ramming a shopping cart into the still-intact door on the left.

Not all of the glass fell away from the steel pane on the first impact, so he rammed the door three more times to clear enough space for a second point of entry. As each blow echoed across the parking lot, the would-be looters winced and looked around nervously. Discretion was clearly one of their unspoken protocols, and this was anything but discreet.

"That was bold," Dan commented.

"I know, right?"

They were silent for a moment, watching as the group reconstituted itself to take advantage of the expanded access. One of the men in line was bouncing on his feet with urgency.

Mike put a comradely hand on Dan's upper back. "Good to see you! Let's get that coffee soon."

"Absolutely."

"You have a card?"

"Uhh . . . sure." Dan pulled out his wallet and produced a business card. Mike did the same, swapping with him.

"Great! I'll shoot you an email once, y'know—"

"There's email again?"

"Yeah."

"Super. Looking forward to it!" *Please don't email me.*

"Me too! Take it easy!"

Dan watched as Mike sauntered off to join the group at the front door.

Two more looters emerged and trotted away, weighed down with bags of food. The group seemed to have settled on a right-of-way in which the left hole was used for exits and the right for entrances. Traffic was brisk, and word seemed to be spreading—new people were arriving in the parking lot almost by the second.

If I don't get in there soon, there won't be anything left.

Doing nothing is a decision.

Having recently learned the perils of leaving his bike unprotected, Dan trotted it over to the fence at the edge of the parking lot and secured it with a U-lock while trying to ignore the butterflies in his stomach.

Then, careful not to make eye contact with Mike or anyone else—especially the couple from his synagogue who'd just arrived—Dan joined the growing crowd at the door.

Not to loot. Just to look.

MAX

The foliage surrounding the duck pond in Memorial Park was just past its peak, and there was nobody in sight except a distant pair of moms pushing strollers. Max leaned his bike against the side of a bench facing the pond, then sat down to try to figure out how to open the can of Skoal that had cost him ten of his last seventeen dollars.

The guy at the gas station had originally asked for twenty. He was definitely price-gouging. But Max had outmaneuvered him by claiming all he had was a ten.

At first inspection, the little green-and-silver hockey puck was as inscrutable as a novelty box from a magic store. Other than the raised *SKOAL* lettering on top, its surfaces were all perfectly smooth, giving no hint as to how it might open.

Max spent a couple of minutes turning it over in his hands with increasing frustration, until his fingernail accidentally punctured a seam just above the WARNING: THIS PRODUCT IS NOT A SAFE ALTERNATIVE TO CIGARETTES label. Following the seam with his nail, he managed to tear a slit through the entire circumference of the packaging.

He pried off the lid. What he found inside looked like almost literal shit—tiny shredded flecks of moist tobacco that gave off a dank, slightly minty smell. He probed it with his thumb, and when he withdrew it, little bits of the stuff clung to the pad. He tried to flick them away, but they didn't flick very well.

This was going to be messy.

Max grabbed a loose pinch between his thumb and forefinger and held it up.

Where does it go? On my tongue?

The thought of putting it in his mouth was not appealing.

He returned the pinch to the tin and tried in vain to flick the stray bits from his fingers as he reconsidered his plan.

Maybe I should smoke it instead.

No, that's dumb.

The whole reason he'd bought it was because smoking sucked. Plus, the stuff was probably too damp to catch fire.

He picked up another pinch and examined it.

Why aren't the pieces bigger? Did I get the wrong stuff?

There was no way the gas station guy would let him return it. And he didn't have the money to buy anything else. Lacking any better option, he put the pinch in his mouth.

Eeegh. It's so loose!

Where does it go?

He used his tongue to push it down past his front teeth, against his lower lip. Somehow, it fit there. Then the saliva began to flow.

So much saliva.

Oh God. TOO much.

Max leaned over and tried to spit onto the grass, past the edge of the concrete slab where the bench was anchored. But the plug of dip, wedged in front of his lower teeth, was pushing his lip out so far that it messed up his spit mechanics.

So instead of spitting, he drooled.

"Hey, uhhh . . . ?"

It was a girl's voice, coming from behind him. Max managed to disconnect the rope of brown spit from his lip, and it fell onto the concrete with a soft *spuck*. Then he turned his head to the voice.

Kayleigh Adams was looking down at him, like a vision straight from his fantasies. What must've been her little sister, a younger and less hot version of Kayleigh, stood beside her. They were both holding buckets. Kayleigh gestured with hers.

"Sorry to bother you. Do you know if it's okay to take water out of this pond?"

Max didn't know the answer. And even if he did, the quantity of saliva flooding his mouth would've made a reply impossible.

The silence quickly became awkward for everybody.

"Like . . . do you think we'd get in trouble if we just filled these buckets?"

Answer her!

He swallowed his mouthful of tobacco spit.

"I think *hhrrgh*—" His reply ended in midsentence when his suddenly burning throat demanded that he cough and he refused, because his mouth was already refilling with spit, and he didn't want to spray it all over Kayleigh.

Max clamped his teeth shut and suppressed the cough with a guttural, wet, inhuman-sounding gargle.

Kayleigh's eyes widened in alarm. "Are you okay?"

WHERE'S ALL THIS SPIT COMING FROM?

It was a deluge in his mouth. He swallowed again. Then, to stop his salivary glands from making more spit, he swept the plug of tobacco out with his tongue and swallowed that, too.

"I'm fine! I just—"

His stomach registered a highly negative opinion of the situation. Max tried to ignore it, but it was impossible to disregard all the saliva that was still flowing into his mouth. He swallowed yet again and gestured at the pond, finally managing to produce an answer.

"I think it's fine. Taking the water. There's plenty."

Kayleigh nodded. "Cool. Yeah. We just don't want to get in trouble."

"Yeah. Totally."

"You're Mark, right? From gym class?"

"Max."

Something very, very bad was happening in his stomach.

"Right! Sorry. I'm Kayleigh." She smiled.

It was the greatest smile in the history of smiles.

His belly convulsed.

"Cool," he managed to say.

"C'mon, Kayleigh," her sister muttered impatiently.

"Well, thanks for your help, Max—"

"Yerghh—" His reply was interrupted when his stomach, which had just contracted into a tightly balled fist, suddenly exploded straight up his throat.

He made it half a step toward the nearest bushes before he vomited all over the lawn.

CHLOE

It took Chloe a lot longer to leave the house than she'd planned, because it turned out to be fiendishly difficult to pack. There were just too many contingencies: she might or might not be playing in the semis in the afternoon, she might or might not be mashing with Josh in the morning, and she might or might not be coming home at the end of the day.

Or ever.

Granted, abandoning the Altman household forever was unlikely in the short term. But anything seemed possible, and she wanted to be prepared for even the long shots, especially when the alternative—being stuck with her family for the duration of the zombie apocalypse—was too terrible to contemplate. If push came to shove, she'd be much better off taking her chances with Josh's family, even though she'd never actually met them; or Emma's, despite the fact that Emma's mom could be every bit as batshit crazy as Chloe's.

So on top of being mindful not to take more stuff than she could carry on her bike, she had to pack with tennis, sex, and eternity in mind—and there wasn't a lot of overlap in that Venn diagram. It took her five minutes just to settle on the most appropriate underwear.

When she finally finished stuffing spare clothes into her backpack and returned to the bathroom to brush her teeth and apply a tasteful amount of makeup, she made a perplexing discovery: the shower curtain had been removed from the tub. She mulled over why that might be all through her final preparations for departure, including the liberation of four of the remaining five protein bars from the kitchen, but the answer eluded her until she exited into the garage.

The shower curtain was spread out on the concrete across most of the empty space where her dad's Lexus was usually parked. Mom was kneeling by the top edge of the curtain, duct-taping what looked like a rain poncho to it.

"What the hell?"

Her mother sprang up, quickly and a little unsteadily, and gave Chloe an overly cheerful smile.

"Hey! How you doing?"

"Fine. What's going on here?"

"Making a rain catcher. It's going to pour tomorrow. And when it does—I'm going to capture the rainwater! I'm creating a tarp here, and then I'm going to hang it up on stakes in the backyard and funnel it into a catch trap."

"That's great, Mom."

You're out of your mind.

"Right? I'm going to get us through this, babe."

Is that your drunk voice? Are you wasted? Already?

Chloe didn't want to know the answer to that question. She went to her bike and slung her racket bag over her shoulder, where it fell awkwardly against her full backpack.

"What are you, running away from home?"

"Just going to Emma's before I have to leave for the semi."

Mom nodded, making a show of looking supportive. "Good luck! I'll be rooting for you. Want me to try to come watch the match?"

"No! It's too complicated. Just—can you move that shower curtain so I can get my bike out?"

"Sure!"

Chloe waited as her mom doubled over the plastic sheet so there was room to wheel the bike out to the driveway.

"Sweetie?"

Ugh. That's definitely your drunk voice.

"Yeah?"

"I really am sorry—"

"It's fine!"

"About everything. I love you *so* much—"

"I know. I love you, too."

The way her mom smiled at her might've been touching if she was sober. Instead, all Chloe felt was disgust.

"Have a great day! Beat the shit out of Rumson!"

"I will! Good luck with your . . . shower curtain thing."

"It's going to be awesome! Pure, delicious rainwater!"

"Sounds great!"

"Bye, sweetie!"

"Bye!"

Nice life, Mom. So pathetic.

JEN

Jen smiled with satisfaction as she watched Chloe pedal off under the weight of too many bags. She was sure her daughter didn't need to bring half that stuff, and equally sure Chloe shouldn't be running off to Emma's with the ACT in three days and a Dartmouth supplement that still needed revising.

But Jen had kept her opinions to herself, and as a result, they'd had a nice little mother-daughter moment. Not for the first time, she marveled at the efficacy of just a smidge of vodka in creating a mental buffer between stimulus and response. It was better than mindfulness meditation.

Even so, it had to stop.

Today was her third morning in a row of day drinking. While justifiable under the circumstances—this was, after all, an emergency—it was also unsustainable, and the time had come to say goodbye for good.

Jen absolutely, positively had to quit drinking.

Which was what made this whole situation so perfect. The epiphany had come to her just minutes earlier, as she'd pulled the first length of duct tape from the roll to begin fusing together the pieces of her rainwater collection apparatus.

No alcohol, no problem.

It was that simple. If things really were going to hell—if the Altmans were truly facing some all-encompassing crisis of indeterminate length, with just forty bucks and their supplies on hand to get themselves through it—then once Jen ran out of whatever booze was in the house, it'd be impossible to get more.

Not only that, but her drinking obsession—which, when she really thought about it, was as much a product of boredom and the lack of productive uses for her time as anything else—would inevitably fade away in the face of multiple, urgent problems that she'd need all her wits and energy to tackle.

All Jen had to do was put herself on a glide path, slowly tapering her consumption as she transitioned to full-time ass-kicking survival mode. By the time the last bottles in the liquor cabinet were gone, she'd be too deep in the daily struggle to even notice.

Ironically, this . . . whatever it was . . . could turn out to be the best thing that had ever happened to her.

No alcohol, no problem!

It solved itself.

And every drink she took brought her that much closer to the solution.

Jen finished taping the first rain poncho to the shower curtain, then went inside to fetch the emergency vodka bottle.

DAN

Once Dan joined the line of would-be Whole Foods looters, it moved all too quickly. He'd only just started to construct a mental shopping list of his most high-priority items—*protein bars, nuts, multivitamins*—when Mike from Simpson Thacher squatted down and waddled through the broken doorway, followed by an older woman in a purple L.L.Bean anorak who lost her balance and almost pitched over onto the broken glass when she tried to copy Mike's technique.

After she recovered and disappeared inside, it was Dan's turn.

When he went into a crouch, his sore thigh muscles complained so mightily that he nearly fell backward on his butt. Feeling a surge of empathy for the woman who'd just preceded him, he somehow managed to contort himself through the hole and into the store, only to discover he had to do it all over again to get through the interior doorway.

After crawling through the underside of a second broken door, he emerged into the produce department.

It was darker inside than he'd expected, and he failed to see the avocados rolling around on the floor until one nearly took him out. There were dozens of them, some ripe enough that they'd been crushed into a slick mash on the floor by prior looters. Together, they posed such a formidable obstacle that Dan decided to forgo the produce section entirely, turning left down the aisle toward the cash registers. He needed to go in that direction first anyway, to get bags.

But thanks to the seasonal floral arrangements, it was a narrow route, clogged with its own treacherous minefield of locally sourced apples. Dan shuffled his feet like a cross-country skier, plowing through the Honeycrisps and past the coffee counter to the first cashier's station.

It had already been stripped of its paper bags. As Dan proceeded to the second station, a woman turned the corner of the checkout line and nearly bowled him over in her haste to get to the exit. The bag she was carrying smacked him in the shin. It must've been full of canned goods, because it hurt like hell.

"Watch it!" the woman hissed at him, like it was his fault. His instinct was to hiss back at her, but he suppressed it.

The floor around the second cashier's station was strewn with bags. He picked up two and turned down the narrow aisle, only to get body-checked again by another exiting looter. This one outweighed him by about a hundred pounds and was moving with all the deference of an NFL lineman blocking on a third and short.

"Jesus!" Dan muttered as the guy practically knocked him over.

"Fuck you," the guy barked over his shoulder.

It was clear that the politesse everyone had been observing out in the parking lot was no longer operative in the semidarkness inside. Dan squared his shoulders and marched into the deepening gloom beyond the registers, determined not to give any more ground.

Almost immediately, he ran into a portable freezer that whacked him at mid-thigh.

Ow! Shit!

It occurred to Dan that on the irregular occasions he'd shopped here, he'd always considered this Whole Foods too small and cramped to make for a pleasant retail experience. All things considered, the West Orange Whole Foods would've been a much better store to loot.

But this was no time for second-guessing. He needed to find the protein bars.

The trouble was, since Jen did all the shopping, Dan had no idea where anything was. He started down the nearest aisle.

Shampoo. Loofahs. Aromatherapy.

What the hell?

The whole aisle was useless. He turned around. As he retreated, his eye fell on a section of empty shelves.

Something there had been very popular with the other looters.

What was it?

He knelt down, ignoring the pain in his legs. Sweeping his hand across a darkened lower shelf, he discovered two large tubs of vegan protein powder.

Protein!

He shook out one of his bags and deposited the jars of protein powder inside. Then he went around the corner to the next aisle.

Pet food. Detergent. Frozen pizzas.

Oh, come on!

These things weren't just useless to him. They shouldn't have been shelved together in the first place.

What idiot laid out this store?

He was moving on to the next aisle when he heard the

pounding. It sounded like a battering ram, and it was coming from the farthest corner of the room, behind the bakery and the deli counter. The sound made his pulse race.

Go faster!

He looked down the next aisle. Drinks and frozen foods. Waste of time.

The pounding was getting louder. People were hurrying away from the noise, back toward the front entrance. Dan decided to forgo the bakery section entirely—it was almost too dark too see over there, anyway—and joined the flow of people moving away from the pounding noise.

Hurry!

But what the hell am I going to get?

The first time around, he'd skipped the aisle closest to the front door in favor of getting bags, so he decided to go there.

It was crowded with people, all of them in a hurry. The shelves were half-naked.

Must be a good aisle.

Dan swam upstream against the flow of looters, past the canned tomatoes—*definitely no*—and the pasta—*maybe?*—toward the darkness at the far end of the aisle.

There were shelves of canned something or other. It was almost too dark to read the labels.

Please, not tomatoes—

Beans!

Dan set down his bag with the two jars of protein powder, shook out the second bag, and started to drop cans into it.

Pinto? Meh.

Black! Better.

The pounding had stopped—but then there was a short, sharp *bang* in the darkness behind him, and flashlight beams began to dance along the freezer on the back wall just a few feet from where Dan was standing.

"POLICE!"

His heart rate skyrocketed. He quickly swept a dozen cans into the bag.

Its handles broke. Heavy with canned beans, the bag plummeted to the floor and—

OOOW!

Landed on his foot.

He crouched down, the top of his foot screaming in complaint along with his sore thighs.

Jesus, did I break a toe?

The flashlight beams were dancing on the shelf just above his head.

FUCK FUCK FUCK HURRY—

He started grabbing cans from the floor and dumping them into the still-intact bag that held the protein powder.

GO GO GO GO GO—

He filled the bag as full as he dared, gathered it in his arm—not daring to risk using the handles again—and forced himself to his feet.

OW OW OW OW—

A beam of light flickered on the shelf in front of him. Someone was shining a flashlight at the back of his head.

GET OUT NOW—

He scrambled toward the front of the store, cradling the bag in both arms and praying he wasn't about to get shot in the back by a cop.

The remaining looters were all headed in the same direction. When he reached the exit, there was such a logjam that the line to get out stretched all the way to the third cashier's station.

On his way to the back of the line, Dan grabbed a second brown paper bag from the countertop and double-bagged his haul as he waited.

Nobody was saying a word. He could hear the clomping of what must be cops, waving their flashlights at the back of the store. Occasionally, a stray beam hit his eye, and he felt like a raccoon caught atop a garbage can. He turned his head toward the parking lot, praying nobody would emerge out of the darkness to arrest him.

Through the window, he could see people fleeing the store. They seemed to be unmolested. There were no cops in sight.

It occurred to him that there was a caffeine-withdrawal headache beginning to stab at his temples. A small standing fridge was just a few feet ahead at the next checkout lane. As he passed it, he retrieved three cans of nitro brew iced coffee and added them to his bag. Then he wondered for a moment if he should make a quick trip to the produce department for fresh vegetables. But he dismissed the idea as a bridge too far.

Don't push your luck.

Soon enough, it was his turn to crouch down and make his escape.

Back in the sunlight, Dan strode quickly to his bike and unlocked it with shaky fingers. As he hung his double-bagged haul of loot on his handlebar and wheeled the bike around to flee, he caught a glimpse of the loading dock at the rear of the store, down by the far end of the L-shaped parking lot.

Denny What's-His-Name's El Camino was backed up to the dock. Several thick-necked men were loading boxes of food into the cargo bed. Dan recognized Barry Kozak among them.

Lincolnwood's former chief of police was laying claim to his share of the spoils.

CHLOE

"So you're saying I can't stay here?"

"I'm saying you don't *want* to stay here," Emma replied diplomatically.

They were wedged into the kiddie-sized seats of the Schroeders' backyard jungle gym, pushing themselves back and forth with their feet as they talked. There wasn't enough clearance for their full-grown legs to really swing, but they'd opted for the location to get some privacy once it became clear that if they stayed inside, Mrs. Schroeder wouldn't leave them alone. She'd glommed onto Chloe from the moment she entered the house, peppering her with questions about what Chloe knew of the crisis (*nothing*) and how her parents were handling it (*by getting shitfaced*, although Chloe kept that to herself).

"I'd rather be here than at my place," Chloe told her friend. "I could sleep on your couch. Or in John's bedroom." Emma's older brother was a sophomore at Tulane, which made it unlikely he'd be coming home unannounced.

"Trust me that you don't actually want to be under the same roof as my mom," Emma replied. "The only thing standing between her and a total breakdown is the Klonopin. And she's running out of Klonopin."

"She can't be as bad as my mom," Chloe insisted.

"She is, though. The thing is? *All* the adults are losing their shit over this. Capitalism's dying! And it's the only ideology they've never known. They're not going to be able to adapt."

"What does this have to do with capitalism?"

"Ohmygod, are you kidding? *Everything*. This is totally the moment where the whole system collapses under the weight of its own contradictions."

Chloe could feel the anxiety rising up inside her. "So, like . . . what does that mean for our college applications?"

"Dude." Emma shook her head gravely. "If shit goes down like I think it will? There's no college. It's just about survival. We gotta figure out how to, like, grow our own food and shit."

Chloe began to cry.

Emma immediately moved to comfort her. "Ohmygod! I'm sorry! I didn't mean to freak you out."

Chloe put her head in her hands and sobbed. She couldn't help it. The idea that everything she'd had spent the last three years building toward could all go up in smoke was just too much.

"Do you know how hard I worked? And it's just going to go away?"

"Maybe I'm wrong! Seriously." Emma hugged her tightly through the swing ropes, which dug into Chloe's arm. "Don't cry! It's okay! It might not be that bad. Like, maybe it'll be over by tomorrow."

"I'm sorry," Chloe sniffled, drying her tears on her sleeve once she'd managed to stop crying. "It's just . . . *guuuugh*."

"I know," Emma agreed. "It's a lot. But I'm probably wrong! Y'know? Like, I bet it'll actually be over soon."

Chloe managed to corral her emotions, but the outburst had left behind a heavy lump of anxiety in the pit of her stomach.

What am I going to do?

Thank God for Josh.

"I just hope I can stay with Josh till this is over."

Emma winced. "Dude."

"What?"

"You hooked up with him *once*. Like, *yesterday*."

"I know! But . . . it's just, like, the chemistry's really good between us."

"Yeah. Well—that's what I thought about Jeremy Friedrich."

Chloe stiffened. This was a completely unfair comparison.

"Just because Jeremy was a dick doesn't mean Josh is, too."

"But think about it—how long did it take me to realize Jeremy was a dick? Like, *months*."

"I tried to tell you."

"Yeah, at the *end*. At the beginning, you thought he was awesome, too!"

Chloe tried to remember if there was ever a time when she'd thought Emma's ex was awesome. "Not even! There was that time we all went for ice cream—"

"That was, like, *months* into it."

"Was it?"

"Yes! And this is my point. You can't always tell if a guy's a shithead after one hookup. Or even ten. Sometimes they're, like, stealth shitheads."

"Whatever." Chloe sighed and shook her head. Emma was starting to annoy her. She'd just tried to take Chloe's future away. Now she was trying to take Josh away, too.

But there was no point in arguing. It was just too hard to put into words the connection she and Josh had forged, especially since it had mostly been nonverbal.

Emma was probably just jealous. She hadn't gotten with anybody in months. And her opinion didn't matter. It was almost late enough to show up at Josh's without seeming desperate. Once Chloe was there, she could make up her own mind.

JEN

The homemade rain catcher as it existed in Jen's head was an elegant adaptation of common household materials—a shower curtain, rain ponchos, duct tape, a snow shovel, a garden rake, two yardsticks, and a recycling bin—into an apparatus as simple as it was efficient.

But somewhere in mid-construction, the reality taking shape on the floor of the garage had diverged from Jen's mental blueprint in ways that befuddled her. The shovel and the rake would have to support the far corners, but how was she going to drive an upside-down rake handle deep enough into the ground to anchor it? And once the rake and shovel were dug in, would they be tall enough to provide the necessary downward slope for all that plastic sheeting?

And what were the yardsticks for? She recalled them as critical to her initial design, but she couldn't remember why.

As she stepped back, physically and metaphorically, to ponder the questions, she took another nip from the rubbing alcohol bottle. There were only about three fingers of vodka left, and she sensed that she was approaching the fulcrum of the not-quite-enough/a-little-too-much teeter-totter. On the one hand, this was a net plus for her overall strategy—the sooner the booze was gone, the sooner she'd be unable to drink it. On the other hand, it was beginning to impair her performance. If she wanted to keep kicking ass, it might be a good idea to put herself on hiatus for a bit.

There was so much to do! Although when she tried to run through the list in her head, she had trouble conjuring everything. Or even most of the things.

Goats.

That was one of the medium-term projects, to be researched now and put into practice later, if the worst-case scenario came to pass and society regressed to a level of medieval subsistence. Goats were perfect. They'd feed on the grass in the yard, and Jen could milk the females.

A cow would be even better.

Where can I find a cow in Lincolnwood?

"Jen!"

The voice startled her. Dan was huffing up the driveway on his bike. A heavy-looking Whole Foods bag swung from one handlebar.

"Whole Foods is open?"

"Kind of." He dismounted clumsily from his bike, leaned it against the back bumper of the Volvo, and limped over with his bag of food to stare at her work in progress. "What are you doing?"

"Making a rain catcher. So we'll have drinking water. What'd you get?"

She resisted the urge to walk around her contraption and peek in his bag. Under the circumstances, it was unwise to get within smelling distance of him.

"What are you doing with the rubbing alcohol?"

"Oh." She'd forgotten she was still holding the bottle in her hand.

Shit shit shit SHIT—

"Sterilizing. Make sure the, y'know—it's clean." She gestured at the plastic sheeting spread out between them. "'Cause we gotta drink from it."

It was a perfectly good answer. But Dan made a face like he didn't buy it.

"Then why'd you put it on top of the oil slick?"

"What oil slick?"

Dan set down the bag. As Jen rose up on her toes and tried to peer into it from across the taped-up curtain-poncho hybrid, he knelt down and flipped over the curtain end to reveal a dark stain on the garage floor.

"*That* oil slick."

"Whatever. It's on the bottom. That side doesn't matter."

His face was still bunched up in a frown. "How's this going to work?"

"Trust me. It'll be great. What food you get?"

"Have you been drinking?"

"*No!* Ohmygod! That's *ridiculous!*"

"Because you really seem—"

"*Jesus Christ*, Dan! You think I'm *insane*? Tell me what food you got."

He stared at her a moment, thrown off balance by the rapid shift in tone and subject. Then he went back to his bag and picked it up with a heavy sigh.

"Beans and protein powder. And some cold brew."

"What the hell?"

"I didn't have a lot of options! It was a very tense situation."

What's tense about shopping?

"Why don't you go back and get more?"

"I don't think you understand." He started to make his way around the plastic sheeting, in the general direction of Jen.

Her pulse accelerated. But he wasn't heading for her. He limped over to the mudroom door and disappeared inside.

Whooo. That was close.

She looked at the bottle in her hand. There was just enough of it left to "sterilize" the water catcher. Plus a little bit extra.

Jen put the bottle to her lips for one last sip.

The mudroom door opened again. Dan was coming back.

She quickly lowered the bottle.

But not quickly enough.

"WHAT THE FUCK?"

"I wasn't drinking it."

"Yes, you were! *Ohmygod, yes, you were!*" He had a look on his face like she'd just murdered one of the kids.

"No, I wasn't—"

"Jen! I *saw* you drink it! You're drinking *rubbing alcohol!*"

"It's not rubbing alcohol—"

"Yes, it is! That's what Kitty Dukakis did! *Ohmygod, Jen!*"

"Calm down—"

"You've got to throw it up! You could go blind!"

He started toward her, his arms out like he was going to try the Heimlich maneuver. She stepped back, raising her free hand in self-defense.

"*Settle down!* It's not rubbing alcohol!"

"How can you say that? I'm staring right at it!"

"I poured it out and replaced it!"

He screwed his face up in a baffled grimace. "What?"

"It's water."

"Why would you put water in the rubbing alcohol?"

"Because . . ."

She had no idea how to finish the sentence.

"And how can you sterilize something with water? Let me see that." He thrust his hand out to grab for the bottle. She moved to protect it.

"Jen—"

"Okay! It's not water. It's vodka."

For a brief moment, it seemed like they were making progress.

But then he went right back to making his you-murdered-our-kids face.

"WHY WOULD YOU DO THAT?"

It was a tough question. Honesty was a nonstarter. But no dishonest reply suggested itself.

"Why *on earth* would you put *vodka* in a bottle of *rubbing alcohol*?"

"It's complicated."

"It sure fucking is!"

He put his hand to his mouth. Now she hadn't just murdered his kids. She'd shot his dog, too.

"Oh my God." Her husband's voice was an anguished hush. "You're an alcoholic!"

"Let's not go overboard."

"You're drinking from a bottle of *rubbing alcohol*!"

"It's not rubbing alcohol! It's just vodka!"

"That doesn't make it better!"

"It's a little better!"

"Give it to me."

Reluctantly, she handed over the bottle. He uncapped it and

gave it a sniff. Then he looked from the bottle to Jen and back again. His hand was trembling.

"Dan. It's not that big a deal."

"Yes, it is! This is a *disease*! You need help!"

The look on his face was simultaneously heartbreaking and irritating. He looked like some astronaut's wife watching the space shuttle explode on liftoff.

It was time for a tactical retreat.

"Look. I understand your concern. But I am aware of the problem. And there is a solution."

"Which is what?"

"If there's no alcohol, there's no problem. And there isn't going to be any alcohol."

"What are you talking about?"

"I won't drink if there's nothing to drink. And we've hardly got any left in the house—"

"There's *tons* in the house! There's a whole liquor cabinet! And a case of wine in the pantry!"

He was looking at her like she was an idiot. Which was infuriating, because her plan for getting sober was excellent.

"That's not that much! I could drink that in a couple of . . ."

She was in mid-scoff when she realized her dismissal of their booze inventory as too easy to consume was not helping her case.

"Do you realize how you sound? Jen, you're deranged! You have a serious mental illness!"

Now his free hand was on top of his head, the palm pressed to his forehead like he'd just watched the Giants miss a game-winning field goal as time expired.

"Will you quit overreacting? This isn't that big a deal."

"Yes, it is! We need to get you into treatment!"

"Oh, Jesus. What are you going to do? Walk me to Hazelden?"

"Where's that?"

"Minnesota."

"Jen, you have a serious problem. And you need to . . . get . . ."

Dan's voice trailed off as he turned his head away for the first time since he'd caught her with the bottle. Something on the street had caught his eye. Jen turned to see what it was.

A man and a woman, both vaguely familiar, were pedaling up Brantley Circle on a pair of touring bikes. They were helmeted, dressed in spandex racing gear, and wearing baggage strapped to their shoulders, although the man's bulging EMS pack looked about sixty pounds heavier than the woman's stylish leather satchel. He had shaggy locks of gray hair that spilled onto his shoulders and a massive, bearlike frame, although he would've been much more intimidating if his middle-aged paunch hadn't been encased in a form-fitting lime green Firenze jersey that made him look like an overstuffed neon sausage.

His companion was nearly as tall but reed-thin and twenty years younger, with cheekbones sharp enough to draw blood and raven hair gathered in a long ponytail.

"Ohmygod," Dan whispered. "Tell me it's not really them."

Jen started to ask who "them" was—but then the man spotted Dan and broke into a grin so big that his teeth were visible from thirty yards away. When he opened his mouth, Jen finally connected his face to his name.

"Dr. Altman, I presume!" Marty Callahan bellowed. "Thank God we found you guys!"

DAN

Dan's first reaction upon seeing Marty and Marina Callahan riding up his street was to wonder if he was hallucinating them. It seemed more plausible than the alternative, especially considering that his grip on reality was starting to feel slippery at best.

It had been, not to put too fine a point on things, an incredibly fucked-up morning. Leaving aside the fact that he still had no idea why the entire technological infrastructure of society had collapsed, Dan had just spent most of his twenty-minute uphill bike ride wrestling with the moral-existential implications of the fact that he'd just committed multiple felonies with no more internal debate than he usually devoted to the question of whether to eat a second bowl of ice cream.

Then he'd arrived home to discover that his wife of two decades was secretly a raging alcoholic. The revelation was both utterly devastating and strangely unsurprising: a number of previously inexplicable episodes, some of which had sat for years like misshapen puzzle pieces refusing to fit into his conceptual understanding of Jen and their relationship, were now clicking neatly into place.

As he'd stood there arguing with her, random memories and their grim implications had begun to ricochet through his mind like stray bullets at a police shooting.

That Thanksgiving at my mom's when she fell asleep at the table—

How am I going to keep the house together while she's in rehab?

Ohmygod, that parent-teacher conference! She was drunk at school!

The kids are going to need therapy.

I'm going to need therapy.

The shock was so severe that Dan's whole body had begun to vibrate when the Callahans first entered his field of vision, a pair of spandex-clad Horsemen of the Apocalypse mounting his driveway to shatter what remained of his sanity.

"Is this some crazy shit or what?" Dan's boss hopped off his bike, setting it down on the concrete and slipping off his heavy pack as he gulped air. "That's a killer hill, by the way." While his statuesque wife dismounted behind him, Marty nodded at the rain-catcher-in-utero, which occupied most of the available space between him and the Altmans. "Can I walk on this thing?"

Jen waved him off. "Lemme get it." She crouched down and doubled over the plastic with a sharp flick of her wrist, clearing a runway for Marty to march up to Dan and administer a sweaty man-hug.

This was no hallucination. Marty smelled and felt all too real.

"*Hola, amigo!* So fuckin' psyched to see you! What's with the rubbing alcohol?"

Dan looked down at the bottle in his hand. "It's . . . uh . . ."

"And what happened to your face?"

Dan reached up with his free hand to touch the fresh Band-Aid he'd applied that morning. "I, um . . ."

Is this really happening?

Marina strode over to Jen and kissed her on both cheeks. "Thank you for taking us in your home."

Taking you where?

As Dan tried to process Marina's statement, she and Marty swapped greeting partners.

"Hey, babe! Looking hot!" Marty crowed as he bestowed a hug and a kiss on Jen. "Sorry I'm all sweaty."

"Good to see you, Marty," Jen said.

Marina gave Dan the double-cheek treatment. Then she took his hands in hers, which were clad in biking gloves, and looked down on him with her dark Slavic eyes.

"Where is your bathroom? I have much need."

Dan just gaped at her, having lost his capacity for speech. Marina was three inches taller than him, and he found her intimidating even when he wasn't dangling on the precipice of a psychotic break.

"Uhhh . . ."

Jen fielded the question, stepping past them to hold open the mudroom door.

"Through here. On the right before you get to the kitchen."

"Thank you so much." Marina disappeared inside as Marty clapped Dan on the shoulder.

"Fuckin' nuts! Right? This whole thing? Swear to God, Manhattan was in full-on *Escape from New York* mode when we left. Can I get some water? I am parched."

When Dan proved incapable of answering, Marty took his silence for a yes and went inside.

Jen glared at Dan. "What the fuck are they doing here?" she hissed.

All Dan could do was shake his head. His vision was starting to go black around the edges, and it occurred to him that he should probably sit down before his brain executed a hard reset.

By the time Dan and Jen entered the kitchen, Marty was gulping down a full tumbler of water poured from a newly opened gallon of Poland Spring.

Dan bypassed him and headed straight for the sink with the bottle of rubbing alcohol.

"Marty, we don't have running water," he heard Jen say in a pointed voice.

"Yeah, I tried the faucet first," Marty replied. "That's why I had to open this."

Dan dumped the vodka in the sink and heard an exasperated grunt from Jen, although he wasn't sure if it was a commentary on his behavior or Marty's. As he put the empty in the recycling, he noticed Monday night's leftover bottle of cabernet by the toaster oven.

"This is all the water we have," Jen was telling Marty as Dan walked the cabernet over to the sink.

That dinner with the Thompsons. No wonder they don't call us anymore.

"I promise I'll get you more," Marty told Jen. "I'm just really thirsty."

"Where you going to get more?"

"I dunno. What's open around here?"

As he disposed of the cabernet, Dan remembered the leftover pinot grigio in the fridge. When he went to fetch it, he noted Jen's eyes following him.

"Dan?" she asked.

"What?"

"Was there any water left at the Whole Foods just now?"

"Your Whole Foods is open?" Marty's voice rose with excitement.

"Not, ummm . . ."

"Dan?" He could feel Jen glaring at the back of his head as he poured the white wine into the sink.

She lied to me. She's been lying to me for years.

She's sick. Literally. She's literally sick.

"Are you okay, dude?"

Dan added the empty pinot bottle to the recycling, shot a glance at the door to the liquor cabinet over the fridge—*do I dump those, too? not in front of Marty*—and then deposited himself in a chair at the table.

Oh, God—that night she peed in the bed in St. Maarten!

"Seriously, are you okay?" Marty asked him. "You look ripshit."

She's got to go to rehab.

Maybe I should ask Marty for a leave of absence.

Dan sighed. "It's been a really long day."

Marty chuckled in sympathy. "Tell me about it. We just rode thirty miles! And I gotta tell ya—there's a real *Mad Max* vibe on the roads. The GW Bridge was fuckin' nuts." He picked up the Poland Spring jug and refilled his water glass.

"Marty, the water—" There was a note of warning in Jen's voice.

"Sorry, babe. Just super thirsty. Swear to God, I'll replace it. ASAP. So what's open? The Whole Foods? You just come back from there?" Marty nodded at the full grocery bag Dan had left on the floor next to the table.

Dan stared down at the bag. The little cans of cold brew sat on top of the pile of canned beans. Realizing there was a caffeine headache stabbing at his forehead, he reached out and took a coffee.

"The thing about the Whole Foods—" Dan started to say as he cracked open the can.

"Hey, can I get one of those?" Marty asked. "I haven't had any caffeine today."

Jen pressed her lips together and glared at him. But Dan nodded his assent.

"Dan. Can we still get water at the Whole Foods?" Jen repeated.

Dan took a long drink of the room-temperature coffee.

That time I called home in the middle of the day—

How did I not see this?

She puked on our wedding night! And I just thought it was funny!

"*Dan!* Is there still water at the Whole Foods?"

Dan sighed and shook his head. "I don't know. I didn't go down that aisle."

"Well, shit," Marty said as he stood up. "We should giddyup! Head over there pronto."

"It's not open," Dan explained. "I mean, it is and it isn't. People were breaking into it."

"Did *you?*" This was news to Jen.

Dan nodded. "Yeah."

"Holy shit, dude!" Marty pointed to the bag of groceries, his eyes wide. "Did you boost this stuff? Did you do a looty?"

"Kind of?"

Oh, right. I just committed a couple of felonies.

"Fuckin' A! I thought they were only looting in the city! We gotta get over there before the good shit's gone." He turned to Jen. "Can you keep an eye on Marina? She's having a really hard time. She got stuck in Bergdorf's yesterday when the power went out? Took her forever to find the exit. I think she's got PTSD."

"That sounds really awful," Jen told Marty.

Dan wondered if his boss had spent enough time with Jen to identify her tone as not only sarcastic, but borderline drunk.

Evidently not. "It was definitely traumatizing for her," Marty said with a grave nod. "Like, 9/11-type shit. You know?"

"Oh, I know. I was there."

"In Bergdorf's?"

"No, 9/11."

"Oh! Right! Holy shit, I forgot! So you know what it's like."

"Tooooootally," Jen assured him.

"Can I talk to you for a minute?" Dan asked his wife.

"Don't you need to get going? While there's still water on the shelves?"

"Not before we talk."

As he watched them stare each other down, Marty's antennae finally started to go up. He might not have known Jen well enough to decipher her tone of voice, but there was no mistaking Dan's.

"Did I interrupt something here?"

"Nothing major," Jen assured their houseguest as she followed Dan out of the room.

JEN

"You didn't have to pour the wine out," Jen snarled.

"I *absolutely* had to pour the wine out! I've got to pour all of it out!"

They were in the den, the door closed behind them to hide the argument from their unexpected houseguests.

"Oh, Jesus Christ, Dan—think about it! If this shit is permanent, that alcohol's worth something! You're pouring out money!"

He just stared at her, less angry than hurt.

She would've preferred angry. It made counterattacking much easier.

"What are we going to do here, Jen?"

"He's your boss. Figure out how to get rid of him."

"That's not what I'm talking about."

Jen sank into the couch with a heavy sigh. "I know I have a problem. Okay?"

"What are we going to do about it?"

She put her head in her hands and talked through them. "I'm going to quit."

"When?"

Fuck you, Dan.

"Now. Okay?"

"I don't think I can leave you alone—"

"Oh, Jesus Christ. I'm not a fucking child! You don't have to—"

"No, you're a person who puts vodka into a rubbing alcohol bottle—"

"*OKAY!*"

"Why are *you* yelling at *me*?"

Jen started to cry. At first, it was involuntary. But when Dan sat down and put a comforting arm around her, she realized the tears conferred a tactical advantage and leaned into them.

"It's okay," Dan told her as he rubbed her back. "We're going to get through this. Just . . . how much more do you have hidden around the house?"

"None."

"Jen."

"I don't! Swear to God."

"If I go out with Marty now . . . will you promise you won't touch another drop?"

"Yes!"

"Do I need to pour out what's in the liquor cabinet?"

"*No!* I swear to God I won't. Okay? And I'm sorry."

"Don't say you're sorry. Just promise me you're going to get help."

"I'm going to get help."

"You *promise*?"

"Yes!"

"When?"

"As soon as the world stops going to hell."

"Jen."

Oh, fuck you.

She took a deep breath. "There's a seven a.m. AA meeting at the church by the train station. I'll go to it tomorrow."

"Swear to God?"

"Yes!"

She felt him pull back a little. "How do you know there's a meeting there?"

"Because, believe it or not, I've been aware there's a problem for a while. Okay?"

"Why didn't you tell me?"

She started to cry again.

"It's okay," he said. "It's okay. We're dealing with it now."

"Please get rid of Marty. They can't stay here."

"I know. But it's going to take me a little while. I think I've got to go to the store with him first."

"Did you really loot the Whole Foods?"

"I don't want to talk about it."

"How did they even find us?"

"Good question. . . . I gotta go." He kissed her on the head and stood up.

"I'm sorry, Dan."

"Don't say that. Just—"

"I know. But I am."

"We're going to get through this. I'm going to help you. Okay?"

"I know. I love you."

"I love you, too."

He started to exit. Then he paused.

"Swear to God you're not going to drink any more today?"

"*Yes!* There's nothing left to drink!"

"There's a whole liquor cabinet! And a case of wine in the pantry."

"I swear to God, I won't touch any of it."

"Okay. I love you. But I'm a little pissed off at you right now."

The feeling's mutual.

When Jen pulled herself together and emerged from the den, Marina was still locked in the bathroom. Marty was standing outside the door, holding a pair of reusable shopping bags that Dan must've given him.

"You sure you don't want to go with us, honey?" Marty called to his wife.

"No," came the muffled reply from inside the bathroom.

"Okay. We'll be back soon!" He turned to Jen and lowered his voice. "Keep an eye on her, okay? She's really fragile right now."

"Sure thing, Marty."

He exited to the garage. Dan, holding two shopping bags of his own, lingered to give Jen a goodbye hug.

"Just so you know," he said quietly, "I checked the levels on everything in the liquor cabinet. And I counted the wine bottles."

"Oh, Jesus Christ—"

"I'm sorry. Peace of mind. I love you. Please don't drink."

"I won't!"

He kissed her goodbye and was gone.

Jen sat down at the kitchen table and considered her options.

The game was up. She absolutely had to quit. There was no question about it. In the morning, she'd swallow her pride and go to the AA meeting. As much as it made her skin crawl, she could put up with the hand-holding happy talk for at least a little while.

It was, she had to admit, long past time for her to sober up.

But quitting right this second was entirely unreasonable. Her buzz was already starting to fade, and she could feel the first warning pangs of her resurgent hangover beginning to throb in her sinus cavity. If she didn't do some maintenance drinking, within a couple of hours the pain would be excruciating, not just physically but emotionally.

There was no point in trying to explain any of this to Dan. She'd either have to water down the vodka in the liquor cabinet or come up with an alternative.

Maybe I can go next door, talk Kayla into some day drinking.

Would she be up for drinking on top of the Xanax?

Maybe I should take a Xanax.

The bathroom door opened. Marina the Minor League Supermodel entered the room, with a look on her face that seemed every bit as traumatized as Marty had feared.

I bet she's game. She's Ukrainian—they drink like the Russians. And what kind of host would I be if poor, traumatized Marina wanted a vodka to soothe her nerves and I didn't——

"Your toilet is broken," Marina informed her.

MAX

The public library was closed. Max sat atop its granite steps with his forearms propped on his knees, staring unfocused into the distance. Every minute or so, he lowered his head, puckered his mouth, and added another dollop of spit to the puddle between his shoes. Other than that, he stayed motionless as a statue.

Physically, he was on the mend: his salivary gland had finally quit dribbling into his mouth like a busted water fountain, his throat no longer burned with the aftertaste of tobacco and puke, his stomach had unclenched, and he'd solved his nicotine problem. The Skoal had been in his system just long enough to generate a faint buzz, while the hockey-puck-shaped container in his hip pocket promised relief from any future withdrawal symptoms, assuming he wasn't dumb enough to swallow the tobacco again.

Psychologically, though, he was a wreck.

The look of sympathetic revulsion on Kayleigh's face as she'd asked him if he was okay while he dry-heaved onto the lawn was seared into his memory so indelibly that he doubted he could ever again imagine himself as the object of anything more than her pity. After he fled the park, sick with shame—and also just plain sick—he'd wandered around for a while on his bike, pausing every couple of blocks to spit bile and survey the community's response to the crisis. Eventually, he reached two conclusions: that civilization was collapsing and he had none of the skills he'd need to survive.

For the most part, the streets were quiet. But what little human activity he did see was ominous. The guy who owned the flower shop on Hawthorne Street was boarding it up like there was a hurricane coming. A house was burning down over on Crawford, and the firemen weren't even trying to put it out. There was some extremely weird shit going down in the parking lot of the Whole Foods—the glass on the front doors was shattered, and cops in riot gear were standing in front of it, waving off a crowd of a couple dozen people that Max would've labeled a mob if they hadn't been so preppy-looking. And half a block from the supermarket, he passed two middle-aged guys headed toward it with shotguns.

This was fucked up. Open carry wasn't a thing in suburban New Jersey. People didn't walk the streets toting guns unless society had gone seriously off the rails.

Max had never played *Dark Ages*, or whatever that game was that Dennis had told him about. But he had enough experience with other postapocalyptic video games to know what he had to do to make it through to the end: wield firearms, scavenge supplies, operate motor vehicles, rescue the occasional helpless bystander, and heal his own bullet wounds.

But those games were cruelly misleading. No amount of familiarity with them conferred an advantage when tackling the real-world equivalent. There were no automatic weapons just lying around on the ground, waiting for Max to pick them up. Riding a motorcycle couldn't possibly be as simple as steering with the left joystick while accelerating with the right trigger button. And even assuming you could scavenge scissors and tape from an empty drawer in the back office of an abandoned warehouse, combining those two items wouldn't magically restore a gunshot victim to full health.

What *did* he bring to the table, skillswise? The ability to edit video on iMovie? A superior grade point average? There was the martial arts knowledge he'd spent the past two weeks acquiring via YouTube. But that was all theoretical. Never having tried to apply it, he had no confidence in its validity. And despite the two weeks' worth of nightly pushups he'd recently banked, his upper body strength was still underwhelming.

He had his imagination, but it wasn't the kind he could put to practical use. In the end, the only solution he'd been able to dream up was to go to the library and look for books on survivalism. Or maybe hunting.

But the library door was locked, its interior dark and silent. Whatever knowledge it contained was as inaccessible to him as YouTube. So he just sat there, perched in front of the entrance, immobilized by an overwhelming sense of helplessness.

He couldn't even serve a volleyball overhand. How the hell was he going to survive the apocalypse?

CHLOE

Josh's parents hadn't exactly been warm and inviting. Chloe had done her best to make a good first impression, but she could practically feel Mr. and Mrs. Houser scowling at her from the living room window as she and Josh pedaled out of the driveway.

"Are you sure your parents are cool with you leaving?"

"Yeah. Why?"

"I don't know. They seemed kind of mad."

"They just want to make sure I get my workouts in. But I lifted this morning. And as long as I'm back in time to do intervals before dark, it's all good. If I can do two-a-day dry land workouts till the pool opens again, I'll actually be in good shape."

It definitely didn't sound like he was planning for the zombie apocalypse. Or any kind of apocalypse.

Is that a good thing or a bad thing?

"What do you think is going on? Like, with everything?"

The knot of anxiety in Chloe's stomach quivered in anticipation of his answer.

"I dunno. It's weird. That whole, like . . . what'd Tucker call it yesterday?"

"A glitch in the simulation?"

"Yeah. That seems like bullshit. Some people are saying it's terrorists? But my parents think it's the Democrats."

"What the hell?"

"Yeah. Like, they think they staged the whole thing so they

can use it to grab power. 'Cause it's the only way they can make socialism work."

Chloe's anxiety spiked as the likelihood of her staying at Josh's plummeted nearly to zero.

Ohmygod! His parents are nuts.

Is he nuts, too?

"That is *seriously* insane," she told him.

"I know, right?" Josh agreed. "*So* insane."

Thank God. It's not him. It's just the parents.

"Hang on a sec." As they reached the corner of Baker and Violet, Josh pulled over to stand with a foot on the curb while he adjusted the straps of Chloe's backpack. He'd insisted on carrying it for her. Chloe had offered a weak protest, but she secretly appreciated the chivalry.

"You okay? I can carry it."

"No! It's easy. I just gotta shorten the straps. Why are you carrying all this stuff, anyway?"

Because I thought I might move in with your family? Except your parents are nuts and they hate me?

"Just to be ready for anything. Like, what if we actually played the semi today?"

She tried not to sound as anxious as she felt. The knot of anxiety in her gut was threatening to turn into a black hole.

"Why wouldn't you play it?"

"Because it's all the way over in Rumson. Like, how are we going to get there?"

"But didn't you hear? Cars actually still work if they're really old."

"They do?" This was news to Chloe.

"Yeah. My mom saw one drive through town yesterday. And I don't know about Lincolnwood? But back at my old school, the buses we took to swim meets were old as shit. So the school district's probably got, like, a beater van or something they can use to get you there."

"I hope so." Chloe felt a welcome flutter of optimism.

"It'll all be good. You'll see."

He smiled at her with those killer eyes.

Ohmygod.

He's amazing.

Josh reached out with one of his powerful hands and drew her to him in an openmouthed kiss.

Except he smells bad.

His breath wasn't great, and his body was worse—he was giving off the vinegary odor of someone who'd gone for a run last night, lifted weights this morning, and hadn't showered after either workout.

Which, as far as she could tell, was true. When Josh broke the clinch, Chloe was relieved in spite of herself.

"So where do you want to go?" she asked. "Brody's?"

"Actually . . ." His smile widened. "I think I got a better idea."

"Really?"

"Yeah. Follow me."

He started up the street. Chloe pedaled after him, doing her best to feed the fragile optimism that was rising up to battle her dread, and hopeful that whatever mystery destination Josh had in mind would include a working shower.

DAN

"I'm so fucking glad you were home, dude!" Marty crowed as he and Dan coasted down Willis Road toward town. Marty's reusable shopping bags were dangling from his handlebars, while Dan had stuffed his own empty bags inside his jacket. "You're a lifesaver. Seriously."

"How'd you know where I lived?"

"Your birthday invitation."

"Oh . . . right."

As part of his effort to work himself back into Marty's good graces, Dan had printed out a hard copy of his birthday cocktail party Evite and given it to Marty on Monday morning—*was that really just the day before yesterday?*—along with handwritten directions to his house. The party was slated for a week from Saturday, and having been reminded of it, Dan briefly wondered how he'd alert the other invitees if he had to cancel due to the ongoing civilizational collapse.

Or for more personal reasons.

Can I still throw a cocktail party if my wife's an alcoholic?

"I thought about trying to get out to Ray's in the Hamptons," Marty said. "But being at the end of an island seemed like a bad idea. Then I thought about Berto's, which would've been perfect—y'know, he's got that place upstate on, like, fifty acres? But good luck finding *that* without Google Maps. You doing okay, buddy?"

"Huh?" Dan glanced over at Marty, who was frowning at him with what looked like filial concern. "Yeah. I'm just kind of . . . trying to process everything."

Marty nodded sympathetically. "I know it must be hard, what you're going through with Jen."

"What do you mean?"

"The drinking. Couldn't help overhearing that argument you were having."

Oh, Christ.

"If you need to talk to somebody? I'm here for you, pal. I know what it's like. We had a writer on season two of the first *Bullet Town*? Had a real bad heroin problem. HR got involved, the whole nine yards. I learned a ton about recovery from it."

"Oh. Wow. How'd the guy recover?"

"He didn't. I had to fire him. Then he died of an overdose. That's the thing—they don't really get better till they hit bottom."

"Jesus!"

"Yeah. You might not want to leave her alone for too long. Hey, this is a really nice neighborhood!"

The leaf-strewn front lawns and handsome Colonials of Willis Road were much more thickly populated than on a typical weekday, when the only signs of life were landscapers and delivery drivers. The crisis had left Lincolnwood's residents not just stranded at home, but unusually social—they clustered in twos and threes at the edges of their property lines, comparing notes with their neighbors under furrowed brows.

"Real Norman Rockwell shit," Marty observed. "How long you lived here?"

"Uhhh . . ." Dan did his best to banish the Marty-implanted thought of Jen drinking herself to death before he could get back home and clean out the liquor cabinet. "Fourteen years? Plus three more in the old place."

"So you know all these people?"

"Actually . . ." A quick mental inventory yielded the disconcerting realization that Dan didn't have a single acquaintance on Willis Road. He didn't even recognize most of the faces they were passing.

"No," he admitted. "It's weird. I don't really know anybody on this street."

"Huh. That's actually good, though, right? 'Cause then you won't feel as bad when you have to kill them and steal their shit to survive?"

"Jesus Christ, Marty!"

"Kidding! It was a joke! Geez."

In the awkward silence that followed, Dan wrestled with the impulse to turn his bike around and return home immediately to protect his wife not only from her own self-annihilation, but the potentially murderous residents of Willis Road.

Oh, God—where are the kids right now?

Don't listen to Marty. He's out of his mind.

Think about something normal.

"So you want to hear my pitches for the replacement episodes?"

"Abso-mundo! Whaddaya got?"

"Okay: guy murders librarian . . . by copying a plot from a murder mystery in the book he checked out from her."

Marty shook his head. "Too highbrow."

"It's not, though. 'Cause get this: the librarian doesn't read! That's one of the reasons the guy—"

"Next!"

"What?"

"Nobody likes librarians. You don't even see them in porn anymore. What else you got?"

"Murder at Comic Con."

"Pass-adena."

"Come on! Just think of the murder weapons we could—"

"*Pass!* Comic Con's over. Even the nerds hate it now. How far away is this Whole Foods?"

In the hour and change since Dan had last been there, the Whole Foods parking lot had undergone a disturbing transformation into what now resembled a bizarre mashup of a police state and a Giants tailgate. The store's entrance, its shattered panes covered over with cardboard, was being guarded by a pair of Lincolnwood cops in riot gear. At the far end of the building, the narrow strip of asphalt that formed the hinge of the L-shaped lot now sported what appeared to be a paramilitary checkpoint manned by four thick-necked white guys in sweatshirts, jerseys, and dad jeans, indistinguishable from weekend football fans only insofar as they were all armed with shotguns.

One of the men was Eddie Stankovic. Mindful of the weaponry, Dan and Marty dismounted from their bikes a respectful distance from the group. When Eddie recognized Dan, he beckoned him forward and stepped out to meet the pair.

What's Eddie doing with that gun?

Has he always owned a gun?

Beyond Eddie and the makeshift checkpoint, Dan could see pallets of boxed food and beverages stacked in front of the loading dock. Denny What's-His-Name's El Camino was still there, its cargo bed piled high with boxes. Parked beside it was a powder blue '68 Cadillac DeVille.

Standing next to the Caddy, Angry-Bald-Sports-Dad-Turned-Emergency-Management-Coordinator Steve Shreckler, dressed in a suit and a long black overcoat, was conferring with leather-jacketed former chief of police Barry Kozak and a uniformed Lincolnwood cop.

"What's up, Dan-O?" Eddie greeted Dan in a brisk tone of voice.

"Hey, Eddie. What's with all the guns?"

"Citizens' militia. Shrek deputized us to keep order. Can you fuckin' believe people were looting this place?"

"Daaaamn," said Marty, with a sidelong glance at Dan.

Eddie sized up the newcomer with suspicion. "Who are you?"

"Marty Callahan. Friend of Dan-O's." Marty stuck his hand out. Eddie didn't move to shake it immediately, possibly because both his hands were occupied by his shotgun.

"*The* Marty Callahan? *Bullet Town* Marty Callahan?"

"That's me!"

"Holy shit!" Eddie lowered his voice and growled in imitation of the voice-over from the original *Bullet Town*'s credits sequence. "'Justice comes with a bullet!'"

Marty beamed. "I wrote that!"

"I know! I heard you talk about it on *Joe Rogan*!" Eddie shifted the shotgun, cradling it in his left arm while he gave Marty an enthusiastic handshake with his right. "Eddie Stankovic, CEO, Capo's LLC. I fuckin' *love* your shows! Only problem with 'em is you got *this* guy writin' for you." Eddie jerked his head in Dan's direction with a smirk. "What's he know about cop shit?"

Marty laughed. "I know, right?"

Dan must've looked sufficiently offended, because Marty gave him an affectionate nudge. "I'm just shittin' you, buddy." He turned back to Eddie. "Dan's actually a decent writer."

"Nah, I know. Just jerking his chain. We kid! Right, Dan-O?"

"Oh, sure," said Dan. *I gotta get out of here.* "Hey, Eddie . . . you know where we could get some drinking water?"

"Also food," Marty added.

"That, too. If it's possible."

"Lemme check." Eddie turned around and yelled across the lot to Shreckler, who was still talking to Kozak and the uniformed cop. "*Hey, Shrek!* C'mere a sec?"

Shreckler reached into the cargo bed of the El Camino, picked up what looked like an assault rifle—*what the fuck?*—and strode toward them with it as Marty commented approvingly on the emergency management coordinator's wardrobe. "That's a nice coat. Think it's Armani?"

Eddie shook his head. "Nah. I bet it's Vince. They got great shit, and it's, like, half the price."

"You got a good eye. Are you in fashion?"

"Sort of. I own a dry cleaning chain."

"Awesome!"

"Yeah, seven locations. Opening the eighth in Glen Rock next month. Throwing a big blowout for the opening. You should come!"

"Love to!"

"What's going on?" Shreckler arrived with an I'm-in-charge-here swagger.

"Can we spare some water for these guys?" Eddie asked. "Maybe food?"

"Who's asking?"

"Marty Callahan."

"Dan Alt—"

Eddie talked over Dan, impatient to give Shrek the news: "You watch *Bullet Town*?"

"Which one? *NYC* or the original?"

"Both." Eddie beamed as he gestured toward Marty with his shotgun. "This guy created them!"

"No shit?" Shreckler broke into a wide grin. "I *love* those shows! You live in Lincolnwood?"

"Right now, yeah. I'm staying with my buddy here."

You're WHAT?

Shreckler's grin began to fade. "When'd you come in?"

"Just now."

"From where?"

"Manhattan."

"How'd you get here?"

"Bike."

"You didn't see the signs?"

Marty's own smile was fading, too. "Uhhh . . ."

"The ones that said, '*Residents Only—No Trespassing*'?" His bald head glistening in the sun, Shreckler shifted his grip on the assault rifle as he glared at the new arrival.

Dan's stomach dropped.

Ohmygod, he's going to shoot Marty.

"I mean . . . I *know* a resident." Marty nodded in Dan's direction.

The emergency management coordinator registered his opinion of Dan's bona fides with a brief, noisy expulsion of breath through his nose.

For a long moment, nobody spoke. Dan watched Eddie's eyes move nervously from Shreckler to Marty and back again.

Then Shreckler's glare broke, replaced by an indulgent smirk. "Nah, it's cool. You're good. We just don't want the wrong kind of people coming in. Gotta protect the community."

"Totally!" Marty nodded vigorously. "I get it. Hundred percent."

"And we're not handing out provisions yet. First, we've got to secure the inventory. Then determine the needs of each household."

"Course! Makes total sense."

Dan nodded along with Marty while wondering how quickly he could flee the parking lot.

"Unless you want kombucha," Shreckler added. "You like kombucha?"

"Who doesn't?"

Shreckler turned to Eddie. "Give them a six."

"Sure thing, chief."

Shreckler started back toward the loading dock, but stopped abruptly when he spied a Latino family of four walking up the sidewalk beyond the parking lot fence.

"*Terry!*" Shreckler shouted at one of the riot-gear-clad cops at the front door as he pointed in the direction of the family. Both the cop and Shreckler began to march toward them.

"Stop right there! You got ID?"

As Shreckler and the cop converged on the terrified-looking family, Eddie motioned to Marty and Dan to follow him past the shotgun-wielding Giants fans at the checkpoint.

"C'mon, I'll hook you up. Pomegranate or apple-ginger?"

"Either one. Your call."

"So what's Ray Liotta like to work with?"

"Great guy. Total pro."

"I knew it! You can just tell by watching him."

"Hey, guys?"

Eddie and Marty stopped and looked back at Dan, who hadn't moved.

"I kind of need to get back to the house."

You know, before somebody shoots me? Or my wife ODs?

Marty nodded. "That's cool, dude! I can find my way back. I'll bring the kombucha."

"I can take you there," Eddie offered. "I live right next door."

"No shit? That's fantastic! I had no idea."

"You sure it's cool?" Dan asked them.

"Absolutely," Eddie assured him. *"Mi amigo, su amigo."*

"Adiós, buddy!" said Marty.

"Great. See you in a bit."

Please don't anybody shoot me in the back, Dan thought to himself as he wheeled his bike toward the street, where Steve Shreckler was supervising the riot-gear-clad cop's frisking of the Latino dad while the man's family looked on in silent terror.

MAX

After staring into space on the public library steps until his butt muscles started to hurt, Max had decided to return home for lack of any better options. On the ride back, his feeling of existential uselessness weighed on him so heavily that he barely made it up the Willis Road hill without having to stop and walk his bike.

When he turned left onto Brantley Circle, he passed his favorite neighbor, Ruby the dachshund. She was trotting up the sidewalk toward her house at the end of a leash held by Judge Distefano. It occurred to Max that he could use some canine affection, so he deposited his bike at the foot of the Altmans' driveway and walked back to intercept Ruby and her owner in front of their place.

As he did, he noticed a familiar pair of bikes propped against the doors of the Stankovics' three-car garage. Ordinarily, the evidence of Jordan's presence would've generated at least a mild adrenaline surge. But to Max's surprise, he felt nothing. In the space of a day, the conflict he'd spent all of his mental energy obsessing over for weeks had ceased to matter to him at all.

That was a relief. But it was also a little scary.

Am I depressed?

"What's up, kid?" The judge gave him an old-man wink as Ruby strained at her leash to greet him.

"Heeeeey, Ruby." Max's mood was so low that the words

came out sounding more sorrowful than friendly. He knelt down on the sidewalk and scratched the dog between the ears. She reared up in a half hop, putting her forepaws on his leg for easier petting. Max started to lose his balance, so he plopped down cross-legged on the concrete and let her jump in his lap.

"I'm sorry," he told the judge. "You in a hurry?"

"To go sit on my couch? I got nothing but time." The judge watched Max and his dog enjoy each other's company with a satisfied smile. "You're like the Ruby whisperer. She's not a fan of a lot of people. But she likes you."

Max shrugged. "She got used to me last spring." In May, he'd filled in as a dogsitter when the judge had spent a week in the hospital.

"How many times a day were you giving her treats?"

"I dunno. Not that many."

"Color me skeptical. I mean, not to take anything away from you. I'm sure she likes you for you. But the bribery probably didn't hurt."

Across the street, the front door of the Stankovic McMansion opened and shut again. Max glanced over his shoulder just long enough to confirm that it was Jordan and Grayson. Then he returned his focus to Ruby as the two oversized teenagers mounted their bikes and headed into the street.

"Whaaat uuup, Aaaaltman?" Grayson called out in a sing-songy taunt as they rode past.

Max ignored him. When they disappeared around the corner, the judge offered some gentle social criticism.

"You could've said hello. You know, a conversation's like a ball. You pass it back and forth."

Max shrugged. "Those guys are jerks."

"Yeah? Which kind?"

Max squinted up at his elderly neighbor. "How many kinds are there?"

"Of jerk? Tons. Wiseass. Bully. Creep. Numbskull . . ."

"What's a numbskull?"

"Y'know—a doofus. Moron."

"Oh." Max considered the options. "Jordan's a numbskull. The other kid's a wiseass."

"Interesting. See, I would've guessed the Stankovic kid was more of a wiseass. On account of his dad's got some of that in him."

Max had an opinion about the Stankovic father-son relationship, although he hesitated before sharing it. Talking trash with an eighty-year-old felt a little weird. But it wasn't necessarily unpleasant. The judge didn't bullshit like most adults. On the few occasions when they'd talked one-on-one, he'd always been disarmingly honest.

"I don't know if he and his dad get along that well," Max ventured.

The judge pursed his lips, mulling it over. Then he nodded. "I could see that. It's a tough thing, not getting along with your dad. Personally, I couldn't stand mine."

"Really?"

The judge had a dad?

"Yeah. He had a real temper on him. Used to take it out on us. It was a different time, though, y'know? Not a lot of talk therapy out there for a longshoreman in the forties. Hey, you hungry?"

"I guess so."

"Want some lunch? I got pepperoni in the fridge that's going to go bad if I don't find somebody to eat it with me."

"Yeah. Sure." Max lifted Ruby out of his lap and stood up. "Let me just put my bike away?"

"Take your time. I got all day."

JEN

Marina had turned out to be a terrible houseguest and an even worse Ukrainian. After Jen had flushed her toilet for her—a thoroughly unpleasant act of benevolence which should have cemented Marina's impression of her host as someone with nothing but her guests' best interests in mind—Jen suggested they relieve the stress of the moment with some vodka. In response, Marina had not only declined to honor her cultural heritage, she'd shamed Jen by looking appalled at the suggestion.

Then she followed up the indignity by chugging almost as much water as her greedy husband. By the time Marina had finished rehydrating, the Callahans had collectively put away most of a gallon of Poland Spring.

Somehow, things managed to get worse after that. When asked if she wanted anything to eat, Marina ignored the clear warning in Jen's "not that we have a whole lot in the way of food" caveat and declared that she was starving. As a result, Jen wound up seething with silent resentment while using up far too much of their remaining mayo to create a tuna salad for her houseguest that Jen couldn't even help eat for fear of destabilizing her iffy digestive system.

Marina pronounced the tuna salad "excellent," which probably wasn't true. But if it was, it would've just added insult to injury, seeing as how Jen's own lunch consisted of vegan protein powder mixed with tap water in a cheap plastic squeeze bottle brought home from Max's tenth birthday party at Sky Zone.

The final indignity was the cruelest: having made her way through ten percent of the Altmans' tuna, twelve percent of their bottled water, and as much as forty percent of their mayonnaise reserves, Marina inexplicably refused to leave the kitchen table even when Jen practically demanded she relocate to the living room.

This made it impossible for Jen to open the liquor cabinet for a discreet maintenance snort of vodka.

Which was absolutely infuriating.

After waiting in vain God knows how long for the statuesque Ukrainian—*literally* statuesque, since all she did was sit there like a block of marble—to get out of the kitchen, Jen finally threw in the towel and decided to kill some time by installing her rain catcher in the backyard.

This did not go well. With the assistance of a trowel, she was able to drive the rake far enough into the ground to secure it as a corner support. But the snow shovel, even after Jen had seated its handle in a carefully dug hole and reburied it, proved stubbornly resistant to staying upright. Jen eventually won the battle, but not until she'd had to bury the shovel so deep that it stood two feet lower than the rake, which she worried would leave the shower/poncho funnel too cockeyed to route the rainwater in the correct direction.

But that issue remained theoretical, because when Jen tried to tape the ends of the funnel to the rake and shovel, the whole thing collapsed.

This all took time. When it was over, Jen was, if not exactly sober, then at least no longer drunk, and the warning signs of a vicious rebound hangover had begun to materialize. So she went back inside, praying that Marina had finally abandoned the kitchen.

Her prayers initially appeared to have been answered. The kitchen was empty, and the liquor cabinet was unguarded. Jen went to the pantry to fetch the stepstool.

The pantry floor was curiously underpopulated. Something was missing.

The wine.

There was usually a case of it sitting there. But the whole box was gone.

DAN!

He must've come home and moved it somewhere.

She quickly dragged the stool to the fridge and hopped up on it.

The liquor cabinet was empty.

FUCK!

She half threw the stool back into the pantry and opened the fridge door.

The bottles of beer and prosecco were gone, too.

She'd just shut the fridge door, a murderous rage filling her head, when she heard footsteps coming up the basement stairs.

He hid it all in the basement. Sonofabitch!

A moment later, Dan emerged.

"Where are the kids?"

It was a perfectly reasonable question, and one to which she recognized that she should've known the answer.

The fact that she didn't just made her angrier.

Stay calm. Don't lose it.

"They're out."

"Where?"

"Chloe went to Emma's, then tennis."

"There's no way she's still got tennis today. It's insane out there."

"Then she'll be home soon."

"What about Max?"

"He's not back yet?"

"No."

"Then he's probably at Dennis's. What's the big deal?"

"It's not safe to be out right now. People are running around with guns."

"Who is?"

"Eddie Stankovic, the guys he plays basketball with—it's like the fucking Wild West out there."

"Where'd you see Eddie Stankovic?"

"The Whole Foods parking lot. They're guarding it with shotguns!"

Okay, that's definitely weird. "Did Marty and Marina leave yet?"

"No." Dan lowered his voice. "Marina's in the living room. She's meditating."

"Seriously?"

Jen walked down the hall and peeked into the living room. Marina was sitting in the lotus position in front of the coffee table, her butt resting on a couch cushion and her unblinking eyes staring at the fireplace.

She was so still that Jen had to watch her for a couple of seconds to confirm that she was breathing.

You crazy bitch. You took my living room hostage. I can't even lie on my couch.

While she stared at the back of Marina's head, Jen considered her options. After briefly cycling through homicide, assault, and chugging Listerine, she opted to retreat upstairs for a nap. And possibly Listerine.

Dan followed her up to their bedroom, limping on his overused legs.

"That woman is *literally* a piece of furniture," Jen told him once they were alone with the door closed. "When are they leaving?"

"I don't know. I'll talk to Marty after he gets back."

"Where is he?"

"I left him with Eddie."

"Jesus, the blind leading the stupid. . . . I'm going to take a nap." She stripped off her pants in preparation for getting under the covers.

Dan looked aghast. "What about the kids?"

"They're fine! They'll come back soon."

"I don't think you realize how fucked up it is out there."

I don't think you realize how shitty I feel.

"Stop worrying so much!"

"Start worrying more! Jesus Christ, Jen!"

She buried her head under a pillow.

"Jen? Jen!"

"The kids are fine! Trust me!"

"What about you?"

You took the fucking alcohol away. What more do you want?

She sat up in bed and did her best to keep her voice at a level that didn't make it sound like she wanted to strangle him. Which she very much did.

"I know I have a problem. Okay? And I'll go to the fucking meeting in the morning. I just don't want to talk about it. I feel like complete shit, I need to take a nap, and I'd *really* appreciate it if when I get up, there isn't a fucking Amazonian fembot in my living room."

"You're really not worried about the kids?"

She ground her teeth and clenched her fists.

Don't blow up.

Of course she was worried about the kids. The fact that she hadn't thought of them until Dan raised the subject filled her with shame. But admitting that, when she had no plans to leave her bed and actually *do* anything about it, would make her look as bad as she felt.

"They're going to be fine," she told Dan. "Just please leave me alone and let me take a nap."

To her surprise, he did.

She fell asleep as soon as she'd sanded down the rough edges of her headache with two Tylenol and three swallows of Listerine.

CHLOE

Almost before she and Josh had even entered the Blackwells' abandoned mansion, it struck Chloe that the difference between run-of-the-mill rich people like Brody Kiplinger's family and actual billionaires like the Blackwells lay in the details.

The Blackwells' stuff was just *nicer*, often in ways that defied explanation. Chloe couldn't identify what made the back patio flowerpot that Josh lifted up to produce a spare basement key so superior to ordinary flowerpots—*was it the material? the design? the seasonal winter cabbage?*—but she sensed it nonetheless.

In the case of the basement door that the hidden key unlocked, it was the material: the knob and trim were made of weapons-grade steel, and the wood was so dense that the door opened and shut with the heavy authority of a bank vault. Set into the stone wall beside the door was a small digital keypad that looked like something out of a Mission: Impossible movie.

Josh knew the code, but it turned out not to matter, because the alarm system only looked omnipotent. Like pretty much everything with a user interface, it no longer functioned.

Chloe didn't pry into the question of how Josh had acquired his knowledge of the Blackwells' household defenses. He'd obviously had some kind of relationship with Tess, but if it wasn't platonic, Chloe didn't want to know any details.

"You sure they wouldn't mind that we're in here?"

"They're pretty chill," Josh assured her. "And I don't think they're coming back for a while."

Navigating the basement rec room in the darkness was a challenge, but eventually they groped their way up to the first floor, where there was plenty of daylight coming through the windows. Settling into the plush upholstery of the living room couch, Chloe felt the stranglehold of anxiety she'd been fighting all morning begin to loosen its grip.

It felt safe in this house. Nothing truly bad, she told herself, could ever happen in a place with such excellent décor.

Then she and Josh started to make out and wound up disproving that theory.

The pheromonal magic of the previous day proved impossible to re-create, mostly because after working out twice in succession with no shower, Josh just didn't smell good *at all*, and his nether regions were particularly rank. Not wanting to embarrass him at such a fragile stage in their relationship, Chloe first tried to solve the problem by suggesting a skinny-dip in the backyard pool. But Josh declined on the dual grounds that it was too cold out and the Blackwells' pool cover was electronic, making it impossible to retract.

Rather than risk the awkwardness of asking him to attend to his personal hygiene, Chloe did her best to gut it out without complaint. But after they relocated to an upstairs guest room featuring the finest bedsheets that had ever touched her skin, and he pressed her a little too urgently to go down on him, she not only couldn't complete the act, she burst into tears, which absolutely destroyed the mood for both of them.

Josh was horrified, and he apologized profusely. Chloe did the same, eventually managing to convey the gist of the difficulty, which proved every bit as embarrassing to him as she'd feared. He retreated to a bathroom and did his best to get clean with the assistance of some bottled water he'd found in the kitchen. After that, they went back at it. Both of them claimed to be pleased with the results, but the awkward silence as they got dressed made Chloe terrified that she'd ruined everything.

By that point, the anxiety had come back with a vengeance, and her body kept sending *let's-start-crying-again!* signals. But she was afraid that if she did, she'd permanently alienate Josh, who didn't seem at all concerned that society might be falling apart but *did* seem terrified of emotional vulnerability. So she resolved to fake a positive attitude.

They went to the kitchen in search of lunch. Both the furnishings and the food were billionaire-grade, although they were of limited comfort, given Chloe's fragile mental state. The fridge, which appeared to have been engineered to withstand a nuclear strike, had actually maintained something close to its working temperature over the thirty hours since the power had gone out. It was stocked with still-fresh berries and organic Greek yogurt, which Chloe combined with some kind of private label granola to create what turned out to be a surprisingly tasty meal.

She and Josh ate it while sitting together on bar stools at the kitchen island. He tried to distract her with some inane patter about his swim workouts, but when she didn't respond, he abandoned the effort.

The silence that followed was almost physically painful.

Chloe didn't even try to fill it. She was too preoccupied with keeping the lump in her throat in check.

"This is really delicious," Josh finally said.

"I know, right? *So* good!" Her lame attempt at cheerfulness, delivered in a trembling yet overloud voice, practically echoed in the big room. She cringed at the sound.

"You think you're okay on time?" Josh asked.

"I should be." Her voice almost broke.

Hold it together!

"I just don't want you to be late for tennis."

"What if there isn't any tennis?" The question tumbled out despite her fear of asking it.

"You'll at least have practice," he told her. "Right?"

"I don't know, I'm starting to think . . . like . . ."

Don't go there.

Screw it, go there.

"What if this is permanent?"

"It's not," he said matter-of-factly. "It's definitely not."

"How do you know?"

"I just do. I mean, there's no way."

Shit, I'm crying again.

She didn't sob or break down, but she couldn't stop the tears from coming. To her relief, Josh immediately put his hand over hers in a tender gesture.

"It's okay. Everything's going to be fine."

She decided to lay her cards on the table. Faking it was just too hard.

"I'm just *scared*. I think this could be really bad. Like, end-of-the-world bad—"

"It's not the end of the world. It's just a little time-out."

"But, like . . . I was supposed to take the ACT Saturday, and the ED deadline's the first, and if I can't take it now, there's no more time, and I'll never get to—"

"No-no-no-no-no." Josh scooted his stool over to bring himself close enough to put his arm around her. He smelled much better now. "It's going to be fine. Everything will just get pushed a little. Like, they're not going to screw anybody. If this goes on any longer, they'll move the test, they'll move the ED deadline, it'll be fine. Trust me."

She'd misjudged him. He wasn't going to run if she opened up to him.

Which was a huge relief, because the alternative would've been unbearable.

"Thank you."

"For what?"

"Just for being here. I'm sorry I'm such a mess." It was embarrassing how much time he and Emma were both having to spend comforting her today.

"It's all good. I get it."

"It just, like . . . it kinda sucks at home right now. My mom's losing her shit. And my dad wants us to ride all the way to my grandmother's on our bikes."

"Where's she live?"

"Outside Boston."

"Jesus. That's, like, *far*."

"I know! And honestly? If this is the zombie apocalypse? I don't want to spend it with my parents! In Boston!"

"So don't. You're almost an adult. You can do what you want."

"But I can't stay home alone. We don't have any food! We barely have water."

"Stay here," Josh suggested.

She let out a little half laugh, hoping it made her sound like the idea hadn't occurred to her. "You think?"

"Why not? The Blackwells aren't coming back till this is over. Pool's full of water. There's plenty of food."

She looked into those killer blue eyes.

Do I ask him? What if he says no?

She decided to risk it.

"Would you stay here with me?"

For a second, he didn't answer, and panic started to flood her brain.

Then he smiled. "Sure. Why not?"

Chloe kissed him hard and deep, wrapping her hand around the back of his head and digging her fingers into his hair. It was tacky with dried sweat, but she no longer cared. She would've crawled inside him if she could.

Eventually, they came up for air.

"Sure you're okay on time?"

Chloe nodded. She was okay now. Not just on time, but everything. Because no matter what happened, she wouldn't have to face it alone.

MAX

It had taken him dozens of tries from his seat on the floor of Judge Distefano's living room, but Max had finally figured out how to toss Ruby's hard rubber ball at just the right angle to bank it off the wall below the stairs and send it ricocheting down the hallway to the kitchen.

Ruby stood next to his leg, watching him intently as she waited for the throw. Max faked a couple of times, making her jerk in anticipation. Then he let loose. The ball disappeared around the corner, and the dog followed it, her collar jingling as she went.

"So this EMP thing," the judge asked from his easy chair, "was a plot device in a video game?"

"Yeah."

"But you're thinking it actually happened in real life?"

"I mean, it makes sense. Right?"

"It does explain some things," the judge admitted.

"Except why did that one guy's car still work?"

"Probably 'cause it's old enough that the starter's not electric. Cars these days, they're computers on wheels, y'know? But not the old ones. . . . What do your parents think of this theory? Does it hold water for 'em?"

"I don't know," Max replied as Ruby trotted back into the

room with the ball and dropped it in front of him. "I told my dad about it, but he didn't really say anything."

When Max reached for the ball, the dog snatched it away again with her teeth. He grabbed it between his thumb and forefinger, and they began a lazy tug of war.

"Well, if it turns out to be true . . ." The creases around the judge's eyes deepened as he considered the implications. "It could be a real issue for some people. I got a medical thing coming up that'll have to get scotched."

"If you need me to watch Ruby—or walk her, or take her to the vet, or whatever—just let me know," Max offered. "You don't even have to pay me. I'd do it for free."

"Good to know, kid. Thanks. Might just take you up on that." The judge watched Max and Ruby continue their tug-of-war. "How come you never got a dog of your own?"

"My dad's allergic."

"Yeah? Sucks to be him."

"Sucks to be me."

"That too."

There was a knock at the door. Ruby abandoned the ball and raced to the entryway, barking as she went.

Max started to rise. "I'll get it for you."

"Sit! Sit." The judge waved him off, then pushed himself up from his seat. "I need the exercise."

Max did as he was told. The judge shuffled past him and went around the corner to the front door, just out of sight.

"Ruby! Settle down!" the judge grumbled.

Over the sound of the dog's barks, Max heard the door open

with a wooden creak, followed by the metallic *click-skreee* of the outer screen door.

"Afternoon, beautiful!"

"Hiya, Judge." It was Jordan's mom. Her voice sounded tired, or maybe drunk. "You want to come to dinner? We're having the whole block over again."

Max winced. *Again?*

"You know, I got a very full social calendar," the judge told Mrs. Stankovic. "But for you, I'll move some things around. What can I bring?"

"You're a doll! Just come with a smile. Unless you don't like sea bass. Eddie just got home from the store with a shitload of it. We gotta grill it tonight, or it'll turn."

"The store's open again?"

"No. But Eddie knows a guy."

"Fantastic. I love sea bass."

"Super! Come by before sunset. Same as yesterday. See you in a bit!"

"Thanks again, gorgeous! Can't wait."

The door closed. A moment later, the judge reappeared, with Ruby at his heels. Max stuck the ball under his thigh, and she jumped into his lap to dig for it.

"So your neighbors are having another cookout."

"I heard." As Ruby dug under his leg in search of the ball, he shook his head. "Hope my parents don't make me go."

"Why wouldn't you want to go? 'Cause Jordan's a numb-skull?"

"A little. But also, there's, like, nobody else to talk to except adults. And the biggest thing is—"

He flung the ball into the hallway. The dachshund took off after it.

"I just hate fish."

The judge settled back into his easy chair. "Then don't go. Things are bad enough right now. You shouldn't have to eat fish at a time like this."

DAN

Overwhelmed by stress and low blood sugar, Dan opted for the self-care of a big lunch, heating up one of the now-defrosted burritos in a pan and smothering it with a generous quantity of pineapple salsa.

In the abstract, he would've preferred the more heroic option of forgoing the calories for his children's benefit. But they were picky eaters, they'd both declared their hatred of the pineapple salsa more than once, and in any case, he didn't know where the hell they were.

He considered going out to look for them, but he didn't want to leave Jen alone for too long in case she went searching for the booze he'd hidden inside Chloe's camp trunk in the basement. Plus, after two trips up and down the hill, his legs were cramping so badly that if he went into town again, he wasn't sure he'd make it back. As the burrito heated up, he stretched and massaged his knotted muscles while considering the most urgent of the many questions he was facing:

How do I tell Marty they have to leave?

Or, alternatively,

How do I explain to Jen why I'm letting them stay?

It wasn't a trivial choice. If he let Marty and Marina stay, and the worst-case scenario turned out to be true, his boss's bottomless appetite could pose a genuine threat to the family's survival.

On the other hand, if this really was the worst case, and Dan threw the couple out on the street, he could be sending them to their doom.

By the time he sat down to his meal, with the pan soaking in the sink under a thin layer of water that it pained him to allocate to cleaning, he'd realized his decision rested on top of a deeper question:

Just how much did he owe Marty Callahan?

They'd known each other over thirty years, but only the first and last four of those had included any significant contact. They'd first met in the fall of '86, when Marty arrived at their freshman dorm as a puppy-dog-friendly, slightly fratty football recruit from suburban Cleveland. He and Dan liked each other well enough, but not so well that they stayed in contact after their rooming groups diverged at the end of the year. When their paths crossed again in an application-only fiction writing workshop the spring of junior year, Dan was surprised to discover that the goofy, bearlike jock he remembered had somehow morphed into a bong-wielding Deadhead with aspirations to become the Martin Scorsese of Generation X.

Dan was in the fiction class on a whim, having gotten in on the strength of a writing sample he'd composed in a few hours the night before the deadline. Marty, on the other hand, had only earned his seat after a three-semester battle of attrition with the instructor. Antonia Studish was a Virginia Woolf aficionado whose aesthetic sensibility was such a poor fit with Marty's own creative gifts that by the third time she rejected one of his application stories—yet another blood-drenched genre piece, this one featuring not a hard-bitten cop or a cynical hit man, but a hard-bitten, cynical cop who was secretly a hit man—she'd begun to suspect "Marty Callahan" wasn't an actual person but an extended practical joke one of her colleagues was playing on her. Only when the large, shaggy, disarmingly sweet Marty materialized during her office hours to beg her to reconsider had she relented and allowed him into the class.

For Dan, the course had almost, but not quite, been life changing. While his stories were stocked with stereotypical (albeit barely fictionalized) characters like overbearing Jewish mothers, they were also clever, intuitively plotted, and reminiscent enough of early Philip Roth that Antonia—who'd opened the first class by announcing that she didn't believe in grading fiction, and every student who turned in their work on time should expect to get a B-plus—abandoned her own rule to give Dan an A.

The effect of that A was briefly, deliriously intoxicating. The Altman family had been producing dissatisfied lawyers for three generations, and once his C-plus in organic chemistry took med school off the table, both Dan and his parents had assumed he'd keep the streak going. But the feedback that Antonia left in the margins of his stories (*great turn of phrase—excellent job revealing character through action—did NOT see that coming, an ending worthy of O. Henry!*) was so encouraging, coming as it did from an actual working novelist whose debut had been rapturously reviewed by Michiko Kakutani, that Dan started to fantasize about becoming a writer himself. The fantasies lasted until midsummer, when— over predinner drinks on the back porch of the family beach house in Wellfleet—Dan casually floated the idea of applying to MFA programs in creative writing after graduation. His mother responded by suffering a panic attack so severe that it required a trip to the Mid-Cape Emergency Center.

Dan was nothing if not a faithful son. Three months later, he took the LSAT and sealed his fate.

After that, other than a few isolated attempts at starting a novel in his late twenties, all of which fell over dead within a few thousand words, he didn't look back until their twenty-fifth Princeton reunion, when a middle-aged Marty Callahan rematerialized in front of him wearing a brand of designer jeans Dan had never heard of and a cashmere hoodie that looked approximately as expensive as a week in the Hamptons. Marty had just wrapped his tenth season as the creator and executive producer of *Bullet Town*, a police procedural about a hard-bitten, cynical cop who was secretly a hit man. It had a weekly audience of fourteen million people, none of whom Dan knew personally. But he did his best to fake it.

"Congrats on your show! It's awesome!"

"Thanks, man!" Marty looked pleased, but skeptical. "You actually watch it?"

"Well, not religiously." Dan had made it through a little more than half of the pilot episode, which he'd ordered out of curiosity on DVD from Netflix a few years after its original air date. "But it's everywhere! You're part of the culture!" (Meaning, *I see ads for your show when I watch football.*)

"Yeah, it's really stuck around." Marty's eyes suddenly widened. "Dude! I just realized—you were there at the beginning! That creative writing class? With Antonia Studish? I literally came up with Vic Stryker in that class!" Marty chuckled, shaking his head at the memory. "And, Jesus, did she hate it."

"Oh, yeah . . ." Dan thought back to that spring, decades earlier, when anything seemed possible, except maybe the idea that Marty's writing would someday be worth millions. "Your sensibility really didn't mesh with hers."

"That's a fucking understatement."

Dan let out a burst of laughter. "Ohmygod! Remember the penis gun?"

Marty practically squealed with delight. "Yes! The penis gun!"

"What were you even thinking with that?"

"Dude, it was brilliant! He was a cyborg assassin with a gun where his junk should be. Which, think about it—you're a robot, you don't need a dick. But if you're an assassin . . . you *definitely* need a gun. Plus someplace to hide it. So why not in your pants?"

"You're right. Makes perfect sense. Very elegant reasoning." A warm bath of nostalgia was flooding Dan's brain. "Oh, man . . . the thing I remember most—this is *so* vivid—is you in your dorm room after class, and you've got that giant bong in one hand—"

"Long Bong Silver! God, I loved that bong."

"And your robot assassin story in the other hand, and you're reading her comments out loud, and she'd written something like—"

"I remember this! Her exact fucking words: 'Penis gun metaphor is *way* too on-the-nose'!"

"And you were, like, 'It's not a metaphor! It's just a penis gun!'"

They were both shaking with laughter. "Oh, man," Dan moaned when he finally recovered enough to speak. "What do you think ever happened to her?"

"Who, Antonia Studish? The critically acclaimed author of *Stamen*? The"—Marty stuck out his lower jaw and adopted a plummy

Thurston Howell accent—"'searing, densely allegorical indictment of Victorian sexual mores'? Dude, I'll tell you exactly—"

"It's *morays*."

"What?"

"It's pronounced *morays*."

"Seriously?" Marty shrugged. "Shit, you learn something
new every day. I'll tell you exactly what happened to her. At least
as of a couple years ago. She's an adjunct professor at Oberlin.
Stamen's out of print. So's her second novel, which tanked. Never
wrote a third one—or at least, she never got it published—"

"Wait—you keep in touch with her?"

"Oh, hell, no! I just hate-google her when I need some inspiration." Marty shook his head. "I just wish she knew how things
turned out for that wide-eyed young kid she shit all over back
in the day. You know, I got a B-minus in that class?"

"Seriously?"

"Yeah! She was all, 'Everybody gets a B-plus! Except you,
asshole!'" Marty's eyes darkened as he stared into his highball
glass. Dan decided against mentioning his own A, which now
resurfaced in his memory as a poignant signifier of roads not
taken.

"I just wish she knew," Marty repeated.

"You don't think she does?"

"Oh, hell, no. There's no way she watches CBS." Then he
perked up again. "So whatcha been up to? Still writing?"

"Oh, no . . . I mean, not like that. I'm a securities lawyer in
the city."

"Like, Wall Street shit?"

"Yeah."

"How is it?"

"Honestly? It sucks."

"Dude, I'm sorry." Marty looked genuinely sorry.

"It's okay. Not your fault. And it doesn't *all* suck. I mean, my wife and kids are great."

"Yeah? How many kids?"

"Two. Girl and a boy. Thirteen and ten."

"Awesome!"

"Yeah. They're great. How about you?"

"No kids. Two wives. I mean, not simultaneously. I only have one right now. But I'm still paying for two."

"Ouch."

"Yeah. Don't get divorced in California. Hey, I got a question: do you deal with any hedge fund guys in your job?"

"Constantly."

"What are they like? I mean, as a class of person?"

"They're assholes."

Marty nodded. "Cool. Hey, can I pick your brain about that sometime? I want to pitch a show in that world."

"A Wall Street show?"

"Yeah. Like, about a guy who's a bond trader by day and—I dunno, a serial killer by night or something."

"Hasn't that been done before?"

"Maybe. Not on CBS, though. And it doesn't have to be that specifically. Just something in that world. So I can try to get the network to shoot it in New York. My wife wants to move there, so I'm thinking, y'know . . ."

"Awesome! Yeah! Call me anytime! I'd love to help out."

Driving home, Dan couldn't get the conversation out of his

head—or the fact that Marty not only seemed rich and happy, but had a global audience of millions. The same thought that had been launching artistic careers for as long as there had been art lodged itself in Dan's mind:

If that guy can do it . . .

A week after the reunion, Dan owned three books on screen-writing, had read two of them, and was waking up at five every day to get in two hours of writing before breakfast. By the time Marty came through town in late summer and bought him lunch at Gotham to pick his brain for the show Marty was calling *Money Men*, Dan was halfway through the second draft of a *Law and Order: SVU* spec. Jen had read the first one and gently warned him to rewrite it before showing anyone else.

Marty was encouraging, sort of. "Everybody's first script sucks," he said. "And don't write more than one spec. After that, do something original."

"You mean, like a pilot?"

"Yeah. That'll suck, too, but at least pilots are more fun to read. So! Tell me all your best Wall Street asshole stories."

Dan only gave Marty his second-best stories. The best ones he kept for himself, eventually deploying several in a pilot script about a crooked law firm that he titled *Lucifer's Counsel*. After Jen pronounced his third draft "actually pretty good," Dan emailed Marty in January:

Hey, so, funny thing . . . I wrote a pilot. Any interest in looking at it?

Marty sent a two-word reply with no punctuation:

send it

Dan did. Six weeks later, after he'd finally stopped thinking about Marty every time he checked his email and was mulling over whether to give up the TV thing and try his hand at a novel, he got a six-word reply along with a phone number:

some good shit give a ring

"It's a great start!" Marty yelled from what sounded like a jet-engine-equipped convertible idling in LA traffic. "You're good at this. Grab a pen, I got a couple notes."

There were more than a couple. Marty rattled off dozens of ideas and criticisms, some contradictory and all based on the script's first ten pages, which was as far as Marty had read.

"I can tell where it's going, though," he said. Dan silently bristled at that, but after hearing the notes, he had to admit Marty was absolutely right about where it was going.

Dan spent the next month doing his best to execute a draft that incorporated Marty's ideas. A few weeks after he'd finished and sent it back, Marty called with what turned out to be life-changing news:

"We got a twelve-episode pickup! I'm turning over *Bullet Town* to my co-EP and moving to New York to shoot the new thing! Gonna run the writers' room out of there, too."

"Holy shit! Congratulations! You got *Money Men* on the air!"

"It's not *Money Men* anymore. We tweaked the concept—now it's called *Bullet Town: NYC*."

"Is it still about Wall Street?"

"Not really. It's about a cop who's secretly a killer. It's a vigilante justice thing—he murders criminals who got off at trial. Kind of like *Dirty Harry* meets *Death Wish*? But fresh. So, you want in?"

"What do you mean?"

"I mean, do you want to come write for me?"

"Are you kidding? Ohmygod! *Yes!*"

"Don't get too excited yet—it's going to be a little tricky to pull off with the network. But I think I can get you in as a diversity hire."

"A diversity hire?"

"Yeah."

"Marty, I don't know if you've ever noticed this about me? But I'm, uh, pretty thoroughly white? And straight. And a guy."

"Yeah, but you're old. That's a thing now."

Marty turned out to be wrong about the parameters of the network's diversity program. Dan didn't qualify, but Marty still managed to get him a lowball offer as a story editor.

For a law firm partner, it was —financially speaking, at least—potentially suicidal. If *Bullet Town: NYC* only ran twelve episodes, or if Marty decided things weren't working out and canned him, Dan's total compensation would top out in the mid-five figures, with no guarantee he'd ever make another nickel as a writer. And to take the job, he'd have to walk away from Wilmer Hale and his comfortable mid-six a year. The senior partners made it clear they wouldn't backstop his TV writing dream. If it didn't work out, he couldn't come back, and he might never see that kind of money again in his life.

Jen, who up until then had patiently humored what she thought of as little more than a slightly nerdy midlife crisis, told him he was out of his mind. Over the next few months, they fought more—and louder—than at any point in their relationship. But with the kids' college money socked away and the mortgage paid off, Dan made his leap of faith.

To say it had worked out well would be an understatement.

Three years into the show's run, he had writing credits on more episodes than anybody except Marty, and he was pulling in as much money as he had during his best years at Wilmer Hale. He had an office in the West Village, an agent in LA, free screeners during awards season, and Ray Liotta's number on his cell phone.

He owed all of this to Marty, which was a substantial life debt even before Dan factored in his monumentally stupid mismanagement of the previous spring's contract renegotiation.

In retrospect, some amount of conflict between the two men was inevitable given the mismatch between their estimations of the *Bullet Town* franchise. To Marty, *Bullet Town* wasn't just his life's work. It was culturally meaningful, widely beloved populist entertainment whose savage dismissal by TV critics only proved that it was operating on a level they were too effete and out of touch to appreciate.

To Dan, it was the pop culture equivalent of Cool Ranch Doritos. And while he was content to help Marty crank out product for a couple more seasons—long enough to earn a co-EP credit and bank some cash in advance of striking out on his own—he considered the job to be a kind of craft apprenticeship for his real creative output, which wouldn't start until he'd punched out of the crap factory.

Dan kept his attitude hidden from Marty all too successfully, which had tragic consequences when Marty called him into his office for a private meeting one afternoon a week before they wrapped the third season.

"I got three words for you!" Marty crowed. "*Bullet Town: Boston!*"

"Cool," Dan said, thinking nothing of the sort.

"Right? Here's the pitch: he's a capo in the Irish mob . . . who's secretly a cop!"

"Sounds great. Does the network want it?"

"They're jonesing for it! We'll write it on the hiatus, maybe shoot it as a midseason. And if it goes—*you'll* be the showrunner!"

"Oh! Wow. That. Is . . ."

"Awesome! Right?"

"It's . . . really flattering."

"Great! So I'll tell the studio, we'll fold the development into your new deal—"

"Whoa-whoa-whoa—"

"Wuh-wuh-what?" Marty already had the phone receiver in his hand.

"I just . . . need a minute. On this."

"What for? Buddy, I'm making your dreams come true."

"Yeah, I—it's just, I was planning on writing my own thing over the hiatus?"

"What thing?"

"It's a, umm . . . it's just, like, a small thing."

"Whaddaya want to do a small thing for? This is a big thing!"

"Y'know, I've had this idea for a while, and—"

"Were you going to pitch it to me?" The phone receiver was back in its cradle, and Marty had a look on his face like a wounded puppy.

"I don't know if it's your kind of show. It's, y'know . . . critic bait."

In the six months since that moment, not a day had gone by that Dan hadn't stopped to wonder what on earth he was thinking when he used the word *critic* in front of Marty.

To be fair, even if Dan hadn't name-checked the only class of person toward whom his boss felt implacable murderous rage, Marty still might've exploded. He just probably wouldn't have thrown things. Dan eventually made it out of the room in one piece, although the same couldn't be said for two coffee mugs and a commemorative tombstone from the original *Bullet Town*'s one hundredth episode. And while Marty ultimately brought him back for the fourth season of *BT: NYC*, Dan's refusal to do the *Boston* spinoff wound up costing him three thousand dollars an episode in compensation, plus every ounce of goodwill he'd accumulated with his boss over the prior thirty years.

As of Tuesday morning, Dan had estimated that he'd earned back maybe twenty percent of that goodwill. Whether it was the result of Stockholm Syndrome or his parents' withholding of affection during his childhood, Dan still pined for the other eighty percent—and one of the many disorienting things about the current moment was that, judging by Marty's attitude since he'd pedaled up the driveway, Dan had just earned it all back.

Now that he'd opened his home to Marty, everything was kosher between them.

Granted, his boss's change of heart was entirely transactional. But even so, having thought it through, Dan realized he couldn't ask the interlopers to leave. It wasn't just their shared history, or the fact that Marty was a very large man with an unpredictable temper. There was also the moral question of whether Dan had an obligation, in times of crisis, to open his home to those in need. Outside of the high holy days, he hadn't been to synagogue since Max's bar mitzvah. But he didn't have to be observant to know what both Rabbi Firshein and the Torah would have to say about the situation.

Having made his decision, Dan was trying to decide how to explain it to Jen when he heard the garage door open. A moment later, Marty strode into the room, carrying a Whole Foods bag.

"Dude! This place is *Chinatown*!"

"It is?"

"I mean, not ethnically. It's super white. But politically? Ohmygod! It's exactly like the movie! 'Cause nobody knows who's really in charge, and it's *all* about the water." He plunked the bag down on the counter. "Where's Marina? She okay?"

"I think she's in the living room. I don't understand this *Chinatown* analogy."

"'Cause you missed the town meeting," Marty said as he trotted off down the hall to find his wife.

"There was a town meeting?"

"Tell you about it in a sec!" Marty yelled from the foyer.

Dan walked over to inspect the Whole Foods bag Marty had just brought in. Inside were four liters of mineral water and six bottles of kombucha in assorted flavors.

"Hey, babe!" he heard Marty call out. "You doing okay?"

The greeting was followed by some low murmurs that Dan couldn't decipher. A moment later, Marty and Marina both re-entered the kitchen. Marty pointed to the bag.

"Did you see I got us water?"

"Yeah. Thanks."

"Told you I'd come through!"

Marty pulled out two of the four liters of mineral water. He handed one to Marina, then unscrewed the top on the second and began to drink straight from the bottle.

"So tell me about this meeting—"

Marina interrupted him. "May I have a glass, please, Dan?"

"Uh . . . yeah." Dan went to the cabinet to fetch her a drinking glass. Marty had already chugged half his liter, leading Dan to wonder if the two of them planned to polish off the entire new inventory of water in one sitting. "So, the meeting?"

Marty set his water down and stifled a belch. "Totally nuts. So, first of all—did you know the town next door still has water?"

"Which one? Ridgelawn?"

"Yeah, that's it. Their tap water's still flowing! 'Cause they get it from a reservoir. And we've got nothing, 'cause we're all well water, and our pumps are down. But that's not our fault! So we gotta get some sharesies from them. It's only fair. But the stupid mayor was, all—" He switched to a falsetto for the imitation. "'There has to be a peaceful negotiation!' And it's, like, come on! They're not just going to give it to us. We gotta lean on 'em a little."

"We?"

"Yeah. All of us."

"Who was at this meeting?"

Marty ticked off the participants on his fingers. "Shrek, Kozak, the mayor, police chief, that dweeby manager guy, plus a bunch of regular shmoes."

"So, like, how many people?"

"I dunno—a hundred?"

"Should I have been there?"

"Maybe? But don't beat yourself up. You got a lot on your plate right now. With the—" Marty held up his fist with the pinky and thumb extended, then tipped the thumb to his mouth a few times in a drinky-drink motion. "But don't worry—the really big meeting's tomorrow morning. You should go to that one. 'Cause we're going to vote on who's in charge."

"*Who's* going to vote?" Dan was having a hard time getting his head around Marty's inclusion of himself when referring to Lincolnwood's citizenry.

"All of us! The whole town. 'Cause the mayor was all, 'This is a democracy!' She gets really emotional, you know? It's counter-productive. But Shrek was, like, 'Fine, we'll vote on it.' 'Cause it's, like, whatever. I mean, the thing is—we got, what? Like, twelve cops on the whole force?"

"I don't know." Dan had never bothered to consider the size of Lincolnwood's police force.

"Something like that. But half of 'em went home and never came back. So there's really just six. And only two of them are still listening to the police chief lady. The other four are on our side—"

"What's 'our side'?"

"The Watchdogs. Oh! Dude. I forgot to tell you! This is awesome: I'm a Watchdog!"

"You're a what?"

"A Watchdog! Shrek deputized me! I'm part of the militia!"

"There's a *militia*?"

"Yeah! We're like fill-in cops. Kozak's the leader. You know Kozak, right? Used to be the chief of police? Supposedly, they're giving me a gun tomorrow. Eddie's a Watchdog, too. That's why he was guarding the Whole Foods this morning. By the way—did you steal his dry cleaning idea?"

"What?"

"Remember the first season finale? When Vargas strung those corpses up on the dry cleaning rack? Did you get that from Eddie?"

"No! Marty! That was *your* idea!"

Marty took a long chug of his mineral water, then nodded pensively. "Y'know, I thought I came up with that? But Eddie was really sure of himself."

"Ohmygod. You didn't let him think it was his idea, did you?"

Marty gave a sheepish wince. "Pretty much."

"*Jesus*, Marty! He's been bugging me about that for years! And it's not fucking true!"

"Don't sweat it. When this is all over, I'll find some room in the budget to throw him a bone. 'Cause right now, dude? Politically? You *really* want to keep these guys happy. And between you and me, you've got some work to do. Eddie thinks you're stuck up. Plus, you stole his idea."

"I didn't fucking steal his idea! It was *your* idea!"

"I know. But that's not what he thinks. Don't worry, though—I can vouch for you. Eddie loves me. Speaking of which: we're all invited next door for dinner. Got a shit ton of fish. Plus some decent Chilean whites. I think we're going to make sangria. Eddie got a bunch of fruit from the produce department, and it's going to go bad if we don't use it."

Marina finished her second glass of water, or possibly her fourth—Dan hadn't been paying attention, but when he looked over at the sound of her empty glass rapping the table, he realized the bottle she'd opened was mostly depleted.

"I will need to wash up," she announced. "Do you have a guest towel, please, Dan?"

Dan stared at her, baffled. "You know we don't have water, right?"

Marina and Marty both glanced over at the remaining pots of tap water on the countertop across the room.

"We've got *some* water," Marty pointed out.

"We're going to need that to drink," Dan reminded them.

"I will only use a little," Marina promised.

"We just gotta freshen up," Marty added. "But don't worry— I can get us all the water we need. Especially once we put the screws to Ridgelawn. I'm a Watchdog!"

"Should *I* be a Watchdog?" Dan found the prospect of a citizens' militia unsettling. But if there had to be one, it seemed prudent to join it.

"Huh." Marty considered the question. "I dunno. They might have enough guys already? But I can put in a word for you. Just don't fight Eddie on that whole dry cleaner idea. He's got a lot of pull with Kozak."

Marty drained the last of his mineral water, then let out a low burp. "Can we get those towels, buddy?"

CHLOE

"They just postponed it," Josh told her. "It's temporary. Every-thing's going to be fine."

It was amazing how supportive he was being. And Chloe desperately needed the support. When they left the Blackwells' mansion, Chloe had thought she was ready for anything. No matter which possible future lay ahead of her, she could roll with the punches.

But it turned out she couldn't. After spending an hour hud-dled on the bleachers in front of the tennis courts, with no sign of life anywhere except for a few stray moms and toddlers on the playground next door, she'd turned into a puddle, crying in Josh's arms for the third time that day.

The whole team had ghosted on her, Coach K included. He hadn't even left a sign on the bulletin board announcing that the semi had been postponed. This was supposed to be the cli-max of her tennis career—or at least the end of it, assuming she didn't play in college. She'd spent ten years working toward this moment.

And it had just disappeared. Nobody had even bothered to leave a note.

It wasn't just the tennis. *Everything* was slipping away. The ACT she'd prepped for. The Common App essay she'd spent so much time to make absolutely perfect—did she even have a hard copy?

The supplementals. The schoolwork. The grades. The recs.

The extracurriculars. The volunteering. The summer internship. All the building blocks of the future she'd spent so much time and effort assembling.

Gone. Poof. Dust. None of it existed anymore. None of it mattered.

An hour ago, she'd thought she was okay with all of this.

She was not okay with this.

Maybe eventually. But not yet.

Thank God for Josh. He was the only reason this was bearable. He'd been incredible, holding her all through her freak-out and telling her the power would come back on and this would all be over by the weekend, even though by now she suspected he no longer believed that, either.

The silences between them that had felt so awkward as recently as lunchtime were oddly comforting to her now. She and Josh didn't have to talk. They understood each other. And as long as they stayed together, they'd be okay, no matter how screwed up the world got.

It was just hard saying goodbye to her old life.

Josh took a deep breath and let it all out in a noisy exhale. He gave her back one last vigorous rub, then ended it with a double pat.

"You should go home," he told her. "Eat some carbs. Rest up for tomorrow. Anything could happen. You know?" He stood up from the bleachers, raising his arms over his head in a stretch. "I gotta jet if I'm going to get my intervals in before dark."

It was cute how he was keeping up the pretense. She wondered if he'd get any exercise at all that afternoon. If he did, he'd stink even worse tomorrow. But that was okay. She had a plan for how they could use the pool water and the gas stove at the Blackwells' to draw a warm bath. They wouldn't make the same mistakes twice—this time, they'd both get clean before they tried to mash.

"Yeah." She nodded and stood up alongside him. "I should get home, too."

There was a lot to do there. She not only needed to pack, she had to decide the right way to say goodbye to her family so they wouldn't freak out when she left them to go live at the Blackwells' with Josh.

A note would be best. That way, by the time they read it, she'd already be gone.

"This is going to be hard," she told him as they dismounted the bleachers.

"Nah." He gave her one last squeeze, then kissed her on the top of her head. "It's going to be great. You'll see."

JEN

It occurred to Jen—surrounded by drunken idiots, her chair cruelly positioned directly across the table from a pitcher of sangria she couldn't drink even as she stewed in an excruciating physical and moral hangover—that if the devil existed and had set out to custom-build her own personal hell, it'd look exactly like the Stankovics' back patio.

She never should've gotten out of bed after that three-hour afternoon nap. It hadn't exactly been restorative, but at least she'd been unconscious.

And right now, consciousness sucked.

Everything sucked. Especially people. Dan sucked, the kids sucked, the Stankovics sucked, and the Callahans triple-sucked.

But the person who sucked worst of all was Jen.

Now that she was sober, or at least no longer drunk, there was no chemical buffer insulating her from the shame of her own bad choices. As she sat there, they burned in her memory like battery acid.

If I'd gone shopping on Monday, we wouldn't have to sit here and eat this shitty fish with these shitty people.

If I hadn't opened the goddamn emergency vodka this morning, Dan wouldn't have busted me. And I could be drinking that sangria right now.

Plus, I'd still have vodka left.

And I could've forced Dan to make Marty and Marina leave.

Her bad choices weren't just in the past. She was still making them every time she opened her mouth.

She shouldn't have yelled at Dan about Marty and Marina when he woke her up from the nap.

She shouldn't have gotten so angry at Max when he refused to go next door for dinner. What was the big deal about letting him stay home and eat peanut butter out of a jar? She'd eventually given up and let him do just that. But she could've saved them both a lot of misery if she hadn't fought him on it for no good reason.

And she definitely shouldn't have made that sarcastic comment to Chloe about not getting any work done on her college apps today. Even if civilization wasn't collapsing, it was Chloe who was applying, not Jen. So why get on her case about not finishing that practice ACT? The fact that Chloe had just shrugged and quietly apologized rather than fighting fire with fire only made Jen feel like an even bigger asshole, although she couldn't shake the suspicion that her daughter's uncharacteristic retreat into pacifism was the result of having spent the day getting high with some delinquent mystery boy.

The worst thing about every one of these interactions was that, even as they were happening, Jen knew she was in the wrong. She watched herself be a complete bitch with the three people she cared most about in the world, while lacking either the strength or the compassion to stop.

By the time they headed over to the Stankovics', she'd resolved to just keep her stupid mouth shut for the rest of the evening—only to regret that decision, too, once she'd failed to intervene in the ugly fight that erupted between Carol Sweeney and Eddie Stankovic.

The specifics of the dispute had been impossible to follow, having something to do with the mayor, the police chief, and some kind of vote that was supposed to happen the next morning. Back at the house post-nap, Dan had tried to explain the situation to her in the course of defending himself for not kicking Marty and Marina out, but Jen had been too furious with him to bother trying to understand what he was talking about.

Whatever the issue, there was no mistaking the fact that Eddie was acting like a misogynistic bully—and if Jen had spoken up like she should've, Carol might not have felt compelled to walk out of the meal on the arm of Judge Distefano, who never returned after escorting her home.

That effectively reduced the voices of sanity at the table to zero, which became all too apparent when the men spent twenty minutes arguing over the qualifications for membership in something called the Watchdogs, which was apparently some kind of militia, but sounded more like a softball league, or maybe a bachelor party outing. Eddie and Marty were members, and Dan, Arjun, and even Eddie's son, Jordan, lobbied them for membership so plaintively that Jen just felt embarrassed for everybody.

Once the fish was gone, Chloe, Jordan, and the Mukherjees had all exited, leaving Jen and Dan alone with the Stankovics and the Callahans. At that point, the conversation descended into an even lower circle of hell.

The two other couples seemed to feed on each other's

stupidity. Having bonded over melodramatic retellings of their recent personal traumas—Marina's harrowing escape from the shoe department of Bergdorf Goodman and Kayla's agonizing ejection from the dentist's chair with her teeth only half scraped of plaque—while refilling each other's glasses through two full pitchers and counting, Kayla was now sloppy drunk and openly worshiping at the altar of her dimwit guest's superficial glamour.

"You're an influencer, aren'tcha?"

"Yes," Marina admitted. "But only in the lifestyle space. I am not a thought leader like Martin."

"Ohmygawd, I can't *wait* to follow you both on Insta!"

Jen began to wonder if she should actually root for society to collapse, if only to deprive Kayla of her Instagram feed.

Meanwhile, on the other side of the table, Martin the Thought Leader was glowing with almost erotic pleasure at Eddie's exhaustive effort to rank the top five episodes of the Bullet Town franchise.

"The Mexican restaurant one! *So* dark!" He lowered his voice to a macho snarl as he quoted Vic Stryker. "'*Try the queso—it's got a little kick to it!*'"

"Dude, I *love* that you love that one! When I was writing it, I was worried people wouldn't get it. 'Cause it's basically, like, a tone-poem homage to Mexican food. Y'know?"

"No, I got it! Fuckin' genius, bro. That one might even be a top three."

Across the table on the opposite side of the sangria pitcher, Dan looked as miserable as Jen felt. So far, none of his *BT: NYC* episodes had made Eddie's list.

"Hey, Marty!" Kayla bellowed from across the table. "Can I ask a totally crass question?"

Is there another kind with you? Jen wondered.

"Fire away!" Marty replied.

"Ballpark figure, not gonna hold ya to it—how much you figure Eddie's gonna get for that dry cleaning idea Dan-O stole from him?"

Dan winced. "I thought we'd covered this," he said in a wounded voice.

"Ya busted!" Eddie crowed as he pointed at Dan with both index fingers.

"Okay, so . . . don't quote me . . ." The Stankovics both leaned forward in their chairs, hanging on Marty's reply. "But I'm thinking probably . . . maybe . . . I dunno, gotta check with business affairs . . . but . . . ten K?"

"Whooooooo!" shrieked Kayla, throwing both arms in the air as she beamed at her husband. "We're going to St. Kitt's on that shit! Pass the sangria, baby!"

"Don't you think you've had enough?" Jen asked her.

The words themselves were ill-advised. But it was the tone of voice that caused the chill to descend over the table.

Kayla sank back in her chair, momentarily stunned as she gaped openmouthed at her attacker.

Shit. That was too harsh.

"Unlike some people at this table," Kayla replied, her voice rising in righteous disgust, "I actually know when I've had enough. So I don't have to get carried home at the end of the night like a fuckin' *wino.*"

"Fuck you, Kayla."

"Fuck *you*, Jen!"

A horrified silence followed. Eddie finally broke it with a barking laugh.

"Catfight, baby!"

"Time to say good night," Dan declared, already on his feet.

DAN

Dan brushed his teeth by flashlight, rinsing his mouth with water from the bathtub. Then he dampened a washcloth and wiped his face with it. He was starting to feel tacky and unclean, but using soap would've required more water than he was willing to expend.

God help us if Marty and Marina find out we've got a full tub up here.

It was enough to last awhile, as long as they didn't have to use it to flush the toilets.

What'll we do when we run out of the pool water in the garage?

After Jen's performance tonight, the odds of their procuring a refill from the Stankovics seemed dicey.

Marty can get more out of them. Although he'll probably use half of it on the way home.

Dan switched off the flashlight and stood motionless in the dark. Anxious dread was vibrating through his body like a low-grade electrical current.

None of this was sustainable. Something had to give.

Maybe we'll wake up in the morning and the power will be back on.

He knew this was magical thinking, but he let himself indulge in it anyway. Enough improbable bad things had happened over the past two days that it seemed fair to imagine an improbable good thing might happen.

Moving by memory in the darkness, he crept back to the bedroom and got under the sheets.

With no familiar background hum emanating from appliances, furnaces, air-conditioning, or distant cars, the silence felt like an abyss. He took a few deep, slow breaths, trying to calm himself enough to sleep.

Jen's voice came from the far end of the bed.

"I'm sorry I fucked up."

Which time?

"It's okay."

More silence.

"They can't stay here, Dan."

"It's not going to be an issue. When we leave, they'll leave."

"When are we going to leave?"

"Tomorrow. I'll pack us up while you're at the AA meeting. We'll leave as soon as you get back." He tried to sound confident.

"It's going to rain."

Oh, Jesus.

"That's okay. We've got rain gear."

"It's not just going to rain a little. It's going to *pour*. It's the leftovers of that hurricane coming up from the Gulf."

"How do you know this?"

"Because I was looking at the forecast right before the power went out."

Dan tried to think back. He had a hazy memory of checking the weather app on his phone and seeing a rain cloud next to Thursday.

"When's it going to start?"

"I can't remember. Maybe by the time we wake up."

That's awfully convenient.

"You're not going to use the rain to try and get out of going to the meeting, are you?"

"You're not going to make me walk into town if it's pouring and forty degrees, are you?" Her voice prickled with defiance.

"Jen."

"Dan."

"You *promised* me—"

"If it's *fucking pouring*—"

He clenched his teeth. This was infuriating.

"You. Have. A serious. Problem—"

"What do you think happens at AA meetings? You think they're going to wave a magic wand over me and—"

"Ohmygod, Jen. *You're going to the*—"

A knock at the door silenced him.

"Yeah?"

They heard the click of the knob, then the creak of the door against the frame. A flashlight beam danced on the floor in front of Marty's feet.

"Hey, uh—do you guys have any more pillows?"

Dan sighed. "Yeah. Can you give us a minute?"

"Oh, sure."

Silence. The flashlight beam held steady on the floor.

"Marty?"

"Yeah, dude."

"Can you close the door and head down to the linen closet at the end of the hall? I'll meet you there in a sec."

"Sure thing, pal."

The flashlight beam retreated behind the door as it closed.

"I'll go to the fucking meeting," Jen muttered. "But if they're still here when I get back? I'm getting shitfaced."

"I sincerely hope you're kidding."

"Get rid of them, and you won't have to find out."

THURSDAY

JEN

She lay awake in the darkness, praying for the sound of rain. But all she heard was the low moan of the wind.

What time is it?

Dan had fished an old alarm clock out of the nightstand the day before. Had he ever set it to the correct time? Did it work? Where was it now? The kitchen?

Who cares?

If she was late to the fucking AA meeting, all the better.

And if she was early . . .

Maybe that bar on Hawthorne would be open.

If I owned a bar and civilization collapsed, I'd keep it open 24/7. That's just a good business opportunity.

She got out of bed.

"Is it time to get up yet?" Judging by the sound of Dan's voice, he was wide awake. He must've been lying there worrying.

"Might as well be."

She took her flashlight to the bathroom, brushed her teeth, and cleaned up as best she could with a damp washcloth. Dan did the same.

If she got too close to him, she could smell his body odor. The same was probably true of her. If not, it would be soon. And there was nothing she could do about it.

Yuuuuugh.

Jen padded downstairs just ahead of Dan, lighting their

way with a flashlight. When they passed the closed door to the den, she could hear Marty snoring on the other side. Entering the kitchen, the flashlight beam revealed multiple unfamiliar elements. Items of clothing were draped over the chairs. Black, camouflage, neon green—

"Oh, for fuck's sake! They washed their clothes!"

"You're kidding me."

A travel size bottle of Woolite was next to the sink, and the two largest pots Dan had filled with water were now empty.

"I can't fucking believe this!"

"Shhhh!"

Instead of lowering her voice, Jen raised it. "Why? Because I might wake them up? Because they're such considerate house-guests?"

She started to yank one of the chairs out to sit on it, then drew her hand back in disgust when her fist closed over a still-damp article of clothing.

"Oh, fucking hell, I touched his underwear! I swear to God, Dan, if they're still here when I get back—"

"I know! I know!" he whispered. "Just please don't make a scene."

She retreated to the downstairs bathroom, because she needed to cry and didn't want to do it in front of Dan. Or, God forbid, Marty and Marina.

The bathroom reminded her of the rubbing alcohol bottle fiasco, and that made the crying worse.

If I'd just saved it instead of drinking it, I wouldn't have to go to this fucking meeting.

Plus, I'd still have vodka left.

Maybe that bar's open.
Except I don't have any cash.
How the hell am I going to pay for a drink?
I'll bring jewelry.

When she left the house half an hour later, Jen had three rings, two pairs of earrings, and a necklace in the pocket of her jeans.

Just in case.

It was still dark, but enough predawn light was creeping in that she could make out the shapes of the houses as she passed. The air was chilly, and the wind was picking up. She hadn't thought to bring gloves, so every few minutes, she had to switch the closed umbrella she was carrying from one hand to the other so she could warm her stiff fingers in her jacket pocket.

Dan had suggested she ride her bike to save time, but Jen had no interest in saving time. Besides, if they actually went through with his borderline insane plan to bike to his mother's house, there'd be more than enough cycling in Jen's immediate future.

Willis Road was deathly quiet, although she glimpsed the occasional flicker of candlelight through a window as she passed. Two . . . no, three . . . no, four households had brought their recycling out to the foot of the driveway.

What's the thought process there? Optimism? Denial? Stupidity? All of the above?

She didn't encounter a live human until she was half a mile down Hawthorne, when she passed a young Asian couple kitted out in Gore-Tex and trekking backpacks. They looked like they belonged on the Appalachian Trail, and it occurred to Jen that they might be headed there.

An older man passed her on a bike. Then, a couple blocks further on, a family of four did the same. All of them were weighed down with backpacks and other baggage.

People were on the move. Dan's plan to flee might be crazy, but others clearly shared it. Jen tried to imagine joining them. But the prospect of all four Altmans trying to survive on the road, with no money, no shelter, and nothing to eat but canned beans and vegan protein powder, was so frightening that her stomach clenched around the day-old boiled eggs she'd had for breakfast, and she had to force the idea out of her head for fear she might throw up.

She reached the commercial strip on Hawthorne, the buildings tinged with purple in the predawn light. Everything was shuttered and chained, including both the bar and the liquor store.

Fuck.

It was too cold to sit outside, and she didn't have the energy to wander the streets. There was no good alternative to entering the Gothic church that loomed over the corner of Hawthorne and Forest.

She walked around to the side entrance, off the little parking area with its reserved spaces for clergy and staff. Her one remaining hope—that the AA meeting had closed for business like everything else in Lincolnwood—was foiled when she saw the little round blue sign with the triangle dangling from the door-knob on a short chain.

If I have to knock, I'm not going in.

She didn't have to knock. The door was open.

Four candles on tall stands, evenly spaced down the hallway, provided just enough light to reach the interior meeting room. Its doors were propped open wide. As she approached, she could hear the murmur of voices.

At least it'll be dark in there.

The only other time she'd been to a meeting in this room, it had been so full when she'd arrived that there were just a couple of empty folding chairs left along the side wall. If that was the case now, she might be able to get in and out without having to talk to anybody.

Her pulse rose with anxiety as she approached the threshold and made the turn into the room.

Candlelight glimmered on the metal surfaces of dozens of empty seats, arranged in concentric rows around an inner circle of eight chairs. Five of them were occupied: by a heavy-set, sixtyish couple in matching pink and powder blue WORLD'S GREATEST GRANDMA/GRANDPA sweatshirts; a middle-aged woman whose creased face showed mileage far exceeding her years; a delinquent kid with neck tattoos who didn't look a day over twenty; and the Honorable Francis V. Distefano.

The judge was seated in the middle of the group, squinting down at an open binder in his lap. As the others paused their conversation and turned to stare at Jen, he looked up. When he recognized her, his eyes crinkled and his mouth turned in a wry smile.

"Welcome!"

The other four alcoholics warbled similar greetings.

"Hey," Jen mumbled.

Keeping her eyes on the floor, she proceeded to a chair at the edge of the inner circle, leaving an empty seat on either side so nobody could reach out and grab her hand, or pat her back, or— *God forbid*—try to hug her.

The next hour promised to be absolutely fucking miserable.

MAX

Shortly after sunrise had brought some light into his bedroom, Max expelled his first chew of the day into the twelve-ounce Poland Spring bottle he'd been filling with spit and used tobacco since the previous afternoon.

After a lot of trial and error, he'd finally established a functional working relationship with his tin of Skoal. The key elements were constant spitting and not expecting too much in return. His efforts had yielded a few mild buzzes, temporary relief from nicotine withdrawal, dehydration, and a lingering taste of barnyard in his mouth. He no longer feared what would happen when the tobacco ran out, because the whole undertaking was so gross that he was starting to welcome the idea of quitting.

There were much bigger problems to worry about now. He'd spent the previous evening gaming out the most likely medium-term consequences of the EMP and had managed to scare himself into what felt like a low-grade panic attack. Even now, after a fitful night of sleep, he felt shaky and weak.

Some of that might be hunger. The victory he'd won in the fight with his mom over whether he had to go to the Stankovics' had turned out to be pretty hollow when he found himself eating peanut butter on stale crackers for dinner. The fact that they were out of crackers now—and pretty much everything else except peanut butter, tuna fish, and beans—was a major factor in his nightmare projection of slow death from starvation.

Or a much faster death from something worse. Like getting curb-stomped by some giant thug the size of that TV producer guy who'd taken over their downstairs den with his hot but scary wife. So far, the guy seemed more goofy than violent. But he was so big that if he went off, Max wasn't sure he could even reach the guy's neck with a karate chop.

The future belonged to guys like that. Barring some kind of miraculous government intervention—which seemed unlikely, because when was the last time the government had rescued anybody from anything? They couldn't even stop school shootings, or admit climate change was a problem—society was going to descend into barbarism. And Max was ill-equipped to handle it.

Is it too late to get a dog?

Not a lap dog like Ruby, but a guard dog. A German shepherd, or a Doberman. The kind that'd kill to protect him out of pure instinct. But also be affectionate, at least with Max. The dog would love him. And he'd love it right back. With a dog like that, he might have a real shot at survival.

But it was probably too late. He'd have to raise it from a puppy if he wanted it to bond with him. And what the hell would he feed it? Peanut butter?

Max shook off the guard dog fantasy. Then he capped his half-full bottle of tobacco spit, hid it in a desk drawer, and went downstairs in search of water and anything that might qualify as breakfast.

Dad was alone in the kitchen, sitting at the table and staring at a can of cold brew coffee. His face was gray and worried-looking. But when he saw Max, he tried to pretend he was in a good mood.

"Hey, buddy! How you doing?"

"Fine. Do we have any breakfast food?"

"Uhhh . . . lemme check." Dad bounced up and started searching for options. "Your mom and I finished the eggs. Sorry about that."

"It's fine. I hate eggs."

"Yeah, that's what we figured. How about oatmeal?" He held up a cylinder with a Pilgrim on it.

"Is it going to be any good?"

"Beats tuna fish. I'll boil some water."

Dad carefully measured out half the remainder of the Brita pitcher and set it to boil in a pot as Max poured himself a glass from a dwindling gallon of Poland Spring.

"Try to go easy on that stuff," Dad suggested.

Max looked around. There was a lot less of both the Poland Spring and the tap water than there had been the night before. "What happened to all our water?"

Dad sighed as he sat down again. "Long story." Then he gave Max one of his concerned frowns, like the kind he used when he tried to explain how important extracurriculars were to the college application process. "How you doing? You okay?"

Max shrugged. "I'm hungry."

"That's understandable. But are you doing all right? With everything that's going on?"

"I'm fine."

"Good. Good. . . . So, uh, after breakfast, you should—"

"Can we get a dog?"

"What?"

"I'm just thinking, it'd be good to have a dog. Like a German shepherd. Or—"

"Yeah. No. Not a good time. Also, I'm allergic."

"But it could be *my* dog."

"I'd still be allergic to it."

"True."

Dad was quiet for a moment. The dog question had thrown him off. "So . . . as I was saying: after breakfast, you should pack your backpack with everything you can carry and still ride a bike. Especially warm clothes. It's probably going to rain later. But as soon as the rain stops, we're getting out of here."

"Where we going?"

"I think Newton. But maybe Wellfleet. We'll see."

Trying to ride their bikes to Grandma's had seemed like a terrible idea when Dad had floated it yesterday, and it hadn't gotten any more attractive since then. If they were going to get murdered or starve to death, it seemed better to do it at home than at some gas station on the highway.

"Why would we go to Grandma's?" Max asked. "You think the EMP didn't hit 'em up there?"

"The what?"

"The EMP."

Dad looked confused. "What's that?"

"The electromagnetic pulse! The thing that caused all this!"

"I don't . . . What *is* that?"

How does Dad not know this?

"I told you about it yesterday!"

"Did you?"

"Yes!"

What the hell did he think was happening?

"Tell me again."

For the second breakfast in a row, Max explained what he knew about EMPs. This time, his dad actually listened—and the information clearly freaked him out.

"So if that's the problem . . . how do they fix it?"

"They don't. I think we're just screwed."

Dad's face turned even more gray. This did not inspire confidence.

Chloe shuffled in, wearing sweats and slippers. "Good morning," she said with a friendly sigh—which was beyond weird, because most days, his sister stomped into breakfast like a sullen T. rex.

"Why are you so happy?" Max asked her.

"I'm not," she replied. "I'm just glad we're all together." She stepped up behind Dad's chair, put her arms on his shoulders, and kissed the top of his head.

Jesus, the world really is falling apart, Max thought as he watched his sister. *Chloe's acting like a human being.*

CHLOE

Chloe had come downstairs to say goodbye in person—although not explicitly, because she didn't want to tip her family off that she was leaving them for good until after she'd made her escape. They'd eventually learn everything they needed to know from the farewell letter she planned to leave on her desk. She'd written it by flashlight before going to sleep, although she was considering a rewrite, because she was worried the first draft had come off too bitchy.

There was no reason not to be nice, especially when she had no clue how long it'd be before she saw them again. *Days? Weeks? Forever?* At this stage of the zombie apocalypse, the future was unknowable.

In any case, Chloe was determined to make this last breakfast count. When she put her hands on Dad's shoulders in a show of affection, he returned the gesture by reaching across his chest to pat her left hand tenderly with his right.

"Hey, pumpkin."

"Hey, Daddy." She felt guilty about abandoning him. There'd be one less mouth to feed without her, but other than that, things wouldn't be any easier for him. Max was deadweight, and Mom was a train wreck.

She was also nowhere in sight. Which was weird, because

Chloe could've sworn she'd heard her voice downstairs a while ago.

"Is Mom still in bed?"

Dad's hand paused in mid-pat.

"No."

"Where is she?"

"She, uh . . . went out."

"Where'd she go?" Max asked.

"Just out for a bit."

"Before the sun came up?"

"Little bit."

"To where?"

"Just to . . . meet somebody."

"Who?" Even Max, who was usually clueless about anything having to do with human social interaction, could smell something fishy.

"Just a friend."

"At six in the morning?"

"It was closer to seven." Dad pointed to a portable alarm clock on the counter, which showed the time as just after seven thirty. "I think that clock's basically right. She'll be back soon."

None of this added up. "Who is she meeting at seven in the morning when nothing's open and nobody can drive? Or even get in touch with each other?"

"I think it was a, uh, work colleague."

"You *think*?"

Just then, Dad's meathead boss walked in, wearing drawstring shorts and a Baja hoodie. "Wazzup, Altmans?"

"Marty!" Dad leaped up. "Just the person I wanted to see."

Marty scanned the room. "Did you see some clothes lying around?"

"Dad—" He was deliberately ignoring her.

"Over there," Dad told Marty, pointing to a small pile of clothing atop one of the kitchen chairs. "And we really need to discuss some stuff—"

"Dad!"

"Sure thing. Fire away. Are they dry?" Marty went over to inspect his clothes.

"*Where is Mom?*" Chloe had come downstairs with the intention of being kind and loving, but her father's evasiveness was infuriating.

"Sweetheart, I really need to talk to Marty alone for a minute. Can you and Max give us a little privacy?"

"Not until you tell us where Mom went!"

Max jumped in on Chloe's side. "Seriously, Dad. Where'd she go?"

There was a pregnant silence as everybody stared at Dad, and Dad stared at the table.

"I'd just tell them," Marty suggested.

"Just tell us *what*?" Chloe demanded.

Dad glared daggers at his boss, who gave him a sheepish shrug.

"Sorry, dude. Didn't mean to get involved."

"Your mother . . ." Dad sighed before finishing the sentence. "Went to an AA meeting."

Chloe felt her stomach drop.

"Is that a good thing or a bad thing?" Max finally asked.

"Good thing!" Marty chirped. "She needs it, dude."

"It's good," Dad assured Max. "She realized she's got a little bit of a problem, and she's getting some help for it. So nothing to worry about. And we can talk about it—but first, Marty and I need to have a conversation about something else. So why don't you guys go upstairs? I'll let you know when breakfast is ready. Okay?"

Chloe and Max both nodded. She walked out of the kitchen, and he followed her. "Is there a breakfast plan?" she heard Marty ask Dad as they reached the stairs.

"I guess it makes sense," Max said when they got to the second floor. "I mean, she *does* get wasted a lot. Kind of weird to start going now, though. Isn't it?"

Chloe didn't reply. She was too busy trying to process the implications of this news. Among other things, her goodbye letter would definitely require a second draft. A decent chunk of it had been devoted to her mother's drinking problem, and parts of what she'd written had just been rendered obsolete.

She also needed to finish packing. Once Mom got home, she and Dad would probably retreat behind closed doors for a Very Serious Conversation, which would give Chloe a window of opportunity to escape to Josh's and—

"Chloe?"

At the threshold of her bedroom, she paused to look back at her brother. He'd kept talking even as she'd stopped listening. His face was wrinkled with anxiety.

"Are you freaking out like I'm freaking out?"

She wasn't sure if he was talking about Mom or the whole situation. But she shook her head, trying to make her voice sound as warm and reassuring as possible.

"No. It's not that bad. Don't worry. It's going to be fine."

Then she disappeared into her room, shutting the door behind her.

DAN

"Why on earth did you do laundry?"

"Dude, if you smelled my bike shorts, you wouldn't have to ask."

"You used half our water!"

"Speaking of which—that's boiling."

"Shit." Dan ran over and turned off the water he'd put on to boil for the oatmeal. "Marty, this water situation is *literally* life or death."

"Dude, first of all: I'm sorry. I didn't think we were using that much. Second: chill out! You're overreacting. I can get us more water! I'm a Watchdog!"

"How? *They* don't have water!"

"Eddie's got a whole pool of it!"

"You can't drink pool water!"

"Yes, you can."

"No, you can't! It's chlorinated!"

"Well, agree to disagree. But whatever. We're making our move on Ridgelawn today. When that happens, I swear to God, I'll get you all the water you need. I brought you some yesterday, didn't I?"

"Yeah—and then you drank it all!"

"'Cause we didn't want to use more of yours!"

Marina slinked into the room, dressed in yoga attire. "Has anyone made coffee?"

"That's a good idea," Marty agreed. "Dan, you got whole bean? Or grounds?"

"We can't make coffee!" Dan seethed.

"Sure, we can. We don't need a machine. We'll just do pour-overs—"

"We don't have *water*, Marty!"

"Dude, why are you so hostile? Is this about Jen? I know it's a lot of stress, being in your situation—"

"It's *not* about Jen."

"It is a serious problem with her," Marina volunteered. "It is normal to be upset."

Dan sank back into his chair. "It's not Jen. It's the entire situation." He took his glasses off, shut his eyes, and squeezed the bridge of his nose between his thumb and forefinger. "We didn't budget for two extra people."

When Dan opened his eyes again, Marty's blurry bulk had stepped forward to loom over the table beside him and was fiddling with something he'd pulled out of his pants pocket.

Dan put his glasses back on just in time to see Marty place a hundred-dollar bill on the table.

"Does that help?" Marty asked.

Yes.

But it also struck Dan as a trap. What he really needed to do was get Marty out of his house. Accepting the money, however badly he needed it, would make that impossible.

"This isn't about money."

"Can it be, though?"

"The thing is, we're *leaving*. I'm taking the family up to my mom's place in Massachusetts. We're going to close up the house.

So I'm sorry, but . . . you guys are going to have to figure out your own situation."

Marty wrinkled his nose. "Why would you go to *Massachusetts*?"

"Because it's not here. And maybe it's—"

The sound of a car horn reached them from the street.

"Oh! That's probably for me. Kozak said he was going to stop by." Marty headed for the hallway to the front door.

At the mention of the Watchdog co-leader whom Eddie had identified at last night's dinner as the man who made the militia's membership decisions, Dan started to stand up.

"Should I come, too?" If for whatever reason they didn't end up leaving town, it seemed like a good idea to align himself with the guys who were running around carrying guns.

"Just sit tight," Marty told him. "You don't want to seem pushy. But don't worry—I'll put in a good word for you."

Dan stayed on his feet for a moment, debating whether to follow until he heard Marty slam the front door on his way out. Then Dan returned to his seat and tried not to stare at the hundred-dollar bill sitting on the table less than a foot away from him.

Marina took the chair next to his. "Dan, can I tell you honestly what I am seeing?"

"Okay." At point-blank range, it was difficult to refuse a request from Marina. Her cheekbones alone were incredibly intimidating.

"I think you are trying to fix your problem by running away," she explained. "But you cannot run."

Why? Because you'll hunt me down and kill me?

But Marina wasn't thinking of the same problem Dan was.

"Jen drinks in the daytime," Marina continued. "My father did this also. It is very serious. And you cannot make her stop just like the, how do you say it? The cold turkey. Because then she will make a seizure."

"I don't think it's quite that bad yet," Dan protested as they heard the sound of the front door reopening, then slamming shut.

Marina frowned and shook her head. "I think you have the denial."

"Check *this* out!"

Marty strode into the room, his eyes glowing as he held up an assault rifle.

Dan gasped at the sight. Outside of the occasional counter-terrorism cop at Penn Station, he'd never seen a weapon like that in real life.

And certainly not in his kitchen.

JEN

The judge, who was apparently the chairperson of the AA meeting, opened it by reading a canned introduction from a laminated script. When he asked if anyone was new to the meeting, five pairs of eyes turned in Jen's direction.

She lifted her hand in a halfhearted wave. "Hi. I'm Jen."

"Welcome!" everybody crowed, as if they hadn't said exactly the same thing when she'd walked into the room two minutes earlier.

Then the judge moved on to soliciting progress reports.

Vince, the kid with the neck tattoos, had sixty-three days of sobriety. Everybody clapped for him.

Leather-faced Sylvia announced that she'd celebrated two years sober at the beginning of the month. Everybody applauded that, too.

World's Greatest Grandma and Grandpa had nothing to report, so they limited their contributions to clapping for everybody while looking self-righteously smug.

Or maybe they were just nice people. Jen couldn't decide how to calibrate her cynicism.

Then the judge announced that this was a "literature meeting," which presumably explained why antique-looking paperbacks titled *Twelve Steps and Twelve Traditions* were on the seat of every third empty chair.

"According to the schedule," he said, consulting the binder on his lap, "today we're going to read . . . Tradition Number Four."

The news elicited scattered chuckles, for reasons Jen couldn't parse. Was there something funny about Tradition Number Four?

The answer was no, which quickly became apparent once the read-aloud began. Jen plucked a copy of the book from the seat next to her and played along as the group read, round-robin style and one paragraph at a time, a mostly incomprehensible essay about some ancient AA group that had tried to open a treatment center and ran it into the ground.

Jen failed to grasp the intended lesson, unless it was that drunk people shouldn't start businesses together, which just seemed like common sense. She couldn't even begin to fathom what the essay had to do with alcoholism, or how reading it was supposed to be helpful to her.

Then, one by one, the members of the group raised their hands to talk. Jen expected to hear a series of convoluted attempts to extract some deeper meaning from what they'd just read. But nobody even tried to do that. In fact, they did the opposite.

World's Greatest Grandma kicked it off. "Diane, alcoholic," she announced in a world-weary voice. "I gotta be honest: I didn't hear a goddamn word of that. Not even the parts I read. My mind's elsewhere. Y'know?"

Everyone nodded. They knew.

"But you know what?" Diane continued. "I'm actually glad we read it. 'Cause it's *normal*. And that's what I needed today. I needed normal. Just to sit in this room, see everybody's face, and read this nonsense. Don't get me wrong—I love the Traditions! They're what keeps this thing going. But I hate the hell out of

Tradition meetings. And the God's honest truth—being able to come in here and get pissed off that it's a Tradition meeting? It makes me feel better. I can't explain it."

She then spent another five minutes trying to explain it anyway, to no success, while repeatedly expressing her gratitude that she lived in Ridgelawn and thus still had running water.

"'Cause no matter how bad things get," Diane pointed out, "it could always be worse. If Steve and I lived three blocks south, it'd be a whole other story."

Jen silently fumed.

I haven't showered in days, and I'm running out of drinking water. What kind of tone-deaf asshole do you have to be to rub my face in—

"By the way," Diane added, "if any of you need to come over? Take a shower, fill some water bottles? Door's open. Just say the word."

Okay, never mind, thought Jen. *That's actually really generous.*

Diane's husband, the World's Greatest Grandpa, was up next. "Steve, grateful recovering alcoholic," he growled. "God help me, if I wasn't sober right now. I'd either be passed out on the couch, no damn good to Diane or anybody—or I'd be out there howling at the moon. When I heard what happened yesterday at the Walmart in Passaic . . ." His jowls swayed as he shook his head in sorrow. "It's a tragedy. Just senseless. And that would've been me. I would've been right there in the middle of it."

Steve then veered off into a long, disjointed recollection of the felonies he'd committed in his youth, and Jen faded out for a while as she tried to devise the most polite way of inviting herself to his and Diane's home for a shower and an explanation of what the hell had happened at the Passaic Walmart.

Vince was next. The veins under his neck tattoos throbbed as he talked. "I walked five miles to get here. Got up in the middle of the night. Didn't even know what time it was. And if I'd known I was coming all this way for a fuckin' *Tradition* meeting—"

Everybody laughed except Vince and Jen.

"Truth is, though, I still would've come," he said. "Last two months, this room's been saving my life every goddamn day. First time I got sober was a gift. But I didn't take it serious. 'Cause I hadn't lost enough. This time around, I'm homeless, I'm broke, I don't know where my next meal's comin' from. Been trying to find a job—"

Jen couldn't help wondering if the neck tattoos were interfering with Vince's employment prospects.

"And then the whole fuckin' world falls apart! But I knew I had to get my ass over here. 'Cause this is the one place on earth where I know people have my back. And if I turn around, you're not going to stick a knife in it."

Once Vince ran out of steam, Sylvia took over. She started by declaring her gratitude for Diane and Steve, who'd let Sylvia and her adult daughter shower at their place on Wednesday.

"One of the things I'm most grateful to this program for—my daughter and I, we're still working through some stuff. She's got a lot of resentments about growing up with an active alcoholic for a mom. But when the lights went out on Tuesday? She showed up at my door. Because she wanted to be with me."

Sylvia's voice thickened with emotion. "And that's a gift. I've got a lot of regrets about the way I was with her back when I was using. I tried to be a good mom. My intentions were good. But I just wasn't *there*. Physically, I was present. But mentally . . . I could never see past my own nose. Even when I hated myself for what I was doing, it was all about me. I could never put her first. I couldn't put anybody first. Y'know? Except Jack Daniel's. I only had room for one relationship in my life, and that was alcohol. And for a while, it cost me my daughter. Once she graduated high school, she was gone. For five years, she wouldn't speak to me."

There was an angry lump in Jen's throat, trying to force its way to the surface.

"But now," Sylvia went on, her eyes brimming with tears, "thanks to this program, when things get bad—and I don't know if any of you noticed, but things are getting pretty damn bad out there—she knows she can count on me. And I know I can count on all of you."

Sylvia looked around the room as she wiped the moisture from her cheeks. "I'm scared to death right now. I don't know what's going to happen. But I got on my knees this morning, and I prayed to God I could be useful. To my daughter and everybody else in my life. And if I can keep that in my head, not pick up a drink today, just do my best to keep moving through the fear . . . I know I'm going to be okay. Thanks for letting me share."

"Thanks for sharing," the others mumbled.

Everyone had spoken except the judge and Jen. Across the circle, his eyes met hers.

Don't look at me, Frank. I got nothing.

"Frank, alcoholic."

"Hi, Frank," everybody said.

"Glad to be here today. Glad to be anywhere, at my age. Especially the way I drank. Y'know, it's a funny thing—you live long enough, you see some shit. And whatever's happening out there, it definitely ain't good. But I was around for the Newark riots, back in the day. They were no walk in the park, either. But we got through 'em. And one way or another, we'll get through this. Walking down here this morning—"

He paused and put his hand to his hip pocket. "By the way, who gets the keys for tomorrow?"

Steve raised his hand. "Right here."

The judge produced a pair of keys on a ring and under-handed them to Steve. "Thanks, buddy. And I gotta say: I love that you and Diane wore those sweatshirts. Made my day."

There were appreciative chuckles all around. "Steve didn't want to!" Diane crowed. "He said, 'They look ridiculous!' I said, 'We need a little ridiculous today!'"

More laughter. The judge nodded approvingly. "Where was I?"

"'Walking over here . . .'" Steve prompted him.

"Right. So I'm thinking to myself, 'What if nobody shows? And it's just me, reading lousy Tradition Four in an empty room?' But it wasn't. And I'm grateful as hell to every one of you for being here: Diane. Steve. Vince. Sylvia. The new kid."

He winked at Jen, then continued. "I don't know what's hap-pening out there. Or what's gonna happen. God doesn't show me previews of coming attractions. And He sure as hell doesn't ask my permission for whatever He's gonna do. All I know is, I didn't drink yesterday. I'm probably not going to drink today. And right now, *just for now*—I'm okay. And that's enough. Thanks."

"Thanks for sharing," the others mumbled.

Silence fell as the room's attention shifted to Jen.

Most of them weren't staring at her. They were looking at their hands, or the floor, or each other.

But they were all waiting on her. To bare her soul, confess her sins, share her fears. Or just shit on Tradition Four. Anything. But *something*. Their silence requested a contribution, just like the rest of them had made.

Having listened to the others, Jen could no longer find it in herself to be cynical. It was a nice thing these people had. They seemed to legitimately care for each other, and to be getting real support. Under the circumstances, that was no small mercy.

Jen strongly suspected that if she opened her mouth, they'd try to do the same for her.

It was too bad she hadn't come in earlier. It might've really helped.

"I'm just going to listen today," she told them.

The judge let the silence linger for a while.

"Anybody want to go again . . . ? No? Okay, we've got a nice way of closing."

DAN

"Is that thing real?" Dan asked Marty, praying the answer was no.

"Pretty sure!" Marty switched the assault rifle's grip to his left hand so he could free his right to fish for something in his pants pocket. "I mean, he gave me this extra clip for it—oh, shit."

As he pulled a boxy ammo clip out of his pants, his wad of cash fell out along with it, tumbling to the floor.

Marty bent over to pick up the money, and the barrel of the rifle swung down in Marty and Marina's direction.

They both screamed.

"Marty!"

"Martin!"

He straightened up, startled. "What?"

"Don't fucking point it at us!" Dan jumped up and backed away, putting the kitchen island in between himself and Marty. "If you don't know how to use it, maybe you shouldn't have it."

"Dude, relax! It's not rocket science. There's, like, three moving parts."

"Is the safety on?"

"Lemme check." Marty turned the rifle in his hands, looking for the safety. "Where do you think it'd be?"

"Ohmygod, Marty. Please put it down."

"Settle! I'll figure it out."

Marina had also moved out of the field of fire and was now

downrange to her husband's left. She pointed past his elbow to a spot on the rifle above and behind the trigger.

"Is that it? There?"

"I think?" Marty raised the gun closer to his eyes.

"*Point it down!*" Dan yelled, ducking underneath the island.

"Dude! Quit yelling! You're making me jumpy."

Dan slowly straightened up. Marty was squinting at the safety switch.

"I mean, it's pretty basic," Marty observed. "'Fire.' 'Safe.' So, like, I just push it toward 'safe.' Right?"

"I don't know! Is it on now?"

"It should be."

Marty pulled the trigger.

What followed was the loudest noise Dan had ever heard in his life, accompanied by a fluttering of his pajama bottoms and a sharp prick of pain on the top of his right foot.

"JESUS CHRIST!"

His ears ringing almost to the point of temporary deafness, Dan looked down at the source of the sudden pain.

A razor-thin, inch-long line of blood was rising on the top of his right foot. Clinging to the calf of his flannel pajama bottoms just above it were dozens of wood splinters.

Just past his foot, the bottom right cabinet door on the island had blown open. When he reached out and pulled it toward him, he discovered an eruption of mangled wood the size of his fist blossoming out from the lower end of the door.

"Oh, fuck! Sorry, dude!"

The ringing in Dan's ears was so loud that Marty sounded

like he was talking under water. Behind him, Marina had both hands clasped over her mouth in horror.

Mercifully, Marty managed to keep the rifle barrel pointed down as he approached Dan, rounding the corner of the island to survey the damage.

"You okay . . . ? Holy shit, look at that exit hole!"

Dan bent over to inspect his foot. A second thin line of blood had appeared, bisecting the first one.

"You fucking shot me!"

"No, dude, that's just cabinet shrapnel." Marty pointed his rifle barrel at the ragged exit hole in the door. "If that bullet actually hit you? Your leg'd be splattered all over the floor right now."

Dan probed the top of his foot with his hand. To be fair, the wound did seem superficial. In fact, his hearing damage might be the more serious injury.

Marina's ears had suffered the same insult. "It was so loud!" she cried. "I cannot hear myself!"

"Marty." Dan glared at his boss. "Get that thing out of my house *right fucking now.*"

"Dude, I'm *so* sorry. I'm totally good for the repair on this." Marty jiggled the rifle barrel in the direction of the disfigured cabinet door. "Do you have a guy who can swap that door out?" He pointed backward, to the opposite side of the island. "'Cause the point of entry's pretty clean. But this exit hole is *nuts!*" He gazed at the weapon in his hands, impressed with its power. "No wonder they want to ban these things."

Chloe raced into the room, followed by Max. When she saw Marty's gun, she shrieked.

"AAAIIEEE!"

"It's cool! The safety's on!" Marty assured her.

Chloe did not seem reassured. Neither was Dan.

"Kids—go back upstairs," Dan told them. "*Now.*"

Max stared in awe at the assault rifle. "Is that an AR-15?"

Marty shrugged. "I guess?"

"Go back upstairs!"

Chloe and Max did as they were told.

"I am seriously sorry, dude. Really. It won't happen again."

"I think you need to leave," Dan said.

"You mean the gun? Or, like, me?"

"Both."

"Oh." Marty pondered this for a moment, then shrugged. "That's cool. We'll just go to Eddie's."

"Really?" Dan hadn't expected ejecting Marty to be this easy.

"Yeah. It's fine."

"What are you saying?" Marina was tugging on her earlobes in a vain effort to restore her hearing.

"We're gonna move over to Eddie's!" Marty explained in a loud voice.

Marina nodded. "Oh! That is good. They are kind." She turned to Dan. "We will leave. I am sorry about your kitchen." Still tugging at her ears, she turned and headed back to the den.

Marty began to follow her, then paused at the kitchen table and stared down at the hundred-dollar bill he'd left there. After a moment's consideration and a brief glance back at his soon-to-be-former host, he dug into his pocket, produced a second bill, and added it to the first before exiting the room.

Dan lurched over to the table and sank into his chair.

Marty almost shot me.

In my own kitchen.

Is this real? Is this actually happening?

At least I got two hundred dollars out of it.

Then Dan looked at the second bill Marty had just laid down and realized it was only a twenty.

CHLOE

It was an hour or so after the gun incident, and Chloe had finished everything except the final paragraph of her goodbye letter, which was giving her fits.

I'll see you on the other side of the zombie apocalypse seemed too jokey.
And anyway, *Hamilton* references were just so junior high school.

PLEASE DON'T TRY TO COME LOOKING FOR ME felt too
hostile, and Chloe had already made the same point more than
once in other parts of the letter.

After everything's settled down, I'll come find you promised too much,
because what if she didn't?

Finally, she came up with a version that felt right, or at least
close enough:

> *If you think about it, I was already going to leave for college in ten months.*
> *This is basically the same thing—I'm just getting an earlier start.*
> *I LOVE YOU ALL SO MUCH! EVERYTHING'S GOING TO*
> *BE OK!*
>
> *Love, Chloe*

The second-to-last sentence was debatable, and the last one
was a bald-faced lie. But she thought it was important to end on a
positive note. As she was writing the last few words, an argument
erupted in the hallway between Dad and Max.

"*NO! We're leaving!* And you haven't even packed!"

"What if I pack and then go over?"

"Absolutely not! It's too dangerous to go out!"

"Then why are we leaving?"

"That's different! We're not leaving on foot!"

"Mom left on foot!"

"*Max!* People are running around with *guns!*"

"Yeah—in our kitchen!"

"The answer is *no! N! O!* Now, get packed! This is serious!"

She heard Dad's feet clomp downstairs. Ever since his boss had almost shot him, he'd gone off the deep end. Now he was running around like a chicken with his head cut off, frantically trying to pack for his batshit crazy bike trip idea while demanding Max and Chloe do the same.

Chloe had complied, sort of. She was packed, but not for Grandma's house. Fortunately, the distinction was lost on Dad. A while back, he'd poked his head in to yell at her for not following orders, then had to stop himself when he saw the overstuffed backpack on her bed.

"You're all ready to go?"

"Yeah."

"Okay! Great! Good job. What you writing?"

"My Dartmouth supplemental."

"Super! Keep it up! We're leaving soon as your mom gets back."

"Okay! Love you!"

"Love you, too!"

Then he'd gone back to yelling at Max, who'd never been any good at manipulating their parents and was taking the brunt of Dad's nervous breakdown.

The insistence on leaving as soon as Mom got home might be a real headache if it actually played out that way. Chloe had been counting on a window of inattentiveness during which she could make her escape without her parents realizing it. In the worst-case scenario—if Dad actually persuaded Mom and Max to set out on bikes for Massachusetts—Chloe was in much better shape than the rest of the family, so she could always pretend to join, then peel off before they got to the parkway and just outrace them.

But she hoped it wouldn't come to that, because such a melodramatic exit would be traumatic for everybody. Better to slip away unnoticed and let them process their grief indoors when they found her letter.

There was a knock at her door.

"Come in!"

It was Max. His hair was greasy and tangled, and two new pimples seemed to have erupted on his face since breakfast.

"Dad's losing his mind," he informed her.

"I know."

"This whole going-to-Massachusetts thing is totally fucknuts."

"Don't worry. Mom will shut him down."

"You think so?"

"Probably. Where did you want to go that Dad won't let you?"

"Just next door."

"To the Stankovics'?"

Max screwed up his face at the thought. "No! Judge Distefano's."

"Why?"

He shrugged. "I dunno. Just want to pet his dog."

"Seriously? She's not even that friendly."

"She's friendly to me."

Just then, Dad bounded back up the stairs and called out to them from the other end of the hallway.

"Leave room in your bags for water and canned goods!"

Max exhaled in a frustrated snort.

"Okay!" Chloe replied in a loud, eager voice. Then she muttered under her breath to Max. "Just play along."

"It's ridiculous," he muttered back.

"Are you packing, Max?" Dad asked in an accusatory tone.

"Yes!" Chloe answered for her brother. "I'm helping him!"

"Okay! Chop-chop! We're leaving as soon as your mom gets home! I don't know what the hell's taking her so long."

"Probably stopped at a bar," Chloe muttered as Dad disappeared into his bedroom.

Max looked at her with concern. "You think so?"

"I don't know." Then, seeing Max's dismayed reaction, she modified her analysis. "No. I'm sure she didn't. Don't worry about it."

"We're not going on this stupid bike trip," he declared.

"Just play along with him. Let Mom have that fight. Stuff some clothes in a bag so it looks like you packed."

"Is that what you did?"

"Kind of."

She started to retreat back into her room. Max stayed in the doorway.

"What?" she asked.

"Do you want to, like . . . help me with my volleyball serve?"

"What?"

"Or just—I dunno, play Monopoly or something?"

The look on his face was crushing. They'd never been all that close, and they'd grown even further apart as teenagers. Over the past couple of years, when she'd thought of him at all, it was as an obstacle—the little jerkoff tying up the bathroom or eating the last of the cereal.

But he was still her brother. And she realized, looking at him just then, that she hadn't been as good a sister to him as she could've—and that a truly good one wouldn't be abandoning him now.

The least she could do was play one last game of Monopoly with him.

But there was no way they'd ever finish it. Monopoly took forever, and at some point in the next hour or so, she'd have to make her escape.

If she started a game, only to vanish in the middle of it . . . would that make her a better sister? Or a worse one?

"Throw some clothes in a bag so Dad thinks you packed," she told him. "I'll go set up the board in the dining room."

JEN

The AA meeting was over, but the drunks hadn't disbanded. Whether it was the small size of the group, the fact that the technological collapse had stripped their personal calendars of any pressing engagements, or just a simple fear of being alone, once they'd wrapped things up with the obligatory hand-holding chant of the Serenity Prayer, everybody hung around for a while.

That included Jen. At first, it was because High Mileage Sylvia and World's Greatest Grandma Diane buttonholed her as soon as the meeting ended with a series of almost-but-not-quite-intrusive questions.

"First time in the program?" Diane asked with a smile.

"Well, I don't know if I'm *in* the program so much as . . ."

"First meeting?" Sylvia suggested.

"Second. The first time was my idea. This time, it was my husband's."

"My first meeting was the state of New Jersey's idea," Sylvia told her. "Wound up saving my life, but I was pissed as hell about it."

"She really was," Diane agreed, throwing a sisterly arm around Sylvia. "This girl came in kicking and screaming. What's your name again, sweetheart?"

"Jen."

"Diane."

"Sylvia."

"Nice to meet you."

"So your husband got sick of your bullshit?"

"More like he, um . . . became aware there was bullshit."

"Bullshit like . . . ?" Diane gently prodded.

Jen was wary of disclosing too much to these women. She was afraid that if she lowered her guard, she'd wind up in a puddle on the floor. But she also didn't feel like she could place her trust in Diane without knowing whether or not she was wearing that WORLD'S GREATEST GRANDMA sweatshirt ironically.

"Like, y'know . . . vodka for breakfast. Well, not exactly breakfast. More like brunch."

"Is that a daily thing?" asked Sylvia. "Or . . ."

"More like a . . . twice-a-week thing."

"Is it working for you?" Diane asked, not unkindly. "Or do you think you might want to quit?"

"Honestly?" Jen could feel the emotions gathering in force around the middle of her chest. If she wasn't very careful about how she handled this conversation, she'd be ugly-crying within seconds.

"I can see the value of it," she admitted, letting the words out slowly. "But with everything that's going on, I'm not sure this is a good time."

The men were talking a few feet away, and as if to underscore Jen's point, Steve's hushed voice reached her ears in the brief silence that followed:

"Where's the military? Why aren't we seeing any helicopter traffic? I was up on the ridge—"

"You mean it's not a good time to quit?" Diane quizzed Jen, drowning out the rest of whatever Steve was saying. "Or it's not a good time to drink?"

Jen thought about it. "Both."

Sylvia nodded wearily. "I know the feeling. You can't drink, but you can't *not* drink."

"Yeah. By the way, I really, uh—" Jen stopped herself. She was about to tell Sylvia that she'd been moved by what the woman had shared about her daughter, but a sudden welling in Jen's eyes told her it was a bad idea to raise the subject if she wanted to keep her shit together.

"That's the sixty-four-dollar question, isn't it?" the judge was saying to Steve and Vince. "How far's it go?"

The women were waiting for Jen to finish her sentence.

"Never mind," she said, shaking her head. "Nothing."

"The way I look at it," Diane explained, "is if I got a problem, and I pick up a drink over it? Then I got *two* problems. You know what I mean?"

Jen nodded. "Yeah. I get that. Can I ask a question?"

"Sure. Go ahead."

"Are you wearing that sweatshirt ironically?"

Diane looked down at her chest and laughed. "Are you kidding me? I am the undisputed heavyweight champion of grandmas! Three hours with me, those kids are *wrecked* with their mom for at least a week."

"She's got seriously cute grandkids," Sylvia assured Jen.

"I'd show you pictures, but my lousy phone died. Couple more days of this, I'm going to forget what they look like."

Eventually, the little party made its way outside. They blew out the candles in the hallway, Steve locked the church door, and the six of them headed up Hawthorne at a pace slow enough to accommodate the judge's geriatric shuffle.

"Don't wait for me," he warned them. "You're gonna get rained on."

They disregarded his warning. The sky was dark and threatening, but the daylight had brought a fair amount of bike and foot traffic, most of it headed south toward the center of town.

"Wrong way, Judge!" a middle-aged man in rain pants and a matching coat called out as he passed by on a mountain bike.

"Where's everybody going?" Vince wanted to know.

"There's a town meeting this morning," the judge explained. "Who's Lincolnwood here? I forget."

"I am," said Sylvia.

"Me too," Jen added.

"You going to the meeting?" the judge asked them.

"What's it about?" Sylvia asked.

"You haven't heard? Apparently, they're going to vote on whether to turn the borough council into a military junta."

Steve chortled. "Seriously?"

"Oh, yeah. No joke. People are gung ho about it. By the way, heads up: first item on their agenda? Invading Ridgelawn to commandeer your water."

"What the hell?"

"Yeah, that's what passes for a good idea these days."

"How would they even do that?" Steve asked. "What are they gonna do? Seize a fire hydrant at gunpoint? Back a truck up to the pumping station?"

"I don't think they've thought it through," the judge told him. "These aren't bright people."

"Are *you* going to the meeting?" Jen asked the judge.

He shook his head. "I'm not a big fan of direct democracy. Plus I gotta get home and walk Ruby before she pees on the carpet."

Jen wondered if Dan would want to go to the meeting. Probably not, considering how intent he was on leaving town.

"Can I get a group opinion on something?" she asked.

"Can't help you," said Steve. "We're not opinionated people."

"Ignore the peanut gallery," Diane told Jen. "Fire away."

"My husband thinks the smartest thing we can do is ride our bikes to his mother's place in Massachusetts."

"*Massachusetts?* Oh, Jesus, no," said Diane.

"He's out of his mind," Steve declared.

"That's fuckin' crazy," Vince agreed.

"Terrible idea," Sylvia chimed in.

"Might not be the best thing," the judge said.

"No." Diane added. "Just no. You gotta hunker down."

Jen nodded. "See, that's what I thought."

"Think about it," Steve told her. "If Boston didn't get hit, too? We'd know by now. Same with Philly and DC. They're close enough, we would've gotten word."

"If you're going to bug out," Vince added, "the only way to go is west. You don't want to fuck with north or east. 'Cause then you gotta get around the city, and it's a fuckin' horror movie over there right now. Especially on the highways."

"Thank you," Jen told them, and she meant it. "Seriously. That's good advice."

By the time she and the judge turned up Willis Road twenty minutes later and left the others to continue north toward Ridgelawn, Jen felt a pang of sorrow at the parting. Emotionally, it was weirdly similar to the night freshman year when she'd first encountered the clique of girls who became her sorority sisters. Kitschy sweatshirts and neck tattoos aside, she sensed that she'd found her people.

And some of them had running water, which was a huge plus.

"Come by later with your family!" Diane told her. "Six eighty-four South Benson! Bring your own towels, you can shower."

"That would be amazing! Thank you so much!"

"Wait—" Steve held his hand up. "There's four of you, right?"

"Right."

"Okay. You're good. Five, we'd have to charge you." He winked at her.

"We'll come by when the rain stops!" Jen promised.

"Watch out for the guerrilla fighters. Apparently, we're gettin' invaded later."

"You're laughing now," the judge warned Steve. "But stay away from your windows. Those people are nuts, and they're packing."

Then Jen and the judge were alone, trudging up the hill toward home.

"I really like them," Jen said.

"Me too," said the judge. "We're out of our minds, every damn one of us. But we're all crazy in the same way. So it kinda works, y'know? We understand each other."

"Yeah. . . . Sorry I didn't talk at the meeting."

"Don't sweat it, kid. There's no rules. Whatever makes you comfortable."

Jen didn't know what to say after that, so they walked in silence for a while. The lack of conversation was starting to feel oppressive when it was broken by the appearance of Carol Sweeney, coasting downhill on a plush-seated cruiser bike with a pet carrier bungeed to the rack over the rear wheel. A backpack and two drawstring bags hung from her shoulders.

"Hey, kiddo!" the judge called out, and Carol steered over to the curb for a brief exchange.

"You coming from the meeting?" she asked.

Jen experienced a brief moment of mortified alarm before she realized Carol was referring to the town meeting, not AA.

"Just out for a little morning constitutional," the judge told her. "But there's a lot of folks headed in that direction." He nodded at the unhappy-looking tabby in the pet carrier. "Does Baxter here get a vote? Maybe I should see if Ruby wants to go."

Carol shook her head with a dark scowl. "I'm done with those people. Going to my sister's in Maplewood. We'll come back when the power's fixed. As long as those idiots haven't burned down the whole town by then."

"Well, safe travels," said the judge. "We'll keep an eye on the homestead for you."

"Thanks, Frank." Carol looked at Jen. "How are you holding up, Jen?"

"Not bad. All things considered."

"Okay. Take care. Watch out for that asshole across the street."

The judge chuckled. "Eddie barks worse than he bites. Take care of yourself, Carol."

"You too!"

Then she was gone, careening downhill to the avenue. Jen and the judge resumed their uphill hike.

Carol had abandoned ship, apparently for the duration.

That meant her house would be empty.

And being Irish, she probably had a well-stocked liquor cabinet.

Oh, for Christ's sake. We're not breaking into Carol Sweeney's house.

It was a ridiculous idea.

Especially when there was plenty of booze left in Jen's basement. She just had to find it.

That shouldn't be too difficult. There were only so many places where Dan could've hidden that quantity of bottles.

An eerie sense of calm washed over Jen. In the space of an instant, a plan for her future had revealed itself.

In the medium term, she'd go to AA and get sober.

In the short term, she was going to liberate the bottles in her basement.

I can't look for them with Dan around.

He'd be watching her too closely. The kids were a factor, too. Not to mention the houseguests.

But Max and Chloe would probably be holed up in their bedrooms. And if Dan hadn't gotten rid of Marty and Marina yet, Jen might be able to leverage their presence.

Marty would likely be going to the town meeting. He'd somehow gotten in with Eddie's goons and made himself a lieutenant in the Lincolnwood Army.

If Jen could get Dan to tag along with him . . .

"Penny for your thoughts," the judge said.

"I'm just thinking my husband might want to go to that meeting."

DAN

"Why would I want to go near those people? They're out of their minds! And they're armed!"

They were standing in the kitchen. Dan had just treated Jen to a tour of the bullet's pathway through the room—after ravaging the island cabinetry and narrowly missing Dan's leg, it had finally run out of steam in the Tupperware drawer—and her reaction had been disturbingly mild.

Somehow, Jen had returned from the AA meeting with her emotions surgically removed. She was no longer bitter and snarling, which was a plus. She'd also reported that the meeting was helpful, and she'd indicated a willingness to go back, both of which seemed to bode well for treating her drinking problem.

But she was far too placid. Normal Jen was a reflexive verbal brawler with an almost biological need to be the loudest person in any household argument. The Jen who came back from AA was no less opinionated, but she paired it with an aura of detached calm that was driving Dan up a wall.

When he'd unloaded on her for coming home an hour late, she'd quietly blamed it on Judge Distefano's walking speed. When Dan admonished her for breaking the judge's anonymity, she'd shrugged it off. When he'd relayed his near-fatal encounter with a gun-toting Marty Callahan, she'd remarked that it must have been very upsetting, while giving no indication that she was upset herself. And when she'd thanked him for getting rid of the unwanted houseguests, her appreciation was nowhere near as extravagant as her anger had been in demanding he kick them out in the first place.

Now she was suggesting it'd be a good idea for him to go to the town meeting, as if they hadn't already agreed they were leaving for good as soon as they finished packing and the weather cleared.

"I just think," she told him, in her semi-lobotomized new cadence, "it's a good opportunity to gather information so we can make an informed choice about what we're going to do."

"We know what we're doing! We're getting the hell out of here!"

"And going where?"

"Newton! Or Wellfleet! We'll call an audible on the road."

"Here's what I see as the problem with that." Every word out of her mouth in that condescending-therapist tone was making him grind his teeth with rage. "If Boston didn't get hit by what-ever this is, we'd—"

"It's an EMD."

"What?"

"EMD. Electro—no, that's dance music. P. EMP. Electro-magnetic pulse."

"Which is what?"

"It destroys anything electronic. Including cars. Except old ones. Because they don't have electric starters."

"How'd you figure this out?"

"I didn't. Max did. It was in a video game."

Jen gave him a blank stare. "And then what? The game came to life? Like *Jumanji*?"

"No! It was already a real thing. Ask Max. He can explain it."

"Regardless of what it was," Jen said, "if Boston didn't get hit, we'd know by now. It's close enough that there would've been some kind of emergency response."

"We don't know that."

"Dan, it's been two days. You can practically walk to New York from Boston in two days. If things up there were functional, the government would've responded. They would've come down here—"

"How do you know they haven't? We're not in the city."

"There would've been helicopter traffic. Or something. Nobody's seen a thing. And not only that—to make it to Boston from here, we've got to get around the city. And it's a horror show right now. Especially on the highways."

"How do *you* know?"

"A guy at the AA meeting told me. Vince."

"Jesus, Jen! You're not supposed to tell me his name!"

"Trust me, you don't know him. Unless you've been buying crystal meth. He's, like, eighteen. And he has neck tattoos."

"Stop telling me this stuff! It's an anonymous program!" It was maddening how determined she was to disregard the AA rules. "We can't stay in this town! I almost got murdered in my own kitchen!"

"And it'll be a thousand times worse on the road. How are we going to defend ourselves? Where are we going to sleep? We're not outdoors people. We don't even own sleeping bags."

"Yes, we do! We have two. I brought them up from downstairs."

"One of those is kid-sized."

"It is?"

"Yes. It hasn't fit Max since he was nine." Jen shook her head. "I think we should just hunker down here. I know where we can get water. And showers."

"Where?"

"Diane and Steve's house. They live in Ridgelawn. I met them at the meeting."

"*Stop telling me* this stuff! That's not how AA works!"

"How do you know how AA works?"

"I've seen it on TV!"

"Dan, you of all people should know TV is bullshit. How many cops commit vigilante murders every week and never get caught?"

"*Oh, you're so fucking clever! Congratulations! You got in a real zinger there!*"

"Why are you screaming?"

He was screaming because she wasn't. And because everything she was saying made sense. Biking to Newton was a terrible idea. But it was the only one he had. And without it, what had he done to protect his family?

Nothing. They were standing in the middle of the road, with a truck bearing down on them. And Dan hadn't moved an inch.

He kicked the cabinet door Marty had shot up. When that didn't give him any satisfaction, he kicked it a few more times, with increasing savagery.

"I'm sorry! It was a joke!" Finally, Jen was showing some emotion. "I didn't mean it that way! Please calm down! Everything's okay."

"No, it isn't! The whole world's falling apart! A fucking plane crashed in front of me! And my boss just tried to shoot me!"

And you're putting vodka in the rubbing alcohol!

How was it that she had the drinking problem, and he was the one who was falling apart? Wasn't it supposed to be the other way around?

Nothing made any sense. He was doing a rotten job of saving his family. And he might've just broken his toe.

Dan abandoned his attack on the cabinet door, staggered over to the table, and slumped into a chair.

"Did you eat enough? Do you want me to make you some food?" Jen went over to the stove and lifted the lid on the pot he'd used to make oatmeal. "Ohmygod. What happened here?"

"I made oatmeal."

"Why?"

"Because I had to feed our children!"

"Thank you for that." She probed the gloopy residue in the pot with the equally dirty long-handled spoon Dan had left next to the stove. "But why oatmeal? It's, like, the world's stickiest food."

"Because I'm an *idiot*! Okay? I wasn't thinking!"

He bent over his knees, put his head in his hands, and raked his fingernails across his scalp.

"It's fine. Don't sweat it. Hey." He heard Jen cross the room. Then he felt her hand on his back.

"It's going to be okay," she told him. "I just have one question."

He raised his head and met her eyes. It was hard to tell if she was looking at him with concern or pity. "What?"

"Tuna or peanut butter?"

He sighed. "Tuna."

Ten minutes later, after Jen had gotten his blood sugar back up with some apple slices and tuna salad made from the last of the mayo, Dan had recovered enough clarity of mind to agree that, from an information-gathering standpoint, it'd be a good idea for him to hurry down the hill and catch the back end of the town meeting.

MAX

Playing Monopoly with his sister hadn't quite satisfied the hunger for emotional connection that Max couldn't articulate to himself, let alone Chloe. But it had done a decent job of distracting him from his panicky dread at the fact that society was collapsing and nobody in the house seemed to have any clue what to do about it.

By the time Mom came home, he owned three houses on Oriental Avenue and was starting to build on St. James Place. But Chloe had just consolidated control over the entire upper-middle-class quadrant from Atlantic to Pennsylvania, and a series of unlucky rolls not only halted Max's construction spree, but reduced him to mortgaging undeveloped properties to make rent when their parents' fight erupted in the kitchen.

Gameplay slowed while they monitored the argument in the next room.

"How come Mom's not yelling?" Max asked.

"I don't know. It's weird. Dad's really losing his shit, though."

After the fighting died down and they went back to the game, the momentum swung decisively against Max. He'd been forced to liquidate half of his houses when Dad emerged from the kitchen, zipping up his raincoat and looking defeated.

"Sorry about the yelling."

"It's all good, Daddy," Chloe told him.

"We're, uh, not going to leave for a while. I'm heading into town right now. Whatever you guys do, don't leave the house. Okay?"

"Okay."

"Sure thing!"

"And keep an eye on your mom. She might be having kind of a hard time."

"Okay."

"We love you, Daddy!"

"I love you, pumpkin! Love you, too, Max!"

Max didn't reply. After Dad left, Chloe gave her brother some unsolicited advice. "You should tell him you love him."

"Why?"

"It's an easy way to get on his good side. Mom, too."

"When have you ever been on Mom's good side?"

Chloe frowned. "True. But it's still good advice."

Two turns later, their mother came into the room, commented approvingly on the fact that they were spending quality time together, and asked if anyone needed anything to eat. Given the dismal state of their food inventory, both Max and Chloe declined.

"Let me know if you want me to make you anything," Mom said. "I'm just going to head downstairs for a bit. Make sure there's no supplies down there that I overlooked."

"Okay."

"Great! We love you!"

"I love you, too!"

Then she was gone.

"See, that was a perfect opportunity. Why didn't you say 'I love you'?"

Max shrugged. "I dunno. Just didn't feel like it."

"Promise me you'll start doing it."

"Why?"

"Just because."

"Whatever. Roll the dice."

Then Chloe got even more weird. She started staring into space, and when Max landed on a built-up Marvin Gardens and would've had to mortgage one of his full sets of properties to make the payment, she told him not to worry about it.

"Seriously?"

"Yeah . . . it's fine."

"Are you quitting on me?"

"No. It's just . . . capitalism sucks."

"Whatever. Your turn."

Instead of rolling the dice, Chloe stood up. "I need to use the bathroom."

On her way out, she paused and looked back at him. "I love you!"

"I love you, too," he cooed while rolling his eyes.

"Say it like you mean it. Even if you don't."

"Leave me alone!" He actually did mean it. He just didn't have any practice at saying it.

"C'mon!"

"I love you! Have fun taking a shit."

A minute had passed before it occurred to him to wonder why she'd gone upstairs without bringing a bucket to flush the toilet.

Then he heard the rattle of the garage door.

He jumped up and ran for the mudroom. When he reached

the garage, she was already in the driveway, walking her bike and wearing her overstuffed backpack.

"Hey!"

She flinched at the sight of him. "Shhhh!"

He considered yelling for Mom. But he stayed quiet.

"I'm sorry," she whispered. "I just can't deal. I'll come back when it's over."

"Where you going?"

"A friend's. You don't know him. It's a long story."

Max stared at her in wounded disbelief. He'd just made his first good-faith effort to connect with his sister in years. It was hard not to take her bailing out personally.

"I love you," she said.

"Fuck you! Then don't leave."

She winced. "I'm sorry. I just have to. Please wait at least five minutes before you tell Mom."

Max watched her disappear down Willis Road. The panicky feeling was already starting to percolate in his stomach again. He lowered the garage door behind her and started to count back from five minutes.

JEN

Dan hadn't put much creative effort into hiding the bottles. Jen found them in the first place she looked, which was Chloe's camp trunk.

But locating them wasn't the hard part. Dan had padlocked the trunk, and she had no idea what the combination was. She ran her flashlight beam all over the heavy red plastic container, looking for a point of entry. When it became clear that there wasn't one—that the trunk had, in fact, been designed to foil attempts at forced entry by delinquent teenage campers—Jen's sense of calm vanished as fast as it had arrived.

It was replaced by a simmering determination to defeat this puny obstacle to her control over the situation.

She balanced the flashlight on a shelf and tried to pry the lid open. That was pointless. She could barely get her fingertips in there.

Then she grabbed the trunk by one of the side handles and tilted it up on the wheels embedded in one of its bottom corners. It was tantalizingly heavy with booze. She jerked the handle back and forth, listening to the hard clink of the bottles inside.

If I break one of them . . . then tilt the whole thing into a bowl and let the liquid leak out of the crack . . .

No. That was absurd. The trunk was far too heavy to lift and turn with any precision. And she couldn't selectively break the bottles inside. She'd just make a mess.

Jen lowered the trunk back to the floor and sat down on the lid with her elbows propped on her thighs and her chin in her hand.

Fucking Dan.

Where else can I get a drink?

Is there mouthwash left upstairs?

The thought triggered a brief attack of conscience.

Jesus Christ, look at you. This is pathetic.

There was no question what she was doing was wrong. The right action was equally obvious: stand up, go back upstairs, and forget the whole idea of drinking.

Give it a rest. Go play Monopoly with the kids.

But her conscience was no match for her lizard-brain compulsion. The blissful feeling of calm she'd briefly enjoyed had come from the anticipation of drinking. Now the calm was gone, but the anticipation had remained, metastasizing into a demand.

There was no arguing with the lizard brain. It had to be satisfied.

Dad's old tools.

There was a big box of them somewhere in the basement. They'd ended up in Jen's hands when her mother had relocated to Florida.

There might be a crowbar in there. There was definitely a saw.

She took her flashlight and went looking for the tools. A few minutes later, she located the box. No crowbar. But there was a hacksaw. She took it back to the trunk and considered her options.

Do I saw through the lock? Or the trunk?

She tried the metal lock first. It was a disaster. She couldn't even figure out how to hold it in place without sawing a finger off. So she opted for the back corner of the trunk, sawing horizontally through it an inch or two below the hinge.

Her progress was surprisingly quick. Within a couple of minutes, the smell of burnt plastic was in her nostrils, and there was a four-inch slit wrapped around the rear edge. She'd just started sawing a second, parallel cut a few inches below the first one when she heard the voice behind her.

"What are you doing?"

Jen sprang up, almost cutting herself in the process, and turned toward her son, his face half in shadow at the outer perimeter of the flashlight beam.

"Heeey!"

How do I explain this?

"I was just, umm . . . I think there might be food in here?"

Max looked past her legs at the newly scarred trunk. Then his eyes traveled back up to meet hers. The look on his face made her sick with shame.

"Whatever." He turned away, back toward the stairs.

"Can I get anything for you? Do you need lunch, or—?"

"No."

He was three steps up, barely visible in the gloom, when he paused to deliver his message.

"Chloe left."

Fifteen minutes later, Jen was sitting at the desk in her daughter's room, Chloe's goodbye letter in her hands, struggling under the weight of self-loathing triggered by her fourth rereading of the paragraph that ended with *I'm glad you're finally getting the help you need.*

It had taken that many readings for Jen's anger to turn inward. The first time through the letter, her fury was directed exclusively at Chloe. Running off at a time like this, while giving them no clue to her destination, was an appalling act of selfishness.

There had to be a boy involved. But who? Not Jeremy Landesman. They were just friends. And not that Aidan kid she went to the junior prom with. That had been over before it started. It must be a new boy, or at least one she'd never talked about.

So how the hell were Jen and Dan supposed to find her?

The second time through the letter, Jen had realized that was the whole point. This wasn't a plea for attention. Chloe didn't want to be found.

By the end of the third reading, the paragraph about Jen's drinking had started to sound less like patronizing nonsense barfed out by a teenager trying to justify her own self-centeredness and more like a sincere expression of pain.

The fourth time through broke her open.

This was all Jen's fault.

All of it.

Her family was falling apart—everything was falling apart—and she was scuttling around the basement like a rat in the dark, gnawing through a box to get a fix.

Max appeared in the doorway.

"I'm going to go over to Judge Distefano's for a while."

"Why?"

"Just to hang out with his dog. There's nothing else to do. And it's right next door. I can come back whenever. I'm not going to run away or anything."

Jen considered the request. There was no good reason to say no, other than the terror she felt at being alone.

"Maybe I should come, too."

Max's face wrinkled with discomfort.

"Please just let me go alone."

She released him with a nod, too defeated to even search for words.

DAN

Jen hadn't been lying about the rain forecast. The sky looked ominous, the wind was blowing stray leaves through the chilly air, and the streets were mostly deserted, although it was hard to say if that was due to the weather or the apocalypse. The only people Dan saw as he rode his bike to Borough Hall looked like refugees, weighted down with baggage and worry. Their forlorn expressions seemed to support Jen's argument for staying put. If nothing else, the Altmans still had a roof over their heads.

But it wasn't sustainable.

They'd be out of food and drinking water in a few days at most. And maybe Newton and Wellfleet were bad options. But if Max's EMP theory was right, then they needed to move *somewhere*, and soon, before the weather got too cold and they ran out of things to eat.

Just thinking about it threatened to trigger a panic attack.

Even more than food and water, Dan needed information. Where had this not happened? How far would they have to travel to get to a place that accepted credit cards?

Or was aid actually on its way, and they just needed to wait it out?

That must be it. Two full days had passed since the incident. There had to be some kind of federal relief effort underway. The town officials must've gotten word about it by now. They'd probably announce it at the meeting. And the vote would put a stop to this Watchdog madness. People in Lincolnwood weren't idiots. Nobody was going to turn political control over to a pack of gun-waving meatheads.

By the time Dan reached Borough Hall, he'd managed to talk himself into a frame of mind that vaguely resembled optimism.

Then he realized he'd gone to the wrong place. The building was locked and empty, with a handwritten sign taped to the door directing him to the gymnasium at Lincolnwood Middle School. LMS was half a mile in the opposite direction from where he'd first turned onto Hawthorne. All in, it was at least a fifteen-minute mistake, which posed a substantial challenge to his optimism.

But he was still reasonably hopeful when he finally reached the middle school, the abandoned cars in its faculty parking lot surrounded by a thicket of bicycles. As Dan reached its outer perimeter, the gym doors on the far side of the lot opened, and a crowd of townspeople spilled out of it.

The meeting was over. When the leading edge of the crowd reached Dan in the middle of the lot, it was clear from the expressions of the people passing him that whatever had happened inside wasn't cause for optimism. Scanning the crowd for a familiar face, his eye landed on a pair of moms from Chloe's grade, tall blonde Stephanie Andersen and diminutive brunette Lisa Cohen.

"Stephanie!"

The women paused long enough for Dan to steer his bike through the throng to reach them.

"I missed the meeting. What happened?"

"Complete shitshow."

"Great news!" said Lisa with venomous sarcasm. "We're a fascist dictatorship!"

"We lose water for a day and a half, and these people fall all over themselves to put the men with guns in charge. They're sheep! These people are *sheep!*" Stephanie addressed her last sentence to the crowd.

"Suck it up, buttercup," a balding guy in dad jeans chuckled as he passed them.

"*Fuck you, asshole!*" Stephanie snarled. The man flipped her off over his shoulder but kept moving, probably because she was taller, fitter, and much angrier than him.

"When this is all over," Lisa declared, "*nobody's* going to admit they supported it."

"Did they say anything about a relief effort?"

Lisa snorted. "Yeah—go line up at the Whole Foods. And the warlords will feed you your rations."

"But I mean, is FEMA coming in, or . . ."

Stephanie shook her head. "No, Dan. Nobody's coming. There's nothing."

"Does anybody know why the power went out? Were there announcements, or—"

"Nothing. Nobody knows shit about shit." The women appeared to be losing patience with his questions.

"Danny Boy!" Marty had emerged from the gym with Eddie, Jordan, and several of the Watchdogs. All of them except Jordan were carrying long guns, although Marty at least seemed to have mastered the basic etiquette of keeping the barrel pointed at the ground and his finger off the trigger.

As he waved to Dan and started toward him, the looks Stephanie and Lisa gave Marty were poisonous.

"Thanks for the info," Dan told them.

The women started walking in the opposite direction, away from Marty and the other armed men. "Say hi to Jen," Lisa told him.

"Will do. Best to Andy and Mike!"

Dan and Marty quickly closed the distance between each other. "Hey, buddy! Sorry again about your kitchen. Are your ears still ringing? 'Cause I can't hear shit."

"Yeah, me too."

"Really sorry, *amigo*. That's my bad." Then Marty's eyes widened as his face split into a grin. "Were you in the meeting?"

"No, I just got here."

"The good guys won! It was awesome! Most people are really supportive. We're going to get through this."

"So what exactly happened?"

"We just voted in the team! We got Shrek calling the shots. Kozak and the Watchdogs backing him up. It's all good."

Dan looked past Marty at the men with guns. Barry Kozak was gesturing toward a sheet of paper he'd just handed to Eddie as Jordan peered over his dad's arm at the document.

"Is Eddie's kid a Watchdog now?"

"Kind of. I think he's, like, a provisional member?"

"So how do you, um . . ." *I can't believe I'm asking this.* "Join the Watchdogs?"

"Oh." Marty's smile transformed into a look of regret. He put a consoling hand on Dan's upper arm. "I'm sorry, dude. I think we're full up. Kozak's only taking new members if you can bring something to the table. Like a gun, or a car, or—"

"What up, Dan-O?" Eddie Stankovic was approaching with his son.

"Hey, Eddie. Hi, Jordan."

"Hey."

Eddie turned to Marty. "We got the list! Ready to saddle up?"

"Yeah, man. Who's driving?"

"Gotta go on foot. But we can eat what we kill."

"Cool."

"What are you guys doing?" Dan asked.

"Just gathering resources," Eddie explained. "How are you? How's your lady?"

"She's fine. How's yours?"

"Real good. You hear the announcement about rations?"

"He missed the meeting," Marty explained.

"Oh. Well, you should head over to the Whole Foods and get in line," Eddie told Dan. "We're giving out food and water. Marty says you could really use some."

"Well, we *had* enough water," Dan started to explain. "But then somebody—"

"Take care, Dan-O!" Eddie interrupted him, walking away.

"Catch you back at the homestead, buddy," said Marty.

He and Jordan followed Eddie off, leaving Dan alone on the rapidly depopulating patch of concrete outside the gym where Lincolnwood's political future had been decided without him.

CHLOE

Josh's mom had been a complete bitch. When she answered the door and Chloe asked for Josh, Mrs. Houser had looked at her like she was some kind of stray animal.

"Josh isn't home."

"Oh." Chloe waited for the woman to offer more information, but she didn't.

"Do you know when he'll be back?"

"He's out for a run. And he's not going out again after that. Have a nice day."

"You too! Thank you for your time!"

Chloe did her best to sound warm and friendly even as the door was being shut in her face.

Walking back to the bike and backpack she'd left at the bottom of the short driveway, her cheeks grew hot with humiliation. She slung the pack over her shoulders and steered her bike into the street, unsure of her next move.

She could go alone to the Blackwells' and wait for Josh to arrive, but the thought of wandering around that massive house all by herself creeped her out.

Or she could camp out somewhere nearby and wait for him to come back. The swings at the playground across the street from his house would've been ideal, but then she'd be in full view if Mrs. Houser looked out the window.

She chose the tennis court bleachers instead. They were far

enough from his house that Josh's mom couldn't see her, but close enough that Chloe would be able to intercept Josh as he came up the street. Unless he arrived from the other direction, in which case she'd have to wave or yell to get his attention.

Chloe hopped on her bike, rode the short distance to the bleachers, and sat down to wait.

Why didn't we make a plan before I left yesterday? Stupid.

Their habit of unspoken communication hadn't served her too well in this case. She looked up at the sky.

Just please get back before it rains.

It was at least half an hour later, and her mind had gone to all kinds of dark places when Josh finally came into view, wearing a sweatshirt and compression shorts as he jogged toward his house from the opposite direction. Chloe jumped up and waved her arms to get his attention.

But he wouldn't look Chloe's way, so she had to yell and hope his mother didn't hear her.

"JOSH!"

He stopped in the middle of the road a few feet short of his property line, cocking his head to one side like a curious retriever.

She waved to him.

He waved back. Then he kept moving in the direction of his front door.

What the hell?

"JOSH!"

He stopped and looked at her again. Finally, he started to jog toward her.

Something was off. The look on his face as he approached was disturbingly blank.

"Hey," he said, slowing to a walk when he was still twenty feet away. "Is your semi today?"

"No."

Of course not. What the hell kind of question is that?

"Oh." Still several feet from her, he stopped and bent his leg back, grabbing his ankle in a quad stretch. "So what are you up to?"

ISN'T IT OBVIOUS?

"Waiting for you."

"Oh. Shit, I'm sorry. I can't really hang out today."

"What do you mean, 'today'?"

"I just gotta stick around home. Y'know?"

Chloe could feel the blood draining from her head. Black spots were starting to dot the edges of her vision.

"I thought . . . we were going to the Blackwells'."

"Yeah, I can't today. Sorry." He switched legs, hopping on one foot to keep his balance.

It's his mother. It's his fucking mother.

"You don't have to listen to your parents," she told him. "They're crazy!"

"No, they're not." He looked offended.

"Are you kidding? They think the Democrats shut the power off! That's insane! You said so yourself!"

He snorted. "Yeah—it's insane of *the Democrats*."

"Ohmygod!" Her stomach had fallen to somewhere near her ankles.

"What?"

"I thought . . . you said you wanted to stay at the Blackwells' with me!"

His eyebrows rose and his jaw fell, stretching out his face like some kind of funhouse clown. "Oh! Damn. I thought you were kidding."

Ohmygod. Ohmygod.

She ran for her bike. He took a few halfhearted steps in her direction.

"Sorry if I gave you the wrong idea. I just can't really be in a relationship right now? Like, maybe once swim season's over—"

Ohmygod!

Chloe threw her backpack on and mounted the bike, nearly falling over in her haste to get away from him.

"Are you okay?"

She righted herself and pedaled off as fast as she could, her eyes welling up and her nose starting to run in the cold air.

Just please let me get to Emma's before I lose it.

JEN

It had taken most of the duct tape and every ounce of her patience, but Jen was finally on the cusp of assembling a functional rain catcher in the backyard.

There were other ways she would've preferred to spend her morning, or afternoon, or whatever the hell it was by now. But the one-two punch of Max catching her hacksawing through a plastic trunk full of booze and Chloe running away while leaving behind written testimony to Jen's failure as a parent had combined to break the spell of her drink obsession.

At least for the moment, she'd admitted defeat. She wasn't going to drink today.

That meant she had to keep busy. When she wasn't anesthetizing it with booze, the relentless interior monologue of *why did I . . . how could I . . . I never should've . . . if only I would've . . .* was almost unbearable. If she didn't do something to distract herself, she'd be slitting her wrists by dinnertime.

Not that there would actually be any dinner, other than peanut butter and canned tuna.

There was no shortage of problems demanding her attention—in fact, a stream of them kept cycling through her head alongside her self-recrimination—but the only ones that seemed solvable were the half-built rain catcher and the dirty oatmeal pot in the sink.

Given the impending downpour, Jen decided to address

the rain catcher first. She marched out to the yard, hopeful that she could make quick work of it, but soon found herself in a quagmire. After several failed assaults and a lot of wasted duct tape, it became clear that the rain ponchos just couldn't be made to work in tandem with the shower curtain. So she stripped them out, even though it meant not only reducing the surface area available to catch rain by almost half, but redigging the holes for the rake and the shovel.

She'd just finished replanting the shovel when the first strong gust of wind whipped up in advance of the storm, launching the recycling bin into the air and pulling the rake out of the ground while partially separating the curtain from it.

Fixing the design flaw this revealed required Jen to weight down the various components with several large decorative rocks from the rear garden.

She was adding the first rock to the bottom of the recycling bin as ballast when she realized Kayla was watching her from the glass sliding door on the Stankovics' back patio. Jen pretended not to see her neighbor, hoping Kayla would get bored with watching and go away.

But instead of going away, she multiplied. Marina joined Kayla at the sliding door, and the two of them stood watching Jen through the plate glass with all the empathy of a pair of Lululemon-clad vultures. Jen ignored them, but she could feel their eyes on her as she duct-taped decorative rocks to the shovel and rake poles, anchoring them in place. Then, as a precautionary measure, she added two more layers of duct tape to the seam that attached the curtain to the recycling bin.

Jen stepped back to survey her creation.

There was no denying it looked like the work of an incompetent third grader.

But it didn't matter how it looked. The only important thing was that it functioned. The proof, Jen told herself, would come when the rain started.

The proof came sooner than that. She'd just turned away to walk back to the house when another gust of wind came through. It lifted the rake out of the ground, ripped it loose of its anchoring rocks, and tore the curtain away from the bin, leaving a long, tape-fringed edge flapping in the wind like a flag of surrender.

Then the shovel tipped over, and the whole thing collapsed in a heap.

Jen was careful not to look in the direction of the Stankovics' house as she retreated back inside, where there was nothing to drown her sorrows with except dry tuna and the beans Dan had brought back from Whole Foods.

CHLOE

Emma was gone. The Schroeders' house was locked and shuttered, with no indication of where they were or when they'd return.

It probably wouldn't be soon. At one point yesterday, Emma had mentioned an uncle outside Philadelphia who was a doctor. Her mother had been lobbying to go stay with him, because he had a big house and the ability to write benzo prescriptions. That must be where they'd headed.

So Chloe was left alone, with no outlet for the stew of humiliation and resentment swirling in her brain, and nobody to help her work through the question of whether the whole thing had been Josh's fault or hers.

He was an idiot. She could see that now. The question was why she hadn't seen it earlier.

Had he lied to her? Or had she lied to herself?

Thinking back, she couldn't recall him making any actual promises other than saying "Why not?" when she'd asked if he'd stay with her at the Blackwells'. He'd been smiling when he said it, so it was possible he really did think she was joking.

When she mentally reviewed the hours they'd been together, what stuck out the most was how much time he'd spent talking about his workout schedule, his hundred-meter butterfly record, and his college recruiting options. At the time, she'd assumed he was just trying to distract her from spiraling down into anxiety by filling their otherwise awkward silences with words. After a while, his monologues on topics like the difference between long-course and short-course race times had started to feel like the verbal equivalent of white noise, and she'd just stopped listening.

But what if he hadn't been trying to distract her? What if meaningless chatter about his swim workouts was actually his conversational A-game?

Ohmygod.

Was he really that boring?

And if he was . . . did that make her feel better about the rejection? Or worse?

She couldn't decide. And it didn't really matter. Either way, it still left her sitting alone outside an empty house while the sky rumbled with approaching rain.

You don't have to go home, Frenchie.

But you can't stay here.

She stood up and walked to her bike.

DAN

The line for rations snaked from the loading dock behind the Whole Foods all the way around the perimeter of the parking lot. The Lincolnwood residents shuffling forward in line alongside Dan weren't interested in talking, so he passed the time by listening to the ringing in his ears.

It seemed to be getting worse. He was concerned it might be permanent.

This upset him less than he would've expected. Under normal circumstances—although that wasn't a fair comparison, because "normal circumstances" wouldn't have included an assault rifle discharging in his kitchen in the first place—Dan would've obsessed over the injury to the exclusion of everything else in his life, spending hours combing through the Google search results for "hearing loss from gunfire" while making and canceling multiple appointments with hearing specialists, both in and out of his insurance network.

But right now, his hearing was a second-order problem, dwarfed by much more immediate concerns like *Am I really going to beg for handouts from a gang of thugs in Patagonia jackets?* and *Why won't they let me join their gang of thugs?*

The latter question took on an added dimension of bitterness when Dan approached the front of the line and discovered one of the men ferrying boxes of canned goods to the distribution table was Arjun Mukherjee.

How the hell is Arjun a Watchdog and not me?

He doesn't even own a gun! And they think he's a terrorist!

Dan hadn't felt this excluded since he'd been picked last for kickball back in elementary school.

When it was his turn to step up to the table, a bearded Jets fan on the other side of it growled, "ID!"

Dan leaned his bike against his hip so he could free both hands to pull out his wallet and produce his driver's license. The man checked Dan's address, then returned it.

"Put your hand out."

Dan held out his hand, palm up. The man grasped Dan's fingers, turned the hand palm side down, and drew a large X below his knuckles with a Sharpie.

Then he handed Dan a pony bottle of water and a can of organic corn.

Dan stared at the puny ration in disbelief. "I have a family of four."

"Next time, bring 'em," the man said. He jerked his head to one side, indicating that Dan should shove off. "You're blocking the line."

The woman behind Dan maneuvered around him and his bike to reach the table. "Hi, Kenny."

"Hey, Brooke."

"Can I get some extra for Haley and Madison?"

"Sure thing. Get the bike out of here, pal!"

Dan stuck the water and the corn in the front pockets of his raincoat and removed himself to the edge of the loading dock, a few yards from where Arjun was tearing open a case of kale snacks.

"Arjun!"

Arjun glanced up from his work and nodded in recognition. "Hey, Dan."

"Do you have a second?"

Arjun glanced in the direction of his nearest co-worker, a gaunt fortysomething in a Yale Squash windbreaker.

"Not now. Sorry. I'm on shift."

"Do you guys need help?"

Arjun and his co-worker traded a look. Yale Squash gave a slight, rapid shake of his head.

"No, we're good," Arjun told him.

Dan did his best to hold his head high as he walked his bike to the street. This was much worse than elementary school kickball.

The sky was threatening rain when he reached Willis Road. But instead of turning uphill toward home, Dan kept riding up Hawthorne toward Ridgelawn. He couldn't stomach the idea of returning to the house with nothing but six ounces of water and a can of organic corn to show for his fact-finding mission.

Half a mile north, he took a right on Greeley, which would take him past the parkway on-ramps. If the Altmans left town for a destination to the north or south, that'd be their most likely route.

He reached the southbound ramp first. It was barricaded with lines of orange Department of Public Works barrels. In front of the barricade, a uniformed Lincolnwood PD cop stood watch with a rifle beside a six-foot-high plywood board with LINCOLN-WOOD RESIDENTS ONLY—NO PUBLIC ACCESS spray-painted on it in giant block letters. Abandoned cars littered the parkway below, several of them with shattered windshields and open doors. A dozen or more mournful travelers walked or biked the road in either direction, most of them carrying baggage.

As Dan approached the barricade, the cop eyed him skeptically.

"You leaving?"

"Not today," Dan replied. "You heard any news?"

"Newark's burning. So's New York. People are getting out of the cities. Just gotta make sure they don't think they can stop here. Need to take care of our own."

"I guess so."

Dan wheeled his bike around and went back up to Hawthorne, then turned right and biked another quarter mile, until the change in the color of the street signs indicated he'd reached Ridgelawn.

He had the vague idea that once he left Lincolnwood, he'd encounter someone who knew what was going on, or who at least didn't seem like they were all in on helping create a fascist dystopia.

For the first mile or so, the streets of Ridgelawn were deserted. When Dan reached the business district, he began to pass isolated pedestrians. None of them looked friendly enough to talk to. Most were lone males, carrying backpacks and examining the buildings they passed with the kind of furtive stares that suggested they were searching for weaknesses to exploit. Very few seemed like locals, and it occurred to Dan that their numbers were increasing as he approached the Ridgelawn exit on the parkway.

When he got to Morton Avenue, with the Mount Carmel Cemetery to his right and Donatello's Steakhouse to his left, he stopped in the middle of the intersection and considered his options. Half a mile to his right was the Ridgelawn parkway exit, and a mile or two up ahead was Paterson. Neither direction seemed to offer much in the way of new information.

If he turned left, he could take Morton Avenue over the hill to Townsend, then follow that all the way out to I-80. But what would be the point? The interstate probably looked a lot like the parkway did. He wouldn't learn anything from seeing it. And he'd have to get over the hill on his aching legs, then back up it from the other side to return home.

The sky was rumbling, and the wind had picked up. Any minute now, it was going to start pouring.

What the hell am I going to do?

The first stray drops of rain falling on his jacket persuaded him that the only smart choice was to admit defeat, turn around, and go home to wait out the storm with Jen and the kids.

If Dan's ears hadn't been ringing, he might have heard the man coming up on him from behind. Instead, his first indication that he wasn't alone in the middle of the intersection came when an unseen fist smashed into his left temple, knocking his glasses off and sending him crashing to the pavement.

MAX

After a marathon session of fetch, Max had finally worn out Ruby. She lay on his lap on the floor of the judge's back patio, licking his hand as he petted her.

The judge raised his eyes from the book he was reading and watched them with an appraising look.

"Just how allergic is your dad?"

Max shrugged. "I dunno. We'd have to rub Ruby in his face to find out."

"Not sure either one of them would enjoy that. But speaking hypothetically . . . if anything were to happen to me, do you think he'd let you take her in?"

"Is something going to happen to you?" It was an alarming thought.

"No! God forbid. Just thinking worst-case scenario. I'm no spring chicken. And Ruby's got a lot of miles left on her. Wouldn't want to leave her an orphan."

"We'd take her. Totally. My dad's not *that* allergic."

A sharp knock came from the front door, loud enough that it made Ruby twitch.

"Did you order a pizza?"

"How would I do that?"

The judge stood up. "It's a joke. Try to keep up, kid."

He exited the patio. Ruby raised her head to stare at the door her owner had just disappeared through. Max stroked her from head to tail as they heard the sound of the front door opening, followed by men's voices, too low to hear.

Ruby strained to get to her feet. Max gathered her in his arms and increased his petting, trying to persuade her to stay with him. When she started to squirm, he let her go. She trotted out of the room. With a sigh, Max got up and followed her.

As he entered the front hall from the kitchen, the judge was talking through the screen door to Eddie Stankovic, who was holding a shotgun. Next to Eddie, Max could see the shoulder of a tall man, but he couldn't tell who it was.

"Kozak didn't think so," Eddie was saying.

The judge shrugged. "What can I tell you? He was misinformed."

"You mind if we take a look?" Eddie asked.

"I do, actually," the judge replied. "I got a friend over right now. It's not a convenient time."

At the mention of a friend, Eddie peered past the judge, looking into the house. Max stepped forward a few paces.

When he did, he realized the second man was his dad's boss, Marty—and he was holding the assault rifle he'd almost shot Dad with earlier that day.

"Should we come back later?" Eddie asked the judge.

"I wouldn't bother yourself, Ed. You're barking up the wrong tree. You boys have a good day, now."

"You too, Judge," Eddie replied. When he shifted position to move off the front porch, Max caught a glimpse of a third person behind him.

It was Jordan Stankovic. He and Max locked eyes for the half second before the judge shut the door.

The old man turned the deadbolt. Then he went to the short table in the hallway, opened its shallow drawer, and placed the large-caliber pistol Max hadn't realized he was holding back inside it.

Max's heart jumped as the judge shut the drawer. "Is that a Colt forty-five?"

"Close," the judge replied. "Beretta nine millimeter. What do you know about handguns?"

"Only what I got from video games."

"I'm not what you'd call an enthusiast," the judge explained. "But back when I was on the bench, I put away a few wise guys. Made my wife nervous that their friends on the outside might get ideas. The Beretta was peace of mind for the both of us. You hungry?"

"A little bit."

"Good. Let's eat something."

With Ruby at his heels, the judge gave Max a reassuring pat on the shoulder and walked past him to the kitchen. But it wasn't reassuring enough to compensate for Max's sense of unease. Life on Brantley Circle was starting to feel more and more like a video game, and he'd always sucked at video games.

DAN

Getting punched in the head and knocked to the ground with no warning would've been disorienting enough. But Dan was severely nearsighted, and losing his glasses added a whole other level of complication to the crisis.

One of his legs was pinned under his bike, and when he turned his head from the pavement, his blurry, green-and-blue attacker was already looming over him, hands outstretched with malevolent purpose.

Dan twisted away from the attack, pressing his hands to the asphalt and trying to push himself up to stand. But he couldn't free his legs from the tangle of his bike. Underneath him, something hard and sharp was digging into his hip.

Then the bike came to life as his attacker tried to yank it out from under him.

NO!

Dan wrenched his legs free and lurched to his feet. Pain signals were flooding his brain, but they were drowned out by the urgency of reclaiming his bike from the blurry shape that had it by the handlebars and was beginning to swing a leg over the seat.

Dan grabbed the man by his fleece jacket and yanked as hard as he could, pulling the would-be bike thief off balance.

The thief countered with an elbow to Dan's face. Starbursts exploded in his already blurry field of vision, and he lost his grip on the man's jacket. As Dan staggered backward, he felt something bang against his hip.

The can of corn—the hard, sharp thing that had dug into him when he was on the ground—was still in his front raincoat pocket.

Dan reached in and pulled it out.

The blurry thief had finally gotten his leg over the seat of the bike and was rising up to bring his foot down on the pedal.

Dan raised the can over his head and brought the metal edge of it down on the back of the green baseball cap covering the man's head.

A howl of pain erupted from the thief as he lost his footing on the pedal and lurched forward over the handlebars.

Dan hit him again with the hard edge of the can.

Another shriek. The man tried to waddle forward as he straddled the bike. Possession of it was no longer an asset—its bulk was preventing the thief from maneuvering away from Dan's attack.

Grunting with rage, Dan clubbed him a third time.

Reeling from the onslaught, the man tried to abandon the bike. But he couldn't get free of it. Handlebars, wheels, frame, arms, and legs were all working at cross purposes as Dan kept hitting him with the can.

Finally, the man stumbled free and began to stagger up Hawthorne toward Paterson. Dan chased him until his fury dissipated enough to realize there was no reason to keep going.

I won.

I fucking WON.

A man had sucker punched him. Had tried to take what was his. And in return, Dan had beaten the shit out of him.

He looked down at the can in his hand. His vision was so bad that he couldn't even read the label. When he held it up closer to his face, he realized it was smeared with fresh blood.

Dan lowered the can, nauseous and dizzy. His ears were ringing. The side of his head was hot with a dull pain from the initial blow. There was a much sharper pain just below his right cheekbone, where he'd caught the elbow.

Now that the adrenaline was subsiding, other parts of his body were starting to cry out in pain, too. Worst of all, his whole world was a fuzzy blur.

Where are my glasses?

Dan turned around. Back in the middle of the intersection, something big and orange was moving.

It was a second man. This one wore a bright orange jacket. He was picking Dan's bike up off the ground.

"*HEY! THAT'S MINE!*" Dan broke into a sprint, scrambling toward the figure as it rose up and jiggled down Morton Avenue in the direction of the parkway.

The orange blur was speeding away much faster than Dan could run.

He threw the bloody can of corn at the man. When it missed its target and clattered to the pavement, he could barely hear it over the ringing in his ears and the growl of thunder overhead.

Eventually, Dan stopped running. The orange blur disappeared into the haze of a world he could no longer see clearly.

He staggered back to the intersection and began to search for his glasses.

By the time he found them, shattered and useless by the side of the road, the rain was coming down on him in sheets.

JEN

Without water, the pot of oatmeal wouldn't come clean. Jen got the big chunks off with a scraper—and, reasoning that no calories should go to waste, she ate them as she went—but the pasty goo had hardened into an unforgiving crust, and after working the sides of the pot in the dry sink basin until her wrists and fingers ached, she couldn't see where she'd even made much of a dent in it.

When she paused to rest her hands and stared out the window, the trash heap that was the failed rain catcher stared back at her from the yard.

Had she been in a less self-pitying mood, she might've been able to resist the temptation to view these twin domestic failures as metaphors. But under the circumstances, it was impossible not to see her own life reflected in the pile of garbage out the window, or the fate of the world in the ineradicable scum clinging to the sides of the pot.

Things fall apart. And when they do, they don't get fixed.
There's no putting any of this back together.
Not this pot. Not my family. Not the world.
I should've gone shopping. I should've gone to the bank.
Now it's too late.
You done fucked up, kid.

Her every thought was a negation. She'd never felt so hopeless. Not that she was ordinarily inclined to sunny optimism. But she'd never gone this far into the abyss.

Partly, that was because whenever she'd felt herself spiraling down in the past, she'd always been able to drown the feeling in alcohol. But there was no medicating it away this time. She had no urge to drink. She was past that. Booze wouldn't help. It'd just put things off, while making them worse.

The only real solution was permanent.

Are there enough pills in the house to kill me?

Probably not.

The gas oven might work if I can figure out how to light the pilot.

But do I really want Dan or Max to find me like that?

Even by Jen's standards, it was a selfish move. The least she could do was spare her family the unpleasantness of disposing of her corpse.

What building around here is tall enough to jump off?

She was cataloging her options when she heard the gunshot.

MAX

"So, at the risk of being a bad host—"

Max opened his eyes. He'd dozed off on the patio couch with Ruby on his lap. The judge was standing over him, his voice just loud enough to wake both boy and dog without startling either one.

"—I'm going to head upstairs and catch a nap myself."

"Okay." Max looked out the window at the threatening sky as Ruby hopped off his lap and stretched herself awake on the floor. "I guess I should get home before it rains on me."

"Probably for the best."

What time was it? Midafternoon? A bump of Skoal would be a good idea.

The judge walked him to the door and held it open as Max stepped out into the prematurely dark afternoon.

"Watch out for that corner of the lawn," the judge warned, pointing to a spot near the edge of the Altmans' property line. "Ruby left a grenade this morning. Haven't gotten my act together to clean it up yet."

"Thanks for letting me hang out."

"Pleasure's mine, Maxwell. Come back anytime."

He decided against telling the judge that his full name wasn't actually Maxwell. As the door shut behind him, a peal of thunder erupted from the sky to the south. Max took the concrete path to the sidewalk, figuring the few seconds he'd save by cutting a diagonal across the lawn weren't worth the risk of stepping in dog poop.

He was twenty feet up the sidewalk toward his driveway when Jordan Stankovic—who must've been lying in wait around the corner of the judge's house—stepped out from behind the shrubbery.

"Hey!"

Max's first thought was to wonder why Jordan was holding a toy AR-15.

Then he realized it wasn't a toy.

"Don't fuckin' move!" Eyes darting between Max and the ground to avoid stepping in Ruby's shit, Jordan quickly crossed the lawn to the sidewalk, blocking Max's route home.

The apparition of Jordan stalking him in a lateral movement while pointing an assault rifle at him matched up so perfectly with an encounter they'd once had in the Call of Duty multiplayer that for a moment, Max wondered if his mind was just playing tricks on him.

"Does he still have it?" Jordan barked.

"What?"

"The Mustang!"

This was no figment of his imagination. It was all too real. Except that Jordan wasn't making any sense.

"What are you talking about?"

"Does he have the Mustang?"

"The what?"

"The car! The fuckin' car!"

Jordan raised the angle of the rifle, pointing it in Max's face.

At such close range, the barrel looked a lot narrower than it did in a video game. It almost didn't seem wide enough for a bullet to pass through.

"Does he have it or not?" Jordan's mouth hung open as he glared at Max with a look of malevolent stupidity.

"I don't know what you're talking about!"

Max's gaze traveled from Jordan's eyes to the base of his neck. It was partially obscured by his hoodie, but there was a tantalizing patch of exposed white skin just above the spot that the YouTube video promised was full of tender nerve endings.

That's where I should hit him with the karate chop.

The trouble was that most of the space between Max's hand and Jordan's neck was occupied by an assault rifle.

This was completely unfair. Jordan had brought a gun to a fistfight. And he wouldn't stop barking nonsensical demands about a car.

"The fuckin' Mustang! Is it in the garage?"

"I don't know!"

"Bullshit! You were in there!" Jordan clenched his teeth and jabbed the rifle at Max's nose. "*Tell me!*"

"*I! Don't! Know!*" Max was starting to tremble.

On top of the anger and the stupidity, Jordan's eyes began to show consternation. He seemed to be wrestling with the question of how to force whatever answer he was looking for out of Max without actually shooting him.

Max stole another glance at his adversary's fleshy neck.

Right there. C'mon.

But he knew he didn't have the courage to attack. Not with a gun in his face.

His gaze traveled beyond Jordan's neck, toward the Altmans' house.

The garage door was open. It wasn't that far away.

Can I run for it? Would he really shoot me?

Jordan's eyes widened. His low-wattage brain had finally generated an idea.

"Tell me or eat the shit!"

"What?"

Jordan jerked his head toward the judge's lawn. "Eat the dog shit!"

Max looked to his left. After a moment's search, he spied Ruby's excrement, half-hidden in the short grass.

Oh, come on.

He looked back at Jordan. "Dude—"

Jordan jabbed the rifle into Max's face again. "Tell me or eat it!"

"I don't know what you're talking about!"

"Eat the shit, Altman!" Jordan took a step back and kicked his foot at Max.

Max took a few placating steps onto the grass. "Jordan—"

"Fucking do it! Get on your knees!"

This is insane.

What's he going to do, shoot me?

With his mom across the street?

Jordan must've sensed he was losing his leverage. Narrowing his eyes, he shifted his aim and fired a bullet into the lawn next to Max's foot.

The roar echoed across the suburban hillside, making Max's ears ring as the round kicked up a foot-high divot of grass and dirt. Jordan turned the barrel back to Max as dogs began to bark on both sides of Brantley Circle.

"EAT IT!"

Max's pulse was skyrocketing. He sank to his knees.

Jordan kicked him in the shoulder, pushing him onto all fours.

"Put your face in it!"

"Jordan—"

Another kick, this one to the back of the head. The force of it knocked Max's face forward to within inches of the shit. He recoiled as the smell filled his nostrils.

"Eat it, bitch!"

The dogs were still barking. The sky rumbled with thunder.

Jordan grabbed him by the hair and pushed his head down. Max braced himself, trying to resist, but the gap between his nose and the shit rapidly narrowed.

Contact was imminent when Jordan suddenly released his grip so fast that Max tweaked a muscle in his neck as his head snapped back.

He heard Jordan make a strange *guuuh* noise that morphed into a yelp.

Max staggered to his feet and turned to see what had happened. His assailant was backing into the street, his now-empty hands in the air and his eyes wide with fear.

Mom was advancing on him. Somehow, the AR-15 was in her hands.

"Get the fuck away from my son," she snarled.

"It was a joke!" Jordan's voice squeaked in terror. "I was kidding!"

"I'm not."

Mom paused to glance back at Max. "Get in the house."

He took a few tentative steps toward home. Jordan began to do the same.

"Not you!"

Jordan froze. Mom began to move around him in an arc, the rifle pointed at the center of his chest. "Think this is funny? Huh?"

"No!" His voice quivered. Mom was about half his size, but she wasn't just holding the gun. She also looked crazy enough to use it.

"Know what I think would be funny?" she asked him. "Why don't *you* eat the shit? Let's see how funny that is."

Before anybody could determine just how funny that might be, Kayla Stankovic burst out her front door with a large-caliber revolver in her hand.

"GET AWAY FROM HIM!"

Dazzle was right behind her, barking frantically. Kayla raised the revolver, holding the heavy weapon in two shaking hands as she trained it on Jen, who returned the favor with the assault rifle.

"Or what? You want to do this? *You want to do this, Kayla?*" Max had never heard such a demonic edge in his mom's voice. She sounded possessed.

"Get over here, Jordie!" Kayla demanded.

With the rifle no longer trained on him, Jordan quickly retreated to his yard, taking refuge behind his mother and her dog.

"Get inside, Max!" Mom yelled over her shoulder.

Max took a few more cautious steps backward, but he stopped at the foot of his driveway when the judge appeared.

The old man had brought his Beretta with him. He kept the muzzle pointed down while he held his free hand up like a preacher, admonishing the women from atop his porch steps like an elementary school teacher reasserting authority over an unruly playground.

"*Ladies!* Think it through! Don't do something you're going to regret!"

Both mothers appeared to be weighing the suggestion when another voice called out from the three-way intersection at the bottom of Brantley Circle.

"*Mom?*"

Chloe stood in the middle of the street, clutching the handlebars of her bike.

CHLOE

Chloe had heard the gunshot when she was still two blocks south of Brantley Circle, walking her bike up the steep hill after the weight of her backpack had proved too much to bear while pedaling.

Since the gunfire had been followed by dog barks and not screams of agony, she'd assumed her dad's boss had just screwed up again. So when she turned off Willis Road, she wasn't expecting to step into the final scene of a Tarantino movie starring Mrs. Stankovic, Judge Distefano, and Mom, with Max and Jordan looking on as extras while Dazzle provided the soundtrack.

Mom seemed to have the upper hand. If nothing else, her gun was the biggest. She was pointing it at Mrs. Stankovic, who was aiming a handgun right back at her.

Chloe's yell of surprise briefly captured everyone's attention. The look of joy on her mom's face upon seeing Chloe instantly validated her decision to come back home.

Once the combatants realized the newcomer was unarmed, they returned their focus to each other.

"Whaddaya say," the judge suggested to the women, loudly enough to make himself heard over Dazzle's barks, "on the count of three, we all lower our guns, go back inside, and try to remember we're in this together?"

It was a reasonable suggestion. As Mom and Mrs. Stankovic considered it, the judge started to count.

"One . . . two . . ." Both women seemed on the cusp of accepting his proposition when Dazzle inexplicably chose that moment to test the boundaries of her no-longer-functional shock collar. With a spasm of barks, the schnauzer lunged across her property line and into the street, headed straight at Mom—who responded by swinging the rifle barrel down at the approaching dog.

"NOOOO!" Mrs. Stankovic and the judge both screamed, although Mrs. Stankovic's scream was much louder.

Everyone braced themselves for bloodshed.

Somehow, though, Mom summoned the necessary self-control to avoid squeezing the trigger. Either that, or she was just waiting for Dazzle to reach point-blank range.

Whether it was her owner's shriek or the murderous look on Mom's face that did the trick, the schnauzer abruptly stopped short, retreating back to her territory as her barks took on a much more subdued tone.

The stay of canine execution lowered the temperature. Mom turned the rifle barrel back in Mrs. Stankovic's direction, but they both seemed to have lost some of their appetite for bloodshed.

"Are we okay?" the judge asked. "Are we good? You want to start the countdown again?"

They didn't need another countdown. Both women gradually lowered their weapons as they began to walk backward toward their respective homes. Chloe took the opportunity to scoot across Mrs. Stankovic's line of fire and past her mother, up the driveway into the Altmans' open garage. Max was already disappearing through their front door.

Meanwhile, Dad's boss had emerged from the front door

of the Stankovics' house. He kept both hands up and out from his body at shoulder level like a surrendering prisoner as he side-stepped around Mrs. Stankovic and gingerly headed in the Altmans' direction.

Chloe parked her bike and unslung her backpack as Mom backed into the garage.

"Sweetheart?" she called to Chloe. "Can you give me a hand with the door?"

"Sure thing." Chloe trotted forward and leaped up, grabbing the handle of the garage door and pulling it down as she landed.

Marty picked up his pace and yelled to the Altmans as he began to disappear from view.

"Wait!"

Chloe paused, holding the door handle just above her head. Marty had reached the foot of the drive. He bent over so he could make eye contact with Mom.

"Jen?"

"Yeah?"

"Can I, uh—can I get that gun back?"

Chloe looked to her mother for a reaction.

The look on Mom's face fell somewhere between amusement and scorn.

"Oh, hell, no." Mom shifted the weapon to her right hand, then reached up and out with her left, placing her hand over Chloe's and shoving the handle downward. Marty disappeared from their sight as the door fell with a clatter and a thump.

"You came back!"

Mom went in for a hug, but with the door down, it was al-

most too dark too see her. Plus, she was still holding the assault
rifle.

"Whoa, Mom—is the safety on on that thing?"

"Oh, Jesus. I don't even know. Let's go inside."

It had started raining buckets by the time they entered the
kitchen. Max was waiting for them in the dimly lit room.

"You okay, sweetie?" Mom asked him as she set the rifle on
the countertop.

"Fine."

Max didn't look fine at all. He looked traumatized.

"Is the front door locked?"

"Yeah."

"Can I get a hug?"

Max submitted to his mother's hug, even going so far as to
return it. When he broke the clinch, she shifted her attention
to Chloe, who'd set her backpack on one of the table chairs.

"Can I get one from you, too?"

They hugged. Chloe was a little surprised at how good it felt.

"I'm *so* glad you're back."

"Me too."

Not really. But my other options sucked worse.

Chloe kept the thought to herself. There was no need to
ruin the moment.

By the time she and Mom separated, Max was halfway down
the hall to the front stairs. Mom called out to him over the sound
of rain battering the roof.

"You sure you're okay? Can I get you anything?"

"No!" He made a U-turn at the foyer and disappeared, clomping up the steps.

Mom sighed and looked at Chloe. "You think he's all right?"

"Why wouldn't he be?"

"You see what that fucking Stankovic kid did to him?"

"No. What?"

"He had him on all fours at gunpoint, trying to stick his face in dog shit."

"Jesus Christ!"

"Teenage boys are such assholes."

Tell me about it.

"So how did you get the gun?" Chloe asked.

"I took it from him."

"From Dad's boss?"

"No, from the Stankovic kid. He didn't see me coming—he was too busy trying to push Max's face in the shit."

"And you just . . . ripped it out of his hands?"

"Yep." Mom sat down at the table. Chloe did the same.

"Who fired it?"

"He did. That's how I knew they were out there. I heard the gunshot."

"And you took it from him? The gun? You just grabbed it?"

"Yeah. Why is this confusing?"

"He could've shot you!"

Mom shrugged. "He was hurting your brother. It wasn't a close call." She turned and gazed back at the rifle on the countertop. "Plus, I got a gun out of it."

Chloe watched her mother stare at the weapon with what

looked like affection. "Good job not shooting the dog, by the way."

"Eh. Kind of a missed opportunity. I always hated that dog." Mom slumped back in the chair and rubbed her face with both hands. Then she let out a long sigh. "I should go up and check on Max."

"I'd leave him alone for a while," Chloe told her. "Give him some time to Juul up."

"What?"

Too much information. "Never mind."

Mom stared at her suspiciously for a moment, then changed the subject. "So what brought you back?"

Somebody was living in my mansion.

After she left Emma's, Chloe had gone to the Blackwells', intending to stay there alone. But she'd found the basement door key in the lock, and two of the Lincolnwood Academy punks—*Tucker? Parker? What the hell were those kids' names?*—doing shots in the kitchen. So she'd abandoned the property to them, but not before taking the key with her.

Now that we've got a gun . . . I could run them out of there.

But would I have to bring my family with me?

Probably.

Maybe that's not such a bad thing.

"Do you not want to answer the question?" Mom asked.

"It's just kind of a long story."

"Didn't work out with the boy?"

"How'd you know there was a boy?"

"Because it was obvious?"

Chloe squeezed her eyes shut in a grimace. "No. It didn't. He's an idiot."

"Most of them are. Especially at that age." Her tone shifted. "So, I, uh . . . read your goodbye letter."

Oh, shit. "I'm sorry."

"No, it was actually kind of good. Well, not good. But it was stuff I needed to hear."

"Did Dad read it, too?"

"No. He hasn't been home since you left."

"Could you please not show it to him? Actually—can I have it back?"

Mom pursed her lips, mulling over the request. "Depends. You going to leave again?"

"No."

"You sure?"

"Yes."

"Then okay."

They smiled at each other.

"Where *is* Dad, anyway?" Chloe asked.

"I don't know. He went to the town meeting. But it must've ended a while ago." Jen cocked her head, listening to the downpour outside. "I hope he's okay."

DAN

Dan was not okay.

Soaking wet, shivering cold, legally blind, partially deaf, famished, impoverished, excluded, deceived, shot at, beaten up, and robbed of the one critical asset he needed to lead his family to safety, it was fair to say Dan had never been less okay.

Worse, he didn't see any reason to hope things might get better.

He didn't see much of anything on that long walk home in the freezing rain. Without glasses, his vision was so impaired that all he could make out of the buildings he passed were fuzzy shapes. Once the sun had set, he couldn't even see those. If he hadn't already turned onto Willis Road by the time it got dark, he might have missed the intersection and wound up wandering the streets until he succumbed to hypothermia. As it was, he barely made it back up the hill to Brantley Circle, his legs trembling and his blistering feet squishing in his soggy shoes with every step. Approaching his house, he thought he discerned a blurry corona of candlelight through the living room window, but it might just as easily have been the spots in his eyes.

The front door was locked. He pounded on it with as much strength as he could muster.

"Who is it?" It was Chloe's voice.

"It's Dad!"

His daughter—actually, a shadowy blur about the same height as his daughter—opened the door, holding a flashlight.

"Ohmygod, Daddy! Are you okay?"

"Kind of . . . ?"

He staggered past her, collapsed onto the stairs, and pulled his shoes off.

"Do you need help?"

"No . . ." His socks were dripping wet. He peeled them away from his gray feet, which were wrinkled and frigid to the touch.

"Dan?" He heard Jen's footsteps coming down the hall from the kitchen behind a jerky flashlight beam. "Ohmygod!"

"Holy shit!" That was Max, arriving from the living room.

All three of them had cursed in horror at the sight of him. That couldn't be good.

"What can we do for you?" Chloe asked.

"Nothing. Just need my glasses. And dry clothes."

"What happened to your glasses?"

Dan hobbled up the stairs without answering and made his way across his darkened bedroom by sense memory.

Fortunately, his spare pair was in its usual place inside the medicine cabinet of the main bath. Once he got them on and his vision resolved—not that he could see anything in the near-total darkness—he stripped off his soggy clothes.

His whole body was shivering. There hadn't been any heat in the house for a while now, and the temperature was dropping inside as well as out. Dan grabbed a towel from the wall rack and dried himself off as best he could.

"Here." It was Jen, the flashlight beam preceding her again. She handed him a pair of long underwear.

"Thank you." He sat down on the toilet seat to put it on.

He couldn't stop shivering.

By the time he got the thermal underwear on, Jen was back with socks, pants, a T-shirt, and a wool sweater. She set her flashlight bottom up on the counter, giving him enough light to see as he dressed.

"What happened to you?"

"Long story. I *really* need food."

"I'm making pasta. I'll heat up some soup for you, too. Come down when you're dressed." She exited to the bedroom.

"Jen—"

"Yeah?" She paused next to the bed, barely visible in the gloom.

"From now on," he told her, "nobody leaves the house without a knife."

She let out a dry chuckle as she leaned over to pick up something she'd left atop the mattress.

"I think we're past knives, Dan."

He figured his eyes must be playing tricks on him, because as she straightened up and walked away, it looked for a moment like his wife was holding an assault rifle.

THE ALTMANS

To the entire family's surprise, the penne with tuna, peas, and shredded parmesan that they ate by candlelight in the dining room actually tasted pretty good. Jen had made plenty of it, and the food seemed to improve everyone's spirits except Dan's; he couldn't help fixating on their dwindling food inventory. To put the meal together, Jen had used the last of the peas and parmesan, most of the pasta, and one of their two remaining cans of chicken soup.

Dan had been the sole beneficiary of the soup, which his wife had insisted he eat for medical reasons. The oatmeal scrapings floating in it did not improve the experience, but he blamed his own poor breakfast decision making for that. In any case, the taste concerned him much less than the fact that the soup did nothing to improve his physical condition. His shivering had turned to chills, his runny nose had metastasized into severe sinus congestion, and he feared he might be suffering from the early stages of pneumonia, or whatever it was that had killed the nineteenth-century president who died after delivering a two-hour inaugural address in freezing rain.

Was it William Henry Harrison? Or Millard Fillmore?

Dan kept the trivia question to himself. He didn't want to worry the others, who were preoccupied with debating Chloe's disturbing proposal for a hostile takeover of the Blackwells' house on Mountain Avenue.

When did my daughter start breaking into other people's homes?

It wasn't just Chloe who was acting out of character. Dan had come home to a very different Jen, about whom the most optimistic thing he could say was that she didn't seem drunk, at least not on alcohol. She was carrying herself with a kind of pirate swagger that might've seemed appealing to the point of being sexy, except that she kept compulsively picking up Marty's gun, which was not sexy at all. It was terrifying, especially since his wife had even less firearms experience than his boss did, and look how *that* had turned out.

For her part, Chloe couldn't understand why her suggestion that they squat at the nicest house in town until the crisis passed wasn't meeting with instant approval from the rest of the family, especially after Mom had soured their immediate neighbors on them by threatening to shoot both the Stankovics' kid and their dog.

"We can take baths with the pool water!" Chloe pointed out. "They've got this huge gas stove, and it still works, and there's a ton of giant pots we can use to heat up the water. Can you imagine how awesome a hot bath would feel? I bet they've got really good soap, too."

"It *would* be nice to take a bath," Jen admitted, drawing her finger across the thin film of oil that had accumulated on her forehead. "I feel gross."

"Right? We're disgusting! And it's not like the Stankovics are going to let us get water from their pool anytime soon."

At her daughter's mention of the Stankovics, Jen reflexively glanced back at the assault rifle resting atop the sideboard. Until she'd liberated it from Jordan's weaselly little hands, she never would've guessed that a gun could be such a powerful source of emotional comfort. Even now, a couple hours into her custody of the weapon, just the act of holding it—one hand cupping the ribbed handguard below the barrel, the other wrapped around the serrated grip with her index finger resting against the trigger guard—still flooded her brain with a dopamine rush of well-being.

The sensation was so empowering that she'd begun to wonder why therapists didn't prescribe AR-15s instead of SSRIs. Thanks to the gun and the residual exhilaration of her standoff with Kayla, Jen was no longer suicidal. She wasn't even homicidal.

What she felt instead was something like omnipotence. Nobody—*nobody*—was going to fuck with her when she had a gun like that in her hands.

Now, looking over her shoulder at the weapon, she had to resist the urge to stand up and retrieve it from the sideboard. Chloe had already started making fun of her for carrying it around, and its presence in the house seemed to unsettle Max.

Which was ironic, because how many hours of her son's life had he spent pretending to shoot people in his video games? Getting worked over by the little Stankovic shit had really done a number on her poor son's head.

"What if we go to the Blackwells', and those private school dickheads are still there?" Max asked Chloe. The afternoon's events had at least temporarily converted him to pacifism, and he wanted to avoid any situation that might result in physical conflict.

Chloe shook her head. "There's no way they moved in. They'll go home at some point. If we get there early enough in the morning, they won't be there yet. And I took the only key—we can lock them out."

Dan winced. "Chloe . . ."

"What?"

Instead of finishing his sentence, Dan withdrew a half-used Kleenex from inside the sleeve of his wool sweater and blew his nose on it.

Max was still worried about the Lincolnwood Academy kids' competing claim on the Blackwell homestead. "What happens when they show up, and we're inside?"

"They won't be able to get in. I have the key!"

"What if they just break a window?"

"Then we'll shoot them."

"Oh my God," Dan moaned.

"What if *they* have guns?" Max wanted to know. As far as he was concerned, the baseline assumption from here on out should be that *everybody* had a gun.

"Buddy, don't sweat that," his mother told him in a soothing voice. "We can handle a couple of snot-nosed Academy punks."

Chloe couldn't help smiling. She hadn't felt this close to her mother since they'd read the Twilight series together over summer vacation when she was twelve.

Likewise, Jen was beginning to appreciate her daughter's cunning. There were clear advantages to squatting at the Blackwells'. Not just the obvious ones, like the water in the swimming pool, the food in the kitchen, and the lack of blood feuds with the neighbors. From Mountain Avenue, it'd be a much shorter walk down to the AA meeting at the church. And on the other side of that coin, Pete Blackwell probably had a phenomenal wine cellar. As long as those teenage twits hadn't emptied it already.

"So is everybody on board with this?" Chloe asked. "We go to the Blackwells' first thing in the morning?"

"It's not a bad option," Jen agreed.

"If we move to the Blackwells'," Max asked, "can we get a dog?"

The women both eyed him with sympathetic befuddlement.

"You realize that makes no sense, right?"

It made sense to Max, in a rock-paper-scissors kind of way: *gun beats dog, but dog beats human.* Depending on the dog. Also, dogs provided affection, which was good for emotional support.

He saw no point in trying to explain any of this to his family.

"The Blackwells had a dog," Chloe noted. "So there's probably a ton of really expensive dog food somewhere in that house."

"Not to get too dark," Jen warned her, "but we might want to hang on to the dog food in case we have to eat it ourselves at some point."

"We're not going to the Blackwells'!"

Startled by the force of Dan's eruption, the other three turned to stare wide-eyed down the table at him.

He'd startled himself, too. Somehow, his wife and daughter had retained a capacity for decisive action that he himself had lost amid the indignities of the past three days, and he could feel the center of political gravity in the household shifting away from him.

But Jen's and Chloe's moral compasses had become utterly fucked, and it was up to him to set them right.

"Are you out of your minds?" he scolded them. "We're not breaking into their house! That's not who we are! We're not going to shoot anybody, we're not going to rob anybody, and we're not going to march in and take over somebody else's home!"

He put so much energy into the denunciation that he gave himself a brief coughing fit, during which the rest of the family meditated on the substance of his objection.

"Dan, you robbed a Whole Foods," Jen pointed out as his coughs subsided.

"That was a fucking Whole Foods! It wasn't people! The Blackwells are *people*! They're our friends!"

"That's kind of overstating it," Jen replied. "They're really just acquaintances."

"And aren't they, like, crazy rich?" Max asked.

"It doesn't matter," Dan declared. "It's the *principle* of the thing."

"Daddy, we're not breaking in," Chloe told him in a quiet but firm—and, frankly, kind of patronizing—voice. "I have a key."

Dan glared across the table at his daughter. "Chloe: you *stole* the key! Don't you see the difference? Does Dartmouth have an honor code? This is not who we are! We don't screw over other people!"

Chloe's lower lip quivered slightly as she met her father's stare.

"What if it's us or them?" she asked.

Before Dan could reply, there were three loud knocks at the front door.

They all turned to stare in the direction of the foyer.

"What the hell?" Jen wondered aloud. The others were thinking the same thing. It was still pouring outside. Whoever was pounding on their door had braved a monsoon to reach them.

The knocks resumed, more forcefully this time.

Jen leaped to her feet and grabbed the AR-15 from the sideboard.

"We need a plan."

Moments later, they were arrayed in the foyer, each with their assigned roles: Dan would fling the door open, Jen would cover the entryway with the rifle, and the kids would shine flashlights into the intruder's face from a low crouch.

"Ready?" Dan had one hand on the doorknob and the other on the deadbolt.

Jen tightened her grip on the gun. "Do it."

The person on the other side of the door began pounding again just as Dan twisted the deadbolt and pulled the door toward himself.

"Freeze!"

The flashlight beams lit up a bearded young man in a yellow rain suit, who reflexively squeezed his eyes shut and turned his head against the sudden explosion of light. Intuiting the presence of a gun despite his temporary blindness, he threw his hands up in surrender.

"Don't shoot!" he yelped. "It's Kevin Leary!"

Jen lowered the gun, her shoulders slumping as the tension left them. Dan peered around the corner of the door. Chloe and Max lowered the flashlight beams away from the young man's face.

The last person they'd expected to see on their porch at that moment was Chloe's ACT tutor.

"Sorry I scared you!" he told them through a grimace, his eyes still squeezed shut and his head turned away as he kept his hands above his head. "But I have a seven o'clock with Chloe."

"Kevin. Right. Sorry!" Jen's eyes traveled from the tutor, to the weapon in her hands, then back again. "*Really* sorry. It's just, uh, been a weird couple of days."

"I know, right?" Kevin tentatively reopened his eyes, then pulled the hood back from his head and unzipped his coat to reveal the straps of a backpack underneath. "How'd that last practice test go?" he asked Chloe. "Did you take 73C?"

Chloe's parents turned to her for a reaction. She looked chagrined. "I didn't have a hard copy. I started one from the book. But I didn't finish. 'Cause . . . I didn't think there'd still be an ACT?"

Kevin nodded, conceding the point. "Yeah, the Saturday test's probably a little up in the air right now. Lot of uncertainty out there."

"Totally," Chloe agreed.

"There really is," Jen chimed in.

"Sooo . . . are we still doing the session?" Kevin asked.

Everyone looked at Chloe again. She peered over Kevin's shoulder at the deluge outside. "Can I, like, take a rain check? I guess literally?"

Kevin slowly nodded again. "Okay. But, uh, the thing is? I have a twenty-four-hour cancellation policy? So I'm going to have to charge you for it. Hope that's cool."

He looked to Jen and Dan for confirmation. They looked at each other.

"Will you take a check?" Dan asked the tutor.

The young man frowned. "I'd really prefer cash."

"I think we all would, Kevin," Jen told him.

DAN

Dan was seeing the ACT tutor out, lighting the path to the street with a flashlight, when Marty emerged from the darkness, wearing shorts and flip-flops under a golf umbrella.

"Heeey, buddy! Mind if I come in for a minute? Kinda need to talk something over with you."

Dan cast a quick look back at Jen, who was standing behind him in the foyer, rifle in hand. Her pose reminded him of a photo he'd once seen in the *Times* of an Iraqi militia fighter on the streets of Mosul.

"It's Marty," he told his jihadi life partner. "He wants to talk."

She cocked her head and narrowed her eyes. Then she shrugged. "Make sure he's unarmed."

Marty was close enough to the door by now to overhear the suggestion. "It's all good!" he promised. "I come in peace."

"Prove it," Jen told him.

Marty closed the golf umbrella and leaned it against the wall by the door, then lifted the hem of his Baja hoodie to reveal a pale, ample belly and no weapon wedged in the drawstring of his shorts.

"Turn around."

He complied, showing them his naked back.

"Fine." She nodded toward the living room. Marty followed her nod, taking a seat on the edge of one of the upholstered chairs that faced the couch. Dan sat down across from him.

Jen remained standing, still holding the rifle as she leaned against the trim at the threshold of the foyer.

Marty gave her an awkward smile. "Hey, Jen? Do you mind if I, uh, talk to Dan alone? Just as, y'know, old friends?"

Jen did not look inclined to agree to the request. Dan felt a flash of irritation at her attitude. This was still his house, too.

"Honey? Can you give us a minute?"

Jen shrugged again, then sauntered off, disappearing from view in the direction of the kitchen.

Dan turned back to Marty. "So what's up?"

His boss leaned forward, peering at Dan's face in the light of the candles on the coffee table. "You okay, buddy? You look like you got knocked around a little."

"I had kind of a bad afternoon."

"Me too, dude," Marty said with a somber nod. "Me too. Shit's getting *loco*."

"Yeah. So . . . ?"

"First of all—" Marty straightened up, furrowing his brow. "I gotta apologize. 'Cause, and I mean, it's ironic, but for a guy who makes his living with words, I don't always do such a great job of communicating to people. Especially the ones who are closest to me. And, dude! How long have we known each other? Thirty-plus years? That's a lot of time in the trenches, brother."

"It's been a minute," Dan agreed.

Marty leaned back, settling into his chair with a wistful smile. "You ever think back to where it all began? That writing class junior year?"

"Oh, sure."

"Fuckin' A, dude. . . . Can you believe that snob gave us *both* B-minuses?" He chuckled to himself. "Joke's on her, isn't it? The joke. Is on. Her."

I got an A in that class. Dan suppressed the urge to correct Marty's memory. "It sure is."

"Right? Oh, man! What a long, strange trip."

Will you just hurry up and ask for the gun back?

Dan let the silence linger until Marty shook his head, bringing himself back to the present. "So with all the history between us, I guess I didn't think it needed to be said. But you're not a mind reader. I get that. So I just want to say, for the record . . ."

Marty paused to sit up straight, shifting his weight forward with a grave look on his face. "Do. Not. Sweat. The *Bullet Town: Boston* thing."

Given the speed and gravity of recent events, it took Dan a moment to recall what the *Bullet Town: Boston* thing even was.

"It's all good, buddy!" Marty gushed, apparently having misinterpreted the blank look on Dan's face as hostility. "I totally forgive you! Water under the bridge!"

"Okay. Thanks, I guess?"

"You're welcome! And, dude: you're a great writer! No matter what HBO thinks. And I'm *so psyched* you've been on my team these last three years."

What's up with that HBO crack? "Well, I'm grateful for the opportunity."

"Me too, brother." Marty thumped his chest twice with his fist. "Comrades in arms."

There was another silence.

"Is that why you came over?"

"That, and, uh . . . slightly awkward ask: I *really* need that gun back."

There it is. "Y'know, I wasn't around when that whole situation went down—"

"It was pretty fuckin' wild, dude. I gotta say."

"Yeah. And *I* gotta say, it was *incredibly* upsetting for my son—"

"I bet! Yeah."

"And I guess the thing I don't understand is, how did the gun wind up with the Stankovic kid in the first place?"

Marty nodded vigorously. "Yeah, yeah. So the way that went down, uh, I was taking a nap? And I thought Eddie was on point. But he'd gone back into town, so, like, there was nobody, y'know, keeping an eye on things? And afterward, Eddie was, like, 'Why were you snoozing?' But I was *beat*, dude! No offense, but I didn't get a real good night's sleep on that pull-out couch of yours."

It had not previously occurred to Dan that the blame for his son's near-murder was traceable back to his own furniture. By the time he managed to parse the logic of the accusation, Marty had moved on.

"And the thing is, we *really* need the gun back. 'Cause the water situation's still fucked. Some of the boys went over to Ridgelawn this afternoon, and those people must've been tipped off or something. 'Cause they were ready for us. So we gotta go back tomorrow in force. And every gun counts. Y'know? It's not like those AR-15s grow on trees. It's actually kind of an honor they gave it to me in the first place. I think 'cause they'd all seen that

BT episode where Stryker shoots up the Mexican heroin ring? So they just assumed. But the thing is . . ."

Marty leaned in further, lowering his voice to confide in Dan. "Even though it's not really my fault the kid took the gun? I'm kind of in deep shit for it. So I really need you to do me a solid and just give it back. Is that cool?"

"The thing about it . . ."

"It'll be good for you, dude! You give it back, it'll be a real plus with the Watchdogs. I might even be able to get you in with them! And the way things are going? Dude. *Trust me* when I say you really want to be on the inside of the tent pissing out with these guys."

Dan took a deep breath, which triggered a round of coughing. "You okay?"

He nodded, then blew his nose before replying. "The thing is . . . I'm not the one who took it. So it's not really mine to give back."

Marty's lip curled. "She's your *wife*, dude. Can't you just tell her to cough it up?"

"He could try—"

The men turned their heads to the foyer entry. Jen must've been sitting at the bottom of the staircase, listening in. Now she was looking down at them, the gun in her hands.

"But the answer's no," she finished. "'Justice comes with a gun,' Marty."

"It's 'bullet,'" he corrected her, visibly miffed at the misquoting of his signature catchphrase. "'Justice comes with a bullet.'"

"Whatever. I don't watch your show."

The reaction on Marty's face indicated that this was not only shocking, but offensive. His stare moved from Jen back to Dan, as if the responsibility for his wife's failure to watch *Bullet Town* lay at his feet, too.

Dan just shrugged helplessly. "Sorry, man."

"Guys, think about it," Marty pleaded. "Be fair! It doesn't belong to you!"

"Then you shouldn't have let that little shit point it at my son," Jen replied. "'Cause it's mine now."

Marty stood up, shaking his head. "I don't think you get the situation here. I didn't want to have to say this? But one way or another, they're getting that gun back. If you don't give it to me now? They're going to come for it later. And that won't be good for anybody."

Dan's pulse quickened at the threat as Jen stepped toward Marty.

"Are you threatening my family?"

"I'm just stating a fact," Marty told her.

"Really? I got a fact for you. If you're not out of my house in three seconds?" She raised the rifle to a firing position. "I'm going to put a fucking bullet in your head."

"Jesus Christ, Jen!"

"One!"

Marty was out the door before she got to two.

JEN

The fight she and Dan had after Marty left resulted in Jen sleeping on the couch. Or at least lying on the couch: the combination of alcohol withdrawal and adrenaline made actual sleep seem more like an aspiration than an achievable goal.

On the surface, their argument was about whether Jen's refusal to give up the AR-15 helped guarantee the family's safety or just threatened it. But after she'd settled in under a pair of blankets topped off by the rifle, with its weight pressing comfortingly down on her rib cage, she replayed the argument a few times in her head and realized the conflict with Dan was more fundamental than that.

The real problem, Jen decided as she thumb-clicked the trigger safety off and on while listening to the patter of rain outside, was that they faced a series of critical yet still unknowable questions—*is this temporary or permanent? should we stay or go? are we still living in a functional society, or a state of nature?*—and her own best guesses at the answers didn't sync up with her husband's.

To Jen's mind, the situation was effectively permanent, since any technological collapse that went on longer than it'd take to die of dehydration (let alone starvation) might as well be forever; their best option was to hunker down, preferably in the Blackwells' better-stocked and more easily defended hilltop mansion; and they should operate on the assumption that all the normal rules of social behavior had gone out the window, and anybody who kept following them was asking for it.

Dan, on the other hand, was behaving as if this was all temporary, and if they couldn't run and hide at his mother's house until things went back to normal, then they should just roll over for the neighborhood goons and hope for the best.

Either that, or he saw things the same way she did, and he just couldn't stomach the implications.

You never know who's swimming naked until the tide goes out.

It was a line she'd first heard in a different context during the financial crisis of 2008, but it seemed applicable now.

What if Dan just can't hack it?

And how the hell did he manage to get his bike stolen?

Maybe losing the bicycle was a blessing. He couldn't keep arguing it was a good idea to flee by bike when they only had three of them for four people.

Even so, they should replace it if they could. Just to keep their options open.

Maybe there's one at the Blackwells'. Except they left town on bikes. So probably not.

Carol Sweeney left on a bike, too. Her house is empty now. It'd be easy to break into the garage. Does she own a second bike? Did she get Pat's in the divorce? How long ago did their kids move out? Did they leave any bikes behind?

As Jen ruminated over Carol Sweeney's bicycle inventory, a thought popped into her head. It had nothing to do with bikes, so she dismissed it as irrelevant.

A moment later, the thought returned.

It was absurd. She shrugged it off.

It came back a third time.

Absolutely ludicrous.

She put it out of her head and tried to focus on actually important questions.

The thought kept coming back.

She told herself it was insane.

But it wouldn't go away.

This is absurd.

Don't be an idiot.

Get some sleep.

It's freezing in here.

The gunmetal had grown cold on her hands. Reluctantly, she moved the AR-15 to the coffee table, rolled onto her side, and tried to deep-breathe her way into unconsciousness, focusing on the sound of the rain.

But the crazy thought wouldn't leave her alone.

It was like a fucking gorilla, jumping up and down on her head.

Finally, she gave in and let the thought turn itself into a plan.

FRIDAY

JEN

For the next several hours, she slipped in and out of consciousness as the rain outside waxed and waned. It was hard to tell
how much time had passed—it might be almost dawn, or still
hours earlier—but eventually, she woke up to silence.

The rain had stopped. It was time to put her plan in motion.

Jen got dressed, put on her jacket and shoes in the dark, collected a flashlight and the rifle, and slipped out the front door.

Carol Sweeney's house had a side entrance to the kitchen
atop a short wooden landing off the driveway, about twenty
feet from her detached garage. Constructed in a less security
conscious era, the side door had half a dozen panes of glass in its
upper third, and the borders of the bottom right pane were less
than a foot from both the deadbolt and the doorknob.

For a determined burglar who wasn't afraid of a little noise,
it was no trick to punch out the glass and reach inside to unlock
the door.

Jen wasn't afraid of a little noise. She cleared the pane with
a few blows from the rifle stock, then let herself into Carol's
kitchen.

Being both conventionally minded and Irish, Carol had a
liquor cabinet, and it was easy to find. Its contents included a
mostly full fifth of Grey Goose.

Attagirl, Carol . . .

It wasn't until Jen had to shove her flashlight inside the

elastic waist of her sweatpants to free a hand that she realized her preparations had been too hasty. She hadn't brought a bag. Considering that the rest of the booze was top shelf and Carol's pantry contained a fair amount of nonperishable food, this was a significant error.

I'm going to have to come back.

First things first: she grabbed the Grey Goose by the neck and lifted it from the cabinet.

The bottle felt good wrapped in her fist, but she didn't feel any compulsion to unscrew the cap. While the voice in her head had been implacable on the subject of acquiring alcohol, it was oddly blasé about drinking it. The bottle, it turned out, was a little bit like the gun. She didn't actually have to fire it. There was comfort enough just in knowing she could.

She let herself back out the side door, broken glass crunching under her feet.

Without the benefit of the flashlight, she could barely see her hand in front of her face, which was why she didn't notice Judge Distefano standing on his porch until he called out to her as she passed.

"Don't shoot. I'm unarmed."

At the sound of his voice, she stopped.

Aaaah, shit.

"Actually, that's not true," the judge added. "I *am* armed. But still."

"What are you doing up this late, Frank?"

"Couldn't sleep. Heard a noise. You?"

"Out for a walk."

"You break some glass a minute ago?"

Awkward. "Yeah, that was me."

"Hope you didn't cut yourself. Got a minute to talk? Something I'd like to discuss with you."

Jen sighed, then started toward his porch.

"Sure. But, ahh, full disclosure—" As she mounted the steps, she held up the vodka bottle. "Probably not the best time to sell me on how great not drinking is."

"Don't sweat it, kid. We're not a proselytizing faith." He wiped the seat of a porch chair with his sleeve, then offered it to her. "Little early in the day for that, though, isn't it?"

They sat down beside each other, looking out into the darkness. "I didn't drink any yet," she explained. "I just stole it from Carol's liquor cabinet."

"Well . . . you do what you gotta do. I've been there."

"So what do you want to talk about?"

"This is going to sound a little melodramatic." He paused. "But I'm dying."

Oh, Jesus.

"We're all dying, Frank."

"Yeah. But I got a head start. Remember when I went in for that stomach thing last spring? Max had to watch Ruby while I was in the hospital?"

"Oh, sure."

"When I went in, they injected this contrast dye to get a CAT scan of my stomach. And it went south. The dye knocked out my kidneys. Ever since, I've been on dialysis a couple-three times a week. Without it . . . sometime in the next few days, the toxins are gonna back up, I'll get uremia, and that's all she wrote. Not the greatest death, apparently. Hurts like hell, and on the way there, I'm going to get loopy and forget my own name."

"Jesus . . . I'm so sorry, Frank."

"Don't be. I had a full life. And Wednesday, I dropped by the parish, got last rites. So I'm pretty squared away. Except for a couple loose ends. And that's where you come in."

"Okay . . ."

"I need somebody to take Ruby. And she's particular. Doesn't like a lot of people. But she likes your son. And he seems to like her, too."

"No argument there. Although. . . ."

"Yeah?"

"How much dog food do you have?"

"Tons. I buy in bulk. Just brought home sixty pounds of it last week."

Jen sighed. "Look, I'm not going to bullshit you. Things could get bad. And I've got four mouths to feed already."

"I get that. And I know what I'm asking's a sacrifice. But there's something else in it for you."

"What's that?"

"Mum's the word on this?"

"Of course."

"I got a '67 Mustang with a full tank of gas in the garage. And it runs."

Holy fucking shit.

"That pack of dress-up GI Joes that's been running around wants to get their hands on it," the judge continued. "But if you take Ruby, I'll throw in the Mustang. Now, she's not that hot on car travel—you'll have to put her in the carrier, bring some hand towels to line it, 'cause she's going to piss herself. But after you drive for a while and she figures out she's not going to the vet, she'll probably settle down."

Jen's head was swimming. "Why us? Why not Diane and Steve? Or somebody you're closer to?"

The judge shrugged. "It's like I said: I didn't make the choice. Ruby did."

Holy shit.

The implications were enormous. Access to a car changed everything. If they could get out before sunrise without attracting notice from the goons next door, they wouldn't even have to leave town right away. They could drive to the Blackwells' and hide out there while they stocked up on food.

We could take baths, siphon extra gas from the cars . . .

Siphon extra liquor from the cabinet . . .

I should put this vodka in the trunk right now, before Dan sees it.

But where would we go?

California.

It was thousands of miles away. Was this happening there, too? It couldn't be.

Dan could find a writing job in California. He'd already been making noises about wanting to relocate once Max went to college.

Max would be happy there. He'd be happy anywhere, as long as he had a dog.

Chloe could apply to Berkeley instead of Dartmouth.

Or Jesus—Stanford.

It was a reach. But this whole experience would make for a hell of a supplemental essay.

And Jen could get sober in California. Just like Erin Tiernan had.

People start over in California. It's practically the state motto—

"You still with me?" the judge asked.

"Yeah. I'm just thinking. It's a pretty good deal."

"Hang on. I'm not done yet. I'll give you the car on two conditions. Number one, you gotta swear to me you'll do right by Ruby."

"Of course! We'd have to—Max would kill us if we didn't."

The judge chuckled. "Funny you mention killing."

"Why?"

"Because that's the second condition."

DAN

Dan sat sniffling at the kitchen table in the light of a scented candle, his Moleskine open in front of him. He stared at the blank page.

I've got nothing. And we're running out of time.

This wasn't a TV show. This was real. The world had gone insane, his family was facing a mortal threat, and he'd never been more in need of creative inspiration.

But he'd lost the thread of the narrative. He was no longer the protagonist of his own story. He was a bystander, a victim, his monogrammed Waterman pen useless for anything except toting up the losses.

Back in his old life—the one that had vanished in an instant at 9:16 a.m. on Tuesday morning—when the creative juice dried up, he listened to music to get it flowing again. Now music was just another thing he'd lost.

What if I never hear "Whole Lotta Love" again?

Or "Tangled Up in Blue?"

As he massaged his swollen sinuses with his thumb and forefinger, a rivulet of snot crept from one nostril. He took a Kleenex from the nearly depleted box on the table and blew his nose despondently.

What happens when we run out of Kleenex?

Jesus Christ, what happens when we run out of toilet paper?

He was trying to remember how many rolls they had left in

the utility room when the familiar creak of the front door interrupted his brooding. He stood up quickly, alert to the possibility of enemy action. But before he made it to the hallway, Jen appeared.

She was still carrying the rifle.

"Where were you?"

"Finding a way out of this." She took a seat at the table, motioning for him to do the same. "I've got a solution. But it's going to involve some unpleasantness. I can handle the unpleasant part. I just need you to promise me one thing."

"What's that?"

She laid the rifle across her lap and leaned over it, staring into his eyes in the candlelight.

"I'm completely sober. I haven't had a drink since Wednesday. And I'm going to quit. For good. Eventually—"

He sucked in his breath to reply. She raised a hand, stopping him.

"*But.* I have to do it on my own time. And I need you to just give me a little space and be okay with that."

"What's your solution?"

"You gotta promise first."

"Promise you what?"

"That you won't hassle me about the drinking. You'll let me handle it."

He watched her for a long moment. Then he nodded. "Okay."

"Really?" His answer seemed to surprise her.

It surprised him, too. But they were in uncharted territory. And between the two of them, she seemed to have a better handle on the navigation.

"One condition," he said. "If you're going to drink, you give me the gun first."

She looked down at the rifle, frowning. Then she raised her eyes to meet his.

"That's fair."

"Okay. Deal. So what's your solution?"

"The judge has a Mustang in the garage. It runs. And he's willing to give it to us on two conditions—"

"Ohmygod!"

"Just wait. First condition: we have to take his dog with us. The second—"

"I'm allergic."

She paused, staring at him in disbelief.

"I have a dog allergy," he reminded her.

"Are you fucking kidding me?"

"I didn't say it was disqualifying. It's just a factor."

"Are you done?" She glared at him. When he didn't reply, she continued. "Good. The second condition: we have to shoot him."

"The dog?"

"The judge."

"What?"

"He's already dying of kidney failure. He just wants us to hurry it up a little. Then we have to bury him in his backyard. Deep enough so starving dogs don't dig him up later."

"What starving dogs?"

"They're theoretical. He's assuming the worst."

Dan could feel himself getting dizzy. If he hadn't already been in a chair, he definitely would've needed to sit down.

"I'll do the shooting," Jen told him. "I just need you and the kids to help me dig the grave. And if we're going to do this, we've got to move fast. I want to be out of here before the sun comes up. What do you say?"

She shifted forward onto the edge of her seat, poised to stand.

"This is really upsetting," Dan said.

"So are the alternatives."

"Where are we going to go? Newton?"

She shook her head. "California. You wanted to move there anyway, right?"

It was true. California was the setting of all the dreams he'd once had for his future. Three days and several lifetimes ago.

Is it possible to dream again?

"That's three thousand miles. Where are we going to get the gas?"

She stood up, looming over him with the rifle in her hands.

"I can get us the gas."

He didn't doubt it. She looked like Patty Hearst robbing a bank.

"Are you in?" she asked him.

Dan nodded.

"Good. I'll go wake the kids."

THE ALTMANS

"It's screwed up they're making us do this," Chloe declared.

"The whole thing is screwed up," Max told her as he worked his shovel into the muddy earth of Judge Distefano's backyard. "I don't know why he doesn't just come with us. There's room in the back seat."

Max's voice was uneven from the lump in his throat that had been there almost from the moment his mother had shaken him awake with the disturbing update.

I've got good news and bad news. The good news is you're getting a dog!

He desperately wanted a dog. But not like this.

It also wasn't how he would've wanted to find out about the judge being sick, or about what was going to happen next. Mom had fucked that part up. She'd tried to make it sound like it wasn't a big deal. Or maybe she just thought all he cared about was getting a dog.

That wasn't true.

"I think he's just giving up," Chloe mused as she heaved another shovelful of upturned earth onto the growing pile next to the ragged three-by-eight-foot hole they were digging. It was over a foot deep, and tougher going now that the black topsoil had given way to lighter-colored, more densely packed clay that was much harder to turn over. "Like, everything's going to hell, and he just doesn't want to deal. You know?"

Max didn't reply. He had to get his mind off the situation and think about something else, or he was going to start bawling. He pursed his lips, working the spit that was accumulating in his mouth into a loogie, then spat onto the grass at the edge of the dirt pile.

"Why are you spitting so much?"

"I just am."

Chloe's face screwed up in disgust. Now that it was starting to get light outside, she could see the lump in his jaw. "Are you chewing *tobacco*?"

"No."

"Ohmygod, you are! That is *so* gross."

"Don't tell Mom and Dad."

"Just don't do it when we're in the car."

"I won't."

They tossed a few more shovelfuls in silence. The predawn light in the yard was turning from deep blue to a pink-tinged gray.

"I feel like we're in the gravedigger scene in *Hamlet*," said Chloe.

"I never read it."

"You will junior year. If you're in Finch's class."

"Is there even going to *be* a junior year?"

Chloe looked over at her brother, pounding the shovel blade into the ground with his heel. "Of course there will be. Don't get dark like that."

"Then quit talking to me about gravediggers!"

She was about to say something snarky, but when he turned his head and she saw the look on his face, she held her tongue.

"I'm sorry."

"Whatever."

Max went back to digging. Chloe stepped over to the picnic table and shut off the Coleman lantern that the judge had given them to see by. With the sun almost up, they no longer needed artificial light.

"Think the judge would care if I use his bathroom?"

"He's not going to care about anything pretty soon," Max said in a mournful voice.

"I just don't want to track stuff on his carpet." She contemplated her muddy feet. "Shouldn't have worn these shoes. We're going to be *so* filthy by the time we get in the car."

"Change them when you're done."

Chloe weighed her options. She had a second pair in her bag, which Mom and Dad were currently packing into the trunk of the judge's Mustang along with the rest of the water and food. But there was no point in fetching clean shoes now, when they still had several feet of grave to dig.

"I'm going inside for a sec. You okay out here?"

"Whatever."

Max watched his sister walk to the door that led to the screened-in rear porch. After she disappeared inside, he waited a few seconds to make sure she was gone. Then he wedged his shovel into the ground and stepped over to the dirt pile. With his back to the house so nobody could see him through the porch windows, he worked the plug of tobacco out of his lower cheek and spat it onto the dirt.

He was staring into space past the hedge that separated the judge's yard from the Altmans', coaxing another mouthful of saliva to rinse the leftover tobacco bits from his mouth, when he saw a cop in a riot helmet run across his backyard.

WHAT THE HELL?

Max bent his knees and ran in a half crouch over to the property line. As he inched up to peer over the hedge, he heard a loud, heavy blow.

HOLY SHIT HOLY SHIT.

Two cops in full body armor had just busted open the Altmans' back door with some kind of mini battering ram. Max watched them enter the house, leading with their rifles.

He turned and ran for the judge's enclosed porch.

The door slammed shut behind him as he leapfrogged the ottoman in front of the judge's reading chair. Turning the corner into the kitchen at high speed, he found himself on a collision course with a balding ogre in a leather jacket who was entering the room from the hallway that led to the open front door.

Max stopped short at the sight of the enormous stranger. Then the man's hand rose, and Max saw the revolver.

Jen would have preferred that the judge not don a suit in advance of his murder-burial. It put them on an awkward footing—a constant visual reminder of *you're about to shoot me, and this is a solemn occasion.*

To be fair, it *was* a solemn occasion. But the constant reminder of her impending duty as executioner was starting to weigh heavily on Jen's mind. As the minutes ticked by, she found it harder and harder to focus on packing the trunk of the Mustang. It was turning into a real spatial-reasoning nightmare, mostly because of the two thirty-pound bags of dog food the judge insisted they pack.

She'd also begun to seriously question her ability to pull the trigger while sober. And the problem with *that* was that she'd squirreled away Carol's Grey Goose in her backpack, which was already deep inside the trunk behind three other pieces of luggage and the remaining gallons of Poland Spring. Besides which, the Grey Goose was earmarked for future emergencies, not current operations.

If Jen needed a drink to drown her conscience, she'd have to get it from some other source. But she didn't want to enlist Dan to retrieve the booze from the half-mangled trunk back in their basement, because under their new arrangement, she'd be obligated to cough up the AR-15—currently resting within easy reach on the roof of the Mustang—in exchange. Her only other options were running back to Carol's house, which she couldn't do without alerting Dan, and asking the judge.

She'd already struck out with the judge. It had been embarrassing.

"Slightly awkward question," she'd muttered to him in an undertone while Dan was preoccupied on the other side of the garage with sawing through a garden hose in the hope of siphoning extra gas from the judge's Prius. "But do you . . . by any chance . . . have any liquor in the house?"

He gave her a pained half smile. "Sweetheart, I'm thirty-six years sober."

"I know. Sorry. Just checking."

The judge glanced over at Dan before whispering a follow-up question. "Do you need to run back to Carol's?"

"Maybe. We'll see."

He didn't seem to be judging her too harshly for the departure from AA orthodoxy, but she couldn't help thinking the exchange had cost her some goodwill a few minutes later when they began to argue over the dog food.

"Do we really need to bring both bags?"

"Are you planning on stopping at a PetSmart? Because if not, then yes."

"It's taking up more space than the human food."

"And if it weren't for the dog, you wouldn't have a trunk to pack in the first place."

"Fair enough. We'll make it work."

"Good on you." He gave her shoulder an avuncular squeeze. "It'd be an easy fit if we didn't have to put the gas can in there. But I wouldn't recommend that." He turned and called out to Dan. "How's it coming over there, Danny?"

By now, Dan was crouched on all fours between the two cars, an empty red five-gallon can beside him. One end of the recently sawed-off hose was snaked deep inside the Prius's gas tank while Dan held the other end to his mouth, trying to get his head lower than the tank so he could get a suction going.

"Not great," Dan reported, hoping the judge wouldn't notice his limbs were shaking. He'd failed to eat anything since dinner the previous night, and low blood sugar coupled with both the frantic exertion of evacuating their house and whatever illness he'd come down with had left him a quivering mess.

Not only that, he had no idea how to siphon gas from a tank. He was terrified of accidentally aspirating the gasoline. "Are you sure this works?" he asked the judge.

"I don't know," the old man replied. "I saw it on a TV show. Does everything you write in your TV shows work in real life?"

"Not even close."

"Just keep trying," Jen told her husband. She took a few steps around the side of the open trunk, stopping in front of Dan as she peered through the passenger window into the back seat of the two-door Mustang. "How much floor space is down there? Can we pack some of the canned goods below the kids' feet?"

"*Max?*"

The judge's shout was taut with alarm. Jen glanced at him, then turned in the direction he was staring, toward the door to the house.

Max had just emerged from the door to the kitchen, walking across the front of the Prius with his hands up like a prisoner.

Stepping into the room behind him was a man whose face Jen instantly recognized, although it took her a second to place the name.

It was Barry Kozak, the disgraced police chief. He was holding a handgun to her son's back.

Jen turned to reach for the AR-15 she'd left on the Mustang's roof.

"*Don't!*" Kozak roared, shifting his target from Max to Jen.

She froze.

"Step back. Both of you. Keep your hands up. Frank, get away from that trunk so I can see you."

With a dismayed grimace, the judge did as he was told. So did Jen.

Still on his hands and knees between the Prius and the Mustang, Dan wasn't sure what the hell was happening.

He saw Jen step backward, her legs passing out of his field of vision.

Then Max appeared, up ahead at the end of the aisle between the two cars. His hands were in the air, and his face was anguished. Seeing his father crouched on the ground, his eyes widened.

"Keep going," the unseen man barked at Max. "Over with the others. Hands up. Don't touch the rifle. Is that the one we gave to the TV idiot?"

Standing beside the judge with her hands up, Jen's heart sank when she saw Kozak's face brighten at the discovery of the missing AR-15.

That son of a bitch. He's going to take my gun away.

Max stepped around his father, careful not to acknowledge him as he joined the judge and Jen against the garage door.

Kozak was grinning. "Looks like I played the right hunch stopping in here."

Crouched out of sight, Dan started to get some clarity on the situation.

It must be Shreckler. Or Kozak. He doesn't know I'm down here.

"I got a little two-for-one going in this house!" the unseen man chortled.

Dan crept forward. The shakiness in his limbs was gone, obliterated by adrenaline.

I've got the element of surprise.

I can tackle him.

He might kill me. But I'd give the others time to get to the rifle.

I can save my family.

I can be a hero—

Then Barry Kozak and his large-caliber revolver stepped around the front corner of the Prius.

"What the fuck? Get up!"

The opportunity for heroism had passed.

"Get up!" Kozak yelled again, pointing the gun at Dan's forehead. He did as he was told, stepping back to join the others with his hands up in a grudging surrender.

Kozak turned his attention to the judge.

"You lied to me, Frank. Said you sold that car."

The judge shrugged. "It is what it is, Barry. Don't take it personally."

"Give me the keys."

"C'mon. Whaddaya gonna do with one more car?"

"Protect the community," Kozak replied with an almost straight face.

"You don't have to do this," the judge pleaded. "Why don't you just let these poor people get out of town? Huh?"

Kozak gave Dan, Jen, and Max an appraising look. Then he snorted. "You three? Want to hit the road in that?" He jerked his head toward the Mustang. "Shit, you'd get eaten alive out there! Be smart. Stay home. Let the big dogs take care of you."

He turned back to the judge, the gun in his right hand as he extended his left with the palm up. "Gimme the keys, Frank. Don't make me take them from you."

The judge didn't move. Kozak took a step toward him, adopting a threatening glare that was wiped off his face by the flat end of a shovel blade humming through the air at high velocity.

The force of the metal crashing against the side of his head sent Kozak staggering sideways over the Mustang's hood. Before he could right himself, Chloe sprang forward, following up her perfect backhand with a second one that finished the job, knocking him senseless.

Kozak's limp body slid off the car, collapsing into a heap on the concrete at Chloe's feet. She lowered the shovel and stared down at her unconscious victim.

"Who *is* that?"

"Used to be the chief of police," Jen explained as she stepped forward to retake the AR-15. "He got Me Too'd for grabbing his secretary's ass."

Chloe reacted to this information with a swift kick to Kozak's rib cage, hard enough that it made the judge suck in his breath in sympathetic pain.

"Whoa! They rang the bell, kid. Fight's over. You won."

"Get his gun," Jen told her daughter, pointing at the revolver on the floor with the barrel of her rifle.

"How did he get in here?" Dan wondered out loud as Chloe picked up Kozak's weapon.

"He just walked in," Max explained. "The door was open." Then he remembered. "They're breaking into our house!"

"Who?"

"The cops! I saw them bust down our back door!"

A moment later, Dan, Jen, and the judge were standing to one side of the bay window in the living room, their necks craned to watch the goings-on at the top of the cul-de-sac next door. Max joined them, having just retrieved Ruby from the foot of the bed where she'd been sleeping.

Out the window, they could see the El Camino parked in front of the Altmans' house. Eddie and Marty were crouched behind the car, peering at the busted-in front door. Eddie was holding a shotgun. Marty appeared to be unarmed.

A gun-toting Steve Shreckler exited through the Altmans' broken front door, flanked by a pair of body-armored cops. He was shaking his head in frustration.

"They're going to come here next," Jen said. "We've got to go."

She headed back to the garage. Dan and Max followed. The judge retrieved his Beretta from the drawer in the hallway and trotted after them.

"Okay, plan B," he called out. "Take the rug from the dining room, you can wrap my body in it—"

"There's no time for that!" Jen yelled over her shoulder. "We gotta leave!"

"You can't go shortchanging me on this, kid! We had a deal!"

They reached the garage. Chloe, with Kozak's revolver in one hand and the shovel in the other, was keeping watch over the ex-cop. A weak moan escaped his still-prone body.

"He's starting to wake up! Should I hit him again?"

"Just get in the back seat," Jen told her. "You too, Max. We're leaving."

"Put Ruby in the carrier!" the judge told Max, pointing to a small dog crate on the wall shelf. Then he held his pistol out, grip first, to Dan and Jen. "Who's doing the honors here?"

They did their best to ignore him. "What about the gas from the Prius?" Dan asked Jen.

"There's no time," she replied. "But bring the hose and the can. We'll find more on the way."

Dan collected the hose and can and took them to the trunk. "Can we lose half the dog food?"

"No!" yelled the judge.

"Yes!" Jen overruled him.

Dan pulled out one of the dog food bags, replacing it with the gas can and the hose. Max was already in the back seat, holding Ruby on his lap in the dog carrier. Chloe joined him as the judge stood watching their parents, still holding his pistol and looking incredulous.

Jen turned to him. "Can we get the keys? Please?"

He shook his head and held out the pistol to her again. "You're not keeping your end of the bargain here, Jennifer."

"Judge, *please!*" Dan begged him. "We're running out of time!"

"Fine. Don't bury me." The old man pulled the car keys from the pants pocket of his suit and held them up to his chest, while offering the gun again. "But if you want the keys, you're damn sure gonna have to shoot me."

Jen and Dan traded a look.

What are we going to do?

"Come with us," Dan told the judge.

"Not a chance," the judge insisted.

"We're going to California," Dan told him. "That's where your kids live, right? We'll take you there!"

"Get real, Danny!" the judge scoffed. "It's the apocalypse out there! You're not even going to make it to Ohio!"

"I'll get us to California," Jen declared. "All of us. You included. Come on!"

"It's three thousand miles!" the judge yelled. "And my kidneys don't work! I'm *dying!*"

"Not yet, though, right?" Jen pointed out. "Just give us a chance! If it looks like it's terminal, I swear to God, we'll pull over and shoot you by the side of the road."

"For cryin' out loud," the judge moaned. "All I wanted was a clean ending."

"It's not going to be clean," Dan admitted. "But it'll be happy. We're not going to let this be a tragedy. We're going to drive till we find you a hospital, and dialysis, and our credit cards work, and we'll *fix* it! Then we'll take you to your kids."

"Aaahhh, Mary Mother of Jesus." The judge's face was furrowed with indecision. He turned to Jen. "Swear to God you'll shoot me if you have to?"

"Swear to God," she promised him.

His face gradually unwrinkled. He uttered a grunt of resignation. "Okay. But put the dog food back in. And bring the shovel. I'm driving."

He headed for the driver's side of the Mustang. After a quick exchange of triumphant glances with his wife, Dan swapped the gas can for the dog food and slammed the trunk shut as Jen fetched the shovel Chloe had left on the hood of the Prius.

"I got shotgun!" Jen called out.

"That goes without saying," the judge told her as he deposited himself behind the wheel.

Dan passed the gas can to Chloe, who was already trying to accommodate the shovel her mother had handed her. After a final glance to confirm that the incapacitated Kozak wasn't about to resurrect himself, Dan squeezed into the back with the dog and the kids.

Jen reached into the front passenger seat and laid the AR-15 across the transmission hump. Then she trotted to the garage door.

"Ready to go?" she called to the judge.

He turned the key in the ignition. The engine roared to life.

Jen yanked up the garage door, flooding the room with daylight and capturing the attention of the cluster of men who were standing in the cul-de-sac next to the El Camino, discussing their next move.

As Marty, Eddie, Shreckler, and the cops all gaped in surprise, she ran back to the car, hopped in, and slammed the door.

"Hold tight," said the judge.

He threw the car into reverse and hit the gas.

The Mustang leaped backward into the driveway. As it crossed the sidewalk, the judge whipped the wheel around, knifing the car ninety degrees and bringing it to a brief, lurching halt before roaring forward to Willis Road as the Watchdogs began to move in response.

"Hang a left!" Dan told the judge. "The parkway's a mess. If you head up Summit to Broadhurst, we can take surface roads to the interstate."

All four Altmans craned their necks to look back as the judge negotiated a sharp left, tires squealing into the turn. When Brantley Circle passed out of sight, the Watchdogs were scrambling to get into the El Camino.

"I think they're coming after us," Jen warned.

"Don't worry, kid," the judge told her. "If I can't outrun an El Camino, I deserve to die."

True to his word, Frank Distefano proceeded to defy every stereotype of elderly drivers Jen had ever held. He took the winding curves of Summit Avenue with the bravado of a reckless teenager. When they started downhill on Broadhurst, he abandoned the main artery in favor of a roundabout descent through the narrow residential side streets, executed as inconspicuously as any muscle car with a V-8 engine could be in the post-technological silence of the autumn morning.

The El Camino never got close enough to appear in the Mustang's rearview mirror. As the topography flattened out and they made their way west through the suburbs toward the interstate, Jen rolled down the window, took a few deep breaths of the cool air, and let the tension in her shoulders subside. Her sober companion was at the wheel, her family was safe in the back seat, and the judge had assured them that the dog in the carrier on Max's lap would eventually quit pissing herself.

Everything was going to be okay.

And if it wasn't, she had a gun in her lap and a bottle in the trunk. One way or another, she was confident they could handle whatever version of America was waiting down the highway.

ACKNOWLEDGMENTS

I wrote the first draft of this book in 2019, back when things like catastrophic social disruption and armed vigilantism by middle-aged suburban dads seemed a lot more fictional than they do now. And while I take some pride in having put "what happens when we run out of toilet paper?" into Dan's internal monologue four months prior to the global toilet paper shortage of March 2020, at this point I'm just hoping nothing else in the book manifests in real life. Turns out it's much more fun to imagine a dystopia than it is to live through one.

Irrespective of how screwed up reality has gotten lately, the town of Lincolnwood exists in an imaginary universe that I couldn't have constructed without the generous assistance of some very kind people who helped make me a little less ignorant in their areas of expertise. Many, many thanks to Jonathan Greenberg, Marisela Santiago, and Susana MacLean for their insights into the New Jersey suburbs; Gary Obszarny and Richard Calbi for their patient explanations of municipal water infrastructure; Sean Koscho, Jason Bhulai, and the late, much beloved Officer Charles "Rob" Roberts III for helping me better understand first responder protocols; Jon Unger and Principal David Kennedy for explaining public school emergency response procedures; Roberto Mignone for the firearms training; Mike Snyder for his electrical engineering knowledge; Ted Humphrey for untangling network television contracts; Elizabeth Derbes for securities law; Dafna Sarnoff for corporate marketing; Daiva Bajorunas for internal medicine; John Malone and Daniella Sarnoff for local municipal government and general suburban living; Etan Zeller MacLean, Aden Malone, Eliav Malone, Tal Rodkey, Ronin Rodkey, and Rahm Rodkey for gently correcting some of my vast misunderstandings of contemporary teen social dynamics; and Jim C. and the late Steve G. for their wisdom on the subject of untreated alcoholism.

Once I finished a draft, the following people were both generous with their time and invaluable in their feedback: Jen Small, Tommy Greenwald, Stephanie Meyers Helms, Jonathan Greenberg, Marisela Santiago, Susana MacLean, and Jonathan Cobb.

As with all my prior books, Josh Getzler found a publisher for the manuscript; I couldn't have asked for a better agent over the past ten years. Thanks also to Mary Pender at UTA, who shepherded the film rights, and Soumeya Bendimerad Roberts, who handled foreign publishing sales

At Harper Perennial, I'm eternally grateful to Sara Nelson for acquiring the book, substantially improving it, and overseeing its release; Mary Gaule for both helping edit and patiently resolving my annoying metadata issues; Robin Bilardello for designing an absolutely fantastic cover; Megan Looney and Lisa Erickson for their marketing expertise; Emily VanDerwerken and Heather Drucker for the publicity help; and Amy Baker and Doug Jones for everything else.

I've probably forgotten some people. If your name isn't included above and should be, please accept my sincere apologies and drop me a line so I can send you a fruit basket or something as penance. Thanks!

ABOUT THE AUTHOR

Geoff Rodkey is the *New York Times* bestselling author of ten children's books, including Kevin Hart's *Marcus Makes a Movie*; *The Tapper Twins Go to War (with Each Other)* and its sequels; *We're Not from Here*; and *Deadweather and Sunrise*, the first book in the Chronicles of Egg trilogy.

He's also the Emmy-nominated screenwriter of *Daddy Day Care* and *RV*, among other movies.

Learn more at geoffrodkey.com, or follow Geoff on Twitter at @GeoffRodkey.